ELLIS ANGELS

The Nurses of Ellis Island Hospital

A Novel by

Carole Lee Limata RN,MSN

Cover Illustration by Frank C Marcellino

Ellis Angels: The Nurses of Ellis Island Hospital is historical fiction. There are well-known actual people, events and places in the novel that play an important role in the setting. Except where noted, all characters, places and incidents are the products of the author's imagination, and are used fictitiously. Any similarity to real persons, living or dead, is purely coincidental and unintentional.

ISBN: 1482615967
ISBN 13: 9781482615968
Library of Congress Control Number: 2014901090
CreateSpace Independent Publishing Platform
North Charleston, South Carolina

Dedication

**This book is dedicated to my grandparents,
Angelina and John Bosco.
They traveled from different parts of Sicily, registered
at Ellis Island, met and married in New York City, and
blessed their family with the gift of the American Dream.**

Table of Contents

Introduction

On October 29, 2012, Superstorm Sandy made landfall, ripping through Atlantic City, New Jersey at 85 mph, and creating storm surges that lifted the level of the sea and flooded the coastline. Wave swells, some as high as fifteen feet, caused major flooding in lower Manhattan, and hundreds of miles of extensive damage along the coast from the southern shores of New Jersey to the beaches of Queens and Long Island, New York.

Smack in the middle of the storm stood the Statue of Liberty Monument on Liberty Island and nearby Ellis Island. Recently refurbished with a new gold torch, Lady Liberty weathered the gusty winds throughout the night as waves pitched and heaved, completely submerging her island platform. In the morning, she remained, as always, standing tall in the harbor. Except for notices posted by the National Park Service that both islands were temporarily closed with all tours suspended, nothing was reported in the news. It wasn't that no one cared about America's beloved landmarks. There simply was too much damage and devastation affecting coastal residents to report on. Lady Liberty's wet feet would soon dry out. Downed power lines, fires, flooded subway tunnels, bridge closures, and power outages wreaked havoc upon the entire tri-state area. In addition, one week after the superstorm, a contentious Presidential Election dominated the headlines.

ELLIS ANGELS

There was another reason the islands weren't considered newsworthy at the time. Most buildings on Ellis Island had been deserted some sixty years ago when the immigrant processing center officially closed. This included the once, state-of-the art, 750-bed hospital that had been abandoned in 1954. Ellis Island Hospital was not one structure, but a series of buildings which made up an enormous complex of more than twenty units. The buildings had been rotting for decades, patiently waiting to be restored, or simply demolished. Broken glass windows no longer offered protection from the wind and salt water, and numerous cracks in the foundation and walls invited weeds, mold and mildew.

In the days and weeks following the storm, the tedious clean-up of Ellis and Liberty Islands was addressed. When power was restored, a variety of electrical pumps were used to flush out standing water. Work crews ripped out waterlogged plaster and wood to eliminate the potential for mold growth and future termite infestations. During the debris clean-up, a partially submerged file cabinet was discovered in the dark recesses of a ground floor office. When the contents of the cabinet were sorted and dried, it was found that the files had belonged to a former Nursing Superintendent, Sister Gwendolyn Hanover. These files were filled with documentation of new nursing procedures, anecdotal notes, incident reports, orientation schedules, and pages from her personal journal. The following story was inspired from these files. It's not a story of angels, phantoms, or ghosts roaming the abandoned property. It's a long buried story of the *ladies-in-white*, *angels-of-mercy*, the compassionate nurses of Ellis Island, and the loving care they gave their immigrant patients.

Part One

Orientation Week

In the 25-year period from 1892 to 1917, when Ellis Island first opened as an immigration center, almost 10 million people from foreign lands entered the United States through Ellis Island.

World War I lowered the tide of immigration to 55,000 immigrants during the war years. When the war ended, the number of immigrants quickly rose fivefold to 250,000 in 1920 and 500,000 in 1921.

Chapter One

〜

April 26, 1920

Monday

There are angels among us when we work and when we play.
There are angels who nurse us, and help us through each day.

Although it was after eight, and the sun had risen over an hour before, there was no sign of light by the docks. Huge, black clouds darkened the sky and appeared to be lingering low, meeting the moist fog slowly rising from the water's edge. Because the young woman could see only a few feet ahead of her, she walked gingerly along the slippery boardwalk. She felt a wet mist on her hands and face. Her light brown hair expanded to twice its normal thickness as moisture clung to each strand, making it a bit curlier and fuller than usual.

She thought. *This hair will surely frighten the immigration officials. Perhaps, I shouldn't have bobbed my hair just yet!*

She stopped, put her bag down, and reached into her pocket. Taking out a blue crocheted cap, she pulled it down hard on her head, covering both her hair and ears, leaving only a few wavy curls swirling around her forehead.

People were boarding the ferryboat when she arrived at the wooden ferry station. "Excuse me. Where would I get a ticket?" She asked a young man at the pier.

"Nay, miss. No ticket necessary for this ride. Just hop aboard." He motioned to her to come aboard with a sweep of his arm and a slight bow.

"Well, thank you, Sir," she said with a smile, and stepped onto the ferry platform.

Once onboard the crowded boat, there wasn't an empty seat to be found. She turned to the boat's railing, looking for a solid spot to steady herself. Men were huddled against the railing three deep. She pressed herself into the crowd in the opposite direction until she found a thin pole attached to the last row of seats, and grabbed it. Putting her bag down, she held on tight with both hands, and was thankful that the ferryboat ride to Ellis Island was a short one.

The young woman took a deep calming breath, as she usually did in crowded places. Then, she studied the others onboard the ferry. The boat was filled with men, many of whom appeared to know each other, and were in surprisingly good morning humor. Amid the swell of the bay, she listened and identified several different languages and broken English with varying accents.

Let's see...Italian, Greek, Russian...an old Irish brogue...and what's that...a language I've never heard before?

Before she could decipher the mystery language, the boat bumped to a stop. As the men moved toward the ferry ramp, she took her place in line. A wave of apprehension quickly washed away the excitement she felt earlier in the morning. Waiting in line to exit, she inhaled slowly. The woman looked up to see an enormous fanciful building with many large arched windows. The top of the building was capped with four spires rising from copper-topped cupolas. Built of red brick and beige limestone, the contrast of light and dark stone softened the stately building, giving it a festive air of a fairytale castle. The woman did not expect to see hundreds of people on the island so early in the morning. A ferry barge, filled with newly-arrived immigrants, had landed minutes earlier. The immigrants were lining up, single file, patiently waiting outside the great Registry Building on Ellis Island.

A uniformed man at the foot of the boat ramp checked off the names of staff members as they exited the employee ferry.

"Name?"

"James Molinari."

"Thank you. Next, name?"

"Timothy O'Brien."

"Check. Next, name please?"

"Angelina Bosco."

"Oh, Miss Bosco! Welcome! Welcome! I was told to keep an eye out for you." Raising his hand, the inspector called out to an older gentleman stationed at the entrance of the building. "Cap Higgins," he called. "Here she is, Sir. Here she is. Miss Bosco has just arrived." Turning to the young woman, he said, "Captain Higgins, Miss, he's here to escort you. See him? Over there by the doorway, he's waiting for you."

"Oh, yes, thank you, but I wasn't expecting…"

"…a royal treatment? Miss, you *ladies-in-white* are deserving of it! The Captain's coming over now."

Captain Higgins, in full uniform, rushed down to the woman, bent over, and scooped up her luggage. He was an older gentleman with grey hair, a bushy grey moustache, and a handsome smile. "Let me take that for you, Miss Bosco. I am most pleased to meet you and welcome you to Ellis Island. I have instructions to first introduce you to the Commissioner, and then, take you to the office of the Nursing Superintendent. Follow me, if you please."

Angelina took her place at Captain Higgins' side as he made his way past the immigrants waiting to enter the processing center. "Are we going straight to the head of the line, Captain Higgins?"

"Yes, Miss, but we won't be taking the Grand Staircase."

The Grand Staircase was the first step in the immigration process. One by one, newly arrived immigrants worked their way up the stairs for their initial medical inspection. Doctors, employed by the U.S. Public Health Service, observed for signs of illness, walking difficulties, and the general appearance of the immigrants. A doctor's chalk mark, placed on the clothes of the traveler, signaled the need for further examination before an acceptable Medical Clearance Card would be issued.

"We'll be taking the staircase in the corner, over yonder." Captain Higgins shouted to Angelina in order to be heard above the clamoring noise.

They climbed nine polished marble steps to the first of many landings, and turned to climb another small flight of nine steps. Angelina followed the Captain until they climbed all seventy-two steps in this manner, and reached the third floor. There, they headed for the Office of the Commissioner of Immigration, only to find it empty.

"He's around here someplace, Miss. He tends to roam, but I'll find him." Captain Higgins leaned over the third floor railing, searching the Great Hall beneath them. "There he is, Miss. There's the Commissioner with the Docs. I'll tell him you've arrived. Wait here."

The third floor of the Registry Room was an open mezzanine level. From the guard rail, Angelina could easily view the Great Hall below. Two large American flags hung from each end of the railing and were visible from every corner of the room. A strong chemical aroma of disinfectants wafted through the air. Looking up, Angelina saw an immense ceiling of white herringbone tiles. Looking down, she saw masses of people, many in dark clothing, standing in line, patiently waiting to be processed. Huge, half-moon windows on both the second and third floors flooded the Great Hall in a pearly-white light. The immense room was divided into horizontal rows by pipe barriers and benches. At the end of each row, uniformed inspectors were sitting on stools behind podium-high desks, conducting interviews.

The Commissioner was talking to a group of four men directly below. He stopped when Captain Higgins approached. Both men waved to Angelina, and began to make their way up the stairs toward her. The Commissioner shook Angelina's hand, and said, "Miss Bosco, you are finally here. I am very glad to meet you. Welcome to Ellis Island. We are in great need of your services."

"It's a pleasure to meet you, Commissioner," Angelina said, nervously.

The Commissioner spoke quickly. "During the war, we had so few immigrants coming through the registration center that the hospital operated at minimal staffing. However, in the first three months of this year, seventy-five thousand immigrants have been processed. That's almost one thousand people a day. When we submitted these first-quarter numbers, we were given the authorization to increase our nursing staff. That is why we are delighted you are here. By the way, Doctor Richmond gave you an excellent recommendation."

"Yes, Sir, for that I am most thankful. I am glad that my qualifications met with your approval."

"I was not only pleased with your nursing qualifications, but with your mastery of both English and Sicilian. Unfortunately, there is no extra funding for hospital interpreters, so your language skills are desperately needed."

"Thank you, Sir, Sicilian is my native language, but I've worked hard at learning English from the start."

"Miss Bosco, I'm sure you are eager to see your room and unpack. Captain Higgins will take you to Sister Gwendolyn now. I've asked her to schedule an orientation day for you this week to observe processing at the Registry Room."

"That will be most interesting, Commissioner."

"It's been a pleasure to meet you this morning, Miss Bosco. I have every confidence that you will have success in your new position here at Ellis."

Smiling her big dimpled smile, Angelina shook his hand, and replied. "My pleasure, Commissioner, and thank you for your most warm welcome."

Angelina followed Captain Higgins as he walked out of the Registry Room, through the Ferry Building, and into a long corridor which ended at the lobby of the General Hospital. The Captain explained that the enclosed pathway they were walking through had been built by the military when a portion of the hospital was used during the war to care for wounded soldiers. Once in the lobby, Captain Higgins led the way past a number of administrative offices until they arrived at the office of the Superintendent of Nursing, Sister Gwendolyn Hanover. The Captain knocked on her door, and announced, "Miss Bosco to see you, Sister."

"My dear, Miss Bosco, it is so nice to see you again. How was your trip this morning? I'm glad you're here. As I told you during your interview in the city, we're suffering from a nursing shortage in the General Hospital this year. Did you meet the Commissioner?"

"Yes, Sister, a moment ago, he said I'm scheduled to return to the Registry Room to observe processing this week." Angelina's voice quivered as she spoke. She hoped she didn't sound too nervous in the presence of the Superintendent.

Sister Gwendolyn explained. "Yes, we feel it's important to understand the registry procedures before you begin your work at the hospital." Turning to Captain Higgins, she said, "Thank you, Captain, for your help in escorting Miss Bosco to my office."

"It's my pleasure, Sister."

"Thank you, Captain Higgins," Angelina said, giving him a quick smile. The Captain winked back just as quickly, without the Superintendent noticing.

"Would you like me to carry the luggage up to the Cottage, Sister?" The Captain asked.

"No, Captain Higgins, that is out of the question," Sister Gwendolyn said, firmly. "You know that men are not allowed in the nurses' quarters."

"Good Day, then, My Ladies!"

"Good Day, Captain." Sister Gwendolyn slowly stood up. She was a woman in her fifties who looked every bit of her years. There were dark grey shadows under her eyes. She appeared pale and tired, no doubt the result of working many long hours indoors. She reached for Angelina's valise. Angelina felt it would be disrespectful to allow the Superintendent to carry her luggage. With her hand on its carry-handle, she insisted, "I can manage, Sister. It's not very heavy."

"Well, then, let me show you the Nurses' Cottage." Sister Gwendolyn led the way as they walked outside along a covered boardwalk which connected the General Hospital to the Nurses' Residence Cottage.

Angelina asked, "Please tell me how I should properly address you as the Nursing Superintendent?"

"I'm Sister Gwendolyn Hanover. In England, a second-tier nurse is called *Sister*. Here at Ellis, the nurses address me as *Sister Gwendolyn*. When I work on the wards, the patients call me *Miss Gwendolyn*. *Miss* has been added to our first names. I don't remember when this practice started. Many of the medical officers are from Virginia and the Carolinas, and naturally addressed the nurses in this fashion. I imagine it caught on because it's easy for the patients, as well. They will call you *Miss Angelina*."

"I call myself *Angie* since I have been in America. May I use *Angie*?"

Sister Gwendolyn smiled. "Of course, from now on, you will be *Miss Angie*."

Angie followed the Superintendent until they reached a brick house where Sister Gwendolyn announced, "This is the Nurses' Residence where you will be staying. We call it the *Cottage*." They entered the house from the back door, and walked through the kitchen to the front of the residence. Sister Gwendolyn showed Angie the community rooms on the first floor. The spacious living room and dining room faced New York harbor. Both rooms had two French-doors that opened onto outdoor sitting porches. A cozy reading room, adjacent to the living room, also had a lovely water view. There were a handful of private bedrooms on the first floor, but the majority of the nurses' rooms were located on the second and third floors of the cottage residence.

The Nurses of Ellis Island Hospital

The women walked up two flights of stairs to the third floor. Sister continued with her tour, giving informative and practical instructions along the way. "Use this chute to send your uniforms, linens, and towels down to the laundry. All uniforms will be delivered with a labeled laundry bag. Place your soiled uniform in the bag before you toss it down the chute so that it finds its way back to you. Of course, linen and towels do not need to be labeled. A bag is not necessary." Sister continued, "There should be three uniforms in your room today. If not, I'll notify Laundry Services at the General Hospital to deliver the uniforms immediately. Fresh clean towels and sheets can be found in this linen closet. At the present time, there are only a handful of nurses living up here on the third floor. However, the rooms will fill up quickly as more nurses are hired." Turning left at the top of the stairs, Sister Gwendolyn walked down the hall, and opened the door to Room 30. "I especially love the views from this side of the Cottage."

When they entered the room, Sister hurried to the closet. "Well, it looks as though your uniforms haven't arrived. When they come, try them on to see if they need any alterations. If you require an adjustment, complete an *LSR*, a *Laundry Seamstress Requisition*. The form will be delivered to you along with your uniforms. I'll leave you now to rest a bit and get settled before Miss Elsie Archer arrives. She'll be here before noon to take you to lunch, and give you the grand tour of the General Hospital."

Angie asked, "Who is Miss Archer?"

"*Miss Elsie*, Dear, we call her *Miss Elsie*. She is the Assistant Superintendent of Nursing in charge of house supervision, education, and orientation."

As Sister Gwendolyn turned to leave, she gave Angie a set of house keys. Angie followed her out into the hallway. "Thank you, Sister. I look forward to meeting Miss Elsie."

"Oh, Miss Angie, Miss Adeline is your next-door neighbor, right here in Room Thirty-One. She returned to us last year after serving in the Army Nurse Corps during the war. You're lucky to have her nearby. She's chock full of information...and energy, too! You'll enjoy getting to know her." Leaving Angie standing in the hall, Sister Gwendolyn smiled, and quickly walked away without saying good-bye.

As Sister Gwendolyn returned to her office on the main floor of the General Hospital, she felt pleased with her choice of the new hire. Her thirty years of nursing experience had given her both the talent and the instinct to pick the good ones out of the crowd. Sister Gwendolyn was impressed with her selection. She was certain that the new nurse would be successful at Ellis Island. Nurses, like Miss Bosco, were desperately needed at the General Hospital. Sister crossed her fingers and said a prayer that the higher-ups would give her the go-ahead to hire additional nurses. She needed at least a dozen more trained nurses by the end of the year for the hospitals to run smoothly.

After the Nursing Superintendent disappeared down the hall, Angie returned to her assigned room to unpack.

What a lovely room. I never imagined it would be so spacious, so light, and so white.

The walls and woodwork of her attic room were painted in hospital-white enamel, as well as the iron bed, two metal bedside tables, a metal desk, a mirrored dresser, and a chair. A pair of white curtains, in desperate need of starch, covered the attic window. The only spot of color in the room were two navy-blue wool blankets that had been neatly folded and placed at the foot of the bed.

Angie opened her valise on the empty desk. Inside the bag, she had one pair of nursing shoes and one pair of white high-topped laced boots. The boots gave her ankles extra support when she worked long hours on the hospital wards. In addition to the plaid dress she was wearing, she had brought along one other dress, a black and white woolen with a crocheted white collar. She carried three delicate wool scarves which were the only keepsake she had from her mother, and an embroidered bed sheet, which she had tea-dyed the previous summer. In addition, packed into her bag, was a pleated white nursing cap from the Bellevue School of Nursing, three pairs of white woolen stockings, a sweater, a nightgown, and various undergarments.

Angie unfolded the bed sheet, took hold of the end corners, and waved it over the bed. After it settled, she carefully smoothed out the wrinkles with both hands. Standing back to examine the effect, she was pleased with the color combination of soft ecru and crisp white. She looked around the room, considering other improvements.

Angie draped two scarves over her bedside tables. They magically turned into gauzy tablecloths. She used the last scarf to cover her chair. She especially loved the swirling paisley patterns and the creamy apricot colors in the scarves. Pleased with her decorating efforts, she smiled.

It will be nice to see these every day when I wake up, instead of wearing them only on special occasions.

Next, Angie's eye went to the small round window under the attic dormer. She walked across the room, and examined the meager white curtains.

I can tea-dye these, and perhaps, embroider a few daisies on them in due time.

Angie opened the curtains, and looked out. The sun had burned off the morning fog, and was peeking out through thinning clouds. Turning to the right, Angie had a view of the left side of The Statue of Liberty as The Lady looked away from Ellis Island and faced the open harbor.

"There you are, My Lady. You were hiding in the fog all morning. Now, I find you outside my bedroom window. Am I the lucky one to have you as my roommate!" Angie happily talked out loud to Lady Liberty. "How different today's greeting was from the first time we met. The years have passed so quickly. It is hard to imagine that I came to America twelve years ago."

Chapter Two

September 14, 1908
8 AM (08:00)

There is a kind of language that only two can share.
No words are ever spoken, but it comes in crystal clear.

"Angelina. Angelina. Where have you been? I've searched all over the ship for you. I looked everywhere. We are landing this morning."

"I've been here, Santino. I slept up here last night."

"I couldn't find you. I knocked on the women's cabins. I knocked so hard that I thought I would break the door. Finally, I noticed the door wasn't locked, and I opened it. I knew I was not allowed in the women's quarters, but I was determined to find you. No one was inside. All the women and children were gone."

"I helped them to come up here," Angelina said.

Taking a closer look at his sister, Santino said, "Angelina, look at me. You look ill, and so thin and frail."

"No, Santino. It is only a cold."

"Have you eaten anything?"

"I took some bread. I couldn't eat. I couldn't sleep. It was freezing cold. Down under, it was worse. Everyone was suffering. They were sick, and the stink was terrible. I helped them all come up to be outside in the ocean air. Mrs. Massino was retching and crying. I brought her children on deck to give her a little rest. I think it helped. The moon-light seemed to soothe the little ones," Angelina explained. "I bundled them as best I could."

"Now, you are sick, Angelina. You gave them your coat and blan-ket. You must come in now. It's starting to rain."

"It is only a mist. Look how everyone is so excited this morning. They forgot how miserable they were last night. I hope we will be able to clean ourselves before we register. If not, we will smell, and give the Americans a terrible first impression. How long will it be until we land?" Angelina asked.

"I think it will only be a few hours more, Angelina. The men say before noon."

"I can't wait to see Giacomo. Are you sure you know where to go to meet him?"

Santino could not contain his excitement. "Of course, he said he would wait for us in Battery Park. Just think, in a few hours, we will be in America, and we will see our brother, Giacomo, once again. It's been four years since he left for America. Soon, we will all be Americans!"

"Santino, it has been only fifteen days since we left Sicily. I miss Celestina so much that I can't bear it. I wish we didn't leave her with Zia Dona."

"We had no choice," Santino said. "Zia Dona raised Celestina as if she was her own when Mama died. She is like a mother to little Celestina."

"She will miss us, Santino. How could we have left our baby sister with our aunt?"

"You will see her again, I promise. I will work hard. There are many jobs in America. I will work and save. In a few years' time, I will buy you a ticket for passage back to Castelvetrano to visit Baby Celestina and Zia Dona. I will. You will see," Santino pledged.

"Such dreams, Santino."

Santino could not be discouraged. "We can have our dreams in America. With my earnings, I will send you to school. In America, that is possible. You will be a lady, an educated one. You will wear fine clothes, a hat, and an overcoat. When Celestina is older, we will send for her. She will be educated in America, also."

"We have come such a long way, Santino. The men up on deck were talking all night. They say there are inspectors at the admission station that give medical examinations. We must pass all their tests before they will allow us into their country. They do not let everyone in."

"What hearsay! I have never heard such nonsense! We were examined by the ship's doctor before we left, and vaccinated for smallpox. Giacomo wrote that he had no problem…no problem at all! You have no need to worry. We can read and write. We are healthy and strong. That is what they want in America: the smart, the strong, and the healthy," Santino said, proudly.

"I was listening to them. They said that it is getting more difficult to be admitted. They are sending people back to where they came from. There are inspectors who can order us to return even if they don't like the looks of us. How can that be? Imagine, Santino. Imagine if we were rejected, and sent back to Sicily. I think I would die if I had to take this trip again."

"Do not worry, Angelina. In a few hours' time, we will be meeting Lady Liberty herself. When I meet her, I will bow to her. I will tell her that I am here to become a good American. I will show her how strong I am, and that I am an able worker."

ELLIS ANGELS

On schedule, the SS Trapani steamed past The Statue of Liberty on Bedloe Island at 11:50 am. Over 1,000 passengers stood shoulder-to-shoulder on the ship's deck to greet Lady Liberty. There were shouts of happiness, tears of joy, and prayers of gratitude amid the hugs, kisses and songs of celebration.

Although Ellis Island was minutes away, the steerage passengers did not step down on land until after 5 pm that afternoon. After passing Bedloe Island, the ship docked at Battery Park, less than a mile away, and waited for landing approval. Brief medical inspections were performed by physicians who boarded the ship, and allowed the passengers in First- and Second-Class to disembark. Because they could afford the expense of the costlier shipboard accommodations, First- and Second-Class passengers were not required to go through Ellis Island for screening and processing.

At 2:55 pm, the SS Trapani steamed on again, and anchored near Brooklyn. U.S. Customs required every ship's Captain to prepare and submit a manifest upon landing. The manifest described the products, and listed the names of the people, that a ship carried to the United States. At this time, the 961 steerage passengers were tagged with their name and the page number where their name could be found on the manifest list. Barges stood ready to tender the immigrants to the Ellis Island Processing Center, but the barges were small and the procedure was painfully slow. Federal immigration officers at Ellis Island met the newcomers. They gave directives in several languages. Many immigrants did not understand their orders and were confused, slowing the process even further. With their belongings in hand, the newly-arrived immigrants entered the ground floor of the Registry Building, and were told to check their baggage. Because they each carried only one small bag and feared losing their possessions, Angelina and Santino moved on to the Grand Staircase.

Men were instructed to go up the large staircase on the left. Women and children were directed to the right. Doctors from the U.S. Public Health Service gave the new arrivals a quick medical assessment, and placed a chalk mark on anyone requiring further inspection. This was the medical inspection that Angelina overheard the men discussing when she was on deck the night before. She knew she needed to look presentable. She flattened down her tangled hair, and wiped her runny nose with her shirt sleeve. Keeping a sharp eye on her brother, Angelina began to climb the stairs, carrying her small bag. The line for women and children advanced slower than the men's line because all children were required to walk, and were not allowed to be carried. Santino was ahead of Angelina, already taking his place in the Great Hall. Angelina's only thought was to catch up to him. Suddenly, a strong hand on her right shoulder stopped her.

A man in uniform turned her around, lifted her chin toward him, and stared into her eyes. He examined her closely, saying something she did not understand. He wrote a large **R** in chalk on the collar of her coat. Shocked that he would dirty her coat in this manner, Angelina attempted to wipe off the chalk mark. The uniformed man firmly took hold of her hand, and abruptly said, "No!" Angelina saw families reuniting at the top of the stairs. She ran toward Santino, but was stopped in her tracks.

Angelina was singled out during the initial medical inspection because she had an upper respiratory infection, a simple cold. If it had been earlier in the day, she would have quickly been examined and allowed to leave with her brother. Because it was after 5 pm, there were many people before her scheduled for their screening examinations. Angelina was ushered into the temporary detention room filled with women and children. She did not understand what was happening. She wanted only to be with Santino. She squeezed herself between the door and the matron standing at the door. The matron sternly stopped her, and pointed to the sleeping section of the room. Angelina sat on a low bunk, certain that she would be deported. She wondered if she would ever see Santino and Giacomo again.

My brothers will never find me. I will be sent back to Sicily. I know this for certain!

Angelina cried so hard her eyes stung. Tears rolled down her cheeks and dripped past her neck, wetting her blouse. She tried to not cry and to be strong, but the tears kept coming and her nose kept running. She wiped her nose with the hem of her skirt. Exhausted, she flopped down on the skimpy canvas bunk, and used her travel-bag as a pillow. Even though she was on land, she continued to feel the rhythm of the ship slowly moving up and down. Weak and dizzy, she soon fell fast asleep.

Back in the Great Hall of the Registry Room, after Santino passed his medical inspection, he waited for his sister until it was his turn for his interview. He was questioned concerning his financial status and his life in Sicily. Satisfied that he had adequate funds and a place to live in America, he was given his Landing Card, the precious pass allowing him to enter the United States of America.

However, Santino was not leaving without Angelina. After unsuccessfully asking many people about the whereabouts of his sister, he was finally able to appeal for help from a guard on duty.

"Aspette, un momento," the guard said, and returned with an interpreter. The interpreter spoke to Santino in Italian, and rushed away to inquire about a teenager named *Angelina Bosco*. Moments later, the interpreter returned. Santino was told that his sister was being detained for a physical examination because she showed signs of an upper respiratory infection. Routine protocol demanded that she obtain medical clearance to rule out such contagious diseases as scarlet fever or diphtheria. The doctors had many other examinations scheduled before closing. Angelina would have to wait in the Women's Detention Dormitory until morning for her exam. The interpreter asked Santino if he preferred his sister to sleep at the General Hospital, the cost would be one dollar per day. The girl would be cleaned, bathed, and given a hearty meal. Relieved, Santino consented to the overnight care for his sister, and paid a dollar toward the first night's hospital fee. In exchange, he was given written instructions with information regarding where and how to check his sister's status. With a heavy heart, Santino left Ellis Island by ferry to find Giacomo, his older brother, at Battery Park.

Angelina was jarred and bumped awake as she was wheeled on a gurney wagon in the cold night air. Her first thought was that she was still on the great steamship, and it had smashed into a giant ocean wave. However, when the wagon stopped, she found herself in a hospital receiving room. She was lifted from the stretcher, and was placed in the arms of a beautiful *lady-in-white*. Angelina did not understand the language the lady was speaking. Nevertheless, she took hold of her hand, and followed her.

The *lady-in-white* led her into a washroom. Clear, warm water was running and filling a bathtub. She carried Angelina's belongings and an additional cloth bag that had a paper label pinned to it. *ANGELINA BOSCO* was written on the paper. The *lady-in-white* attempted to undress the young girl, but she resisted. She would not let the lady touch her. Angelina tugged one way, and the lady tugged the other. Finally, the lady took the young girl's hand, and put it under the running water, motioning to her to feel the water. It felt warm and inviting.

The lady pointed to herself, and said, "I am your nurse, Miss Mary. I am Miss Mary, Maria, me... Angelina, you."

"Maria? Madonna? Mary?" Angelina repeated.

"Sure, my name is Maria. It is Mary, in English, like the Madonna." Miss Mary unbuttoned the first two pearl buttons of her own white uniform. Angelina understood the nurse was trying to tell her to undress and to take a bath. Although she had heard stories of strangers tricking immigrants into stealing their money and their clothes, her instinct was to trust this *lady-in-white*. Angelina undressed, folded her clothes neatly on a chair, and slipped into the warm bath. Miss Mary gently checked Angelina's head for lice before washing her hair. She placed two white towels on the chair next to the bathtub, and left Angelina to soak in private for a few precious minutes more.

A short time later, Miss Mary returned to the room, and held up a towel for Angelina. She wrapped the girl in the thick towel, and draped a smaller towel over the young girl's wet hair. Miss Mary put Angelina's dirty clothes in the bag that was marked with her name, and dressed Angelina in a clean nightgown and knitted socks. Sitting close to a warm radiator, Miss Mary helped Angelina brush and dry her hair. Angelina began to relax, and felt sleepy. While Miss Mary combed her hair into two neat braids, Angelina imagined she was still on the ship for she continued to feel the rocking and swaying of the boat.

Next, Miss Mary took Angelina's hand, and brought her into a crowded ward with twenty-six beds, ten on each side of the room and six beds down the middle. She placed Angelina's belongings on a bedside table, and patted an empty bed near a window. Angelina jumped up onto the bed. Miss Mary took hold of her wrist, and put a thermometer in her mouth. Then, Miss Mary tucked her under crisp tight sheets and a heavy wool blanket. She smiled down on Angelina and stroked her forehead softly, saying words that Angelina did not understand. Angelina felt safe, warm, and protected.

Too bad I can't stay in America. I would have liked it here.

Suddenly remembering that she was going to be kicked out of America and sent back on the first boat headed for Sicily, Angelina began to cry. Miss Mary kissed her forehead. As she leaned over, Angelina smelled a sweet fragrance of soap and lavender flowers. A second *lady-in-white* came into the room, carrying a tray. Miss Mary positioned the bed pillows so that Angelina could sit up. She placed a tray of food on a small table that fit snuggly over the bed. On the tray was a large bowl of thick, hot vegetable soup, a piece of cheese, an apple, a glass of milk, and a roll and butter. Angelina devoured every morsel of the food.

She wondered: *Why would Miss Mary treat me so well if they are planning to send me to prison, and put me on a ship returning to Sicily? This lady, dressed in white, makes me feel like everything is going to be all right.*

Later that evening, Miss Mary returned to the ward, sat down on a chair next to Angelina's bed, and held the young girl's hand until she fell off to sleep.

The next morning the police came.

They are here to arrest me, and send me back to Sicily!

"You are Angelina Bosco?" asked a uniformed young man who spoke Italian.

"Yes," Angelina answered.

"How old are you, Miss Bosco?"

"Thirteen."

"What is your date of birth?"

"July 1, 1895. Am I going back to Sicily today?" She asked in Sicilian.

"No, Angelina, you have a cold. This is Doctor Wall. He needs to examine you to help you get better." Although the man spoke Italian, a dialect different from Angelina's native Sicilian language, he injected many Sicilian words into his translation so that Angelina was able to understand him.

Angelina worked up the courage to ask, "Are you a policeman?"

"No, I'm an interpreter from the Registry Room. My name is Fiorello. I speak many languages. I will translate the doctor's questions for you. Doctor Wall wants to know how long you have been ill."

"I started to catch a cold two nights ago when I slept outside on the top deck of the ship."

"Were you sick before that?"

"No."

"Does your throat hurt when you swallow?"

"Yes."

"The doctor wants you to open your mouth, like this, *ahhhh*, say, *ahhhh*."

"Ahhhh."

The doctor put a tongue depressor in her mouth, and pushed down on her tongue. He looked into her throat, and appeared to study it for a moment. Then, he touched the back of her throat with a wooden stick. Next, he put his thumb and forefinger under her chin and palpated her neck.

"The doctor wants to listen to your chest to hear how you are breathing. He will use this stethoscope," Fiorello told the young girl.

Confused, Angelina questioned what she heard, "Test a rope?"

"This is a stethoscope. The doctor uses it to hear the sounds that your heart and lungs make."

The doctor continued to quietly examine Angelina. Then, he said something to the interpreter that Angelina did not understand.

"What is he saying?" Angelina asked.

"The doctor has written an order for you to stay three days in the hospital for observation. He is going to carry a specimen to the laboratory to test and identify the type of germ in your throat. It is a good sign that your temperature is not elevated. You may not have a serious illness that will prevent you from entering the United States. However, the doctor wants to be certain that you are not harboring a streptococcal infection that can lead to scarlet fever."

"I cannot stay here. I must leave to find my brothers."

"Your brother, Santino Bosco, knows you are here at the hospital, and that you are safe. He's been told where to get information concerning your status. We will send word to him with instructions that we will have your test results ready in two days' time. Today is Wednesday. If your tests are negative, you will be able to leave with your brother on Friday evening or Saturday morning."

"You are not sending me back to Sicily?" Angelina questioned.

"No, we are not deporting you. It is our duty to make absolutely certain that everyone is healthy and strong when they enter the United States. We don't want people spreading diseases to others and making them sick."

"Are you sure that my brother knows where to find me?"

"Yes, Angelina, he has written instructions. Look, here comes Miss Mary. She was worried about you, and stayed late last night, past the time her shift ended."

"Please, Signore Fiorello, please thank Signora Maria for taking care of me last night."

"Yes, I will thank Miss Mary. She is your nurse. Call her *Miss Mary*. In America, Maria is Mary. She is here to help you get well."

"Miss Mary," repeated Angelina.

Fiorello spoke to Miss Mary, and turned again to Angelina, "I thanked her for you. Do you have anything to ask the doctor?"

"No, but I wish to thank him, and to thank you also, Signore Fiorello."

"You are most welcome, Angelina." The doctor spoke to Miss Mary, and the two men walked on to the next patient.

Miss Mary disappeared, and returned with a breakfast tray laden with food. On the tray was a bowl of hot oatmeal, a hard-boiled egg, a banana, two slices of white bread, and a glass of milk. Angelina had never tasted bread like this before. It was soft, but tasted delicious. After breakfast and throughout the day, Miss Mary swabbed the back of Angelina's throat with a brown Argyrol antiseptic solution. She showed Angelina how to gargle with salt water by counting from one to ten in English. Miss Mary worked on her ward during the day-shift from 07:00 to 19:00 hours, and appeared to never rest while caring for the young women on her ward. She made certain that all her patients were clean, neat, and tidy. She helped the girls comb their hair, and showed them the latest American hairstyles, while teaching them many English words and phrases. Throughout the day, a man in a white uniform came into the ward pushing a stainless-steel snack cart. Miss Mary helped him distribute glasses of milk and fruit snacks to the children on the ward.

On Friday afternoon, Miss Mary brought the interpreter, once again, to see Angelina. "We have good news for you, Angelina. We are happy to report that Doctor Wall has written a discharge order for you. Your throat culture showed no sign of a contagious germ. You will be able to leave the hospital early tomorrow morning. Your brother was notified this afternoon. He left word that he will come to pick you up tomorrow. Miss Mary wants you to follow her to select a clean outfit to wear home."

Miss Mary brought Angelina into a room filled with donated clothes. The Italian Immigrant League had sorted and collected piles of clothes donated by wealthy New Yorkers. Most of the dresses were far too big for Angelina, but Miss Mary found two pretty dresses that fit her in the children's section.

The next morning, Miss Mary helped Angelina into her American dress, and braided her hair. Angelina followed Miss Mary through a long corridor until they came to the lobby discharge room. Santino and Giacomo were waiting for her, just as Signore Fiorello promised. Angelina put down her bag. She ran into their arms, hugging them tightly. Her brothers jumped with joy, lifted her up, and twirled her in the air.

Watching them, Miss Mary laughed. Angelina ran back to Miss Mary, kissed her on the cheek, and said, "Thank You, Miss Mary", using the English words she learned from the *lady-in-white*.

"You're most welcome, Angelina, it has been a pleasure to make your acquaintance. I wish you the best of luck, my dear."

Holding hands, the three siblings ran to the dock to take the ferryboat to their new life in America.

Chapter Three

❧

April 26, 1920

Monday
11:30 AM (11:30)

*Some say there are angels beside us each day.
Always watchful, ever careful, they are guiding our way.*

Angie was lost in thought when three sharp knocks on her door startled her enough to make her jump. "Oh!" She said. "Who is it?"

"Laundry Maid, Matilda, Miss."

Angie opened the door to find a young girl, no more than eighteen, carrying three, freshly-starched, white uniforms, two nursing caps, and one navy-blue, wool cape. Matilda appeared to be relieved to hand over the heavy bundle to Angie.

"Thank you, Matilda. I'm Angie."

"Nice to meet you, Nurse," Matilda said, with a slight curtsey and a smile. She pulled a paper from the pocket of her white apron. "Here is the *LSR* form you will need, if anything needs fixing."

"Thank you, again," said Angie.

"Have a nice day, Nurse."

Angie closed the door, and inspected the crisp, white uniforms. Matilda had delivered three, identical, size-six, white, shirt-waist dresses. Each uniform had twelve pearl buttons evenly sewn from the collar of its pleated blouse to the hem of its flared skirt. Angie removed the top uniform from its wooden hanger, and unbuttoned its buttons. She slipped out of her dress, eager to try on the official uniform of an Ellis Island Nurse.

Securing the uniform and fastening the waist-flap that was designed to carry her bandage scissors, Angie caught a glimpse of herself in the mirror. Her short bobbed hair had settled down into soft waves which gently framed her face. As she placed her pleated nursing cap on her head, she stood back to get a full view of herself in the dresser mirror. Angie carefully examined her reflection. *I think this will do nicely.*

For all of her twenty-four years, Angie Bosco never considered that she was beautiful. When she looked in the mirror, she saw features quite satisfactory for a young woman. She stood five-feet, four-inches tall. She had dirty-blonde hair, plain hazel eyes, a simple nose, and a basic mouth. She never knew that her classic features blended together perfectly to form a soft and stunning face. Angie looked at her reflection and simply saw herself as adequate. She did not see what others saw when she cared for her patients, diligently carrying out her ward assignments. If she had the ability to view herself through different eyes, she would have noticed the sparkle in her eyes and the delightful dimples in her cheeks when she smiled. There was no doubt about it. In twelve years, the frail, awkward, immigrant girl had transformed into a graceful and beautiful *lady-in-white.*

The Nurses of Ellis Island Hospital

Miss Elsie Archer struggled up the second flight of stairs to the third floor of the Cottage grumbling about the feeble-minded architects who neglected to include an elevator in the design of the nurses' residence. Her arthritic knees burned with each step. She was almost sixty and pleasantly plump. Her clenched lips formed a constant frown, and her thick neck, heavy eyebrows, and wire eyeglasses made her look like the meanest of schoolmarms. She had worked on the wards of the hospital for sixteen years since its grand opening in 1902 until 1918, when Sister Gwendolyn removed her from direct patient care because of her severe rheumatoid arthritis. That was two years ago. Now, she was assigned to house supervision and education of the new hires. Although she looked prudish and strict, she loved meeting and teaching the young nurses who put their heart and soul into their work as she had always done.

Angie was fully capped and uniformed when Miss Elsie came to call on her.

"No, no, no, no!" said Miss Elsie, shaking her head when she saw Angie in uniform.

Feeling foolish, Angie asked, "Is something wrong? Is it my nursing cap? Am I wearing the wrong nursing cap?"

"No, you have a choice. You can wear either your nursing school cap or the nursing cap chosen by the Public Health Service. Most nurses take to wearing the *PHS* cap because laundry services will clean and starch it regularly at no charge."

"Well, that's convenient. In that case, I will wear the *PHS* cap, too. Are you Miss Archer?"

"Yes, Dear, I am Miss Elsie Archer, Nursing Superintendent Two. I will be giving you your orientation. I'm sorry I scared you. It's your badge. You don't know our custom. I'm glad I arrived before you went downstairs."

"My training school pin?" Angie looked puzzled. Just then, Angie heard her stomach groan, and hoped Miss Elsie was standing far enough away so that she didn't hear it, too.

"Yes, your school pin. Years ago, we called them *badges*," Miss Elsie Archer explained. "They were worn like military badges to identify trained professional nurses."

"I thought they represented the school we attended," Angie said.

"I suppose that's why we wear them nowadays. You're wearing the pin in Sister Gwendolyn's spot."

"I'm sure I don't understand, Miss Archer."

"Call me *Miss Elsie*. Only our Superintendent fastens her pin in the very spot you have your pin. She closes the top button of her uniform and pins her badge there, close to her neck. Miss Elizabeth and I, Superintendents Two and Three, secure our badges between the first and second buttons."

"What do I do?" Angie asked.

"As a Chief Nurse, it is the custom to wear your top button open, and to secure your badge on your right lapel, like this." Miss Elsie unpinned Angie's school pin, unbuttoned the top button of her uniform, and repositioned the pin in the proper place.

"I see. Thank You, Miss Elsie."

Miss Elsie took a closer look at the midnight blue and gold pin with the engraved name, *Bellevue School of Nursing*, encircling a laurel wreath. A crane, standing on one foot, was featured in the heart of the pin.

"Such a lovely pin, I've always admired it. It's the very first of its kind designed by Tiffany and Company. Do you know why a bird was chosen as a symbol for nursing?"

Beginning to relax with Miss Elsie, Angie answered, "The bird is a crane, an ancient symbol of constant vigilance. The crane on my pin is standing on one foot, and is holding a rock in the other. The crane was chosen to protect his king through the night. If the crane should fall asleep while on duty, the rock will fall to the ground, and wake him."

"Well, I learn something new every day. My, you look quite fine, my dear. How about a little lunch? It seems to be getting warmer outside. I do believe you won't have any need for your cape this afternoon, Miss Angie. Put your room key in your pocket, and we'll be off."

Angie locked her door, and followed Miss Elsie, as she slowly made her way down the stairs. Leading the way, Miss Elsie exited the rear of the Cottage. They walked together along the covered walkway until they reached the lobby of the General Hospital. From there, they entered a large dining room. They found two empty spots on a bench at one of the long tables, and sat down. "Over two thousand meals are prepared throughout the complex every day," Miss Elsie explained. "Lunch is served in the Hospital Dining Room, but breakfast and supper are delivered every day to the nurses in the Cottage Dining Room."

A young girl, in a striped dress and white apron, brought them each a glass of water, and asked if they wanted coffee, tea or milk. She served them the beverages they ordered, and then, brought two plates piled high with boiled beef, mashed potatoes, and overcooked green beans.

American food, thought Angie, remembering how her Aunt Dona prepared crisp green beans smothered in fragrant garlic olive oil and fresh tomatoes. *I miss those green beans, but I do not miss Zia Dona.* Nevertheless, not only did Angie eat everything on her plate, she wished she had a second helping, but dared not ask for more.

After lunch, Miss Elsie suggested they begin the hospital tour outside. Miss Elsie walked very slowly and carefully down the ten stairs from the main hospital entrance to the sidewalk, putting both feet on a step before attempting to descend to the next step. The warm sun was shining brightly, shimmering silver highlights on the water. A soft harbor breeze encircled them and carried the scent of freshly cut grass. "Well, this day turned into a beautiful one, after starting off so dark and gloomy. A good sign, don't you think, Miss Angie?"

Angie nodded in agreement. "Oh, yes, it looked like rain this morning."

"How much do you know about Ellis Island?" Miss Elsie asked, as they walked side-by-side.

"Well, Miss Elsie, I know that the island originally was three acres. Now, it's grown to more than twenty."

"That's correct, Miss Angie, to enlarge the island, they used landfill. It consisted of the earth and gravel taken during construction of the city's subway tunnels."

"I didn't know that, Miss Elsie."

"We talk as if the complex is three separate islands: Island One, Two and Three. Actually, Ellis is one large island."

"I can see that," Angie agreed. "It's shaped like the letter *E* with three peninsulas jutting out from a main stem."

"I never looked at it from that perspective, but, yes, it is. The top line represents Island One where the immigrants come when they first arrive. The middle one is Island Two, where we are currently standing. It houses the General Hospital, the Psychopathic Pavilion and the Cottage."

Angie added, "...and The Contagious Disease Hospital is on the bottom line."

"Island Two and Island Three are sometimes called the *South Islands*," Miss Elsie said.

"Like the islands of the South Seas?" Angie asked.

"Not quite, it's because they are facing south."

"How can they be south if the Statue of Liberty is east?"

"You have a good sense of direction, Miss Angie. Picture the **E** tilting slightly forward to the right. The very tip of Island Three is the most southern point on the complex. Like this," Miss Elsie said, turning Angie toward the tip of Island Three. "That direction is south."

"I see, therefore the Statue of Liberty is not directly east but slightly south-east. She is facing the open harbor, standing ready to welcome everyone," Angie said.

Miss Elsie explained, "Actually, the French sculptor, Bartholdi, had something different in mind when he designed the statue. He called her, *Liberty Enlightening the World*, and intended her torch to be a symbol of America, shining new light on the old ideas and the established traditions of Europe."

"Well, that's something I didn't know. I know that she's a green color because her copper has oxidized, but I've always wondered why her copper is never polished and shined up bright," Angie said.

"She's made of copper the thickness of two pennies put on top of each other. The patina that she's acquired living near the water is actually thicker than her delicate copper, and provides protection for it." Miss Elsie continued, "Let's walk down to the Ferry Building to begin our tour of Island Two."

At the Ferry Building, Miss Elsie pointed toward Island One. Angie looked up to see a flock of seagulls flying overhead. Miss Elsie said, "Directly ahead of us are the Dormitories and the Laundry

Building. Can you see the large white tank and the tall tower to the left of the Registry Building?"

"Yes," Angie nodded.

"That's our water tank and beyond that, the power plant. It generates all the electrical power for the facility. Ellis Island is entirely self-sufficient, you know. The furnaces heat the radiators on the hospital wards, keeping everyone toasty warm in the winter. There are also a carpenter and a glazier on the grounds," Miss Elsie added. "We even have our own fire station." Miss Elsie turned, and pointed to a series of bungalows on Island Three. She told Angie that the cottages were added as the complex grew and developed. "Most are for medical staff housing. Over the years, extra offices were needed for medical records, transcription services, bookkeeping, and research."

Angie continued to follow Miss Elsie as they circled the grounds of Island Two, deliberately slowing her pace to match that of the older nurse. The first building they reached was a small hospital called the *Psychopathic Pavilion*. Miss Elsie began, "This hospital has a fifty-bed capacity. The immigrants, who are classified as mentally ill, are housed here while they await deportation. The hospital is designed to be a safe place for temporary detention and not an asylum. There is a fenced outdoor space on the roof to expose the patients to fresh air during the day."

"I've heard that Ellis is recognized as one of the top centers in the country for mental health testing."

"Yes," said Miss Elsie. "A bunch of highfalutin scientists from up north come down to do their research. Medical students and interns come and go all the time. However, I sometimes wonder if all their work actually proves anything, except that their proposed theories aren't viable. Do Englishmen have higher IQ levels than men of other nationalities? Nonsense! Are certain facial features reflective of intelligence? Preposterous! Such notions always sounded like poppycock to me from the start!"

As Miss Elsie approached the General Hospital, she explained that the decorative façade of the 275-bed hospital appeared to be three large buildings, but the hospital was actually divided into seven sections, each attached to the other at right angles. "You'll get a better idea of the design when we walk around to the back. Let's go," said Miss Elsie. The rear of the hospital faced the waterway between Island Two and Island Three. The seven sections of the buildings formed three U-shaped courtyards, creating a park-like setting down to the water's edge. Here, the hospital had verandas on the second and third floors to provide patients with daily exposure to the healing powers of fresh air and sunshine.

"The basement runs from one end of the island to the other. We can walk through the entire distance underground. It's almost two city blocks long. We'll start here at the North Wing." Miss Elsie guided Angie down a ramp, and opened one of the double doors marked *RECEIVING*, where food and supplies were delivered to the hospital. They passed the Morgue and an autopsy room. "The nurse brings the deceased here after postmortem care. She fills out the three identification tags found in the morgue pack," Miss Elsie instructed. "Two tags are placed on the body, and the third outside the shroud."

"That's routine procedure, isn't it?" said Angie.

"Yes, however, it's important to note that the morgue is not manned at mealtimes and after ten pm…twenty-two-hundred hours, military time. The nurse must register the deceased at those times. Being alone in the morgue, in the middle of the night, can wear a little on your nerves. Have someone accompany you the first time you need to go there." Miss Elsie continued down the hall. "Here are the employee locker rooms for staff who travel from the city by ferry each day. Next, we have the Laundry Receiving and Distribution Center which occupies a large portion of the basement. This is also the laundry for the nurses who live at the Cottage. If your uniforms need alterations or mending, bring them to the seamstress at this laundry. Don't forget to fill out your *LSR* form when you drop them off."

After passing the laundry, Angie saw a door marked *STERILIZATION*. "I've heard so much about the giant autoclave on Ellis Island. Is this where it resides?"

Miss Elsie laughed. "No, that's at the Contagious Disease Hospital on Island Three. I'll take you there tomorrow. This is where you will bring your unit supplies to be sterilized."

"Doesn't the nurse sterilize on her unit?"

"Only the small jobs, we boil tweezers and rubber gloves. Efficiency studies showed us that we can save nursing time, and do a more effective job, when sterilization procedures are done at one central location."

"That's extraordinary," Angie said.

"Yes, the nurse cleans and washes her used instruments, always taking the precaution of keeping the instrument sets intact. She brings them here to exchange them for freshly sterilized packs. Imagine the time this saves the operating-room nurses. By the way, the surgical arena is above us on the third floor. Let's go up, and take a peek. Then, we'll work our way down."

Angie and Miss Elsie took the elevator to the South Wing Surgical Pavilion on the third floor which housed two operating rooms and a recovery room. An identical surgical suite was located on the North Wing. Daylight from the skylights on the roof provided the extra light surgeons often needed for their most delicate surgeries.

"I noticed two solariums on the roof of the hospital this morning. It feels as though we are standing under one of them right now," Angie said.

"Yes, that's exactly where we are. The ORs, the *operating rooms*, do actually look like glass-covered sunrooms when you are standing outside the hospital."

The nurses moved on to the Recovery Room. There, men and women were being closely monitored by a nurse as the patients recovered from their ether after surgery.

"This side of the hospital is called the South Wing. It houses female patients. The North Wing is primarily for male patients." Miss Elsie added, "There is a small children's residence on the first floor. A number of children live here who are not sick. Their parents have been admitted as patients. They have no place to go while they wait for their parents to be discharged. Classes are scheduled for them throughout the day. Red Cross Volunteers teach English, American History and Hygiene. When they leave here, those little ones know more English than their parents. They actually become their translators."

The nurses crossed over to the North Wing Men's Medical Wards. Then, they worked their way down to the first floor, where Miss Elsie showed Angie the North Wing Children's Wards. The tour ended at the central Administration Building which housed the Pharmacy, the Dining Room, Medical Records and a large Auditorium. Looking at her pocket watch, Miss Elsie said, "Where does the time go? I must give you some free time to allow you to get settled at the Cottage, and to wash up for supper."

"What time is supper at the Cottage?"

"Evening supper is served at eighteen-hundred hours for the night shift and nineteen-forty-five hours for the day shift. That usually gives the day nurses adequate time to give report, walk back to the Cottage, and wash before supper. Tonight, you're welcome to go to either the early or the late sitting. You'll find everyone down there at suppertime. It's a good opportunity to meet the nurses living at the Cottage. Do you remember how to find your way back to the Cottage from here?"

"Yes, I think I do. Is it this way?" Angie pointed toward the South Wing.

"That's correct. You have a good sense of direction. Miss Angie, I'll meet you here in the lobby tomorrow morning at zero-seven-hundred-hours for another day of orientation. Don't forget to eat your breakfast before you arrive. It's served in the Cottage Dining Room, beginning at zero-six-hundred hours."

"Will do, Miss Elsie, I promise!"

"And Miss Angie…"

"Yes, Miss Elsie?"

"Try to go to bed early tonight, and get a good night's sleep!"

Chapter Four

April 26, 1920

Monday
9 PM (21:00)

Sometimes in your wandering, you'll recognize a friend.
No end and no beginning, just a long enduring trend.

Angie Bosco carefully opened the box of lavender-scented soap she saved for a special occasion, such as this, her first night on the island. Buying the expensive olive-oil soap was one of the few luxuries she allowed herself. She enjoyed the scented tissue paper the soap was wrapped in, and could not resist inhaling its fragrance, which was both uplifting and relaxing at the same time. Angie opened the middle drawer of her dresser and removed her nightgown. She carefully tucked the delicate tissue paper in between her folded nightclothes. A hot soak in the bathing room down the hall was just the remedy Angie needed to unwind before she went to sleep in her new surroundings. With her bathing supplies in hand, Angie opened her door. A tall, slender woman was standing directly in front of her.

"Hi, I'm Adeline Fermè. I live next door, Room Thirty-One. We're neighbors. Welcome to the Cottage!"

"Hi, I'm Angie Bosco."

"I didn't knock on your door. I was just about to. How did you know I was standing out here?" Adeline asked.

"I didn't. I was going down the hall to take a bath," Angie said.

"That's a coincidence. A bath sounds wonderful. The bathing room is two doors down. There's another bathing room on the second floor if the one up here is occupied. This was your first day, right?"

"Yes." Angie answered.

"Did Miss Elsie give you the grand tour this afternoon?"

"Yes, she did. She's very knowledgeable."

"She knows everything there is to know about this hospital," Adeline said. "Her face can scare you half to death, but as mean as she looks, that's how kind she is to all of us."

"I agree. In fact, everyone I've met today has been very welcoming," Angie added.

"I know. I have to tell you that we're a great bunch of people. I love working here. I couldn't wait to come back."

"Yes, Adeline, the nurses at supper told me you were stationed in France during the war."

"Supper, did you say supper? That's where I was going when I saw the light under your door. I couldn't resist calling on you." Adeline talked quickly. "I have an idea. Come with me."

"Where? Haven't they stopped serving supper?"

"You don't think they would actually let this *lady-in-white* starve because she worked late on the wards. You must come with me to learn one of the most important lessons there is to discover around these parts." Adeline smiled a big wide-mouth smile.

"What's that?" Angie asked.

"Finding late supper after you worked overtime on the wards. It's a very important aspect of your orientation, I assure you."

"I believe you. What should I do?"

"Close your door, and follow me. I'll show you how it's done." Adeline turned and disappeared down the hall, giving Angie just enough time to snatch up her room key and put down her things. She hurried after Adeline, running to keep pace with her. Angie caught sight of Adeline, jumping down the stairs, two steps at a time. She reached the dining room as Adeline turned on the lights, and was taking a covered tray from the kitchen cart.

"Ah, it's here already. That didn't take very long. Lucky me, I'm starved." Adeline sat down at a round table close to the window. Outside, the water shimmered under the lights of Bedloe Island.

"How beautiful, what a lovely sight," Angie said, taking in the view of the harbor.

"Yes, it's so peaceful and serene at night," said Adeline.

"Where did your supper come from?" Angie asked.

"From the kitchen staff at the hospital," Adeline answered.

"How did they know to deliver it here at this time?"

"I was delayed on the unit tonight. On my way back to the Cottage, I stopped off at the hospital lobby. I filled out an *FRF*."

"*FRF*, what's that?" Angie asked.

"Sorry, *FRF* stands for a *Food Requisition Form* to order a late-night supper. It's used to request meals after regular meal hours. You check off what you need from the menu of the day. The kitchen workers require thirty minutes from the time the *FRF* is dispatched to them. I'll show you where the forms are stored tomorrow. Sit down. Would you like my cup of tea? You can make coffee, or boil water for tea in the kitchen anytime. There's lemon, sugar, and honey stored in the cabinets. Milk is in the icebox if you ever want a warm cup of milk before retiring. Tell me a little about yourself. What nursing school did you go to?"

"Bellevue, I see that you went there, too, Adeline. I noticed that you're wearing the nursing school pin. I graduated two years ago."

"Ah, Bellevue, I must confess, I got into a little trouble before I graduated. Not my grades, they were fine. I was caught leaving the grounds without an evening-pass." Adeline talked quickly, scarcely taking a breath. "I graduated fourteen years ago. My first job was with the Settlement Nurses, working downtown. I met two sisters, Margaret and Ethel. They were nurses. Tenement neighbors called upon them to care for women after the women attempted to self-abort their pregnancies. One woman died before the nurses arrived. They began to teach the cycle of ovulation to the tenement women. Margaret published a newsletter on the subject. It created a great deal of controversy. Many considered it scandalous. She was facing jail time for distributing her article. However, her husband quickly planned a trip to Europe, and persuaded her to leave with him. That was about the time I applied to work here."

Adeline paused for a second to catch her breath. "There's something special about working here, although the patients and their stories will break your heart. I enjoy working with the children. At first, they are terribly frightened to be here, but kids are kids. They somehow manage to find friends, play, and even fight when they can't understand a word of each other's language."

"I've been watching for jobs to open up here for quite a while. I..."

Angie didn't finish her sentence. Adeline jumped up, ran to the kitchen door, and stomped her foot on a cockroach. She calmly walked back to the table, and sat down.

"Bugs," she said, and began a story about her wartime experiences. "I'd been working here at Ellis for a few years when war was declared. I wanted to enlist immediately, but instead, I volunteered to teach the Red Cross Nurses who were deployed here at Ellis Island before going overseas. Then, I signed up for the army corps. I was stationed in Northern France in La Roche Guyon, where the small town converted its only hotel into a military hospital. My assignment was on the gas wards, treating soldiers who were poisoned with chlorine and mustard gas. Those horrid gases burned and destroyed their mucous membranes. The boys suffered so, especially when we ran short of medication and supplies. The war was rough, much rougher than I could have ever imagined, but that's then, and now is now. I have to admit, it's great to be back."

"You're so courageous. I'm impressed." Angie gulped, awed by both Adeline's bravery and her years of nursing experience.

"It didn't feel like bravery at the time, just felt like the right thing to do. I was born in Avignon, in Southern France. My parents emigrated when I was four. I'm an American citizen now.

"I am one, also. Adeline, you don't have much of an accent."

"Neither do you. English came easily to me because I was young. I attended school here in New York. I'm bi-lingual, a necessity for working at Ellis."

"I'm certain that's why my application was processed so quickly. Adeline, you haven't touched your food. Slow down and eat. You could use a little more meat on your bones."

"I eat all the time, just thin naturally. Okay, I'll eat. You talk. When did you come to America, Angie?"

"I was thirteen when I came with my brother, Santino. My oldest brother, Giacomo, came first, and worked for many years. He paid our passage, and rented an apartment for us. He helped Santino find a job. My brothers encouraged me to study and finish school instead of working. I graduated high school with honors. Then, they insisted I marry."

"Marry?"

"Yes, they chose a *paisan*, a friend from our home town. He had become an American citizen, and had a good job."

As Angie spoke about her marriage, she felt the familiar ache in the pit of her stomach. *Why did I mention my marriage tonight?* She reluctantly continued her story. "I wanted to study nursing, but my brothers were persistent. They insisted that marriage was the proper next step for an American woman. I married. Eight months later, my new husband died of influenza."

"That's awful, Angie."

"At the funeral, my pastor encouraged me to apply to nursing school, and persuaded my brothers to allow me to become a nurse. The priest wrote a strong reference letter for me, and contacted the monsignor. They remembered me as a young teen, and submitted their references using my maiden name. Because of this, I resumed using my family name. I first applied to St. Vincent's School of Nursing. They had reached their quota of lay students for that year, and forwarded my application to Bellevue. When I received my admission letter, I was happier than I'd been for a long time. After I graduated, I worked downtown at the Foundling Hospital. There aren't too many hospital jobs that pay well in the city. I jumped at the chance to work here when I heard there was an opening on the family wards as a Chief Nurse."

"I'm glad you did, Angie."

Angie was beginning to feel more comfortable with the older nurse. "Perhaps I should tell you one thing more."

"What's that?"

"I had gotten pregnant. I didn't know anything about family planning in those days."

"It's 1920, a new decade. A woman can now decide when she wants to have a child. She can plan for a family."

"At the time, I didn't know. I was sheltered by my brothers."

"So, you have a child?" Adeline asked.

"No, my baby was stillborn, very premature."

"I'm sorry to hear that, Angie. Do you think you will feel badly when you work on the family wards? You'll be supervising nursery and postpartum, working with new mothers and babies."

"I've thought long and hard about that. I believe that I might actually find it healing. Does that make any sense to you?" Angie asked.

"Yes, of course, it does. I understand, and you are needed desperately. We've had a number of pregnant women admitted lately. My friend, Margaret, should teach classes here. She believes that birthing is a woman's choice, and that choice is her right, like voting. Oh, have you heard?"

"What?" Angie asked.

"Only one more state and the Nineteenth amendment will be the law of the land. Women will have the right to vote. I can hardly believe it. The bill was passed last year. Thirty-five states voted in favor of it. Now, only one more state is needed to reach a two-thirds majority. It looks like that state might be Connecticut. If it is, I'm going to request two days off to lobby the senators in Hartford."

"Have you done that before?" Angie asked.

"Yes, especially when things are this important. After the fire at the Triangle Factory, nine years ago, I had to get involved. So many young women died in the fire because the doors were locked, and the fire escape collapsed. The girls could not get out of the building. We needed safety regulations in the workplace. I believe one woman can make a difference, but many women together can make real change happen."

"Wow. That's impressive. How can I get more involved?"

"Come to the city with me on Sunday. Teddy Roosevelt's sister is speaking at the Red Cross. She is very knowledgeable about what's happening on the political scene, especially as it relates to women. If women will be voting in the presidential election this year, we need to be informed."

"I'll definitely go. If I'm scheduled off, I'll request a pass. If I'm going to vote, I want to learn more about what's going on. I don't even know who's running for president."

"No one knows. They haven't chosen candidates yet. The Republicans are looking at Senator Harding from Ohio. The Democrats may select Governor Cox from the same state. Oh, this is exciting. I can't wait."

Once again, Angie stopped Adeline to remind her to eat. "You need to finish your supper, Adeline."

"Yes, you're right, but I don't know how I'm going to get the gals over to the city to vote on Election Day. They'll have patient-care assignments. Sister Gwendolyn won't be able to give all of them passes to leave the island. Hey, here's an idea! Sister could apply for a polling station right here on the Island. There ought to be enough people working on that day to justify it. I'm going to have to look into this right away. Perhaps, I'll ask Alderman Fiorello. He knows us. He was an interpreter here during his law school days. I'll wager a nickel that he'll know what to do."

"Right now, you're going to finish eating before you disappear on me," Angie said.

Adeline laughed. "Okay. I need someone like you around to calm me, and remind me to eat. What's on your agenda for tomorrow?"

"Tomorrow, I'm meeting with Miss Elsie. On Wednesday, I'm orienting at the Registry Room."

Adeline frowned. "They are quite strict at the Registry. There are so many rules. It's terribly formal, I'm afraid."

"Yes, it does seem extremely regimented."

"So regimented it makes me want to scream! Aaaahhhh." Adeline pretended to scream. "Well, the good news is that it's only one day, just in and out, and you'll be through."

"Just like the immigrants," Angie said.

"Just like the immigrants," echoed Adeline.

"Is there anything I should know before I go?" Angie asked.

Adeline finished her supper, and stood up to return her tray to the cart. "Did you finish your tea?"

"Yes, ages ago, Adeline."

"Here, put your cup on my tray. The kitchen crew will pick up the cart in the morning."

As the two women climbed the stairs to return to their bedrooms, Adeline asked, "Now, what was it that you wanted to know?"

"Oh, I was wondering if there is anything I should know before I go to the Registry Room on Wednesday."

"Well, do you really want to know?" Adeline asked.

"Yes, I really want to know." Angie answered.

"Okay, if you really want to know, there are only three things to remember."

"Three things?" Angie questioned.

"Number One: Do nothing to interfere with the screening process. No one around here is entirely comfortable with it, but we respect it. It's the law. Number Two: Don't eat too much of the food. You'll gain weight and blow up fast."

"Okay. I'll remember that. What's Number Three?"

"Number Three: Don't get involved with the physicians. Things get complicated. Most are from the South, and they marry Southern gals. The others are Jewish. The nurses are Catholic. Jewish men marry Jewish women. Catholic men marry Catholic women. That's it, don't mix religions. Keep it simple."

"That's it?"

"That's it. That's all you need to know. Do you want me to explain anything more?"

"No explanation needed."

"Thanks for keeping me company tonight. It was great to meet you. I'm glad we're going to be neighbors." Adeline grinned.

"Good Night, Adeline, I enjoyed meeting you. Sweet dreams."

"Angie, Good Night. Don't let the bed bugs bite!"

Angie could not help but smile to herself as she opened the door to her room. *This has been quite a day, not only did I find Lady Liberty living outside my bedroom window, I met a friendly neighbor. What was the meaning of her advice? I would never interfere with the registration process, nor would I ever allow myself to get romantically involved with a physician. Such notions, it's not proper to even think such thoughts. However, knowing how I like to eat, perhaps I should heed her warning, and watch my diet. What a kick she is.*

Angie looked at the small alarm clock on her dresser. She picked up the clock, wound it up, and set the alarm for the next morning. It was late, almost 11 pm. She collected her soap, towel and nightgown. Then, Angie locked her door and hurried down the hall to the bathing room. The small room was toasty warm. When she turned on the bathtub faucet, the water flowed steamy and hot. Angie shut off the water when the tub filled, and eased into the soothing hot water. She relaxed as the heat seeped into her bones.

Ah, this feels good. This is what I needed at the end of this busy day.

As Angie soaked in the tub, she reflected on her conversation with Adeline.

I wonder what Adeline would have thought if I told her the truth about what really happened to Pasquale and the baby six years ago? I try so hard to forget. So many people have left me. I wonder if there will ever be a time when someone stays long enough to help me mend the pieces of my broken heart.

Chapter Five

January 13, 1914

For many years I wasn't real. I couldn't think. I couldn't feel.
Stories I would never tell. Places where I dared not dwell.

"Angie! Angie! Come quick! Pasquale has got my brother! He won't let him go!" Esther cried.

Angie opened the door to find little Esther standing in the hallway in tears. "What is it, Esther? What's happened?"

"Angie, you must come right away. You have to stop Pasquale. He's got Leo. He's beating him up."

"Where are they?" Angie asked, grabbing the keys that were hanging on a small hook near the front door.

"Downstairs, Angie. Come!"

Angie closed her apartment door, and followed Esther down three flights of stairs. Outside, a crowd of men and boys were huddled around Pasquale and Leo. With one hand, Pasquale held the little boy by his jacket collar. With his other hand, he shoved a fistful of snow in the boy's face.

"Boy, you ain't so tough now, are you?" Pasquale cried, victoriously.

"Please Mister, I didn't mean it. Put me down," Leo begged.

"PASQUALE STOP!" Angie shouted. "Leave the boy alone."

When Pasquale turned to Angie, he lost his grip on the small boy. Leo twisted himself free and ran, punching his way through the crowd until he disappeared down the street.

"Pasquale, what gets into you? You act like a fool sometimes. You should know better. You are a grown man," Angie scolded.

The crowd roared with laughter. Pasquale's face blazed red. He shouted, "Angelina, go home! You do not know your place." Angie turned, and went back into the apartment building. Pasquale followed her. Inside the apartment, Pasquale's anger continued to rage, fueled further by his wife's composure.

"Come," she said. "I was starting to make *Pasta Fagioli*, your favorite. You will feel better after you eat."

"I don't want anything to eat. No wife of mine is going to humiliate me in front of the others!" Pasquale declared.

"What did the boy do to you, Pasquale?"

"That hooligan threw a snowball at me," Pasquale answered.

"A snowball...Pasquale, this is about a snowball? He is the landlord's son."

"Landlord or not, he is not going to make a fool out of me," Pasquale announced.

"No, you can do that all by yourself!"

Angie was chopping an onion for the beans she was preparing when Pasquale grabbed the knife, and pointed it at her. "What do I have to do for you to take me seriously, Angelina?"

Pasquale pushed the knife into Angie's arm, breaking the skin. Instinctively, Angie moved her arm away. The knife slipped deeper and cut her. Angie screamed. She ran into the bathroom, trailing blood behind her. Pasquale followed the trail. "What have I done? Forgive me, Angelina. I lost my temper. I am sorry. Here, let me help you."

"Pasquale, it is always the same. You are sorry afterwards, but never before. You lose your temper every day. Today is no different from yesterday, and tomorrow will be the same."

"No, no, Angelina. I will change. You will see. I can be a good husband. I will be a good father to the baby. I will make you proud of me."

"Pasquale, someday your temper will get the best of you. Believe me, it will."

Pasquale calmed down that night. All was peaceful until the following afternoon when Santino stopped by to visit his sister after his workday. He noticed the large bandage on Angie's arm, and demanded to know what had happened. Angie refused to tell him. Santino persisted until Angie finally recounted the events of the previous evening. "Please, Santino, don't say anything. Pasquale is sorry. He lost his temper. It was an accident."

"Angelina, you are my sister and with child. That is no way to treat a woman who is carrying a baby."

"He will change, Santino. He is young. Please, don't say anything. Please." Angie begged.

Santino agreed to not talk to Pasquale about the incident, and he did exactly as he promised. However, he did report the story to his brother, Giacomo. Together, the brothers decided to teach Pasquale a lesson that he would never forget.

On his way home from work, Pasquale heard rumors that Angie's brothers were on the lookout for him. He hurried home. With each step, his rage percolated. Once home, his temper flared. He slammed the door with all his might, and took hold of Angie. Shaking her, he screamed, and slapped her again and again. Angie squirmed free of his grip. She fell down, and he kicked her. She crawled into her bedroom.

Bruised and beaten, she fell across her bed and cried. An hour passed. Angie became aware of a sensation of wetness. She looked down at her skirt, and saw blood. She screamed. Pasquale came running into the room.

"Pasquale, I am bleeding...the baby...something is wrong. You must get help right away. Go quickly! Call Mrs. Bellini, the mid-wife! Hurry, Pasquale. Run!"

Pasquale rushed out of the apartment building and into the street. The brothers were waiting in ambush. They grabbed Pasquale by his collar, and pulled him into the alley. The story they later told was that it took only one strong punch to bring Pasquale to the ground. "That should teach you a lesson, Pasquale!"

The brothers left Pasquale lying among the garbage cans in a pile of dirty snow. Pasquale came to minutes later. When he opened his eyes, he was alone in the alley. Angie's brothers were gone. Struggling to stand, Pasquale stumbled, hitting his head on a fire escape ladder which was hanging five feet above the ground. The collision stunned him. He fell unconscious for a second time that evening. However, this time he did not regain consciousness until the following morning.

Angie was alone throughout the long night. She knew she was cramping and bleeding heavily. She cried when she felt a gush, and then another. Something was wrong. She waited for hours for help to come. None came.

In the early hours of the morning, the superintendent of the apartment building found Pasquale lying in the alley when he was collecting the garbage cans for morning pickup. He helped Pasquale to Angie's apartment. That's when they found Angie, asleep in bed with her still-born baby beside her.

ELLIS ANGELS

As Angie slowly recovered and grew stronger each day, Pasquale's health deteriorated. It started with a cold…a cough…and then…a fever. The fever roared for three days. Angie called for a doctor who immediately ordered Pasquale to be admitted to the hospital. Angie's brothers rushed Pasquale to the nearest hospital, but it was too late. Pasquale died of influenza that evening.

Chapter Six

April 27, 1920

Tuesday
7 AM (07:00)

As I learned my lessons, I stepped up among the fools.
All the world is not a theatre. It is the best of schools.

The office that Miss Elsie shared with Miss Elizabeth, the Night Supervisor, was in Nursing Administration, which was located directly off the main lobby of the General Hospital. Miss Elsie always arrived for work at 06:00 hours to begin her morning rounds. After rounds, it took her fifteen minutes to put the finishing touches on the orientation binder she was preparing for Miss Angie. She finished the project promptly at 07:00, just in time to meet Miss Angie in the hospital lobby.

"Good Morning, Miss Elsie."

"Good Morning, Miss Angie. How are you this fine morning?"

"Very well, Miss Elsie, and yourself?"

"Excellent, my dear, did you get to bed early last night?"

"Oh yes, Miss Elsie, of course I did!"

"Well, let's proceed to Island Three to complete your tour of the complex. Then, you'll know your way around the entire island. Let's take the enclosed walkway. It's still dark out."

ELLIS ANGELS

Angie followed Miss Elsie down the hall and through a passage-way until they reached the 450-bed Contagious Disease Hospital which was not one building as its name suggested, but a series of eighteen structures connected by one endlessly long central corridor. The plain exterior of the white-brick, red-roofed buildings indicated that more thought had gone into the plan to limit the spread of disease from one building to another, rather than to a decorative design. The buildings were strategically staggered, and required walking and turning through several hallways before reaching an entrance door. The larger wards, housing the most contagious patients, were connected by curved corridors which formed half-moon courtyards outside.

"Assignment to the wards is determined by disease, age and sex," Miss Elsie explained. "For example, there are specific wards for scarlet fever, measles, whooping cough, diphtheria, and tuberculosis. Men, women and children are assigned to separate wards. Let's go in. I'll show you."

The first building they arrived at housed the laboratory. When Miss Elsie opened the door, Angie recognized the familiar hospital smell of disinfectant and bleach. "Here, the lab folks work, day and night, to identify and confirm the diagnosis of every disease that comes our way. A wrong diagnosis can mean cross-contamination of patients."

Returning to the central corridor of the Contagious Disease Hospital, they stopped at the hospital administration building. The women climbed the stairs to the second-floor patient library. The library room contained over 5,000 donated books, written in a variety of languages. A series of empty classrooms were on the third floor. Many of the rooms would be used later in the day by the volunteer teachers.

From there, they walked down two flights of stairs, and quietly roamed through various long and curved corridors, passing the many different ward buildings of the Contagious Disease Hospital. The wards were numbered consecutively, but the placement of their entrances was staggered and irregular. "So the germs have a harder time hopping from room to room," Miss Elsie laughed.

She continued. "At one time or another, we have treated every known contagious disease from every part of the world. I can recall cases of typhus, cholera, yellow fever, smallpox, and malaria. I've even seen the plague."

Windows in the doors allowed the nurses to check inside the rooms without entering them. As they passed the wards, Angie studied the layout of the large rooms. The standard twenty-four bed unit had twelve beds lining each side of the room. The desk of the chief nurse was positioned in the center of the unit. If extra patient beds were needed, six more beds could be placed in the middle of the room; three beds in front of the nurse's desk and three beds in back of it. The high ceilings and the light from the tall windows made the wards feel bright, airy and spacious.

In the isolation section, there were a number of private rooms which opened to outside verandas. Each room had a single bed and two sinks. Miss Elsie explained the rationale for using the double sinks before Angie had an opportunity to ask. "A clean sink and a dirty one; one is for spitting out the germs, and one is for washing them off."

They followed the first floor corridor to a back door, exited the building, and walked up a number of steps. They entered a cavernous room. "Take a look at that!" Miss Elsie announced, as both nurses stared into a giant autoclave. It was ten-feet high with enormous doors that opened on both ends.

"I've never seen anything like it." Angie said.

"It's used to sterilize mattresses so that they can be used over and over again. I believe it's one of the largest autoclaves in the country."

The next building held an enormous autopsy amphitheater for teaching and research. The last stop was a section of rooms dedicated to laundry services. "Imagine the thousands and thousands of sheets and towels that are washed here each and every day, and that's in addition to the laundry services on Islands One and Two."

"The laundry needs at this hospital are enormous."

"Yes, the machines are running twenty-four hours a day. Look, the sun is starting to peek out," Miss Elsie said. "Let's make our way back to the nursing office. I've prepared an orientation binder for you. I'd like to show it to you before we go to lunch."

Outside, the women walked side-by-side in the morning air until they reached Miss Elsie's office on the ground floor of the General Hospital.

"Come and sit down," Miss Elsie instructed. "You're scheduled to observe *processing* tomorrow at the Registry Room. I want to tell you a little about immigration law before you go."

"I was very interested in immigration, and did research on my own. I wanted to know more about the rationale for the medical inspections and screening interviews," Angie said, sitting down in Miss Elsie's office chair.

"What did you learn?" Miss Elsie asked.

"Well, here's what I read. Tell me if this is correct. Laborers first came from China and Japan sixty years ago to build the railroads in the west. Then, workmen were needed for the industries that were prospering in the east. Thousands of Irishmen, facing famine in

Ireland, came to America because of the boundless opportunities to find work here. When Northern Europeans were immigrating, there were no restrictions. However, the next wave of immigration brought Europeans from Southern and Eastern Europe. Some were escaping brutal religious pogroms and others, poverty. The cities were filling up with people who dressed, spoke, and lived differently from the folks in town. Americans were beginning to get uncomfortable with the growing number of immigrants."

"Yes, go ahead. Continue," encouraged Miss Elsie.

"People were ambivalent. They knew that the immigrants contributed to America's resources and wanted to share the American dream, but they questioned if the door should be left wide open for everyone to enter. About forty years ago, the first restrictive law was passed, called *The Chinese Exclusion Act*. It stopped Chinese immigration completely for ten years. After that, efforts to control immigration continued. A new law was passed which called for inspection and deportation of aliens who were criminals or had the potential to be a public charge."

"In others words, they wanted to stop criminals and prostitutes from coming to America, and to identify those people who would not contribute to America's growth and prosperity," Miss Elsie added.

"Let's see, that would be anyone unable to work, like pregnant women, single mothers with children, retarded or slow-witted people, and those with a debilitating illness."

"Don't forget people with contagious diseases," Miss Elsie added. "I outlined *The Immigration Law of 1891* in your orientation folder." Miss Elsie opened her binder. "Here it is on Page Twelve."

Angie leafed through her papers and found the page. She read out loud, quoting the exact words of the 1891 law: "All idiots, insane persons, paupers and persons likely to be a public charge, persons suffering from a loathsome and dangerous contagious disease, persons who have been convicted of a felony, or misdemeanor involving moral turpitude, polygamists, and any person whose ticket and passage is paid for."

"That would be *contract laborers*," Miss Elsie said.

"I don't understand why *contract laborers* are not allowed into this country if they have an authentic job waiting for them when they arrive."

"In return for their passage to America, they sign a contract before leaving home. They agree to work for fewer wages than American citizens. That creates competition for jobs and takes work away from able Americans."

"How is *moral turpitude* defined?" Angie asked.

"Known prostitutes, unmarried pregnant women, or an unmarried couple living together."

"I see," said Angie.

"It's not always easy to identify the people who truly should be deported. That first-line responsibility rests on the shoulders of the medical officers, doctors of the U.S. Public Health Service. Their job is to make medical recommendations for exclusions in an effort to protect the American public. These young men are doing their best to fulfill their duties, but the work takes a great emotional toll on them. Because of this, they rotate assignments between the hospitals and the registry."

"The whole experience can be devastating for so many."

"However, most immigrants are processed through the Registry Room in less than four hours from start to finish. Do you have any questions about anything thus far?" Miss Elsie asked.

"Yes," Angie said. "There's something pressing on my mind. Why would the government build an elaborate medical center for poor foreigners at a time when the public wants to limit immigration?"

"That is an excellent question, Miss Angie. When Congress appropriated the money to build the hospitals, it was in direct response to demands from the public to protect American citizens from the communicable diseases they believed the immigrants carried."

"Tell me more," said Angie.

"It all began with the development of steerage class on the giant steamships," Miss Elsie explained. "Ships going to Europe were filled to the brim with lumber and grain from America. These exports were bulky and heavy in weight, and the ships were built accordingly. Returning ships carried European exports that were considered light cargo, such as fine lace, fabric, tea, and cork. Empty space remained on these ships. The steamship companies developed the brilliant plan to fill the America-bound ships with people. They advertised the American dream to Europeans. Thus, safeguarding their profits both ways, but giving little concern as to who was traveling on their ships to America. Problems arose when steerage conditions were so dreadful that diseases developed. The federal government was forced to establish ship inspections with strict entrance requirements. Before the Contagious Disease Hospital was built, a ship could be quarantined in the Narrows for weeks before her passengers were allowed to enter the United States."

"I see, and a ship that is out-of-service does not make money," Angie said.

"A safe place was needed as a dumping ground to lift the quarantines. The shipping companies contributed to the funding of the hospitals," Miss Elsie said. "In addition, there's a tax on every immigrant entering the country, and a steep fine for those who don't pass the Ellis Island medical inspection. The hospitals now operate in the black with the shipping companies paying large sums of money. Patients are charged only nominal fees. So, you are absolutely correct in your reasoning. The hospitals aren't charity hospitals. They weren't built out of the goodness of the hearts of the American public."

Angie nodded, "I'm beginning to understand that the hospital business is about dollars and cents."

Miss Elsie agreed, "Yes, my dear, of course, it's all about money. It's a business like any business."

"But what about healing the sick?" Miss Angie asked.

"My dear," Miss Elsie answered, "...why, that's the reason you are here!"

Chapter Seven

❧

April 27, 1920

Tuesday
8 PM (20:00)

Patiently, I practiced and rehearsed my lines each day.
I studied, and I memorized what I should know and say.

REGISTRY ORIENTATION SCHEDULE:
APRIL 28, 1920
PREPARED BY: MISS ELSIE ARCHER,
SUPERINTENDENT OF NURSING, II

Line Inspections 07:30 – 09:00

Eye Examinations 09:00 – 10:00

Legal Interviews 10:00 – 11:00

Testing Rooms 11:00 – 13:00

Examinations 14:00 – 17:00

Hearings 17:00 – 19:00

ELLIS ANGELS

Before preparing for bed, Angie reviewed the orientation schedule for the following day. It was going to be a long and busy day at the Registry Room, and Angie wanted to make the best of it. If she was going to spend time observing the registration process, she wanted to learn more about the procedures. She noticed that Miss Elsie summarized these on Pages 13, 14, and 15 of her orientation binder. Angie sat at her small desk, and read.

Now let's see if I understand this correctly, she thought after reading three pages. *To begin, the immigrants arrive on the island by barge because the water around the island is too shallow for the ships to dock. On the first floor of the registry, they are asked to check their baggage. Many immigrants are reluctant to do this because they are carrying all their worldly possessions. The preliminary inspection begins when they are asked to walk up the Grand Staircase. Physicians, who are trained in diagnostic symptoms, observe the immigrants overall appearance and specifics, like gait, stature, and skin tone, as well as the movement and color of their extremities. The doctors put a chalk mark on anyone requiring further testing. Letters in chalk represent specific ailments. Umm, perhaps, I should memorize the coding system.*

Angie read the codes that Miss Elsie listed on Page 14.

PAGE 14

MEDICAL INSPECTION CODES
PREPARED BY: MISS ELSIE ARCHER, SUPERINTENDENT OF NURSING, II

B = Examine Back
BD = Breathing Difficulty Noted
CT = Conjunctivitis or Trachoma
D = Test for Contagious Disease
FT = Examine Feet
G = Goiter Noted
H = Possible Heart Problem
K = Possible Hernia
L = Lameness Noted
N = Examine Neck
P = Full Physical Needed
PG = Pregnancy Noted
R = Respiratory Infection
S = Examine for Senility
SC = Examine Scalp Further
T = Examine Throat
X = Evaluate for Feebleminded
X (Circled) = Evaluate for Insanity

How could any person, even a trained physician, identify these symptoms in a matter of seconds? It's almost an impossible task. The eye exams are after the line inspections. Eighty percent of the immigrants pass medical screening and are given a Medical Clearance Card. Next, they wait in the Great Hall for their legal interview.

Page 15 of Miss Elsie's report listed a variety of questions that an immigration officer might ask during a legal interview.

PAGE 15

SAMPLE LEGAL INTERVIEW QUESTIONS
PREPARED BY: MISS ELSIE ARCHER,
SUPERINTENDENT OF NURSING, II

What is your full name?
What is your nationality?
What is your occupation?
What is your age?
Are you able to read and write?
What is your marital status?
Are you a polygamist?
Have you ever been in prison?
Have you been in the U.S. before?
Have you ever been in a poorhouse?
What is your final destination in the U.S.?
Are you going to join a relative?
What is the name of your relative?
What is the condition of your health?
Have you signed a labor contract?
Did you pay for your passage?
How much money do you have?

If all goes well and the immigrants pass the legal inspection, they are given a Landing Card. Next, they return to the first floor to retrieve their baggage. After that, they are free to leave. It's possible that they could be processed in three to four hours from start to finish.

"Simple enough," said Angie out loud. "That's if all goes well. However, in my case, things didn't go smoothly. I want to learn more about what happens when the immigrants don't pass inspection, and get detained and deported. Well, I'm certain I'll find out tomorrow. It is lights out for now, and time for sleep."

Angie took off her robe, and jumped into bed, snuggling under her crisp sheets and heavy wool blankets. A sliver of moonlight slipped through an opening where the window curtains met. The light rested on her mother's scarf that was draped over the bedroom chair.

"Mama," Angie whispered, and closed her eyes.

"Angelina, Angelina, Wake up! It's time to get up, Sleepy-head. Today is the first day of a new year and a new century. Come, you will miss the celebration."

"Mama, today is also my birthday!"

"No, not your real birthday, today is your half-birthday. You are four and a half years old today. Your birthday will be in six months on July 1st," Mama said, lifting off the feather-down bedcovers. "Angelina, you are getting to be such a big girl. I can hardly lift you, now that I am pregnant again."

"Mama, may I wear my white party dress?"

Giving Angelina a big hug, Mama said, "Yes, you can wear it for the New Year's Day celebration. Papa is already up and dressed. He is having his breakfast, and waiting to take us to church."

Angelina went to the Piazza Garibaldi with her parents and brothers to attend the January 1st holy day mass at the Mother Church. Piazza Garibaldi was decorated with flowers and red and green ribbons. After Mass, the people of Castelvetrano gathered in the town square for lunch and dancing. One large table was filled with bowls of olives, platters of baked fish, dishes of winter squash with onions and tomatoes, and frittatas made of eggs, potatoes, and peppers.

When the band began to play, Papa danced with Mama. After the dance, Papa took Angelina up into his arms and danced with her. Angelina laughed as he twirled her around and around. Suddenly, Papa stopped. He placed Angelina gently on the grass before he fell to the ground. Mama screamed. Everyone rushed to Papa. Papa was not breathing. There was no heartbeat.

"Papa, Papa...no, no, no!" Mama cried.

Papa died of a heart attack on New Year's Day while he was dancing and celebrating the start of the twentieth century with his family and friends. That day, Mama's heart broke also.

Six months later, Mama died giving birth to a baby girl on July 1st. It was the day Angelina turned five, and became an orphan.

Chapter Eight

∾

April 28, 1920

Wednesday
8 AM (08:00)

Beggars and thieves stay far from our shore.
If we let you in, you'll bring in more.

Dr. Abraham Goodwin took a deep breath of sea air in preparation for the blast of kerosene fumes that would greet him when he opened the door to the Registry Building. The Great Hall was strangely quiet, in sharp contrast to the usual morning activity at this time. A troop of janitors were busy mopping the floor, and wiping down the benches and walls with a diluted bleach solution. Dr. Goodwin heard the echo of his footsteps as he made his way across the Great Hall and up to Captain Higgins' third-floor office.

"Good Morning, Higgins, mighty quiet down there this morning," he said, after knocking on the door, and opening it.

"Morning, Doc. The SS Touraine from La Havre was running late. She only arrived ten minutes ago. There's a nurse assigned to observe processing today, but as you can see, there are no immigrants to process this morning." Captain Higgins sighed as he passed the orientation schedule to Dr. Goodwin.

Briefly glancing at the schedule, the doctor said, "I see. The nurse was to start with initial screening when the immigrants first land and await their fate by being acutely scrutinized by my colleagues."

"Yes, but this morning calls for a little flexibility in the schedule."

Dr. Goodwin smiled, "You know that the good nurses are not the most flexible of God's creatures, Higgins."

"I know, my boy. I thought if we could juggle the schedule around, she could work with you while you examine the children who were detained last night. After that, she'll move on to preliminary screening later in the morning."

"Work with me? I have almost fifty exams scheduled before lunch. Do you know how much time that gives me for each examination? Five minutes…and I'll need extra time if she's around to slow me down. Don't look at me like that, Higgins! Okay. Okay. I know. If these are orders, I'll comply. Go ahead. Send her down to my office when she arrives, but she is to do nothing but observe."

"She's already waiting there, Doc. You'll find her sitting outside your exam room."

"Well, Higgins, you've done it again, haven't you? You owe me a beer for this one."

Even before Dr. Goodwin left the Captain's office, he formulated a plan to keep the new nurse out of his hair, and away from his exam room as much as possible.

While Angie waited, she couldn't resist taking a peek at the empty exam rooms. She inspected the stocked supply closet, memorizing the placement of each shining instrument that had been carefully placed on the shelves of the instrument cabinets. Before she left the room, she knew where to find the basics that were required when assisting with examinations: cotton swabs, tongue depressors, bandages, and tape. When she was satisfied with her investigation, she sat down and waited in the hallway.

Earlier, Captain Higgins had informed Angie that there would be a change in the day's schedule. "The next group of immigrants won't arrive until late morning so preliminary inspections won't begin until then. No problem," he said. "Dr. Goodwin has a large number of exams scheduled this morning. He'd like you to work with him."

Angie was deep in thought when Dr. Goodwin approached. "Miss Angie Bosco, I presume?" He said with a chuckle. Angie looked up to find the handsome doctor smiling down at her. He had dark wavy hair, dark eyes, and an olive complexion. Although he was an unusually tall man, towering over six-feet tall, when he spoke he made an effort to bend slightly in order to look directly into Angie's eyes. Angie knew that most physicians were not in the habit of doing this. She felt a bit uneasy for a moment, but appreciated the attentiveness. If this was a sample of his bedside manner, his patients would feel special and cared for.

"Yes, and I imagine you are Doctor Goodwin whom I'm to work with this morning."

"That is correct. While I was walking here, I had an idea. It would be extremely helpful if you would introduce yourself to Matron McKenna in the Women's Detention Dormitories. Have her show you the setup there so that you know your way around. When we have *no-shows*, it's best to know where to go to locate our patients so that we stay on schedule."

"Certainly, Doctor Goodwin, where would I find her?"

"The Women's Dormitories are down the stairs and to the right. Follow the signs."

ELLIS ANGELS

Angie found the dormitory rooms, and introduced herself to Matron McKenna. Each large room had a capacity to sleep 90 people in small triple-stacked bunks. At times, many more people squeezed into the dorm to sleep overnight. The space of each bunk was no bigger than a compartment in steerage. Matron McKenna reported that 83 women and children had slept there the night before. A woman traveling alone was automatically detained until a family member came to sponsor her. A mother and her children would be detained until her husband or another relative claimed her. The cost of their meals and lodging was charged to the steamship companies as a penalty for transporting unattached females to American soil.

Each dormitory bunk was designed to be folded flat during the day, converting the space into a large dayroom. The dormitory was a riot of activity. Women were waiting patiently on a long line to wash their clothes at the many sinks along the rear wall. Children snaked themselves through the crowd. After lunch, the children would be rounded up, and allowed to play on the hand-crafted wooden swings and see-saws on the rooftop playground. Morning classes in Sewing, Needlepoint, and English, taught by Red Cross Volunteers, were beginning to assemble.

Angie recognized some of the languages she heard in the room: Romanian, Slovenian, Finnish, and Portuguese. However, there were so many that she found herself getting a bit confused. Social Workers had already arrived to assist the women in locating their relatives in America. Volunteers were distributing clean, donated clothing. A representative from the Hebrew Immigrant Aid Society was helping a woman compose a telegram. Another volunteer from the Italian Immigrant League was writing an appeal request to the Board of Special Inquiry.

Matron McKenna showed Angie the enormous dining room adjacent to the dormitories with tables so long that forty people could sit at one table. A framed sign on every wall in the dining room read *NO CHARGE FOR MEALS*, in English and four other languages. Piping hot meals were prepared three times a day. Breakfast of oatmeal, boiled eggs, milk, and bananas had already been served at 07:00 sharp. Snacks of milk, apples, and bananas were wheeled into the dormitory in stainless steel carts, and were served frequently throughout the day. The matron brought Angie into the kitchen where workers were washing hundreds of white porcelain dishes. The cooks were in the process of preparing lunch of corned beef hash, cabbage sprouts, and peas. One of the matron's duties was to record the number of meals served at mealtimes in the daily bookkeeping report used to invoice the steamship lines.

Returning to the exam area, Angie was introduced to Dr. Mildred Brown, the only female medical officer hired by the U.S. Public Health Service. Angie went to work at once, assisting both Dr. Goodwin with the children's exams, and Dr. Brown with the women's exams. As the morning progressed, the three effortlessly eased into a smooth work pattern. Angie kept the doctors on schedule and anticipated their every need, offering them the correct supplies before they requested them. She seemed to instinctively know how to soothe an anxious woman by holding her hand, giving her a light pat on her shoulder, or simply sitting with her while the doctor examined her child. She helped the children undress, and when necessary, lifted them on and off the exam booth tables.

Dr. Goodwin remained focused on his patients. He appeared annoyed when Angie lingered in his exam room. Angie sensed that he needed his space. She knew not to hover over his patients during his examinations. She kept her distance, and managed to stay out of his way, while still providing what he needed to work efficiently.

The exams went smoothly. Dr. Goodwin gave medical clearances to the majority of the children he examined. When Angie removed the bandage on the arm of one five-year-old boy, the doctor noted that the cut required stitches. Angie prepared a sterile area on a nearby rolling cart, and carefully opened a sterile suture needle, using her best aseptic technique. She filled a metal beaker with antiseptic solution, and removed a pair of sterile scissors and tweezers from the cabinet. Anticipating that the doctor might need additional gauze sponges, she opened a package of three, and dropped them onto the sterile field. Angie assisted Dr. Goodwin as he sutured the boy's arm. After the procedure, Dr. Goodwin showed Angie how to complete the Medical Clearance Cards required for discharge. Angie knew that assigning her to clerical work was his way of keeping her out of his exam room.

The next patient was a curly-headed three-year-old boy who had been detained to rule out an eye infection, possibly conjunctivitis. Dr. Goodwin tested him thoroughly, and found his eyes were mildly bloodshot but clear of infection. Angie was in the process of signing his Medical Clearance Card when she noticed that the little boy was scratching his head. Upon further examination, she discovered head lice. She returned the boy to the doctor, who promptly sent him to the treatment room for de-licing, which would include a head shave.

Dr. Goodwin next transferred a ten-year-old boy to the General Hospital for evaluation because his broken arm had been cast in Germany. His mother reported that the plaster had been applied six weeks earlier, and the doctor felt that it was time for the cast to be removed. Dr. Goodwin promptly gave Angie the assignment of coordinating the transfer paperwork.

The morning passed quickly. Angie enjoyed working with the families. Before lunch, Captain Higgins sent a messenger to call for Angie, asking her to report to the Great Hall. The immigrants from the Le Havre steamship had arrived. The preliminary screening process was about to begin. Angie hurried to leave. She said good-bye to Dr. Brown, who looked genuinely sad to see Angie go, and thanked her.

As Angie was preparing to leave, Dr. Goodwin was called out of the exam area for a brief hallway conference. He stopped, and watched Angie as she walked away.

How did Miss Angie know where to find the supplies I needed in the utility room? She comforted my patients so naturally and easily. She appears to be in quite a hurry to leave. Perhaps, I should have made more of an effort to make a better first impression.

Dr. Goodwin was a romantic. However, his romantic yearnings were not directed toward finding a mate. Since the good doctor had graduated from medical school seven years before, he had been searching for his perfect nurse. He dreamed of harmoniously working side-by-side with her. His dream nurse was efficient, smart and caring. To him, most appeared stern, structured and detached. Some were talkative, others too quiet. Some were overly helpful, others not helpful enough. Some challenged him, others complied too easily. *His* nurse would magically know what he was thinking to anticipate his needs. She would calm his patients, giving them sound information without stealing his spotlight. Until that morning, he hadn't met anyone that came close to the nurse of his dreams.

In the preliminary screening area, Angie was given instructions to: "Quietly observe, do and say nothing!"

For the next forty-five minutes, she stood beside Dr. Adams, and watched him work the *six-second examination*. As the immigrants passed, the medical officer had only seconds to make an assessment and a recommendation using the chalk mark code. The doctors were well-trained. Over the years, each had developed a keen eye to uncover the slightest deviation from the norm. When Dr. Adams marked **K** for hernia, Angie didn't see any indication of a hernia. He used the **X** mark frequently on people who simply looked confused and dazed, either seasick or exhausted from the lengthy ocean voyage. Angie felt relieved when she actually observed a limp on an older man who was marked with an **L**.

Next, Angie was assigned to observe the notorious eye exams which the immigrants feared with dread. She stood behind Dr. Gibbons. She watched him manually lift hundreds of eyelids looking for indications of conjunctivitis and trachoma, a disease which caused the eyelids to turn under, scratching the cornea and ultimately causing blindness. Dr. Gibbons worked fast and efficiently using only a hook that resembled Angie's boot-lace hook. An antiseptic towel was draped over his shoulder. Between exams, the doctor wiped both his hands and the boot hook with the damp towel. Angie knew both eye infections were highly contagious. She silently questioned his sterile technique.

If trachoma is contagious, it's possible that the doctor could be spreading the germ from person to person during the eye exam.

Angie did not challenge his practice. Captain Higgins' instructions echoed in her ear: "Quietly observe, do and say nothing!" Her two years of nursing experience had taught her to file this observation away for a more appropriate time, and to first discuss this with a supervisor, such as Miss Elsie.

The Nurses of Ellis Island Hospital

Once given their Medical Clearance Card, families were reunited, and waited in the Great Hall for their legal interview. Angie observed the officers asking the many questions that were listed in her orientation binder. Most immigrants passed the legal inspections easily. One young man from Vizhnitsa, a village in Bocovina, was detained for further investigation. Through the use of a Romanian interpreter, he answered that his brother's employer promised that a job would be waiting for him upon his arrival in America. He was scheduled to appear before the Board of Special Inquiry to clarify his statement. If the committee determined that a job had been prearranged for him, the young man would be labeled a *contract worker*, and deported.

Immigrants were given a reading test. When asked to read from a book written in Greek, Angie was almost certain that an older Greek woman was not reading a section from the assigned tablet, but may have been reciting a prayer. The officer did not appear to notice. Angie was amused by this, but could not say a word for she had repeatedly been instructed to: "Quietly observe, do and say nothing!"

After a short lunch break, Angie reported to the Mental Testing Section. She was paired with a young intern who was friendlier and more approachable than the medical officers in the Registry. Dr. Philip Scott was coordinating the psychological tests. He gave Angie a thorough overview of the testing center. He carefully explained how patients were evaluated, and outlined the details of the testing procedures.

People who were marked with an **X** and a circled **X** were sent to *Testing* to be evaluated. It was thought that diminished mental ability interfered with finding and maintaining stable employment. Feeble-mindedness and insanity were reasons for deportation under the Immigration Act of 1907. A series of intelligence tests were chosen, and a unique classification system had been developed based on the test results. Those having the mentality of a three-year-old were labeled *idiots*. Those having the mentality of a three- to seven-year-old were called *imbeciles*. Lastly, those having the mentality of an eight- to twelve-year-old were *morons*.

"I've never heard the term *moron* used before," Angie commented.

"That's because we invented it," Dr. Scott answered, patiently. "We needed to create a category for a feeble-minded person who was not obviously mentally retarded, just a bit slow."

Angie nodded, "So, you made up a name?"

"That's right. The word *moron* means *foolish* in Greek," Dr. Scott explained.

"Well, that's interesting, I wonder if that expression will ever catch on." Angie had never learned of this type of selective labeling in nursing school. She wondered if this was the *poppycock* that Miss Elsie talked about on her tour yesterday.

The Mental Testing Station offered a number of testing levels. The first test was a basic intelligence test. A variety of universal puzzle shapes were used. If results were poor, an interview with an interpreter followed. After that, the person was allowed to rest and refresh for twenty-four to forty-eight hours before attempting the second round of tests.

Angie stayed two hours in the Mental Testing Station until Captain Higgins appeared at 17:00 to escort her to a Hearing Room. He explained that a Board of Special Inquiry Hearing was where the decision for deportment was made by a panel of, at least, three committee members appointed by the Commissioner of Immigration. It was the final opportunity for an immigrant to appeal a legal issue or medical concern made by the medical officers of the U.S. Public Health Service.

Hearings were in session when Angie and the Captain arrived at the miniature courtroom. Three Board members were seated behind a rectangular table with two interpreters. A wooden railing, in front of the desk, separated the Board from the immigrants waiting in the observation area. Captain Higgins opened the railing gate, and beckoned Angie to sit on the last empty chair behind the desk. He stood beside her and waited until the case in session was determined before he whispered introductions to the officers. He smiled at Angie as he left, motioning to her to be silent by putting his finger to his lips.

The first five hearings were male, mental-defective cases. Each case progressed swiftly, and all five cases took less than one hour to resolve. The psychological and intelligence test results were presented to the committee. The Board members determined that all five men, two from Syria, one from Armenia, one from Turkey, and one from Czechoslovakia, were to be deported.

The next case was a nineteen-year-old boy from the town of Mattmar, Sweden in the province of Jantlind. He had been detained because he did not have the required twenty-five dollars necessary to enter the county. His uncle from Rhode Island had been notified by telegram. He appeared at the hearing with the money to sponsor his nephew. The Board approved the boy's Landing Card. However, the boy was given a stern warning that he would be required to find employment in the United States. His case could continue to be eligible for re-evaluation for three years.

The last case was a mother and daughter from the town of Sveksna, Lithuania. This was a small border town near Mamel, Germany that was occupied by Germany during the war. It was reported that the mother had not passed the vision test. She was almost blind. The mother and daughter had traveled together, and planned to live with the mother's sister who had come to America before World War I. Unfortunately, it was determined that the mother could not be granted admission, but the daughter would be allowed to enter if her aunt and uncle could be contacted. The old woman begged for mercy from the board. With the assistance of an interpreter, she told them that she could not return to Sveksna. Their home had been destroyed by the Germans, and she was not able to live alone. The board postponed the case, requesting more time for further investigation.

At 19:30 hours, Angie left the Registry, and was relieved to leave the noise and confusion behind her. It felt good to be outdoors after the chaos of the Registry Room. A cool evening breeze was stirring. Angie walked briskly, not only to keep warm, but to escape Island One as quickly as possible.

Back at the Cottage, Angie bumped into Adeline coming down the stairs as she was going up. Adeline was excited, "Hi! I was wondering where you were. Guess what? You're orienting with me tomorrow!"

"I am?" Angie asked.

"Yes, Miss Elsie confirmed it this afternoon. I'm going to teach you how to wash those pretty little favas-infected scalps at the Contagious Disease Hospital."

"Sounds...um...great. Adeline, I really don't know much about the condition."

"Well, you'll know after your firsthand experience tomorrow. Hurry now, and come to dinner. I want to introduce you to my girls. They're already in the dining room," Adeline said.

"Do I have time to wash up, and change my shoes? My feet are killing me."

"Of course, but shake a leg," Adeline laughed.

"In a flash!" Angie answered.

Angie ran to her room, slipped out of her uniform, and washed up. She quickly changed her shoes. She was down in the dining room in a matter of minutes.

"That was fast." Adeline said when she saw Angie. "Everyone, this is Angie Bosco, our newest recruit. Angie, this is Mabel and Dorothy. They work in CD with me. "

Dorothy was taller and thinner than Adeline with a long, narrow face. Her black hair that had been worked into two tight braids that crowned her head. Mabel was five feet tall, plump and round, with a shiny, clean-scrubbed face and rosy cheeks.

"Hi. It's nice to meet you. What's CD?"

"It's short for the Contagious Disease Hospital. Now, here are the *twins*, meet Ruth and Rose. They work nights at the General," Adeline said.

Ruth and Rose appeared to be the same height and weight. They were both dressed in navy-blue. Their short blonde hair was trimmed like Angie's, in the latest bob style of the day. However, they didn't look identical which made Angie ask, "Hi, nice to meet both of you. Are you really twins?"

"No, Adeline calls us *twins* because we look alike," Rose said.

"There's definitely a resemblance. It's a pleasure to meet you. I am hungry. I almost forgot about supper tonight. I was so upset after spending the day at the Registry."

"Say no more," said Ruth.

"You're not alone," said Rose.

"I hate going there," said Mabel.

"The docs aren't too happy either, but they take their responsibility seriously," Adeline added.

Dorothy agreed. "They are good at what they do. Their job is to protect the American public from the diseased and the demented. They became doctors to heal the sick. Now, they feel that they actually punish the sick, the very people who need their help and assistance most."

"I know what you mean," said Angie. "One doctor who I worked with today was a bit of a grouch. He didn't seem to want me interfering with his patients. I felt like I couldn't do anything right."

"Who was he?" Mabel asked.

"He was Dr. Goodwin," Angie answered.

"No, it can't be. He's one of the good guys on this island." Adeline said.

"Cute, too," said Dorothy.

Mabel added, "Fit and fine…and over six feet tall."

"Tall, dark and handsome," Rose said, "with piercing brown eyes that look right through you."

Angie laughed. "Yes, he's the one. Well, I must admit, he was kind to his patients, but if he's one of the good guys around here, oh dear, I can only imagine what the others are like!"

Chapter Nine

❧

April 29, 1920

Thursday
6:15 AM (06:15)

Beware of the demons that live inside of you.
Tenacious, stubborn demons will thrive and cling to you.

Angie was fully dressed in her uniform, and was adjusting her navy-blue cape when Adeline knocked on her door. Adeline was also in her Ellis Island uniform, complete with cap and cape. Her long brown hair was pulled back into a loose bun. Perfect finger waves gently framed and softened her narrow face. "Morning, doll, I'm glad you thought to wear your cape. It looks a little blustery out there this morning," Adeline said.

"Morning, Adeline. Wow, your hair looks great."

"Thanks, I washed, and set it last night."

Angie yawned. "I didn't sleep well last night. The wind was hollowing for hours. It kept waking me. Is it like this all the time?"

"Only sometimes, but don't worry, Angie, you'll soon get used to the sounds of the sea and the wild wind whipping around the Cottage. Are you ready for breakfast?"

"Just a little something before we go out there." Angie said, and followed Adeline downstairs to the dining room. Breakfast of hot

Wheatena, hard boiled eggs, and cinnamon toast had been assembled. Angie helped herself to a bowl of Wheatena. She was topping it off with a pat of butter and a dollop of orange marmalade when she noticed Dorothy standing behind her.

"Morning, Angie," Dorothy said. "I want to introduce you to Imogene and Gertrude. They work in surgery at the General Hospital. You'll be seeing a lot of each other. Imogene...Gertrude...this is Angie Bosco, our new nurse."

Both Imogene and Gertrude had streaks of grey sprinkled throughout their dark hair and appeared to be in their late forties. They were older nurses who radiated competence and experience.

"Hi, call me *Gertie*. It's nice to meet you. Where will you be working?"

"I'm assigned to the Women and Children's Unit," Angie answered.

"Oh, really, Miss Elsie has been forever floating me to the women's wards. I've cared for more than my share of babies since the beginning of the year," Imogene moaned.

"What do you mean?" Angie asked.

Adeline quickly interrupted. "That's the very reason Sister Gwendolyn is hiring more nurses. Guess what? Angie is going to work with me in CD today."

"Oh, no, CD...Contagious Disease, really Adeline? Couldn't Miss Elsie find something other than that for the new recruit to do today? She'll get the heebie-jeebies over your scalp treatments, and run scared right off this Island." Imogene warned, sarcastically.

"I doubt that!" Dorothy and Mabel replied in unison, as they sat down to eat their breakfast.

Preferring not to eat with the younger nurses, Imogene and Gertrude sat at a nearby table for two. Imogene turned to Angie, and said, "Well, good luck to you, honey, you'll need it."

Ignoring Imogene, Mabel turned to Adeline, and asked, "Will you have time to bring Angie to my trachoma unit today?"

"I hope so, if I don't have many new patients requiring scalp treatments. When would be the best time to come, Mabel?"

"We do the therapies in the early afternoon before naps and in the evening before bedtime. The treatments are so painful and upsetting, it helps if the patients sleep after receiving them," Mabel said.

Overhearing the conversation at the larger table, Imogene interrupted, "Oh my, the new nurse has to observe both favus and trachoma treatments on the same day. Is it your intention to scare the bejesus out of her during her first week of orientation?"

"Be nice, Imogene!" Adeline said.

"Is it really that bad?" Angie asked.

"Everything you've heard and more." Imogene added.

"Imogene, stop!" Mabel said, and continued on with her explanation. "We are having some success with blue stone and silver nitrate therapies, especially with the children. They burn away the diseased tissue to generate fresh, healthy growth. However, blue stone is copper sulfate, and the process is both painful and slow. It takes the longest time before we see even the slightest results. Many of the sulfur compounds and experimental mixtures that we tried before copper sulfate turned out to be ineffective."

Imogene looked annoyed. "Ladies, can you postpone this conversation until *after* we eat?"

Everyone at the table agreed. They stopped talking about work long enough to eat their breakfast. When they finished, they exited the Cottage through the rear door, and walked along the boardwalk to the lobby of the General Hospital. There, Imogene and Gertrude took the elevator up to the Surgical Department. Angie, Adeline, Dorothy, and Mabel continued on, walking to Island Three. A strong wind rattled the glass window panes lining the enclosed walkway. It was cold and drafty. The women walked quickly to keep warm.

"Adeline, I have to admit that I don't know much about favus infection. I've never actually seen it. I've only read about it in my textbooks. It's like ringworm, isn't it?" Angie asked.

"Similar but different, although both are fungi," Adeline said.

Dorothy couldn't resist the temptation. "What? You mean ringworm isn't caused by a round worm."

"I know. I often hear that from my patients. They think that a worm actually enters their body," Mabel said.

Adeline explained. "Yes. Ringworm is the more contagious fungus. It can spread like wildfire, especially in crowded places, such as schools, hospitals, and certainly steerage quarters. People can get ringworm on different parts of their body...their skin, feet, hands, scalp, genitals...almost anywhere."

"Favus is contagious, too," added Mabel.

"Yes, Mabel, but favus appears to be a more sensitive type of fungus. It isn't able to survive outside the body as long as ringworm. Favus grows on the scalp, under the hair follicles. It only spreads to the patients' fingernails because they scratch their heads."

When they arrived at the Contagious Disease Hospital, Dorothy headed off to *TB*, the Tuberculosis Unit, and Mabel to *Trach*, the

Trachoma Unit. Angie and Adeline continued walking until they reached the ward dedicated to isolating favus scalp infections. The spacious ward was well-equipped to care for thirty children. Extra-large floor-to-ceiling windows on the south wall were cracked open, allowing fresh air and light to enter the room. The children were awake and dressed for the day, having been assisted with their morning care by the matrons on night-duty. As she entered the room, Adeline was suddenly surrounded by six little girls with gauze-covered heads who all wanted to hold one of Adeline's two hands. The boys were chasing each other in an impromptu game of tag.

Bertha, the night matron, greeted the nurses and gave a quick report, mentioning two new admissions. "They are the Stanescu twins from Romania who arrived last night, Mariana and Melita. They will need their first treatments this morning. I was able to reach Paulo before he left yesterday. I asked him to help us today when he had some free time because he is originally from Slovakia, and speaks Romanian."

Adeline turned to Angie to explain. "Paulo is our janitor. He might be able to interpret for us, so that the girls won't be terribly frightened. I give the first two scalp treatments...depilation and debridement. First, I remove any hair growing in the affected area. Then, I remove the diseased scalp tissue. After that, the aides take responsibility for keeping the scalps oiled QID, *four times a day.*"

When Bertha left, Adeline and two aides gathered the children for breakfast. While the children sat at the table and waited for their food to arrive, Adeline cranked up the gramophone, and put a record on. The children immediately started to sing the song *Swanee* when the music began. The next record that Adeline played was *Over There*

"Sing along," she said, and the children sang the words to the wartime song. "Singing the songs helps them practice their English. These little ones catch on very quickly."

"Yes, it's wonderful, but how did such an expensive Victrola find its way to an immigrant hospital?"

"A donation from an old flame," Adeline answered.

"Seriously?" questioned Angie.

"Yes, I'm absolutely serious. When young men aren't ready to commit, they donate gramophones to the charity hospital of their choice to assuage the guilt," Adeline smiled, but did not elaborate.

After breakfast, Red Cross volunteers arrived to teach English classes. They lined up the boys, and led them to a classroom for a one-hour lesson. Thirteen little girls remained on the unit and played quietly. The ward was filled with many different types of toys that had been donated for the children to play with. However, Angie noticed that the little girls gravitated toward the baby bottles and dolls, ignoring the tinker toys and erector sets.

The nurses put on surgical gowns, and turned their attention to the twins from Romania. They were four years old. Both girls wore their black hair plaited into thin braids, tied with blue ribbons. "Hi, Mariana, my name is Adeline." Adeline gave the little girl a squeeze as she lifted her up, onto her lap. Mariana smiled up at her. "Let's see what we have here," Adeline said in a friendly voice. She untied the little girl's meager braid to take a peek at her scalp. An inch of hair circling the crown of Mariana's head appeared to be healthy growth. Underneath, the child's scalp was a mass of honeycomb-like infections with irregular tufts of hair growing from the center. Each honeycomb was two to three inches in diameter, and was made of small, yellow, hollow, pea-sized cups. When Adeline touched the encrustations with her gloved hand, they disintegrated into a dense, white powder. Thick, olive-green pus erupted from the hollows.

"Look, Angie, this is a severe case of *favus sulphureus celerior*. All of her hair will have to be removed. We must attend to this today."

"Yes, I see, it smells awful, almost like a dead mouse." Both the smell and the oozing pustules made Angie gag, but she tried her best and successfully stifled the reflex.

"We'll have to wait for Paulo to come to explain the situation to the girls, or they will be terrified when we shave their hair. First, I must check in with the matrons covering the Boys Measles Unit. Come with me. Leave your gown here. We'll look for Paulo along the way."

Angie followed Adeline as she walked down the curved corridor in the direction of the measles units.

"These boys are always getting into some kind of trouble. They're almost ready to be discharged, and are scheduled to go home at the end of this week. They've become close friends because they were all on the same boat that left Cobh, Ireland," Adeline explained. "They were taken off the ship, and admitted two weeks ago."

When Adeline and Angie entered the measles unit, the brightly lit ward was filled with cherub-faced little boys, rosy-cheeked with fair skin and dark black hair. The window shutters were open, and streams of light flooded the room. Ida and Lauren, the ward matrons, were in a tizzy. "The boys will not leave the shutters closed," Lauren reported. "We have written orders to keep the room dark to avoid eye irritation, but the boys hate being in the dark. We close the shutters, and no matter what we say, they ignore us. They open the shutters when we turn our backs and leave the room. They all follow the ring leader, Stephan O'Gill."

At the mention of his name, Stephan stopped picking his nose, and looked up.

"I didn't do nottin', Miss Adeline. She's a liar!"

"Stephan O'Gill, you are the leader of this pack. Everyone knows that the boys obey your every command. You open the shutters, and they follow your lead. Since you've been here, I've never given you a punishment, but this time I might be reporting you to the doctors," Adeline scolded.

"They can't do nottin' ta me, Miss," said Stephan.

"Well, maybe they will detain you, and not discharge you with the others this week," Adeline threatened. "I can take away your snacks today, too."

"Aw, you wouldn't do that, Miss Adeline. You're too pretty to be so mean. Why, just look at me...nottin' but skin 'n bones...a growin' boy."

"Promise me you'll behave today, Stephan."

"Oh, you know I will, Miss Adeline. I promise," Stephan said, smiling innocently and looking up at Miss Adeline with big, blue, angelic eyes.

"Now, stop picking your nose, Stephan. Go wash your hands. I want to hear nothing but a good report when I return this afternoon."

When the nurses left the measles ward, they searched for Paulo. They found him stocking supplies in the janitor's closet.

"Good Morning, Paulo. How are you today?"

"Just-a-fine, Miss Adelina, and-a-you?"

"I am having a good day, Paulo. This is our new nurse, Miss Angie. She'll be working at the General Hospital, but she's assisting me today on the favus unit."

"It's a pleasure for sure-a, Miss Angie. Glad to meet-a-you!"

"Paulo, would you have time this morning to interpret for two Romanian twins who were admitted yesterday evening?" Adeline asked.

"Sure enough-a, Miss Adelina, anything for you. Misses Bertha asked-a-me-last night. When do you want-a-me to come?"

"As soon as you have free time, Paulo."

"Now's a-good, Miss Adelina."

"Perfect," Adeline said, smiling.

They returned to the favus ward. On the way, Adeline described the scalp treatments to Paulo. She told him exactly what to explain to the little twin girls. When Paulo was introduced to the twins, he was able to translate everything that Adeline requested. The girls appeared to understand. Paulo was happy to report that the girls knew they had a serious hair problem. Their mother promised that the medicine in America would help them grow healthy hair.

Adeline smiled, "Please tell them that I will start their treatments today. The treatments will not hurt. I have medicine that will stop the hurt, and allow them to heal and get better. Tell them that the bad hair has to come out so that new, strong, healthy hair can grow in."

Paulo said, "It's gonna be-a-fine, Misses. Their mama told-a-them not to be afraid and to be-a-brave and-a-strong."

"Thank you, Paulo, I appreciate your help. It makes a big difference."

"You're-a-most welcome, Misses. I get-a-back to work now," Paulo said, and left the ward.

"Okay, let's get started. This is our protective gear," Adeline instructed. "First, put on your rubber apron, and then, these surgical gloves."

ELLIS ANGELS

After gearing up, Adeline went to work. She wrapped the longer tufts of hair growing from the center of Mariana's head around a ruler, and pulled. In seconds, the clump of hair came out easily, and without struggle. Mariana didn't appear to feel the pulling. Angie was reassured that Melita wouldn't feel her hair being pulled, and repeated exactly what Adeline did with Mariana. The nurses then handpicked the shorter tufts of hair until the center of each scalp showed only the honeycomb infection. They shaved the hair around the crown of the girls' hairlines. Next, they scrubbed the little girls' scalps with a mixture of carbolic acid and Balsam of Peru, an antiseptic with a pleasant vanilla aroma taken from the bark of the balsam tree. Finally, they sprinkled a layer of boric acid powder and brushed on a thick coating of cod liver oil, carefully filling each red hollow space with the oil. They covered the girls' heads with white cotton kerchiefs, securing them with a knot. Adeline unrolled two feet of three-inch gauze. She wrapped the gauze around the flannel kerchiefs and fashioned a big side bow on Mariana's head.

"Very stylish," said Angie.

"In the summertime, I dye the gauze cherry-pink for the girls. I boil the strips in water with six beets, and dry the gauze out in the sun on the side porches of the Cottage," Adeline explained. "Okay, we're finished for now. Some of the pustules will begin to rot and die within twenty-four hours because they are smothered by the oil. The aides will keep renewing the oiling. Lard is sometimes used instead of oil. Both do the same thing. They drown the fungus. We've tried every treatment from alcohol and peroxide to bleach, but this recipe of carbolic acid, balsam, boric acid, and oil is highly efficacious. One medical officer is experimenting with X-Rays in an attempt to kill severe infestations. Tomorrow, I'll start

94

debridement. I'll use a tongue depressor to scrape the scutula, then wash, treat, and oil again."

"How long will it take to heal?" asked Angie.

"The scalp will heal in three to four months. The Settlement Nurses in the city sometimes follow-up. They try to check on the children every six months after they are discharged," Adeline said.

Angie and Adeline were in the process of cutting the ends off the gauze bows they had made, when Ida burst into the room, screaming. "Miss Adeline, come quick. It's Stephan, he's on the roof!"

"What in the world? How did he get there?" Adeline questioned.

"After you left, the boys were teasing Stephan. He told them he was leaving, and no one could stop him. They actually dared him to go, and he did. Stephan went right through the open window, and straight out onto the roof. Miss Lauren ran for the guards from Psych Pavilion. We thought that they might know what to do."

Angie and Adeline stopped what they were doing, and ran out into the cold to search for Stephan on the roof of the hospital building. "There he is," someone shouted. The wind was blowing wildly. Young Stephan sat frozen on the tile roof.

"Stephan, are you okay?" Angie screamed, at the top of her voice.

"Please, come down, now," Ida cried.

"I can't, Miss Ida. I keep slippin' when I try. I'm scared, Miss Ida."

"How did you get up there, Stephan?" Adeline called up to him.

"I followed the tiles to the top, but some of 'em tiles broke. I can't get past 'em now," Stephan cried back.

"Okay, Stephan, sit still. Stay right where you are. Don't move! We'll get help," Adeline shouted.

Just then, Lauren ran toward them with an announcement. "The guards won't come because they said they don't want to catch measles."

"Oh dear, the boy is no longer contagious," Adeline said.

"What shall we do?" Ida asked.

Hearing the commotion, Paulo came outside. He offered his assistance in an effort to save the boy. "I go-up-a, Misses. I go to fetch-a-the boy. No one care if I get-a-the measles."

"Wait, no Paulo, you might get hurt. There must be an alternative."

Angie had an idea. "Yes, there is. I saw a fire alarm in the hallway. Lauren, come with me!"

Someone screamed, "Wait!"

"Look, Misses!" Paulo pointed toward the roof.

When Adeline looked up, she saw a tall man in a white lab coat standing behind Stephan. In an instant, he snatched Stephan up into his arms. Very cautiously, he made his way back down to the window. Both the boy and the man entered the same open window that Stephan had escaped from.

Everyone ran back into the building to find young Stephan still clinging to Dr. Abraham Goodwin. Dr. Goodwin examined the boy for scratches and injuries.

"You saved me life, Doc," cried Stephan.

"Well, nothing's broken. You seemed to have survived. Stephan, you must settle down. In three days' time, I promise that I will discharge you, and you will be able to go home with your parents."

"I'll be good. I will, Doc." Stephan looked very serious and determined.

Ida said, "Hooray, Dr. Goodwin, you saved the day."

Dr. Goodwin explained. "I came in during my rounds. The boys looked upset and frightened. They told me what happened. I went out to get Stephan, without thinking."

"I'm so glad you came when you did, Doctor. We can't thank you enough. Oh, I want to introduce you to our newest nurse, Miss Angie," Adeline said.

"We meet again," Dr. Goodwin said, shaking Angie's hand. "It was a pleasure to work with you yesterday. Where will you be working?"

"Mother and Children's Unit at the General Hospital," said Angie.

"We'll be working together. I'll look forward to that."

"Thank you, Doctor, I will too. You have a special knack with the children."

Dr. Goodwin's special knack with the boys, however, could not get them to settle down. The boys were overexcited as they circled around Stephan, calling him *one brave American*. They were jumping up and down when the kitchen matrons wheeled in the lunch cart. Lauren and Ida looked helpless. They could not get the boys to sit down.

"I have an idea," Angie whispered to Adeline. Adeline laughed, and nodded. Angie disappeared.

The room was still in an uproar when Angie returned, rolling in the Victrola. She wound its side-crank, and put a record on. The music played. It calmed the boys. They soon sat down to eat their lunch of potato-leek soup, apples, and cheese with white bread and butter.

Suddenly, Adeline grabbed Angie, and said, "I'm starved. It's lunch-time. Let's go, and get our lunch. Then, we'll head over to Mabel's in time for the trachoma treatments."

"All this excitement and it is only lunchtime." Smiling, Angie asked, "Is it like this every day?"

"Well, every day does hold a new surprise...and I love it, Angie."

"I believe you, and I know I'm going to love it, too!" Angie said, taking hold of Adeline's arm as they hurried off to the Dining Room.

Chapter Ten

~

April 30, 1920

Friday
7 AM (07:00)

Suddenly she woke up, and found to her surprise,
That teachers there were many, always at her side.

Sister Gwendolyn Hanover, Superintendent of Nursing, was pacing the floor when Mickey knocked at her office door.

"Top of the Mornin', Sista!" Mickey said.

"And the balance to you, my lad. What can I do for you today?" Sister Gwendolyn asked.

"Cap Higgins sent me over, Sista. He said to tell ya that the work crew will be here to put up the walls this mornin'. He said it would be fittin' if you met 'em on the ward along about eleven to tell 'em exactly where you want 'em up."

"Yes, of course, Mickey. Tell him, I will definitely be there. Thank you, Mickey, for coming to deliver the message to me," Sister Gwendolyn said.

"Aw, taint nothin', Sista. Goodae, Sista."

"Good Day to you, too, Mickey." Sister called out, as Mickey turned and left the room.

There was no doubt about it. Sister Gwendolyn had procrastinated. She would be required to make a decision this morning. Three weeks before, she submitted a work order for a ward renovation, but she had not included the specific details of the ward conversion along with the requisition form. She visited Ward 220 on the second floor of the South Wing daily for inspiration, but could not decide how to transform the large room into smaller workable units to create a Mother and Children's Unit with separate spaces for ante-partum patients, postpartum patients, and newborns. If the large room was quartered into four separate ones, two rooms would not have windows and two would not have doors. The military had converted many of the smaller rooms into large wards during the war. As a result, the nursery and labor room had been sacrificed. A maternity patient would now be assigned to a bed anywhere on the women's wards. Her newborn would simply be placed in a crib beside her. Sister Gwendolyn thought.

This is not the standard in modern hospitals, and quite an unacceptable practice.

Today, Sister Gwendolyn would not only be faced with making a final design decision, she would also have to confess to the nurse recruit that the Mother and Children's Unit, the unit she was assigned to, did not, as yet, exist. Sister Gwendolyn had managed to stall the young woman during her first week by scheduling her to work with Miss Elsie and Miss Adeline. Today, Miss Angie was expecting Sister Gwendolyn to orient her to the Women and Children's Unit at the General Hospital.

On schedule, Angie Bosco arrived at the Superintendent's office at 07:00 sharp.

"Good Morning, my dear Miss Angie, how are you this morning?"

"I am fine, Sister Gwendolyn. How are you?"

"Fine. Fine. Are you satisfied with your accommodations at the Cottage?" Sister Gwendolyn asked.

"Oh, yes! I love my room," Angie answered.

"Have you had an opportunity to meet any of the other nurses, Miss Angie?"

"Yes, they are quite a fine group of women, and have been most welcoming, Sister."

"I am happy to hear that. Miss Angie, I have a little challenge that I would like to discuss with you this morning. First, let me ask you if you have any questions or concerns about the hospitals thus far."

"The hospital is much bigger than I imagined. There are more than seven hundred and fifty patient beds in the complex. I counted less than thirty nurses. That's one nurse to twenty-five patients," Angie said.

"My, I am impressed, Miss Angie. You have the makings of an administrator. You are already calculating nursing ratios. In addition, we must factor in day and night coverage to the ratio numbers. As you know, many of our best nurses left when the hospital census declined during the war years. We haven't rehired to the pre-war number."

"How many chief nurses are now on staff?" Angie inquired.

"There are twenty-eight chief nurses. In total, thirty-one nurses are employed here, including the three superintendents: Miss Elsie Archer, Miss Elizabeth Turner and myself."

"How do you determine ward assignments?"

Sister Gwendolyn explained. "Let's see, ten chief nurses are on the schedule in Contagious Disease because of our concern for cross-contamination. Seven are on the day-shift, and three on nights. Then, I try to assign one nurse to the Psych Pavilion, whenever I can."

"That's eleven," said Angie, adding up the numbers.

"The remaining seventeen chief nurses are assigned to the General Hospital. There are four nurses in surgery and recovery on the day-shift, and thirteen in medicine, covering both the day and night shifts," Sister Gwendolyn said. "We rely heavily on the matrons and aides. They are a great asset. We have over one hundred on staff. Nursing duties of the chief nurses have expanded to include teaching them."

"What procedures are the aides permitted to perform?" Angie asked.

"You will be surprised at what we taught them. In addition to bedside instruction, Miss Elsie teaches formal classes. She has regularly scheduled classes in aseptic technique, enemas, catheterizing, and dressings. Miss Elsie worked very closely with the chief nurses to create an educational curriculum that meets the needs of both the nurses and the patients. After the classes, the work of the novice aides is supervised, and must be approved by two registered nurses before they are allowed to perform the procedures without supervision."

"That sounds exciting to me. I love to teach, and share what I've learned," Angie said, eagerly.

"One important role of the chief nurse is to oversee the work of the matrons and aides. You will be supervising, teaching, and making appropriate patient assignments for them. I don't want my nurses scrubbing floors and cleaning windows."

"But...it's our job to keep the wards clean."

"Yes. However, there are charwomen employed here at the facility to do all the scrubbing of the wards. You are responsible to keep your wards sparkling clean, but you are not to waste valuable nursing time cleaning. We must all work smart to make the best use of the time and talent of our trained professional nurses."

"Will you be hiring additional nurses soon?"

"The government higher-ups make the budget decisions. They want to be certain that immigration numbers will continue to rise."

"With the exception of the war years, immigration has been steadily increasing since the turn of the century. Do you anticipate a change?"

Sister Gwendolyn continued to explain. "There's talk of putting barriers on immigration, and perhaps stopping it completely. Unemployment is on the rise, and jobs are beginning to get scarce. Unfortunately, the unemployed city folks blame the immigrants for taking their jobs, as well as for everything else: crime, disease, and over-crowding in their neighborhoods. The *upper-crusts* are gradually moving uptown and away from the immigrant *riff-raff.*"

"I've been reading about that in the newspapers," Angie said.

Sister Gwendolyn added, "There are a great many people who believe in America, and welcome the strong workers who boost the economy. They believe that America has always been a melting pot, made rich by the addition of resourceful people from foreign lands. Then, there are those who are fearful and afraid for their jobs. Many, especially the labor unions, now want a halt to immigration."

"Would that really be possible?"

"It's possible, of course, but highly improbable. Congress is still in session on that one. A handful of congressmen are researching ways to restrict the number of people permitted into the United States. One proposal on the table is to establish a quota number for every country, and put a limit on the number of immigrants coming into America each year. When the country's quota is met, immigration from that country would be closed until the following year."

"Do you think that would happen?"

"Truthfully, I don't really know." Sister Gwendolyn sighed. "We will have to wait and see the results of their investigation." Both women were silent for a moment as they considered the outcome of such a ruling.

Angie thought this was an opportune time to ask Sister Gwendolyn a question that was on her mind. "Sister Gwendolyn, does a nurse named Miss Mary work here?"

"No, there's no one named Mary currently on the nursing staff at Ellis Island. However, there were two over the years that I recall. What is Mary's last name, Miss Angie?"

"I am afraid I don't know, but she worked here twelve years ago."

"Yes, that would be Miss Mary O'Connor, a very fine nurse...a very fine nurse indeed. God bless her."

"She was kind and beautiful with golden hair," added Angie.

"We lost her during the war. She was one of the first nurses to enlist, and the first of our many casualties. While overseas, she became gravely ill. I learned of her death less than a year after she left us to go to war. I was heartbroken when I received the news that we lost such a lovely lady. A great many of our nurses, who were stationed in France, died of influenza. The news was devastating. We have honored them by entering their names on a bronze plaque in the Cottage Reading Room. Have you had an opportunity to go in there this week?"

"No, Sister, I'm afraid I haven't had time."

"Well, do go in. Have a look around when you have a free moment. You will see Mary O'Connor's name included on the memorial on the wall. How did you know Miss Mary?"

"I met her once when I was a young girl. I believe she inspired me to go into nursing, Sister Gwendolyn."

"Yes, if anyone would instill inspiration for nursing, it would have been Miss Mary. I will always remember her. Now, Miss Angie, about the Mother and Children's Unit..."

"I can't wait to see it, Sister Gwendolyn."

"Well, that's what I want to talk to you about. The workmen are coming this morning to divide one of the largest wards into smaller units."

"This morning?" Angie asked.

"Yes, we lost our nursery and labor room during the war. They were converted into a larger ward to care for wounded soldiers. It is my wish to redesign Ward 220 on the second floor. It's directly under the surgical wing. Would you be interested in assisting me, Miss Angie?"

"Of course, you mean that you were waiting for my input before designing the unit? I can't think of anything better!"

"Indeed, my dear, that's why I waited until after you arrived and had your orientation. Let me show you the space. Perhaps, you'll have some ideas for us," Sister Gwendolyn suggested.

Angie's face glowed with excitement. "Oh yes, of course, let's go."

Sister Gwendolyn could not be more pleased with Angie's reaction. She jumped up from her chair, and said, "Follow me!"

Angie followed Sister Gwendolyn out of her office, through the main lobby, and into the South Wing. They took the elevator to the second floor. As they exited the elevator, they entered the first door on their left. Sister had chosen Ward 220 because it was directly below the surgical suite and adjacent to the elevator in the event of an emergency delivery or Cesarean-Section. Ward 220 was empty. It was extremely large, and there seemed to be room for more than fifty patient beds. The inside wall had two doors to the corridor creating two entrances into the room. A panel of large windows lined the opposite wall. "There is a work crew coming this morning. They are ready to work if we can direct them concerning how to divide this room into smaller units without giving up hallway access and light," Sister Gwendolyn said.

"I think I might have the solution, if perhaps they can install doors," Angie said.

"I'm certain they can put in a door here and there. What do you have in mind?" Sister Gwendolyn asked.

"Oh, Sister, yes, I think I see it. Divide the room completely in half from the window wall so that every side of the room has light. If we were to build a door in the new dividing wall, the nurses would have access to both sides of the room without having to go out into the hallway. When there are no maternity patients, these rooms can be used for overflow. Let's call them Ward 220A and Ward 220B. They can be one large unit or they can be divided into separate spaces with maternity patients on one side and medical or surgical patients on the other."

"Of course," said Sister Gwendolyn.

"Now, come, here in 220B. Let's build two walls in an **L** shape in this corner. This section would receive light from the windows, and can be used as a nursery or a procedure room when there are no babies in-house," Angie said, excitedly. "Let's put another door in one of those walls to close it off. We can put the door right here."

Sister Gwendolyn walked over to the corner of the ward where Angie was standing. "I think it would work very well…very well indeed!"

"Yes," said Angie, "and the morning sun that comes in through these windows is perfect for the babies. The hotter sun in the afternoon would be too strong for them. The sunlight does help to decrease their jaundice color, you know."

"Ah, so you've had that experience working with newborns, also." Sister Gwendolyn answered in surprise.

"Oh, yes, one of my nursing instructors at Bellevue demonstrated this color change to the class. She was originally from England and cautioned us that the physicians will say that this practice is an old wives' tale."

"I've had many a conversation with a medical officer about that very same notion. Of course, they continue to insist that there is no scientific rationale for the infant's change in color," Sister Gwendolyn said.

"I know, Sister. Oh, look, I can see a little baby in her crib, right there in the corner, all ready to be wheeled out to her mother. It's perfect. This arrangement for the unit might work quite well."

As she looked across the room, Sister Gwendolyn squinted a bit, and smiled. "Why, Miss Angie, I believe your recommendations may be just the solution I was looking for. I do believe I am beginning to see your vision. I can almost see the tiny nursery built in this corner of the room. Yes, my dear, I believe I do actually see it!"

Part Two

Ladies-In-White

In an effort to curb the flow of immigration to the United States after World War I, Congress passed the Temporary Quota Law of 1921. This law was to be in effect for one year. However, it was renewed in 1922 and 1923 in an attempt to stop the large number of foreigners coming from Southern and Eastern Europe.

Each country's quota number was calculated at 3% of the people from that country who were living in the United States during the census of 1910. Because there were more Englishmen and Irishmen in the USA in 1910, the law favored admitting Northern Europeans over others. This law gradually decreased the number of immigrants coming through Ellis Island to a steady average of 250,000 people annually for the next three years.

∽

Chapter Eleven

Three Years Later

September 13, 1923
11 AM (11:00)

Always guarding, ever vigil but we deny they're near.
We can believe in angels. Just trust that they are here.

Angie took a minute from her busy morning to quickly take an assessment of Ward 220B. At the moment, all was peaceful and in order. With the support of Sister Gwendolyn, Angie had worked patiently and diligently to create a safe hospital setting for new mothers who delivered their babies at Ellis Island General Hospital. It had taken over a year to obtain the necessary equipment, but together, they were persistent in acquiring what was needed for the nurses to efficiently care for their patients.

As Angie surveyed the ward, she checked the expiration date on all the sterile packages stocked on the unit. She noticed that one delivery pack was close to expiring with a date of 09-14-23 written on the label. Angie walked down the hall to the storage closet to exchange the outdated pack for a fresh one. Just as she was closing the closet door, Angie heard the screams.

"JESUS, MARY, AND JOSEPH, HE'S COMING RIGHT NOW!"

"Oh, no," said Angie, stopping to listen more attentively.

"MOTHER MARY, PRAY FOR ME," the screaming continued.

That's Maggie McGuire, thought Angie as she ran back toward Ward 220B which she had left minutes earlier.

Fannie, the nurse's aide, came running out to meet Angie in the hallway. "Miss Angie! Miss Angie! Come quick! Mrs. McGuire says the baby is coming right now, and her sheets are wet with brown poo-water."

When I last checked her, her cervix was 6 centimeters dilated, thought Angie, rushing to meet Fannie.

"Please, Miss Angie, please come. Please come, quickly," Fannie begged.

Angie rubbed her hands together to heat them as she ran to Mrs. McGuire's bedside. She softly placed her warmed hand on Maggie's rock-hard abdomen. Maggie's uterus was contracting sharply. Angie grabbed her Pinard horn, the fetal stethoscope. She had it poised and ready to listen for the baby's heartbeat when the contraction ended. Feeling Maggie's abdomen soften, she carefully positioned the Pinard horn to listen to the baby's heart tones. The rhythm of the baby's heart was slow and irregular. She looked at the clock on the wall and counted the heartbeats. The baby's heart was beating slowly at 100 beats per minute.

Something is wrong.

Angie lifted Maggie McGuire's bed covers to find her bed soaked in a tan liquid. This meant that Maggie's amniotic sac, her *bag of waters*, had ruptured. The color of the amniotic fluid should have been clear, but this tinge of light brown meant that the baby was releasing some of his first meconium stool. This was always an indication that the baby was not getting all the oxygen he needed.

Hypoxia is a sign of fetal distress! Maggie's baby is not getting enough oxygen. The baby's heart is slowing down.

Angie turned, and reached for a pair of rubber gloves and lubricant to prepare for a cervical check. When Angie gently slipped her gloved hand through the vaginal canal, she noted that the cervical opening had softened and enlarged to the size of all five fingers of her hand.

Fully effaced and dilated at ten centimeters, she calculated.

Angie noted that the baby was preparing to enter the birth canal. As Angie wondered if there was time to transfer her patient to the Delivery Room on the third floor, another strong contraction erupted. Maggie McGuire cried out once more, "HELP ME, JESUS!" She appeared to be starting to push her baby out.

"Run, Fannie, run, please. Find Doctor Collins, upstairs!" Angie took a deep breath. Then, with a calm, softer, and slower voice, Angie said to Fannie. "Doctor Collins is scheduled for surgery this morning. He is upstairs in the operating room. Take the elevator. Find Miss Gertrude. Tell her that delivery is imminent. The baby may be in trouble."

Angie wheeled the green oxygen canister closer to Maggie's bed. She turned on the oxygen meter, and adjusted the black oxygen mask on Maggie's face. Angie waited for the contraction to ease. Then, she turned Maggie onto her left side, facing her. Angie spoke softly but firmly. "Maggie, look at me, look into my eyes. You are doing great! Breathe with me, breathe with me, dear. Breathe how I am breathing. It will help you not to push right now."

When the contraction subsided, Angie had an idea. She gently slipped her gloved hand through the birth canal. If the baby's head was presenting in the most common posterior position, Angie knew that she would be able to feel the very back of the crown of his head. Angie felt encouraged that the baby's head was in the correct position for a vaginal delivery. Tugging in a little further with her gloved hand, she identified the baby's neck, and could actually feel the umbilical cord wrapped around it. With each contraction, the cord was tightening around the baby's neck, shutting off his much-needed supply of oxygen. The low oxygen level was slowing down the baby's heart rate. This caused the baby to release his meconium stool before delivery. Angie felt beads of sweat forming on her forehead. She tucked a finger under the umbilical cord, and was relieved when it loosened just enough so that she could lift it over the baby's head. Angie softly eased her hand out.

Miss Gertrude rushed into the room with a stretcher, and announced, "Collins is in surgery. He has a bleeder in the *OR*. Is there time to bring her upstairs to surgery?"

"We can try, Gertie, if we hurry." Miss Gertrude positioned the stretcher so that it was parallel to Maggie McGuire's bed. Angie repositioned the oxygen tubing. She loosened the soiled bed sheet, and grabbed hold. Gertrude did the same on the other side of the bed. "One, two, three," they said in unison, and lifted Maggie McGuire, bed sheet and all, onto the stretcher.

Angie grabbed the sterile delivery pack, and placed it on top of the stretcher. The nurses ran with Gertrude in the lead, pulling the stretcher, and Angie pushing it from behind.

At the doorway, Maggie McGuire screamed, "NURSES, HE'S COMING OUT!"

Angie and Gertrude abruptly stopped in their tracks. "Better check!" Gertrude said.

Angie peeked under the bed sheet to see a small circle of black fuzz appearing.

"No time, Gertie!"

Instantly, both nurses abruptly swung into reverse, as Angie pulled and Gertrude pushed. Gertrude placed the delivery pack on the bed, and opened it quickly and carefully to maintain the sterility of its contents. Gertrude had no sooner taken out her pocket-watch in anticipation of noting the time of birth when the head of the baby suddenly emerged. Angie carefully guided the baby's shoulder as it came out slowly. She knew that after the shoulder delivered, the baby would quickly swoosh out. Angie braced to hold on tight to the baby. This was the part she always dreaded, concerned that the slippery wet baby might fall from her hands. Angie felt her own heart thumping in her chest, and her blood rush and redden her face. She maintained the tightest grip as a baby girl slipped out. Before placing the newborn on her mother's abdomen, Angie used both hands to hold the baby upside down until the baby cried. It was hoped that gravity would prevent the baby from breathing in mucus. Gertrude handed Angie a thin catheter from the delivery pack. Angie quickly suctioned the baby's throat and both nostrils by softly sucking on the end of the tubing. Luckily, the fluid she retrieved was clear. She felt reassured when she saw no brown particles of meconium in the tube.

A good sign, thought Angie, feeling relieved.

The baby howled.

Ah, Angie sighed…*an even better sign!*

"It's a girl!" Gertrude called out, "11:22."

"It's a girl, Mrs. McGuire!" Angie cried.

"Here I was calling her a *he* all this time," Maggie McGuire said. "God bless my darling daughter."

Gertrude took two metal clamps and a pair of scissors from the delivery pack. She handed Angie the two clamps. Angie quickly secured the umbilical cord leaving a space of an inch between the clamps. Gertrude used the sterile scissors to cut the cord. Next, Gertrude removed two flannel blankets from the delivery pack. She carefully smoothed out the first one on top of the bed. She opened up the second blanket, and used it to lift and carry the baby to the bed. Using the blanket, she rubbed off the thickest patches of the waxy *vernix caseosa* and mucous.

Angie turned her attention to Baby Girl McGuire to listen to her heart rate. She tapped her finger on the bed to the rhythm of the baby's vigorous heart rate. Gertrude counted the taps with her pocket-watch. "That's 140 beats per minute," announced Gertrude.

"Book normal, she is," said Angie, "with good muscle tone."

"…And her color is nice and pink now," Gertrude added. "She seems to be showing no signs of respiratory distress."

Angie swaddled the baby tightly and placed her in her mother's arms. The baby's eyes were wide open. She stared at Maggie McGuire as if to say, "So, you are my mother. I've been waiting to meet you." Maggie McGuire started to cry as she gazed at her baby daughter.

Tears welled up in Angie's eyes, also. She looked down on the mother and baby, and said, "Welcome to the world, Baby Girl McGuire. I'm glad you've arrived safely."

Gertrude could not help but smile. "Now, we must wait patiently for the placenta to deliver. Come, Fannie! Come. Help me change the bed while we wait."

Shocked and stunned, Fannie had been watching the delivery of Baby Girl McGuire from the doorway. She appeared dazed, and unable to speak. Finally, she said, "I've never seen a baby born before. Why was the baby in trouble?"

"Stress," said Angie.

"How could she be stressed? What's she got to be worried about, Miss Angie?"

"I don't mean emotionally stressed, the baby was physically stressed. In nursing language, we would say that she was *in distress*," Angie explained.

Gertrude called to Fannie. "Come, Fannie, bring over those clean sheets and that cart. Let's make a fresh bed for Mrs. McGuire, and I will teach you a little more." Gertrude wrapped up the used delivery pack, and placed it on the cart. Then, Gertrude and Fannie removed the soiled bed linens.

"Do all mothers poo when they deliver?" Fannie asked.

Gertrude explained. "The mother didn't poo. The baby did. It was a signal to us that she wasn't getting enough oxygen."

"How does the baby get oxygen, Miss Gertrude?"

"When the baby is in her mother's uterus, she gets air and nourishment from her mother through her umbilical cord."

Angie massaged Maggie McGuire's abdomen, preparing to deliver the placenta. Gertrude reached for a clean bed sheet with one hand. With the other hand, she gave Angie a round metal basin. Angie carefully positioned the basin. She waited. She knew it was important not to pull or tug on the cord to allow time for the placenta to deliver naturally. Soon, the placenta plopped out into the basin in one full piece. Gertrude examined it thoroughly for any missing pieces which might have remained in the uterus. Angie checked for tearing and trauma to the perineum before positioning a thick wad of white cotton to absorb the bleeding.

While Fannie held the baby girl, Angie tucked a clean sheet under Maggie McGuire. Gertrude pulled the sheet out from the other side.

Angie pushed the stretcher as close to the bed as possible. Each nurse took hold of her side of the sheet. "One, two, three," they said together, and lifted Maggie McGuire onto the clean bed. When Maggie McGuire was safely returned to her bed, Angie checked the flannel perineum pad. It was thoroughly soaked through with bright red blood. She discarded it in a basin, and replaced it with a clean, dry cotton flannel. Angie rechecked Maggie McGuire's bottom after several minutes. When she removed the pad, blood gushed out. Angie's face turned ashen. Once again, she felt her own heart pumping wildly.

"What's wrong, Angie?" Gertrude asked.

"She's going through the pads too quickly. Her uterus feels a bit boggy. It's not tightening up enough," Angie said, as she vigorously massaged Maggie McGuire's uterus to stimulate a contraction.

"We need Collins to check her, stat!" Gertrude said, "Fannie, run upstairs again. See what's keeping him. Angie, I examined the placenta carefully. It was intact."

"Good, Gertie, I think I feel some tightening now. Can you help me position Mrs. McGuire to put the baby to breast?"

Angie removed the new mother's soiled gown, and placed a clean one around her shoulders, leaving one breast exposed. She grabbed an extra pillow from the stretcher, and arranged the pillow under Maggie McGuire's arm for extra support. In an effort to assist Maggie McGuire to breastfeed, Angie rolled the new mother's left nipple between her thumb and forefinger to stimulate the release of oxytocin. Next, she positioned the baby close to her mother, and stroked the side of the baby's cheek to encourage the baby to latch on to her mother's breast. The baby rooted for a moment, caught hold of her mother's nipple, and sucked six times with gusto. Then, she stopped to rest.

"Ouch," said Maggie McGuire. "I feel the labor pains again."

"That's your uterus contracting," Angie said. "It's a good thing. Breastfeeding releases a hormone that tells your uterus to contract to stop the bleeding."

Gertrude added. "The contractions help you to heal, and get you back into shape, Mrs. McGuire."

As the new mother continued to breastfeed, Gertrude and Angie gave each other a big hug. "Thank-you, Gertie, you were great. I have to admit that I got a little scared there for a moment."

"Me, too, honey, me, too," Gertrude whispered.

"Thanks for coming down to help me when I needed you, Gertie."

"You did a fine job, Miss Angie. I came as soon as Collins said that he couldn't leave the OR. I knew you were in trouble, or you would have brought your patient directly up to us."

"I'm glad you came," Angie said, calmly.

"My baby and I thank you wonderful *ladies-in-white*. You are my *angels-of-mercy* in my hour of need." Maggie McGuire said, smiling radiantly.

For a moment, everyone was silent, standing quietly, absorbing the joy and wonder of the moment. Suddenly, Fannie broke the silence as she entered Ward 220B to make an announcement. "Doctor Collins is here, Miss Angie. Miss Gertrude, Doctor Collins is here. He's right behind me. He said he's ready to attend to the delivery of Mrs. McGuire now!"

Angie looked at Gertrude.

Gertrude looked at the new mother.

Maggie McGuire looked at her baby.

Angie winked at Gertie, and Gertie winked back. The nurses grinned at each other as Dr. Collins entered the room. "You're just in time, Doctor!" They said with a giggle.

Chapter Twelve

❧

October 29, 1923
4 AM (04:00)

Protecting you and guarding tight,
The angels watch you through the night.

LOG BOOK: WARD 220 (A AND B)

ENTRY NUMBER: *17432*
DATE: *October 29, 1923*
SHIFT: *19:00 to 07:00*
TIME: *04:00*
CENSUS: *21*
STATUS: *Stable*
UNUSUAL INCIDENTS: *None*
SIGNED: *Angie Bosco, R.N.*

Sitting at the nursing desk in the center of Ward 220B, Angie signed her name slowly and carefully in the last column of the log book. As the nurse in charge of six wards, this was almost her last log entry before daybreak. Her sleepy head tilted slightly to the right as her heavy eyelids gently closed. Suddenly, her head jerked. The pen in her hand dropped. She woke up in an instant, like the crane on her nursing school pin that awakened when a rock fell from his foot.

Stay awake, Angelina. You must stay awake.

There simply was no doubt about it. Four o'clock was the toughest hour of the early morning, especially for those who didn't regularly work the night-shift. Angie rotated to *nights* one week every month, and there was no getting used to that hour of the morning.

The first four hours of the shift were always hectic. After the supper trays were collected, there were a number of nighttime treatments. *HS* medications were distributed at the *hour of sleep*. By one o'clock, everything suddenly settled down. The heaviest jobs were accomplished. At two o'clock, it was fun to be awake in the middle of the night, knowing that the people in the big city were sound asleep. Snaps of fatigue arrived around three, but were easily overcome. Four o'clock in the morning, however, was serious sleep time. The body wanted to lie down, and put a head on a pillow. It was a struggle to stay awake especially on a night as quiet as this. Five o'clock brought renewed energy with vital signs, morning care, and charting to be done.

Walk, Angelina. Walk to stay awake.

Angie stood up. She surveyed the still ward, carefully tiptoeing to check on her sleeping patients. When she passed Mrs. Ryan's bed, a tangle of long, thick, auburn locks popped out from under the blankets. "Top of the morning to you, Miss Angie!" said Katie Ryan, giving Angie a smile so wide that her blue eyes sparkled.

"…And the balance to you, my dear!

"Oh, Miss Angie, do you have some Irish blood in you?"

"Not exactly, Mrs. Ryan, I learned your Irish greeting right here on Ellis Island from my Irish patients. How are you feeling?"

"I was hoping I would be able to leave today, but my legs are more swollen than yesterday." Katie Ryan lifted her blanket. She uncovered her legs to show Angie. "See!"

"Yes, I see, that's why you were admitted to the hospital last week. Your edema needs to be closely watched during this pregnancy, Mrs. Ryan."

Katie Ryan looked concerned. "I never had this with the others."

"You were younger. Your boys were born when you were in your twenties. You're almost forty now. Our bodies have a way of quietly changing on us," Angie said.

"I think I may need to go to the bathroom, Miss Angie."

"I will bring you a bedpan, Mrs. Ryan."

"Do you think it would be all right to get out of bed and walk?" Katie Ryan asked.

"The doctor ordered bed rest until your blood pressure stabilizes. Let me take your vital signs now."

Angie adjusted the blood pressure cuff on her patient's upper left arm. When she finished taking the blood pressure reading, she said, "Good, your blood pressure is a bit lower today. I would like you to sit up, and dangle your feet for a few minutes. I want to repeat the reading while you're in a sitting position."

"Certainly," Katie Ryan said.

Miss Angie helped her to sit up. "I am certain those handsome lads of yours are missing their mother."

"Yes, Miss Angie, but I know they are all doing well under their father's watchful eye. They came for Sunday visit this week."

"Yes, I met them, all four of them, one lad more handsome than the other, and taking after their parents in the looks department."

"Thank you, Miss Angie. They've already found work in America."

"All four did?"

"Yes," answered Katie Ryan. "I am so proud."

"Oh, Mrs. Ryan, that's wonderful. How old are your boys?"

"Sixteen, seventeen, eighteen and nineteen...Mike, my husband, says that with all five of them working, it won't be long before he finds a big sunny apartment for us, and takes me home to wait for the baby."

"I have no doubt about that, Mrs. Ryan. Tell me, do you want a girl this time after having four boys?"

"It doesn't matter to me, Miss Angie...boy or girl...as long as the child is healthy."

"Yes, of course, I agree."

"Do you think I will be allowed to leave soon?" Katie Ryan asked.

"Perhaps in a few days, the doctor wants to continue to check your blood pressure and observe you for edema. When is your baby due, Mrs. Ryan?"

"Early January..."

"Why, that's ten weeks away. If all goes well, the doctors will monitor your blood pressure and discharge you long before your due date. Your baby will be born in a big city hospital."

Katie Ryan looked at Angie with concern. "I never delivered at a hospital before. The others were born at home."

Angie took another blood pressure reading, and said. "I'll get that bedpan for you now. I'll be right back."

Upon her return, Angie placed a portable screen around Katie Ryan's bed. She helped her onto the bedpan, and patiently waited behind the screen until Katie Ryan was ready for her. "Would you like a bed bath now, Mrs. Ryan?"

"No, I'd like to try going back to sleep in this cozy bed right now."

Angie tucked Katie Ryan into her bed. "You treat me like a princess, Miss Angie. Thank you."

"Your most welcome, Mrs. Ryan, see you in the morning."

Ward 240 was the last unit to visit on her four o'clock ward checks. Angie always prepared herself for the unusual when she stepped into the corridor in the middle of the night. Last month, she discovered a naked man roaming the hallway. He wandered off his ward, dragging a blood transfusion pole. When he met Angie, he asked her for directions. "My dear," he said, "can you direct me to the exit of this fine establishment?" Angie immediately covered him with a sheet. She calmly answered, "Yes, of course, Sir, follow me." She walked with him to the Men's Wards on the North Wing, searching for Miss Ruth. She found her on Ward 237. Angie and Ruth dressed the patient in a hospital gown, and tucked him into his bed.

When Angie went out into the hall, she met an attractive young woman pacing the floor. The woman looked worried and upset. "What's keeping you up, Miss Morales?"

"No comprendo the en-gee-lish, Senorita Angelina."

"Oh, sorry, dear," Angie said, repeating her words in her native language of Sicilian.

"You speak Siciliano, Senorita Angelina?" Fabiana Morales asked, now speaking Sicilian.

"Yes, I am from Sicily," Angie answered.

"My Nona, my grandmother, was from Sicilia. She spoke Siciliano to me when I was a little girl," Fabiana explained. "I can also speak Lunfargo."

"That's a type of Spanish, isn't it?" Angie asked.

"It is a mixture of both Spanish and Sicilian. You would be able to understand it easily, Miss Angie. It is a special language developed by the Sicilianos who live in South America."

"I am curious. How did your nona come to live in Paraguay from Sicily?" Angie asked.

"Nona immigrated to Argentina from Sicilia. She was introduced to my grandfather in Argentina. They married and raised a family. Years later, when my mama was betrothed to my papa, mama traveled to Paraguay to live with papa's family on their ranchero. That was where I was born, after they married. Eventually, my grandparents came to live with us on the ranchero until they passed." Fabiana continued, "After papa died, mama arranged for me to marry a Sicilian man, a *paisan,* who lives in America. It was her hope that I would bring her to America soon after I married him. Last month, I travelled by train and horse carriage to the port of Cartagena to catch the ship that sailed to America."

"That was the ship that came up through the Caribbean, was it not?" Angie asked.

"Yes, the sea was a magic color of blue. I was happy then, and did not have a care. Now, I am awake with worry, Miss Angie. I will soon be deported. I do not want to go back to Paraguay. I will be a great disappointment to mama. She sold the ranchero and went to much trouble to make the financial arrangements with the Siciliano, but he would not consent to marry me when he saw me."

"But, you are so beautiful!"

"No matter, the bump on my neck is too large." Fabiana frowned. "He took one look at my big neck, and called the wedding off. He travelled from Jersey to sign for me, but when he saw me for the first time, he said that he would not marry a deformed person."

"Yes, I know. I read about that incident in your chart. I think he behaved poorly. You have a goiter on your neck that is curable." Angie explained, "That's why you were admitted to the hospital. Your goiter is responding wonderfully to the treatments you are receiving. It is actually shrinking quicker than anyone could have ever imagined."

"I know, and that is the problem. Soon, they will deport me," Fabiana said.

"Yes, you need a sponsor. There is an admission rule that an unescorted woman cannot be admitted. It's believed that a woman is not as employable as a man in America, but we know that's not always true," Angie said, with a wink.

"Yes, I am a very hard worker. My nona has a brother living in America...in Transylvania," Fabiana said.

"I don't believe that's in America, Fabiana."

"Yes, it is!" Fabiana insisted. "It is next to the New York State. I saw it on a map."

Angie smiled. "Well, then, perhaps, you mean the state of Pennsylvania."

"Yes, that's it. Mama told me that if I needed assistance, he would be the one to call for help."

"Do you have his name and address?" Angie asked.

"Mama wrote his name and address on a postcard. I was to mail it to him when I reached America, but I lost the postcard when I was traveling. I no longer have his address, but of course, I know his name," Fabiana told Angie.

"There are people here that help locate families of immigrants. I will talk to them in the morning, and submit a request. Someone from the IAS will come and meet with you right here at the hospital," Angie said.

"The IAS...what is that?" Fabiana asked.

Angie explained. "The Immigrant Aid Society, it was established to assist travelers, like yourself, with these types of problems. They may be able to locate your uncle and notify him by telegram."

"Oh, do you think, Miss Angie?"

"Yes, I will dispatch a request for their services now so that they will receive it when they arrive at their office this morning," Angie said, decisively.

Fabiana showed a faint smile. She asked, "Would my great-uncle be allowed to sponsor me?"

Angie explained. "If your uncle can be reached, he will be asked if he is willing to sign for you. He must agree that, if you do not find work, he will support you so you won't become a burden to society."

"I see. Thank you, Miss Angie, because soon they will be scheduling my deportation hearing. My goiter is shrinking very quickly. Do you think there will be enough time to find my uncle?"

"I hope so, Miss Morales. I surely hope so." Angie walked with Fabiana until they reached Ward 240. She helped Fabiana climb back into her bed. "Please try to sleep now. Say your prayers. Dream that everything works out exactly as you wish. I will say a prayer for you, also. I promise to talk to the IAS people before I leave the hospital this morning."

"Senorita Angelina, you are my guardian angel. Perhaps, that is why you are named Angelina."

"Why, thank you, Senorita Fabiana. That is a most thoughtful thing to say."

At 05:10, Dr. Abe Goodwin began his morning rounds by first stopping at the nurse's desk.

"I thought I would check my patients before I begin my day at the Registry. Did anything noteworthy occur last night, Miss Angie?"

"No, but I was wondering, Doctor..."

"About what?" Dr. Goodwin asked.

"I don't understand about Miss Morales' goiter. I learned that a goiter was irreversible. When I administered iodine treatments in the past, they stopped the growth of the goiter, but never shrank it. What's making her goiter shrink so quickly, Doctor?"

"I've seen a goiter respond to treatment like this only once," Dr. Goodwin answered. "It was a similar case of severe iodine deficiency in the early stages of growth. The person had been exposed to only trace amounts of iodine in his diet, like so many people living in Paraguay."

"Is that because Paraguay is land-locked? Fish from the ocean is a natural source of iodine, isn't it?" Angie asked.

"Yes." Dr. Goodwin explained, "Many people there develop goiters caused by a lack of iodine in their food supply. Miss Morales had only been exposed to trace amounts of iodine in her native country."

"Now," Angie said, "since she is receiving iodine regularly, her goiter is responding, and actually beginning to shrink."

"Yes, because she is young and strong. Let me take a look at her chart. You know, I recently read that the Morton Salt Company will be adding iodine to our salt next year as a preventative measure."

Miss Angie retrieved the chart. She handed it to the doctor. "That sounds like a smart thing to do."

"What strength *Lugol's Solution* did I order? Four percent... hummm...that's eighty-six percent water, ten percent potassium chloride, and four percent iodine, BID, *twice a day.*" Dr. Goodwin calculated his formula on a scratch pad. "Miss Morales' goiter is shrinking very quickly."

"Too quickly I'm afraid, Doctor."

"What do you mean?" asked Dr. Goodwin.

"Well, it is shrinking so quickly that her case will soon be up before the board for a deportation hearing," Angie said.

"That is the protocol, Miss Angie."

"Doctor Goodwin, she told me that she has a great-uncle in Pennsylvania, but she lost his address. Perhaps the IAS can find him to sponsor her. If only she had more time."

"She doesn't have an address?" The doctor asked.

"No, only a name." Angie said.

"That's a long shot, Miss Angie. You know, rules are rules." Dr. Goodwin appeared unemotional, as he continued to write in the medical chart, "...but if a goiter shrinks too fast, that could lead to complications as well."

"Yes, Doctor Goodwin, I know, that's my concern."

Dr. Goodwin closed the chart. "Duty calls," he said. "Have a good day, or at least, a good sleep after working all night."

"Good Day, Doctor. I hope everything is quiet at the Registry Room for you today."

The next two hours rushed by. During the early morning check on her patients, Angie noted that Mrs. Padua was bleeding from her surgical site. Without delay, Angie notified the house officer, and prepared to transport her patient to the operating room. Next, Mrs.

Tucci's temperature was severely elevated when Angie took her vital signs. The house officer ordered a crushed-ice bath, stat, to prevent complications from a high fever. Angie was in the process of preparing the bath, when a patient on the other side of the room became disoriented, and called for assistance. After that, there was morning care to attend to, and breakfast trays to be distributed.

Angie didn't have time to chart or pick up the doctor's orders until after 07:15, when she carefully reviewed all her paperwork before leaving the hospital and stopping at the IAS office. It was only then that she noticed Dr. Goodwin had written a new medication order for Miss Fabiana Morales. Angie was surprised when she read Dr. Goodwin's revised order. She felt her cheeks flush and her heart race.

Oh my, Doctor Goodwin changed Fabiana's treatment order!

Taking a fountain pen and a blank medication ticket from her desk, Angie slowly transferred Dr. Goodwin's order for Miss Morales onto the medication card. She wrote:

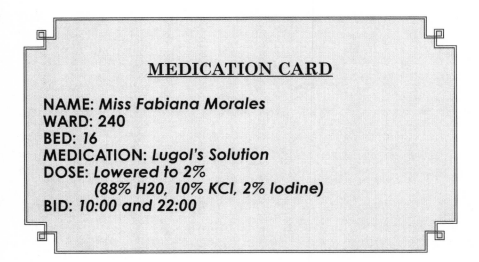

MEDICATION CARD

NAME: *Miss Fabiana Morales*
WARD: 240
BED: *16*
MEDICATION: *Lugol's Solution*
DOSE: *Lowered to 2%*
        (88% H20, 10% KCl, 2% Iodine)
BID: *10:00 and 22:00*

Chapter Thirteen

⟋⟍

November 6, 1923
9 AM (09:00)

In a heart connection, you never really part.
Each time somebody leaves you, you hold them in your heart.

Dr. Mildred Brown had just finished her third physical examination of the morning when she heard the screams coming from the corridor. Her immediate thought was that there was a fire in the Registry Room. Her first concern was the safety of her patients. She called to them to follow her, and exited the exam room in search of Dr. Abe Goodwin. She met him in the hallway.

"What was that? What's happened?" Dr. Brown asked.

"DR. BROWN! DR. GOODWIN! COME QUICK!" Matron McKenna shouted, running toward them.

The doctors rushed to Matron McKenna with a troop of patients following behind. When Matron McKenna realized that the doctors were running in her direction, she turned and called, "Follow me!"

"What is it, Miss McKenna?" Dr. Goodwin asked.

Matron McKenna stopped, and inhaled deeply, trying to catch her breath. Between breaths, she made an attempt to explain. "A baby was born, Docs. It's in the bathroom, a sickly looking thing, it is." The Matron pointed toward the Women's Detention Dormitory. "There!"

When they arrived at the crowded dormitory, the immigrant women cleared a path from the doorway entrance to the bathroom to allow the doctors to pass. A group of ladies were attempting to calm an angry woman who was screaming out of control. Another group huddled around a young woman on the floor. When the doctors pushed their way through the crowd, they found a pale teenager, who looked no older than sixteen, sitting in a puddle of blood holding a tiny infant in her arms.

"We found her here on the cold tiles, holding the scrawny thing," one woman said.

"We called her mother right away," said another.

"Is it alive, Doc?" asked a third.

More comments flowed from all directions and in all languages.

"I've never seen one that small before."

"It looks like a wrinkled old man."

"Her mother's having a fit. She didn't know her daughter was pregnant."

"She won't let go of the thing."

Dr. Brown knelt down on the bloody floor. She placed the newborn on his mother's lap. The baby, still attached to his mother's umbilical cord, was limp and lifeless. His color was blue-grey. Dr. Goodwin reached for the stethoscope that was draped around his neck. He strained to listen for a heartbeat in the noisy room. "I hear something," Dr. Goodwin reported, "but it's faint and very slow. This little guy may be less than three pounds."

Dr. Brown struggled to untie her shoelace. She pulled and tugged, but it would not come lose.

"Hurry Millie," Dr. Goodwin said, taking out his pocket knife.

"It won't come lose," she said, frustrated, but continuing her attempts to unfasten her shoelace.

"Ah, here we go!" Dr. Brown said with relief as the shoelace released. She quickly used it to tie the baby's umbilical cord. After she made a tight knot, Dr. Goodwin cut the cord with his knife. He began to rhythmically tap on the baby's chest using his index finger. "We don't have any equipment here," Dr. Brown sighed. "If we were at the hospital, he might have a chance."

Dr. Goodwin attempted to stimulate the baby to breathe with no success.

"Take the baby, Abe," said Dr. Brown. "Take the baby to the nursery. Run, Abe. Take the baby to Miss Angie at the hospital. I'll stay with the girl."

"Do you think there's time, Millie?"

"The baby is dying," Dr. Brown said.

"Okay, I'll do my best." Dr. Goodwin opened his jacket, and tucked the tiny infant deep inside, holding him close to his body to keep him warm. Then, Dr. Abe Goodwin ran. He ran and ran. He ran across the Great Hall and through the tall doors of the Registry toward the pathway that led to the Hospital on Island Two. He ran through the Lobby to the South Wing and up one flight of stairs to the Mother and Children's Ward. He didn't stop until he reached Miss Angie. "A baby boy!" he said, opening his jacket to reveal the infant.

"Come!" She said.

Angie took the doctor into her makeshift nursery tucked away in the corner of Ward 220B. A small table, covered with a bed sheet, had been placed near the radiator. Angie lifted the sheet to reveal a twelve-inch-high glass enclosure surrounding a thin crib-mattress on top of the table. It took both hands for Angie to lift the heavy glass surround, and place it on a nearby counter. A metal bin, filled with worn flannel blankets and four bricks, sat on top of the radiator near the window. Angie quickly wrapped two bricks with the flannel blankets, and placed the warm bricks at the end of the waist-high table. She opened a warm blanket, and motioned to Dr. Goodwin to put the baby on the blanket. She loosely draped another blanket around the baby keeping his chest exposed. While Dr. Goodwin washed his hands at the sink, Angie suctioned the baby's tiny nostrils and mouth by gently sucking on the end of a thin piece of tubing. A portable green oxygen tank was nearby. Dr. Goodwin turned the valve to *full*. He placed the rubber tubing three inches away from the baby's nose.

The doctor and nurse carefully studied the infant boy. He remained flaccid on the mattress, except for the movement of his chest. His breaths were shallow and labored. Each time he took a breath, his chest rose sharply creating a hollow pit beneath his sternum. His color remained pale grey.

Angie took a moment to wash her hands at the sink. She dabbed a cotton ball in alcohol, and used it to clean the bell of Dr. Goodwin's stethoscope. She handed the stethoscope back to the doctor. He placed it on the baby's chest, listened for thirty seconds, and reported the heart rate. "It's very slow."

Angie attached a miniature black oxygen bag and a child's-size mask to the oxygen tubing. The too-large mask covered the baby's entire face. When the bag filled with oxygen, the doctor gently squeezed it. The baby's abdomen expanded and filled with air. For a moment, the baby's color appeared to change slightly. As the doctor continued the administration of oxygen, Angie removed several more threadbare flannel baby blankets from the radiator. They were warm to the touch. Angie rolled them tightly, and placed them in a circle around the baby. She began light chest compressions using only her index finger.

Minutes passed without a reassuring response from the tiny baby. "His heartbeat is weak. His lungs are not developed enough to utilize the oxygen." Dr. Goodwin said, sadly.

"I hate to give up on him, Doctor."

"He is very premature," Dr. Goodwin said. "Perhaps the best thing to do is to let nature take its course."

"Can we try a little longer…a few more minutes, Doctor?"

"Another five minutes," said Dr. Goodwin.

Dr. Goodwin and Nurse Angie worked with their hands and their hearts for five minutes more to no avail. The baby remained lifeless except for the slight movement of his chest and abdomen. "Shall we disconnect, and let him rest peacefully?" Dr. Goodwin asked.

"Yes," Angie said with a tear in her eye. She turned off the oxygen valve, and walked to the sink. She filled a beaker with a quarter-inch of tap-water, and slowly poured the water over the baby's head. "I baptize thee in the name of the Father, the Son, and the Holy Ghost. Amen."

Awkwardly making the Sign of the Cross, Dr. Goodwin asked, "What if the parents are not Christian?"

"Then, the ritual is meaningless. It's only significant if it represents the intention of the parents."

They stood on each side of the table in silence as they stared down at the baby. Angie had a thought and said, "I feel I should hold him." She swaddled the baby in a warm blanket, sat, and gently rocked him. Dr. Goodwin kneeled down beside her, and listened with his stethoscope. "His heartbeat is very weak." Angie continued to rock the baby as Dr. Goodwin watched.

"May I hold him?" He asked.

Angie stood and lifted the baby up to Dr. Goodwin. He cradled the baby in his left arm, and listened with his stethoscope in his right hand. A minute passed. "He's left us...nine fifty-eight," the doctor announced.

"I shall note that," Angie whispered. She reached for the baby in Dr. Goodwin's arms. She returned the baby to the table. "I'm sorry, Doctor Goodwin."

"We did our best," he said softly.

"Where is his mother?" Angie asked.

It wasn't until that moment that Dr. Goodwin told Miss Angie the details of what had occurred at the Registry earlier.

"Oh my, the poor girl, where do you think she is now?" Angie asked.

"I suppose they may have transferred her to surgery. Let's go upstairs and inquire." Dr. Goodwin said, as he turned to leave. "It's my responsibility to inform the mother. We may need an interpreter, but I don't know what language she speaks."

"Wait!" Angie said. "Your uniform is soiled. Perhaps, you should change to a surgical gown before you leave."

Dr. Goodwin took his jacket off, and placed it on a nearby chair. Angie helped him into a clean surgical gown, and tied the three sets of gown strings attached to the back of the gown. After she covered the baby with a single flannel blanket, she locked the nursery door.

They took the elevator up to Surgery where they found Miss Imogene at her desk at the nurses' station in the alcove entrance of the Recovery

Room. "The mother's in Recovery with Dr. Collins," Miss Imogene announced. "They are trying to piece the story together. Captain Joseph brought an interpreter who speaks both Greek and Armenian."

Dr. Goodwin entered the Recovery Room. Plump, kind-hearted Captain Joseph was talking to the interpreter who, in turn, spoke to the young mother.

Angie returned to the nursery to attend to the baby. After she weighed and cleaned him, she realized that she did not have the information to properly identify him for postmortem care. She swaddled the baby in a flannel blanket with only his face showing, and walked up to the third floor.

Miss Imogene was writing at the desk in the nurses' alcove. When she saw Angie carrying the baby, she dropped her pen and cried, "Great Scott, Miss Angie, what are you doing? Are you out of your mind? Cover up that baby immediately!"

"I was thinking that perhaps the mother might want to see her baby before I transferred him to the morgue, Miss Imogene."

Miss Imogene scolded Angie. "Where would you get such a new-fangled idea? You, insolent young nurses, are all the same. You have no respect for established protocol. I am calling Miss Elsie this very minute. She will never allow this."

Angie pleaded, "She doesn't have to know. Please, let me go in and ask. Let me ask the mother if she wants to see her baby boy for one special moment to say good-bye to him."

With one hand on her hip, Miss Imogene waved the index finger of her other hand. "No, no, no! I most certainly will not allow you with *that* in my Recovery Room. This is highly improper, and you are impertinent. I am going to find Miss Elsie this instant."

Miss Imogene stood up from her desk, and stormed out of the nurse's station, leaving Angie in the hallway with the baby in her arms. She motioned to Dr. Goodwin through the recovery room window. He nodded, and came out into the hallway to ask what Miss Angie needed. Angie asked him if the mother wished to see her baby boy before she transferred him to the morgue. Dr. Goodwin returned to the mother's bedside and spoke to the interpreter, who then translated the doctor's question for the mother. When the young mother nodded agreement, Angie entered the room with the baby.

The mother stared at the tiny face peeking out of the blanket. She reached up for her child, cradled him in her arms, and kissed his forehead. Seconds of silence slipped by. She whispered something in her native language to the interpreter. The interpreter said, "She asks for a priest."

"Please tell her that I baptized her baby when he passed, but I will also call for the priest to come immediately," Angie said.

When Angie turned to leave the room, she saw Miss Gertrude peeking through the recovery room window. She had been called by Miss Imogene, and was watching as the scene inside unfolded. "I know, Gertie, I'm in for it now," Angie said. "Did Miss Imogene call you?"

"Yes, of course, Angie, she is furious. She left in a huff to look for Miss Elsie. She told me to keep an eye on you. So, that's exactly what I was doing."

"But you didn't stop me?" Angie questioned.

"Well, let's just say, that I got here too late to stop you, and leave it at that. You know, we've never considered such a thing before. In my day, I suppose we just assumed that it would upset a mother to see her dead newborn baby, but as I was watching you, all of you together in there, I almost wanted to cry. From the outside looking in, it all seemed right, very peaceful and perfect. I believe it was the correct thing to do."

"I didn't mean to make trouble, Gertie. I thought that if this was a home birth, the parents would have the opportunity to see their child, and have private time to mourn. Oh, I mustn't forget, the mother asked for a priest."

"Yes, of course."

Miss Gertrude sent a request for a messenger to notify the on-duty priest that he was needed in the Operating Arena. While they waited for him, Angie watched Gertrude make two, blue and white, beaded, identification bracelets. Using surgical tweezers, she carefully picked up a number of small white beads with the letters that spelled the mother's last name. She finished off the bracelet with tiny blue beads to identify the infant as male. These bracelets matched the mother to her child. Miss Gertrude gave Angie the bracelets, along with the second page of the mother's medical record for morgue documentation. When the priest arrived, Angie entered the recovery room with him. She attached one bracelet to the baby's ankle. She gave the other bracelet to the young mother. The priest baptized the baby for a second time at the mother's request.

When the mother was ready, she lifted the baby up to Angie. Angie carried the newborn out of the recovery room, and found three faces staring at her. Miss Imogene, Miss Elsie and Miss Gertrude were at the nurses' desk, waiting for Angie.

Before they could say anything, Angie said, "I apologize if I upset anyone today. It was not my intention to go against protocol."

Miss Elsie answered. "Actually, that was what we were discussing. We have no written protocol for a situation such as this."

Miss Imogene looked at them in disgust. "Well, there will be after today. I am writing an incident report, and sending it off to Sister Gwendolyn immediately."

Miss Elsie was the voice of reason. "Let's all calm down a bit. I am certain Sister Gwendolyn will want to know the specifics of what developed here today. We will all want to discuss this at a more appropriate time in order to make a suitable decision about the proper procedure in a case like this."

Gertrude agreed. "Perhaps, it is time to rethink what's been done in the past. After all, it's 1923!"

"Well, in my opinion, there is nothing to discuss," Miss Imogene insisted. "Such disrespect, she countermanded my orders!"

"Settle down now, Miss Imogene. It's been a difficult day. Right now, Miss Angie, I suggest you carry that precious bundle to the morgue. Register him with these papers. Do you want me to accompany you? It's noon already. You might find that the attendant is on his lunch break. You will be alone in the morgue."

"I'm certain that I can handle it, Miss Elsie."

"Well, then, go ahead, Dear. We will continue this discussion at a more appropriate time."

"Yes, Miss Elsie."

Angie took the elevator down to the basement. No one would have suspected that the bundle she carried was a newborn. When she reached the morgue, Angie rang for the attendant, but as Miss Elsie predicted, no one answered. Angie used her house key to open the door. She entered the still and quiet room. Inside, there were eight ice compartments against the back wall and one separate walk-in closet. Looking around, Angie found written instructions on the wall. She was to enter the identifying information in the morgue log book, place the deceased in the closet, and leave the supporting paperwork on the desk in the center of the morgue.

When Angie opened the door to the tiny closet room, she found a gurney inside. There were two small shrouds on the stretcher which appeared to be those of children. It seemed extremely impersonal to simply place the newborn on the stretcher and leave. Angie stayed in the room a few minutes, but the room grew too cold to linger. She felt that she needed to say something before she left. "Baby, you are so tiny and brave. We are all proud of you. You lived only a few hours, but now you have done something that all of us living here on earth have not yet accomplished. You passed through your short life, and already experienced death." Angie took a deep breath. She kissed the baby blanket once, and then, again. "One kiss is for you and one is for my baby. Perhaps, you'll meet in Baby Heaven. If you do, tell him that his mother loves him and thinks about him often. Good-bye, baby. I'm sorry I failed you."

Angie filled out the required paperwork, and left with a heavy heart. She returned to the Women and Children's Ward to clean the nursery and resume her ward duties. Dr. Goodwin was in the nursery, examining a miner's headlamp attached to a battery that was the size of a shoebox. "I came back to pick up my uniform jacket in order to have it cleaned at the laundry. I saw this handy device on the counter. I couldn't resist looking at it. Where did it come from?" Dr. Goodwin asked.

Angie explained, "The Edison Company approached the Surgical Department to test a new alkaline storage battery designed to be used with coalminers' head gear. They sent four sample prototypes to the OR. When the headlamps arrived, one was defective. It didn't shine as brightly as the others. I asked the Edison representative if I could save it for small surgical procedures. He said that he was required to return it to Mr. Edison to determine the reason for its malfunction. However, three weeks later, he surprised me by sending a brand new one in the mail. His only request was to write him with feedback every year."

"That's remarkable. We can use it in so many ways," Dr. Goodwin said, earnestly examining the instrument.

"I worry that our nursery equipment is not adequate," Angie said.

"We didn't have a chance today. Nothing would have saved the little one, Miss Angie, nothing. The baby was too young, less than six months. His lungs had not matured. What do you have here? Let's see…oxygen, suction tubing, warmed bricks, blankets, and hot water bottles. Where did all this come from?"

"I gathered up any supplies that I thought might come in useful someday."

The doctor asked, "Did you make this glass enclosure also?"

"I didn't. I asked the glazier from the glazier shop on Island One. I talked to him one day when he was repairing a broken window in the main corridor downstairs. He came up, and took measurements that same afternoon. He offered to make the enclosure to my exact specifications, even cutting out these little squares and polishing the edges. I glued cotton muslin around them so that we wouldn't scratch our arms on the glass when we cared for a baby. I cut up an old sweater, and sewed the sleeves to the cotton. See. The openings can be kept open, or tied with ribbons.

"What will you use to maintain the temperature?"

"Warm bricks and hot water bottles…a premature infant does not have enough fat to keep his temperature stable. He will lose body heat very quickly. I bought fabric on Orchard Street. I keep it wrapped and sterilized. I would use it to cover the top of the glass enclosure. It's sheer enough to see through, but it will keep the heat from escaping quickly."

"This is very impressive, Miss Angie. Where did you learn to do this?"

"I went to the Infant Incubator Exhibit at Coney Island."

"I've seen that advertised, but I thought it was a scam," the doctor said.

"I did too! I went with Miss Adeline. She was eager to show me the exhibit because she knew of my interest. We paid the dime admission, and went in. Inside, everything appeared to be running efficiently, like a miniature hospital. We were so impressed that we introduced ourselves to the nurses who were on-duty that afternoon. Of course, when they learned we were registered nurses, they gave us a behind-the-scenes tour. They brought us to meet their supervisor. She is originally from France, and thoroughly enjoyed meeting Adeline. Then, we were introduced to the Medical Director. He invited us to dinner with his wife and daughter at his home a mile away in Sea Gate. We accepted his invitation, and dined with his family that evening. The doctor urged us to return. He invited us to come back to spend time working more closely with his nurses. We now go every summer, and spend a whole day there."

Dr. Goodwin appeared interested, and had many questions to ask. "Is it actually on the Coney Island Boardwalk where everyone passes?"

"Not quite, but it is in a busy section of Luna Park with heavy foot traffic. The doctor charges ten cents to observe feedings, and to listen to a lecture on the care of premature infants given by one of his nurses. The money he earns from the exhibit is used to care for the babies."

"Is he a real doctor?"

"Of course, he is a real medical doctor. He is an MD. They were caring for six babies the last time we visited. All the babies were growing beautifully with no signs of complications.

"It sounds like an extremely unsterile environment, Miss Angie."

"On the contrary, the doctor upholds the most sterile standards. He employs registered nurses who work around the clock."

"Isn't he exploiting the babies like freaks?" Dr. Goodwin asked.

"I thought the very same thing before we went and met the staff. It's the only resource of its kind available in the entire city. Hospitals are reluctant to take on the challenge of caring for premature infants. The doctor offers hope to new parents, and he doesn't charge them a cent for his services."

"How does he find babies to care for?"

"The hospital administrators in New York and New Jersey work with him. When a premature infant is born, the hospital informs the parents of this treatment option. The doctor comes to the hospital to examine the baby, and to meet with the parents. If the parents agree to release their newborn to his care, they sign a contract. It states that the baby will be returned to the parents when the baby reaches five pounds, eight ounces in weight."

"Is that so?"

"Yes, but there's one thing I don't understand. While the hospitals endorse Dr. Martin's work, they continue to refuse to purchase his incubators to care for their premature infants. The equipment is not extremely expensive, and could save a life. The doctor even offers rental programs."

"I suppose this specialized type of care requires a great deal of one-to-one trained nursing care. It would not be cost effective for one infant. I don't believe that the Commissioner would ever approve such an expense to care for a child of an immigrant. The infant could develop medical complications and brain damage, and potentially be a burden to society for the rest of his life."

Shaking her head, Angie said, "Yes, you're right. I suppose they are required to consider everything, aren't they?"

"I believe so," said Dr. Goodwin emphatically.

"I can be so naïve about such matters. Sometimes, I wonder why I work here."

"I know I do, almost every day. I suppose the answer is simply to do some good, Miss Angie."

Dr. Goodwin heard himself talking, but he could not take his eyes off of Angie. He found himself gazing into her warm hazel eyes and wondering.

Are all hazel eyes the same soft color of green sprinkled with brown speckles?

"Yes, we try to do the best that we can, and hope that we make a difference in some small way." Angie stared back into Dr. Goodwin's eyes, and thought.

Oh my, his eyes are as brown and delicious as dark chocolate fudge!

Chapter Fourteen

～

November 6, 1923
8:15 PM (20:15)

There's no need to despair,
We're given only crosses that we can bear.

"Miss Adeline, why are you still working at this hour? It's almost eight-thirty! I want you to know that I forgot my cape, and nearly froze to death coming out here to CD tonight." Angie put her hands on her hips as if to scold Adeline. "I waited for you to go to dinner tonight. When you didn't show up, I came to look for you."

"Oh, Angie, you're just the gal I want to see. Tell me what happened today. Everyone's talking about it. There are a million versions of the story floating around. Now, tell me exactly what happened. I want every detail. They said you saved a baby."

"No, the baby died." Angie said, sadly.

"I heard he was only a few pounds. How could he possibly live?" Adeline asked.

"He was two and a half pounds when I weighed him," Angie reported. "His mother had been pregnant less than six months."

"Six months and he was alive! That's extraordinary, isn't it Angie?"

"Yes, he was so tiny. His mother is only fifteen years old," Angie added.

"I heard that the girl's mother never knew she was pregnant," Adeline said. "She went crazy. She's being detained at the Psych Pavilion. Sit down. Tell me everything."

"I will. Are you ready to leave Adeline? Can we order our dinner? I haven't eaten tonight, and my feet hurt."

"I'm covering for Miss Maude. She was scheduled to report for the night shift at seven. Her mother was ill. She called for Maude to help her today. Maude's traveling from Brooklyn, and is running late. She's taking the eight o'clock ferry. She'll be here at eight-thirty." Adeline looked at the clock on the wall. "That's only a few minutes from now."

"Okay, we'll order late dinner after Maude comes to relieve you. I must be really hungry because I can already smell the onions," Angie said, inhaling deeply.

"Perhaps, they served onions at dinner tonight. Sit down. Tell me what happened." insisted Adeline.

Angie began, "Okay, the family is from Armenia, from a village called Smyrna. When the Turks invaded Smyrna, the girl's father was brutally killed."

Adeline interrupted, "You mean the baby's father was killed?"

"No, the teenage girl's father was killed. She and her mother survived the Turkish invasion. They escaped on a French freighter making its way to Greece. The mother's sister lives on the island of Corfu."

"The teenager's sister?" Adeline asked

Angie clarified, "No, the teenager's aunt lives in Corfu, Greece."

"Okay, I think I'm getting the story straight now. Go on," said Adeline.

"I'm trying to," said Angie, continuing her story. "The two older ladies have a brother in Boston. They contacted him. He invited them to live with him, and immediately sent money for all of them to come to America. The women were detained in Corfu while they waited for their passage papers. It took them a year to obtain final approval. There were many other Armenian refugees living in Greece at that time. The young girl met an Armenian boy traveling with his family. They fell in love and secretly married, so she says. They told no one about the marriage because changing the paperwork would delay passage for both families. When the boy's family obtained clearance, the boy left for America with the marriage certificate. Of course, the young lovers had a plan. He was to write her with his location in America. However, the girl and her mother were approved to travel only a short time after the boy's ship sailed. There wasn't time to wait for a letter from America. The girl and her mother arrived yesterday. They were detained until the uncle from Boston came to sponsor them."

"What happened to the aunt in Greece? Did she travel with them?" Adeline asked.

"I heard that the girl's aunt wasn't ready to leave Corfu. She decided to stay and come after her financial affairs were in order. By the way, do you know that the doctors at the Registry completely missed the pregnancy during their initial screening yesterday? Can you believe that, Adeline?"

"No, I can't. What a hoot. They claim they never miss a trick, and actually missed a six-month pregnancy. Someone's going to be in hot water for that one. Okay, what happened next?" Adeline demanded.

"The women slept in the Women's Detention Dormitory last night," Angie explained. "The girl never told her mother that she was pregnant. Her labor started this morning. She had stomach cramps, and thought she had diarrhea. She went into the bathroom, sat down on the tile floor, and delivered her baby. The women in the dormitory found her. They ran to get the doctors at the Registry."

"Then, what?" Adeline asked.

Angie continued, "The baby died. The girl doesn't know how to locate the baby's father. No one believes the marriage story, and the girl will probably be deported for moral turpitude."

"...And they will deport the grandmother for insanity, no doubt. Now, when were you called to the Registry Room to save the baby, Angie?"

"I wasn't. Dr. Goodwin brought the baby to me."

"He brought the baby to your nursery?"

"Yes, we worked on the baby for twenty minutes in the nursery with no success."

"You and Dr. Goodwin?" Adeline asked.

"Yes, Dr. Goodwin and I," Angie answered. "He was extraordinary. Later, I got into an altercation with Miss Imogene because I carried the baby up to see the mother after the baby expired."

"You did...what?"

"I brought the baby to the Recovery Room because I thought the young mother might want to say *good-bye* to her baby. When Miss Imogene saw me with the baby, she went on the warpath."

Adeline smiled. "I bet she banished you from her OR. She's done that before, you know!"

"No, Ad, she ran to find Miss Elsie to file an incident report," Angie explained. "After she left, I asked Dr. Goodwin if he would approve of asking the mother if she would like to see her baby. He was in favor of the idea. He talked to the mother, and I brought the baby to her."

"I can only imagine what happened when Miss Imogene found you."

"The fireworks started when she returned with Miss Elsie. She really has it in for me."

"She has it in for anyone under thirty years old. She gives everyone a hard time in the beginning."

"Well, I'm not exactly the new girl. I've been here three years. Ad, I thought I would be dismissed for sure. I was called down to the Nursing Office at the end of my shift."

"Was Sister angry?" Adeline asked.

"No. I was surprised. She had already interviewed Imogene, Gertrude, and Dr. Goodwin. She wanted to hear my version of the story."

"Oh my, you got yourself into a pickle today. What did Sister do after you reported what happened?"

"She didn't say much. Apparently, there is no written procedure for an incident like this. She said that, technically, I did nothing wrong, and that I was following doctor's orders. You see, Dr. Goodwin told her that I was operating under his orders."

"No? He covered for you. He's quite the gentleman, isn't he?"

"Adeline, when the baby was taking his last breaths, he asked me if he could hold the baby in his arms until the baby expired."

"Oh, that's just like him, so sensitive. I think you like him."

"Stop!"

"Angie Girl, you are blushing," Adeline teased. "Now, don't be falling for any of the doctors. Things get complicated."

"I'm not falling for anyone. Umm, Ad, what is that smell?" Angie walked around the ward, sniffing. "It smells like onions in here, like raw onions or something rotting. It's coming from that corner. Is it some sort of a new treatment?"

"I don't smell anything, and do not change the subject, Miss Angie. We were talking about the doctor. Promise me you won't start dreaming about him."

"I have no dreams, Adeline, and definitely am not carrying a torch for him or anyone. We simply work together. I feel he is a very competent and caring doctor. He certainly doesn't like me in a romantic way. He has never given me any indication that he has feelings for me."

"Okay, but you need to get out more to meet new people, Angie."

"I go out with you, Ad."

"Sure, you go to political meetings and rallies. I'm talking about going out, and making new friends. Come with me tomorrow night." Adeline pressed.

"Where are you going?" Angie asked.

"Out with a friend, and I can ask him to bring along a friend for you, too. We can double-date."

"Who are you going with, Ad?"

"Come out with me, and meet him," Adeline said, looking away from Angie. She turned in the direction of the Victrola that was in the corner of the room.

Angie studied Adeline's face. Then, noticed the Victrola tucked away in the corner against the wall. "Oh, no, Adeline, not *Victrolaman*, not him, not *Mr. No-Commitment*, are you seeing him again? Why would you think that things will be different this time?"

Adeline purposefully steered the topic of their conversation back to the subject of onions. "Okay. I confess. They are raw onions, Angie. I admit it. They are under the children's beds."

"What are onions doing on the unit?"

Adeline explained, "Well, two weeks ago, little Katarina's mother came to visit her. She gave her a large onion cut in half. Her instructions to Katarina were to put the onion under her hospital bed, and to keep it hidden there. She told her that the onion would absorb the bad germs, and help her to heal quickly."

"Horse-feathers, that's an old wives' tale, Adeline."

"Yes, but Katarina's chicken-pox healed in record time. She went home without a pox mark on her body," Adeline said. "So, one by one, the others asked their mothers for raw onions. They want to heal quickly, without scars, and go home like Katarina."

"That's baloney, you don't believe that sort of thing do you, Ad?"

"If it helps them to believe they will get well, what can it hurt?" Adeline said.

"Just our noses, it stinks! Miss Adeline, are you giving me the run-around? Did you fabricate this onion story because you don't want to talk about *Victrolaman*?"

"No, the onion story is true, but I have to confess that I'm confused. Angie, I really don't know what to do."

"Tell the charwomen to clean up all the onions tomorrow. Throw them out. Tell the girls that the onions did the job, and grabbed up all their germs. If they want onions, their mothers could bring them fresh ones."

"No, I'm talking about *Victolaman*, I mean Harry. His name is Harry. Angie, I don't know what to do about him."

"Don't start things up. Don't go out with him, please," Angie pleaded.

"Things have already started up, Angie."

"Well, stop it, cancel your date."

"I can't."

"You have to."

"I can't. I can't help it. I love him."

"Love, really Adeline, love? What about marriage and children?"

"You know, Angie, perhaps I will never marry, maybe never have a child. I may be getting too old anyway. I just know that he is the one for me, the Real McCoy. I tried breaking up with him years ago, but he came back into my life."

"Tell me, Ad, how do you know he's *the one*? How do you know for sure? I don't think I really know what love is."

"Well, the first thing I love about him is that he is fun and not afraid to try new things. He's adventurous."

"Like you, Ad!"

"Like me? Well, I suppose you can say that, but he is cool and calm about it," Adeline explained. "You know how excited I can get sometimes. Well, he seems to *get* me, like he knows my heart. It's like he understands what I need. When I get excited, he's composed. He runs a tremendous business, but nothing ever seems to rattle him. Most importantly, I feel relaxed and safe with him."

"He sounds like a good match for you, Adeline. I can't wait to meet him."

"Come out with me tomorrow night. I'll introduce you."

"I can't."

"Why, Angie? You always have an excuse."

"No, I mean, I'll go out with you, but not tomorrow. I promise, Adeline. My brothers are meeting me at the ferry building after work. They meet me for supper once a month. They've never canceled. It's important to them, and me too. It's the only time the three of us get together. Look! There's Maude, right on time. Hurry, give report so that we can order supper and eat."

Angie waited quietly while Adeline reported off to Maude. At the end of her report, Adeline gave Maude a detailed account of Angie's heroic efforts to save the premature baby born at the dormitory that morning.

"Bundle up," said Maude. "It's damp and drafty in the corridors. You don't have your capes with you. Take a blanket or towel to wrap around you when you walk back to the Cottage."

As Maude had reported, the enclosed pathway to Island Two was cold and windy that night. Adeline and Angie were glad they had taken a flannel blanket to put around their shoulders. They heard the wind howling as it whirled around the curved walls and windows of the corridor. "Adeline, that can't be the wind! It's too loud. It sounds like screaming. A child is screaming. She's in trouble. She needs our help."

"Angie, that's not the wind. We're passing the trachoma unit, and it's time for the *HS* copper sulfate eye treatments before bedtime."

"Oh my, Mabel described how painful the treatments are, but I would have never imagined this. It sounds as if a child is being tortured. Do the children receive medication for the pain?"

"The treatments are extremely painful," Adeline explained. "The children are given a mild dose of Phenobarbital, an hour before the treatment to ease them into sleep."

"Phenobarbital could be dangerous for a child," Angie said.

"The small dose helps them to go right to sleep. A good sleep relieves the pain, and enhances the treatment," Adeline explained.

"Oh, Adeline, it must be so difficult to work there, and there are so few recoveries."

"Yes, recoveries are few and far between but they happen. We are finally having some success with the blue stone treatments. We celebrate when someone is healed and discharged. One seven-year-old boy showed only mild improvement after four months of hospital care. He was about to be deported. His father petitioned the Board of Special Inquiry for more time. The doctors supported his request. They were using a new treatment regime, and wanted more time to continue it. Miracles of miracles, the board approved his treatments for another six months. The boy would either be deported or released at the end of the six-month extension."

"What happened to him?" Angie asked.

"His trachoma was cured. He was discharged to his father's care last week. We had a party for him," Adeline continued. "Lately, there have been other success stories among the children. They seem to respond best to the treatments, and are able to grow new tissue after the diseased tissue is destroyed."

Angie frowned. "Those little one have been given such heavy crosses to carry. I don't know how they get through it."

"Angie, we all have a cross to bear."

"But we are so fortunate in so many ways, and so lucky to be healthy, Adeline."

"Angie, you are not without your crosses. I know you've had your share of challenges."

"Yes, but I've been given the strength to carry mine," Angie said.

"I believe we're only given the crosses that we are able to carry. Look, Angie, we're here already. Let's order dinner. I'm hungry!"

"Okay, I wonder what they're serving for supper tonight."

"Liver smothered in onions, no doubt," Adeline said, with a giggle.

"No, Ad, I think fried cabbage and onions."

"Perhaps onion soup," Adeline said, "oozing with cheese and topped with a thick slice of bread, the French way."

"Grilled sausage," said Angie, "mixed with onions and green peppers, fried in olive oil and garlic, the Italian way."

"Angie, will you make sausage and peppers for me when I come to your big house in the country when you are married to a nice, fat, Italian papa with six little bambinos running about?"

"Yes, and will you make me French onion soup in your Fifth Avenue apartment when you are married to a handsome Frenchman, surrounded by your seven children?"

"Two, I'm getting old," Adeline said, laughing.

"Three, you're in great shape," insisted Angie.

Adeline took Angie's hand as they hopped up the steps in the hospital lobby to order their supper. They filled out one *FRF* for two dinners, and submitted the *food requisition form* to the kitchen through the pneumatic tube system.

"Hurry, Angie, hurry. I'm half frozen," Adeline said, starting to shiver.

Adeline's chattering teeth made Angie laugh. "Okay, let's make a run for it before we both die of hunger and cold!"

When the nurses reached the Cottage, they ran up to their rooms, slipped off their soiled uniforms, and hurried to take quick showers. They crept down to the dining room in their nightclothes and slippers to find their supper waiting on the kitchen delivery cart. While they ate, Adeline told Angie stories about her adventures as a Settlement Nurse in the city. She helped Angie forget about her troubled day.

Before going to sleep that night, Angie thought. *What a day! How very special Adeline is to me. She always has a way of making me feel better. I will never forget the day she taught me how to laugh, the day we went to Coney Island.*

Chapter Fifteen

One Year Before
July 2, 1922

The infant in the isolette struggled all night long,
While suction and oxygen hummed a hopeful song.

Sister Gwendolyn did not look pleased. "Miss Angie, I cannot approve another day-pass for the both of you this month. We are very short of nurses. Many of them need to go home in the summertime to visit their families. When Miss Adeline goes off on a cause, you always follow behind. Where is she taking you this time?"

"Coney Island," Angie mumbled.

"What, Coney Island? Did you say, Coney Island? You must enunciate, my dear, enunciate!" Sister said sternly.

"Yes, Sister."

"Do you really need a day off to go to the beach when I know the nurses go swimming right here on Island Two? Don't think that I'm not aware of it."

"I don't, Sister Gwendolyn."

"Probably not, but I've seen Ruth and Rose sneak in a swim on hot afternoons. So, now, you ladies want to go to the *Nickel Paradise*, do you?" Sister was annoyed.

Angie explained. "We weren't planning on going to the beach. We were hoping to spend the day at the Infant Incubator Exhibit in Luna Park."

"You were what?"

"We've been invited to observe the nursing care of the premature infants at Luna Park."

"How did this come about, Miss Angie?"

"Adeline and I were introduced to the Medical Director and the Nursing Supervisor last summer. They invited us to spend a day there shadowing a registered nurse. We weren't able to return last year, but thought we might write ahead to schedule a whole day this season."

"How very interesting, and how will you use this information in your clinical practice? I mean, there haven't been many premature infants born at this hospital in recent years, Miss Angie?"

"I know, Sister, but this is an opportunity to learn a very specific type of nursing care that may be useful someday."

"Yes, I suppose it could be. I have actually heard of this doctor at Coney Island. What is his name?" Sister Gwendolyn asked.

"Dr. Martin, Sister, Dr. Martin."

"Yes, that's it, Dr. Martin. We thought he was exploiting the infants when he opened the exhibit years ago, but he has now gained the respect of many pediatricians around the city."

Angie explained. "Adeline and I met him at the exhibit last year. He is an experienced physician with an outstanding track record. His techniques have successfully saved over eighty-five percent of the infants under his care, including some who were only six months gestation."

"Would you be interested in sharing what you learn with Miss Elsie and Miss Elizabeth? If Dr. Martin's nurses have developed something unique, and their outcomes are as successful as you say, perhaps you could document these techniques for future practice."

"Oh, yes, certainly. I would be glad to. I think that's a wonderful idea, Sister Gwendolyn."

"Please give me a moment. Let me look at the schedule." Sister Gwendolyn studied the master schedule. "Let's see. Do you think you could possibly wait until August? I can't find an opening for you in the month of July."

"August would be perfect, Sister."

"Let me see. I need a day that both of you can be off. I suppose it will be far safer for the two of you to travel together instead of sending one of you off alone. Perhaps, Monday, August 4th would work from eight in the morning until about ten-thirty at night."

"August 4th it is, Sister. Thank you."

"Miss Angie, you must promise to take notes, and report what you learn to Miss Elsie."

"Yes, Sister, I promise."

"Please be sure to return on the ten o-clock ferry, no later dear. I don't like the idea of the two of you roaming around Luna Park after dark, and taking the trains back to the city so late at night."

On August 4th, Angie and Adeline boarded the 8 am ferry that delivered them to Battery Park. From there, they rode a streetcar up to the Brooklyn Bridge stop of the *BMT*, the Brooklyn-Manhattan train line. Adeline showed Angie how to buy the newly-minted subway tokens for five cents each, and how to use them at the turnstiles that were recently installed at the entrance of the station. At Flatbush, the women changed trains for the Brighton Beach Line which took them directly to Coney Island.

Angie and Adeline found empty seats in the first car of the train. The wicker seat for two had to be adjusted so that they could sit facing each other. Because the seat backs could be modified in this way, a group of four people could sit together, or two could sit privately, simply by using the lever to move the back of the seat in either direction. Leather straps hung from the ceiling and swung from side to side as the train joggled along the tracks. The rhythm of the train, shaking and jerking, added to the anticipation of their arrival at the last stop, Coney Island.

The train's exit ramp opened onto a wonderland of intoxicating aromas. The smells of Coney Island were irresistible, even at 10:30 in the morning. A bouquet of cotton candy, pulled taffy, roasted peanuts, and chocolate fudge drifted from the many sweet shops that lined the enclosed walkway leading down to the street. Out on Surf Avenue, the smell of freshly cooked hot dogs and chunky potato fries floated through the air.

"Adeline, everything smells delicious!"

"Yes, I'm hungry for a hot dog myself, but we must resist. Remember that Dr. Martin gets upset when his staff eats concession food. One of the wet nurses was almost fired last year when she was caught sneaking out at night to buy a nickel hot dog."

"I remember that he hired a wonderful French cook to prepare nutritious meals for his staff. He wants the wet nurses to eat only the healthiest foods so that the babies thrive. I hope the cook is on duty today and makes lunch for us. What was her name?"

"Emelie."

"Yes, Emelie, I wonder what she will cook today?"

"I think we are definitely getting hungry. We must be strong, Angie, or the doctor will smell hot dogs on our breath. Let's keep walking."

"Okay, but can we each buy one tonight?"

"Sure, let's plan on it, Angie."

They walked quickly to the Luna Park entrance where a large heart-shaped sign told them they were at *The Heart of Coney Island*. After they showed Dr. Martin's introduction letter to the young lady at the admission booth, they were admitted to Luna Park without paying the entrance fee. Once inside, Angie and Adeline were turned around and lost in the fairytale play land of exotic towers and make-believe castles. It wasn't until after they passed the *Loop-the-Loop* and the *Dragon's Gorge*, did they notice a sign shaped like an arrow that read:

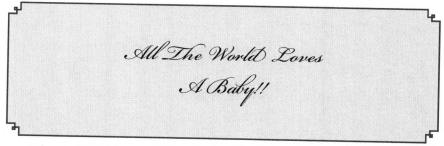

All The World Loves
A Baby!!

They walked in the direction of the arrow, and passed the skating rink. Then, they saw a large castle-like building marked:

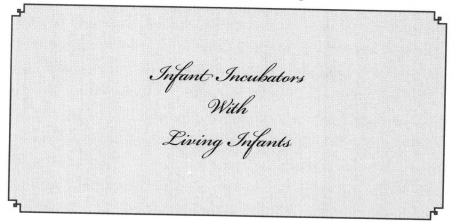

Infant Incubators
With
Living Infants

Angie and Adeline continued to follow Dr. Martin's instructions, and entered the building from the side entrance. An elderly servant answered the door. She called for Madame Louise, the Nursing Supervisor. Madame Louise came promptly to greet them. She insisted on giving them an opportunity to rest after their journey, and offered them a mid-morning snack of tea, cheese and crackers. While they drank their tea in the dining room, Madame Louise outlined her plans for the day and told them about the institute.

"The nursing staff lives here on the top floor from the beginning of May to the end of October. Dr. Martin and his family live a mile away in their Sea Gate home. They also keep a small apartment upstairs in the event that the doctor wishes to stay overnight to observe a newly-admitted infant. The nurses work eight-hour shifts. Three nurses are on-duty at one time. They are all registered nurses who work as private-duty nurses during the winter when we close our doors to the public. Dr. Martin only accepts newborns in the spring and the summer months."

Angie and Adeline were paired with a registered nurse to observe her nursing care with special concentration on I & O *(intake and output)*. Madame Louise explained that the babies were weighed twice a day. They had already been weighed earlier in the morning, but another weigh-in was scheduled for that evening. An evening-shift nurse would show them the weigh-in procedure before suppertime.

There was much to see throughout the day, and the time passed quickly. Angie and Adeline were given instructions on how to calculate the exact amount of infant feeding for each baby based on his most current weight. The babies were fed breast milk pumped from the three wet nurses employed at the facility. The nurses demonstrated two types of feeding methods which they used when an infant was too small or too weak to suck from a baby bottle. The tiniest babies with under-developed suck and swallow reflexes were fed by a gavage tube to their stomach or by a nasal method using a funnel-shaped spoon. For the nasal method, a small amount of breast milk, no more than a teaspoon, was slowly drained into the baby's nostril. Angie was amazed to see this type of feeding demonstrated. She knew that the feeding liquid could easily go into the baby's lungs and be aspirated, but the procedure was done quickly and efficiently with no adverse effects on the babies.

"How can it be?" Angie asked. "I would have thought the milk would go directly into his lungs."

"You must tip the funnel like this, ever so slightly, so that the milk goes down very slowly," the nurse instructed.

The nurses stressed that carefully recording the *output* of the babies, the amount going out, was as important as measuring the *input*, the amount taken in. They did this by documenting both the number of diapers the baby used and the baby's bowel movements. They also recorded the approximate amount of any feeding that was regurgitated by the baby. Vital signs were charted on the smallest babies every hour, and every four hours on the hardier ones. Temperature, heart rate, and the number of respirations per minute were then marked on a graph.

The paying guests from Luna Park began their slow parade through the hospital-like quarters during the afternoon feedings. They walked quietly through the infant incubator room, and stood behind a railing that separated the public from the premature infants.

The babies lived in glass incubators that hung from each wall of the room. Fresh outside air was pumped through pipes into the filtered incubator chambers. The temperature of the incubators was monitored and maintained by a simple heating system. Two glass doors opened like kitchen-cabinet doors for observation and easy access to a baby. Every hour on the hour, one of Dr. Martin's registered nurses gave a half-hour lecture on the care and feeding of the infants. After the lecture, a nurse brought in an older baby, showing him off for the public to "*ooh*" and "*aah*" at his little booties and tiny clothes.

Angie and Adeline were invited for supper. The long table in the Dining Room was set for fifteen people. They dined with the doctor, his wife, their daughter, six registered nurses, three wet nurses and Madame Louise. A young maid served a salad of lettuce greens, cucumbers and tomatoes. This was followed by fresh codfish, pan-fried in a light egg batter, topped with lemon sauce and capers, and served with boiled potatoes, sliced carrots and garden peas. Assorted cheeses and red grapes were offered after dinner. Dessert was home-made blueberry cobbler.

While they ate, the doctor explained how he transported infants from the hospital to Luna Park. He employed a chauffeur to assist him with driving to and from the many hospitals he visited. He felt a driver was necessary because he often had to attend to an infant during transport. After examining the newborn baby, he met with the parents at the hospital. He contracted with the parents to provide care for their infant at no charge, and to return the baby to them when the baby reached five and a half pounds.

His current concern was that he discovered that many of the new parents were not emotionally ready to accept their tiny baby at discharge time. After months of separation, the parents remembered a small, frail and fragile infant. The doctor identified a need to teach them how to care for their babies prior to discharge. He was experimenting with a concept of providing transportation for the parents so that they could visit the institute for instructions at least once a week. His chauffeur picked the parents up, drove them to the center for a hands-on lesson, and then, drove them back home.

After dinner, Angie and Adeline thanked everyone and bid them good-bye, promising to return the following summer. They left the quiet, calm and order of the doctor's well-run facility, and were immediately jolted into the frenzied excitement of a summer night at Luna Park.

Out on the promenade, masses of people strolled along. Thousands of light bulbs lit up the electric quarter moons which surrounded the park, giving the playground an illusion of midday. Goat-pulled carts and a procession of real elephants, carrying paid passengers, added to the spectacle of the evening.

A Luna Park Barker called out to the nurses. "Step right up! Step right up! Come and try your luck. Take a spin for a free ride! Hello, ladies, step right up. Come talk to me. My name is Archibald. What's yours, little lady?"

"Hello, I'm Adeline."

"Adeline, take a spin. A zero will win."

"How much does it cost?"

"Nothing, not one cent, tonight is *Free Spin Night*. No strings attached. Spin the wheel. You'll win if a number with a zero appears. Spin and win! There are six numbers with a zero on the wheel."

"Okay, Archibald, I'll try." Adeline spun the wheel hard, but unfortunately the arrow did not stop on a number with a zero.

"Better luck next week, Adeline. Come back again and try your luck. How about you, little lady? What's your name?"

"Angie."

"Okay, Angie, it's your turn. Spin the wheel."

Angie gripped the wheel, and spun it with all her strength.

"Round and round it goes, where it stops, nobody knows!" Archibald pretended to look astonished when the arrow slowed down and stopped at the number 40.

"Two free tickets, right here, you saw it folks! The number forty wins a prize tonight. It's as easy as that. Look, Angie's won two free rides on the *Loop-the-Loop*. Come one, come all. Try your luck. Here you go, Angie, take these tickets to the *Loop-the-Loop* ride before ten o'clock tonight to claim your free ride."

"Oh, Angie, how wonderful, let's go. The *Loop-the-Loop* is over there."

"No, Adeline, we don't have time. We must start back. We have trains to catch."

"It's only eight o'clock. We have two hours." Adeline said as she pulled Angie in the direction of the *Loop-the-Loop*.

"No, we can't stop. There's not enough time. We'll be late."

"The tickets are free. They're only good for tonight. We have to go!" Adeline insisted.

Angie continued to walk toward the Luna Park exit. "We will be late for curfew. It took us over two hours to travel to Coney Island this morning."

"No, Angie, the trains run more frequently in the evening. We won't have any problem making our train connections tonight. I know. Believe me. Even if we are late, no one will ever know. Look, here's the *Loop-The-Loop*!"

Angie looked at the roller coaster with two 360-degree circles looping around the track and froze. "That's it? I can't, Adeline."

"What? Are you scared?" Adeline asked.

"Scared? I'm terrified. I've never been on a ride like that before."

"Oh, Angie, that's all the more reason to try it. I know you will like it."

"No, I don't think I will like it."

"There's nothing to be afraid of Angie. It's so much fun. You won't believe how much. All you have to do is to scream when the car goes down fast."

"No, Adeline, I couldn't. I'm afraid."

Adeline teased Angie. "Are you afraid to scream...or...afraid to go on the ride?"

"Both!" Angie said.

"Then, you must do it. You must always face your fear. When fear is holding you back, you must be brave, and crash right through it. Tonight, you must go on the *Loop-the-Loop.*"

"Really?"

"Really, Angie, have I ever been wrong? Come on. It's fun!" Adeline took Angie's hand. She pulled her toward the ride.

"But..." was all Angie could say.

They showed the two free tickets at the ticket booth, and were ushered onto a short line to wait for the next train of cars. Adeline continued to give Angie instructions above the shrieking and squealing of the passengers on the roller-coaster ride. "Half the fun is screaming."

"Oh, Adeline, I could never scream like that."

"Try it. You'll be surprised."

Angie followed Adeline as the *Loop-the-Loop* car roared into the station to drop off and pick up passengers. The women boarded the ride. Terrified, Angie braced herself, and strapped herself in tight. She pressed both feet hard against the front of the car, and tugged the safety bar closer to her waist.

Up, up, up, the car went. Angie held her breath.

Up, up, up, it climbed further. Angie shut her eyes.

When the car began its rushing descent, Angie heard Adeline scream. She heard the others scream, as well. She opened her mouth. She tried to scream, but nothing came out. Adeline screamed as the little car approached the first circle and looped them upside down. When the car approached the second loop, Angie attempted to scream once again, but was unsuccessful. Her stomach felt odd as the car raced. A bubble of a giggle floated to the surface. The little car twisted and shook, and jiggled and jerked. Angie started to laugh. Adeline screamed when the car bumped to a stop. She heard Angie laughing. Her laughter was contagious. Adeline laughed along with her. They laughed so hard that they couldn't catch their breath. Tears ran down their cheeks. Angie never remembered laughing so hard.

When they left the roller-coaster ride, they hurried to the Luna Park Exit, and ran down Surf Avenue as fast as they could to catch the Brighton Beach train to Flatbush.

"No time for a hot dog," Angie said, as she pulled Adeline into the train station.

Waiting for the train, they started to laugh. They laughed when they changed trains in Flatbush to catch the BMT train to the city and when they caught the street car downtown. They were still laughing when they missed the 22:30 ferry. The nurses had to wait thirty minutes for the next ferryboat to arrive.

Once back on Ellis Island, their laughter stopped as they hurried to the Cottage and quietly tip-toed into the house and up two flights of stairs to their rooms.

Sister Gwendolyn had been waiting for them in the Nurses' Reading Room. She was relieved when she saw that they had finally returned safely. Smiling and shaking her head, she watched them go up the stairs from the hallway.

When they reached their bedrooms, the nurses hugged each other good-night. Adeline winked at Angie. "See Angie, I told you, no one will ever know that we were an hour late."

Once again, Angie and Adeline burst into laughter!

Chapter Sixteen

❧

November 12, 1923
7PM (19:00)

She challenged both the old and new
And found a different point of view.

Journal of Gwendolyn Hanover
Date: November 12, 1923
Entry Time: 19:00
Journal Notation:

Heaven only knows what gets into the heads of my nurses nowadays! Why in my time, no nurse would ever dare challenge authority
the way these youngsters do today. We would be dismissed, and immediately sent packing for home if we spoke up the way they do. No one
ever complained about their work load, staffing shortages, or patient
safety. We all did the best we could with what we had, and understood
our place.

Apparently, it's 1923 and anything goes!

Ever since women were given the right to vote, my nurses now
believe that it's their duty to challenge established procedures to effect
change. They all have an opinion, and everyone wants to be heard.
They will actually criticize another's work and confront that person,
face to face. If they believe things should be done a certain way, they

accuse the other of neglect and ignorance. Oh my, things were so much simpler in the old days. As the Nursing Superintendent, I was respected. I made all the hospital decisions with no questions asked. Now, we have meeting after meeting. Everything must be discussed, inside and out, with everyone!

This morning's MMM, our Monday Morning Meeting, was no exception. At the top of the agenda was Miss Imogene Phillips' (Miss Imogene) complaint about the young nurse, Miss Angie Bosco (Miss Angie), who brought a newborn infant, recently deceased, to his mother in Miss Imogene's recovery room six days ago. Miss Imogene considered this action to be highly improper. She reported the incident immediately to the house supervisor, Miss Elsie Archer (Miss Elsie). However, after careful assessment, Miss Elsie determined that she could not discipline the young nurse because Miss Angie was following doctor's orders. Although highly shocking, the doctor stated that he asked the mother if she wished to see her baby prior to post-mortem care. Because of this, I could not reprimand Miss Angie.

Miss Imogene has been in my office every day since, to complain and criticize my actions. In my humble opinion, Miss Imogene, of all the nurses here, should be experienced enough to know better. That is another issue. Miss Imogene is my peer. Perhaps, she feels that she should be making the rules. Who knows what the old nurse is thinking? I don't know why she always has to make things difficult for the young *ladies-in-white*. She gives them a hard time until they pass her test. I have a notion that the person I would like to give a good old-fashioned warning to is Miss Imogene herself, but dare I go there?

Delving in further, Miss Elsie and I discovered that there is no specific protocol for this particular type of situation. Protocol #78 simply describes routine postmortem care. It contains line-by-line instructions, detailing what the nurse should do to label and prepare the body of an adult or a child. The nurses need a written protocol for an infant death. Of course, if they could agree among themselves on the proper action to take, the problem would be solved. The sixteen nurses who attended the meeting could not come to a decision. Eight nurses believed that the mother should be protected from the trauma of seeing her dead baby. The remaining eight nurses argued that this was a unique opportunity for the mother to mourn her child. After carrying her fetus in her womb for nine months, doesn't the mother deserve the opportunity to meet the baby that was growing inside her?

Needless to say, after twenty minutes of discussion, nothing was settled. The only alternative left was for a higher authority to decide. They agreed that if the superintendent would write the protocol, they would follow it. I suppose that, in itself, is something coming from this group, but do they realize that they are now telling me what I should and should not do? First, they want the opportunity to vote. When they cannot come to a conclusion, they proclaim it is the supervisor's responsibility. Such is a democracy, I suppose!

So, now, I sit here after hours, attempting to come up with the fairest of solutions. If the nurse were to initiate such a discussion with the parents of a newborn, I now know that half the nurses would be uncomfortable with this sensitive topic. Perhaps, in this case, I could call upon the physician to use his judgment and make the final decision.

Of course, then I would be criticized for contributing to the paternalism that already exists in this institution.

I dislike making a determination when everyone is not in agreement, but alas, it is my job. I pray that I will make the correct decision while being true to myself and fair to both the nurses and the patients involved. I must put myself in the patient's shoes and imagine what it would be like to be a young mother who is only fifteen years old.

I am madly in love with the father of the baby. We are abruptly separated. I carry his baby in my womb. I grow to love my dear little baby with all my heart. I am forced to leave my homeland and all that has become familiar to me. I am thrust into a strange world, following my love to a new land. I am embarrassed by my pregnancy. I feel that it's not safe to reveal my secret to anyone, even my own mother. I confide only to my baby. Suddenly, and all too soon, my baby is born. He is so tiny. The doctors whisk him away. I am frightened for him, but hopeful that they will be able to help him. Then, I receive the worst news imaginable. A stranger tells me that my baby is dead. Do I believe him? Perhaps, they have stolen my baby. Who can I trust? After all my love, all my worry, and all my care, my baby has died. When I ask to see him, will they deny me, or will they assist me through my mourning? Will they give me the opportunity to whisper good-bye to my precious little one?

Well, Sister Gwendolyn, it seems as though you have been given your answer tonight!

GENERAL HOSPITAL LOG BOOK

ENTRY NUMBER: 104,489
DATE: November 12, 1923
SHIFT: 07:00 to 19:00
CENSUS: 276
STATUS: Stable
UNUSUAL INCIDENTS: See Attached Addendum to P78

ADDENDUM TO PROTOCOL 78:
Infant Post-Mortem Procedure
Following the death of an infant, the Nursing House Supervisor will be called immediately. The Nursing Supervisor will ask the mother if she desires to see her child prior to post-mortem care. If either parent wishes, the Nursing Supervisor will provide a private viewing area for the parents so that ward patients and nursing staff will not be disturbed. The mother and father will have access to the infant viewing area until the end of the shift, or for a minimum of four hours.
Respectfully Submitted By: Sister Gwendolyn Hanover, R.N., Superintendent of Nursing, I
Date of Revision: November 12, 1923

Chapter Seventeen

∿

November 30, 1923
7 AM (07:00)

The dream has died and hope is low.
It's almost time to let it go,
But fate steps in and helps it grow.

After receiving the 07:00 nursing report given by Miss Ethel, the night nurse, Angie began her morning rounds, checking each and every patient on her assigned wards. Rounds included visually assessing each patient and recording their vital signs. Once a week, after completing her rounds, Angie counted the narcotic medications that were stored on her units.

On November 1st, during one of her medication checks on Ward 240, she noticed that the bottle of codeine tablets was only half full. This was unusual because she couldn't recall a single patient who had a physician's order for the administration of codeine the previous week. After carefully reviewing two weeks of patient charts, she could not identify even one patient who had received the medication. Because of this, she decided to change her weekly routine to a daily one. Throughout the month of November, she counted the narcotic medications every morning after rounds.

She developed a simple system of recording the date, the name of the narcotic medication, and the number of tablets remaining in the bottle. If there was a change in the tablet count, she immediately investigated who the narcotic was prescribed for, and who had administered it. She carefully documented this in her notebook. Her daily calculations had gone smoothly until this particular morning when she found eight codeine tablets missing and unaccounted for.

Today, there was one patient on the ward with a doctor's order for codeine. It was Mrs. Cara Brunne, a two-day, postpartum patient who had delivered a seven-pound, eleven-ounce baby girl onboard the SS Franconia. Mrs. Brunne had been admitted to the hospital at noon yesterday. Her physician ordered pain medication for her. If she requested it, Mrs. Brunne could receive medication for pain Q4H (*every four hours*) PRN (*pro re nata, as needed*). Angie held her breath as she continued her investigation. If indeed, Mrs. Brunne had complained of pain and received codeine yesterday evening and throughout the night that would account for five pills given in nineteen hours at: 13:00, 17:00, 21:00, 01:00 and 05:00.

Angie reviewed the hand-written medication sheet and the nurse's notes for Mrs. Cara Brunne. She found that there were no references of c/o (*complaints of*) pain, and no entries on the pharmacy record.

Did Miss Ethel forget to complete her charting?

Angie knew this was a possibility but it was highly unlikely. Miss Ethel, a careful and precise nurse, might have been distracted, forgetting to initial one dose, but she would not miss all her medication entries. In addition, Miss Ethel had not mentioned that Mrs. Brunne complained of pain when she discussed the case in her morning report.

Strange...codeine tablets were missing earlier this month. I must report this to Sister Gwendolyn, but first let me check on Mrs. Brunne.

Angie went to Mrs. Brunne's bedside, and found her sound asleep. Her dark brown hair was spread out on her pillow, tangled and dirty with sweat and grime from her long sea voyage. Miss Ethel had reported that Mrs. Brunne cried throughout the night and hadn't slept. Angie didn't have the heart to wake her.

She's finally sleeping. I'm glad she's getting some rest. Poor thing is exhausted and upset to be caught in the middle of this quota law. I'll help her to shower when she wakes. Then, I'll check her for bleeding and tearing.

"Good Morning, Miss Angie," a cheerful voice came up from behind her. "How are you this fine morning?"

Angie turned to see Dr. Goodwin. She greeted him with a soft whisper. "Good Morning, Doctor," she said, touching her finger to her lips. "Mrs. Brunne didn't sleep well during the night. She was terribly worried about her baby."

"Is something wrong?" Dr. Goodwin asked. "I came in this morning for the Brunne Baby's discharge exam."

Angie tiptoed away from the patient's bed, and pushed the baby's crib into the nursery. Dr. Goodwin followed her. "They aren't allowing the baby to be discharged with the mother. They're deporting the baby."

"What?" Dr. Goodwin asked in amazement. "Impossible! Now, I've heard just about everything. How can anyone deport a two-day-old baby?"

Angie explained. "It's the Quota Law. The Austrian quota is closed for the remainder of the year. It will soon be the first of December."

In an effort to curb the flow of immigration, Congress passed the Quota Law in 1921. Its purpose was to temporarily stop the large number of foreigners coming to America, especially those from Southern and Eastern Europe. Each country's quota number was calculated at 3 percent of the people from that country living in the United States during the 1910 census. Since there were more Englishmen and Irishmen in the USA in 1910, the law favored admitting Northern Europeans. The law had been renewed in 1922 and 1923. As a result, immigration numbers, as well as the hospital census, had slowly declined. The effect that it had on nursing was that no new registered nurses had been hired since the beginning of the year.

While Dr. Goodwin performed a head-to-toe assessment of Baby Girl Brunne, Angie reported on the Brunne case. "Mr. and Mrs. Brunne emigrated from Austria in 1914, nine years ago. He is a fish-monger by trade, and established a thriving business at the Fulton Fish Market. Seven months ago, Mr. Brunne sent his wife to Austria to visit her dying mother. While she was there, Mrs. Brunne discovered that she was three months pregnant. When her mother passed away, Mrs. Brunne left Austria. Unfortunately, she had stayed in Austria almost four months. That was longer than she had planned to stay. By the time she started her preparations to return home, she was 34 weeks pregnant. She traveled by train to Germany, and waited a week in Bremerhaven to catch the next steamship sailing to America. On the first day at sea, there was a small engine fire on the ship. The ship was rerouted to the closest port for repairs, which was Southampton, England. The passengers were detained until it was announced that the German ship would not be making the Atlantic crossing. People were transferred to the SS Franconia, an English steamship that was due to sail to America in two days. Although she was more than eight months pregnant, Mrs. Brunne declared that she was six months along when she boarded the ship in Southampton. The voyage to America took nine days. On the last day at sea, Mrs. Brunne went into labor. The ship's doctor delivered a healthy baby girl. The SS Franconia landed yesterday morning. Mrs. Brunne was immediately admitted to the hospital. Last night, they informed her that after discharge from the hospital, she was eligible for readmission to the United States, but the baby would not be granted a landing card. You see, the baby is considered a citizen of Austria because his parents are Austrian. This year's quota for admitting Austrian immigrants is closed."

"This is pure Ellis bunk," said Dr. Goodwin, beginning the newborn examination. He placed his index finger near the baby's left hand. The baby grabbed it with a tight grasp. Next, Dr. Goodwin took hold of both hands of the baby, raised her slightly and gently released her. The doctor observed for symmetry in the infant's response. Next, he gave the wicker crib a slight jolt which startled the baby girl who opened both arms and legs as an immediate response to the jarring. "Good Moro reflex and strong startle and grab reflexes," said Dr. Goodwin. He recorded these reflex responses as WNL *(within normal limits)*. He completed his examination of the baby, and found the baby to be in satisfactory condition to leave the hospital.

He sighed. "This baby cannot be separated from her mother. Her mother will have to return to Europe with her. In this way, they are shutting out the parents, and getting rid of the whole lot of them."

"This hard working family will be forced to leave their home and business. Perhaps, we should say something on their behalf," Angie suggested.

"What can we possibly say, Miss Angie?"

"We could tell them that we are concerned for the health of the baby. She is far too young for a transatlantic voyage. Perhaps, I can ask Sister Gwendolyn to make a formal recommendation to the Board."

"They wouldn't consider it, Miss Angie."

"Yes, I know, Doctor, I suppose I am only wishing out loud."

Throughout the morning, Dr. Goodwin could not stop thinking about the Brunne family. Instead of lunching at the hospital, he went outside, hoping the fresh sea air would clear his head. It was a crisp, sunny day. There wasn't a cloud in the sky. The seagulls were flying in full force. A tiny mouse scampered onto the sidewalk, stopped, and stared at the doctor for a moment. The mouse then scurried away in the direction of Island One. Dr. Goodwin was deep in thought as he followed the mouse down the path.

What can I do? I'm only a government employee. I have no power. No one will listen to me. I am certain that my opinion will not carry any weight against their interpretation of the law, but I am a physician and the baby is too young for a return oceanic voyage. I have a duty to protect the child. Would it hurt to ask who was in charge of the Brunne case today?

At the Registry, Dr. Goodwin was walking up the stairs to Captain Higgins' office when he was stopped by Captain Joseph who was walking down the stairwell. Dr. Goodwin had a special fondness for Captain Joseph because he was a cheerful and good-natured man who always wore a welcoming smile. This was in sharp contrast to the sober and serious faces of many of the Ellis Island officers. That afternoon, Captain Joseph appeared exceptionally jubilant. "Doc, you wouldn't believe what happened! We had a happy ending right here on Ellis Island!"

"A happy ending, Captain, I haven't heard many of those coming from the Hearing Board."

"Guess what, Doc? She was married after all!"

"Who?" Dr. Goodwin asked.

"Your patient, Doc, the young mother who delivered her baby in the john of the women's dormitory."

"Is that right? Last I heard, they were getting ready to deport her for moral turpitude, and her mother for insanity," Dr. Goodwin said.

Captain Joseph explained, "They were. They were ready to close the case when the young man from Armenia showed up with the marriage certificate. It verified the girl's story. They really were married in Greece."

"How did they find him?" Dr. Goodwin asked.

"A little detective work on the part of the girl's uncle. He came down from Boston and started an investigation. He located the boy living with his family downtown," Captain Joseph said excitedly.

"What about the grandmother?"

"The grandmother expressed her desire to live with her sister in Greece. If she leaves voluntarily, she is eligible to reapply for admission in one year. Her brother paid for her return passage. She's leaving tomorrow morning. The girl left with her husband an hour ago."

"That's wonderful news! Captain, did you happen to hear anything about the Brunne case?"

"Yes, they're in Hearing Room D, debating the case right now. Doc, the panel is not in agreement. I never saw anything like it. Chairman Cooper's taking the position of considering the mother and

179

baby as one entity. He's arguing that the father's Fulton Street business creates jobs, and is a community asset. The others are standing firm behind the quota law and will not budge."

Dr. Goodwin headed toward Hearing Room D to listen to the debate. As he entered the room, the discussion was underway:

"The mother was working toward American citizenship."

"The mother is Austrian. Her child is an Austrian citizen."

"The mother and baby should be considered one person."

"The mother and baby are two separate people."

"It was the mother's wish to return to the United States. Therefore, it was the wish of the baby."

"The baby was not aware of her mother's wishes."

Dr. Goodwin raised his hand. "Mr. Chairman, may I have permission to speak?"

"Please state your name and position for the record," the Chairman requested.

"I am Dr. Abraham Goodwin, U.S. Public Health Service Physician. I have recently examined Baby Brunne. The baby is in excellent condition to be discharged to his mother's care. However, I would like to address a practical concern. It is this doctor's opinion that a two-day-old baby is far too young to survive a transatlantic ocean voyage."

Dr. Goodwin's recommendation stimulated further questions from the panel:

"What would be our most responsible action?"

"When would it be safe for the infant to travel?"

"Should the baby be detained at the hospital?"

"If so, who should bear the burden of the expense?"

Dr. Goodwin raised his hand for the second time. "Mr. Chairman, may I have permission to speak?"

"Please state your name and position once again for the record," Chairman Cooper said.

"I am Dr. Abraham Goodwin, U.S. Public Health Service Physician. May I ask this question to the panel? Has the panel considered where the baby was actually born?"

"Please clarify your question, Doctor Goodwin."

"Has today's esteemed panel considered that the actual place of birth of Baby Girl Brunne was not on Austrian soil but on the SS Franconia, an English steamship sailing under the flag of England? In this case, a child born under the English flag is born an Englishman, is he not?"

Chairman Cooper made an announcement for further discussion. "Doctor Goodwin asks the panel to determine the citizenship of Baby Girl Brunne. Is she a citizen of Austria or a citizen of England?"

One member of the panel answered quickly. "Indeed, the child is a citizen of England!"

"Who here is in favor?" The Chairman asked.

"Aye."

"Aye."

"Aye."

"Aye."

Chairman Cooper made a request to the court clerk. "Please report the status of this year's quota number for England."

"The quota remains open, Sir," the clerk quickly answered. "The English quota is ten times that of the Austrian quota. The English have not met their quota for 1923."

The panel huddled.

"This panel has come to a conclusion, Chairman Cooper. The panel concurs that the baby born on November 28, 1923 on the SS Franconia is indeed a citizen of the country of England, and is to be admitted under the English quota."

"Decreed," said Chairman Cooper, as his gavel went down with a bang.

Chapter Eighteen

Christmas Day

December 25, 1923
6 AM (06:00)

Patients, friends and family,
All in perfect harmony!

When the children in New York City woke up in the early morning hours on Christmas Day to peek at the holiday treats in their stockings, Nurse Angie Bosco woke up to go to work. *It's really not so tragic to work on Christmas,* Angie thought as she dressed in her uniform. The day always passed quickly with everyone in a happy holiday spirit. There were festivities and entertainment planned for patients, families, and staff throughout Ellis Island. Holiday treats and live music helped everyone forget their struggles for at least one day.

Angie gave the buttons of her size-eight uniform a little tug. *Can't say I wasn't warned. Adeline told me about eating carefully from the start.*

"I will not go up another dress size this year," Angie declared, remembering the trays of homemade cookies, fruit breads and candies that the volunteers from the immigrant aid societies delivered to the hospital during the holiday season.

Everything was too delicious, and I ate too much. No more sweets for me, after today, of course. For the kitchen cooks had proclaimed that they would make 350 loaves of cranberry-orange-nut bread for the Christmas Day celebration on Ellis Island.

I'll start my reducing plan on January 1st after the New Year's Day dinner with the family.

If Angie worked on Christmas Day and missed the family holiday dinner, her sisters-in-law always planned a repeat performance of the menu on New Year's Eve or New Year's Day. Angie treasured the family gatherings with her two brothers and their families. She loved preparing the holiday meal with her five nieces and nephews.

The meal started with an antipasto table spread of assorted cheeses, salami, fresh tomatoes, roasted peppers, anchovies, and marinated vegetables. The star of the antipasto tray was the *caponata,* a tasty mixture of sautéed eggplant, celery, tomatoes, and olives which Santino's wife, Rosa, bottled after Thanksgiving to have plenty available during the holiday season.

Primo piatto might be freshly-made manicotti crepes filled with a delicate ricotta filling, followed by plates of chicken, meatballs, pork neck bones, and two hard-boiled eggs that had slowly simmered together in the tomato sauce for hours. Oven-roasted chicken with potatoes and onions was usually the *secondo piatto*. This was served with a green salad dressed with the juice from a whole lemon, olive oil, salt and pepper.

Angie would arrive early at Giacomo's apartment house on 116th Street. His wife, Isabella, always gave Angie the assignment of making the meatballs. She started with four thick slices of Italian bread that had soaked in a bowl of warm water for ten minutes. After the bread softened, she squeezed out the water with her hands and swished in two pounds of chopped beef, two eggs, a small handful of fresh parsley, a sprinkle of grated cheese, and salt and pepper. When the ingredients were thoroughly mixed, she formed twenty-four perfectly even little balls, and lined them up on the countertop before frying them.

After that, she would help Isabella and the children cut snakes of pencil-thin dough to make the holiday *struffoli,* honey balls molded into a beehive shape and sprinkled with multi-colored candy. Some Sicilians called this dessert *pignolati,* symbolizing the pinecones that Jesus played with as a child. Isabella always packaged and set aside a small batch for Angie to carry back to the hospital to share with the nurses at Ellis Island Hospital.

Santino and Rosa would arrive laden with packages of bread, cookies, and presents. Their children pushed a baby carriage full of *vino rosa.* Santino had discovered that delivering his homemade wine during prohibition was always uneventful if the bottles were bundled up like a newborn and transported in the old baby carriage.

Rosa would proudly show off the trays of cookies laden with fig-filled *cucidati* cookies and pine nut *pignoli* cookies. Thinking about the cookies made Angie's mouth water. She wished she could spend Christmas day with her family.

Next year, if I am on-duty, I might sleep over on Christmas Eve, and travel to work in the early morning.

At the hospital, the nurses were assigned to work four out of the five most requested holiday shifts. Angie had chosen New Year's Day as her first choice. She had already worked Thanksgiving and Christmas Eve, and would work Christmas Day and New Year's Eve. The big family meal would be January 1st, the first day of 1924.

Breakfast buffet for the nurses at the Cottage was already assembled when Angie arrived at the Dining Room. A small pitcher of warm maple syrup and a honey bowl were next to a large serving pot of hot oatmeal and a plate of hard-boiled eggs. A covered china bowl contained a holiday treat of browned breakfast sausages. A beautiful platter of peeled orange slices, sprinkled with rose water, brightened the table. Two trays of the cranberry-orange-nut bread were there, as promised, evenly sliced, and placed over delicate white doilies.

Angie served herself breakfast and sat down, waiting for the others to join her. The tiny wreath in the dining room reminded her of the Christmas decorations that were on every hospital ward this time of year. A twelve-foot Christmas tree in the auditorium was decorated with strings of popcorn and cranberries, clove-studded oranges, peppermint candy, and handmade origami ornaments in the shape of boxes, cranes, and paper airplanes.

Christmas Eve was always special on Ellis Island. It began with a celebratory dinner of fried flounder filets, cabbage, and boiled potatoes. After dinner, St. Michael's Boys' choir sang Christmas Carols while Dr. Collins, dressed as Santa, and Miss Gertrude, as Santa's Elf, distributed Christmas packages to everyone in the auditorium. The patients unable to attend the celebration were visited on the wards by Captain Joseph wearing a Santa suit.

Volunteers from both the Presbyterian and Episcopal Missions had spent weeks collecting presents. They assembled large gift bags to give to every patient in the hospital and every detainee at the Registry. Although the well-to-do grumbled about the large number of immigrants in the city, it was their donations that provided the Christmas gifts that were distributed, and their generosity was astounding.

The gift bags were so bulky that they were stored in huge barrels, and wheeled to the auditorium in laundry carts. Mission reports, listing the contents of the gift bags, were posted throughout the halls of the hospital. Little girls received a doll, a picture book, crayons, pencils, hair ribbons, and a hairbrush. The presents for the boys were a harmonica, a ball, books, pencils, handkerchiefs, and a comb. Tucked inside the men's packages, were an assortment of toiletries, hand towels, a tie, a pair of socks, and books. Women's gift bags were packed with an apron, a sewing kit, a pair of stockings, a necklace, a writing tablet, and pencils.

"Morning, Adeline, Merry Christmas to you!"

"I came by to give you a big Christmas kiss!" Adeline grabbed a slice of cranberry-orange-nut bread from Angie's plate as she gave her a kiss on the cheek. "Got to run, Angie."

"Eat something, Adeline."

"I am eating…see…cranberry-orange-nut bread." Adeline took a bite. "It's delicious. Remember, I'm covering for Miss Elsie so that she could go home for the holiday. I'm running a little late already."

"Okay, Miss Supervisor, see you later. Stop by on your rounds." Angie gave Adeline a hard-boiled egg to take with her. "Eat it later. Promise!"

"Yes, I promise," Adeline smiled, as she scurried away.

Angie finished her breakfast, and walked to the Mother and Children's Unit. There, she found two memos on her desk. Angie read the first one.

MEMO TO ALL CONCERNED

VISITING HOURS EXTENDED ON

**CHRISTMAS DAY,
DECEMBER 25, 1923**

**VISITORS ALLOWED
FROM 13:00 TO 16:45**

The second memo announced an hour of entertainment planned for Christmas evening.

TONIGHT!

ALL ARE INVITED - PATIENTS, FRIENDS, FAMILY, STAFF!

TO A MUSICAL VARIETY SHOW FROM 17:00 TO 18:00

IN THE HOSPITAL AUDITORIUM FOLLOWING VISITING HOURS

ADDITIONAL FERRIES WILL RUN BETWEEN 18:10 AND 19:00

Angie posted the memos at the entrance of the ward. She began her day by checking all the patients assigned to her care. As she worked her way through the wards on rounds, she quickly assessed each patient. She worked fast and efficiently throughout the morning to get the majority of her work finished before visiting hours.

Fannie interrupted her mid-morning to call her attention to Captain Joseph from the Registry. He was dressed as a jolly, fat Santa, and was happily distributing holiday presents to the bedridden patients on the wards. Angie took a moment to thank him for sacrificing his holiday to be with them. He told her that it cheered him to come into the hospital, as he would otherwise be spending the holiday alone.

Soon after lunch, Adeline knocked on the window of the ward. "Hi, Angie, I'm reminding everyone that visiting hours are extended today."

"Yes, how could I forget? Once the visitors arrive, there's no getting our work done. After that, I'll start taking patients down to see the show. I'm trying to organize my charting and paperwork now. By the way, what's the show going to be tonight, more carolers?" Angie asked.

"No, it's a real treat. An entertainer called *Ragtime Jimmy* is coming. Miss Elsie received confirmation last week. She didn't tell anyone because she wanted to surprise us." Adeline said, excitedly.

"Really, Adeline?"

"Yes, he's coming with his jazz band. I've heard him perform a number of times." Adeline leaned over to Angie and whispered in her ear, "...at the speakeasies, you know."

"Oh, Adeline, that's sounds like fun. I've never been to a real speakeasy."

Adeline smiled. "Well, you must come with me the next time I go, my dear. Keep it hush-hush until it's announced this evening."

When Adeline left, the first of the many visitors began to arrive. They carried flowers, cookies, and baskets of apples and bananas. Angie never interfered with the visitors, preferring to give the families the privacy they needed. She sat quietly visible at her desk in the middle of the room in order to be available to anyone who might need assistance.

Katie Ryan was surrounded by her family. She waved to Angie from her hospital bed. "Miss Angie, come and meet my boys."

"Hi, boys!" Angie greeted the handsome group of redheads, and shook hands with each one of them. "Let me see if I remember your names. You are Patrick, Sean, Michael, the Second, and...don't tell me, Davin. Did I remember your names correctly?"

"Yes, you did, Miss Angie, but in America, I'm called *Dave*," said Davin.

"Yes, and I'm called *Mickey*," added Michael the Second. "How did you remember our names?"

"Well, I've seen you many times these past ten weeks. You've all been so good about visiting your Mother every Sunday."

"We miss her," said Sean. "It won't be too long now, will it?"

"I really don't know. It's difficult to predict an actual time. The doctors thought that your Mom would be discharged weeks ago, but her legs are swollen and her blood pressure is elevated. We're all hoping that she stabilizes, so that she can soon go home with you. I heard that you're all working and contributing to the family income."

"Yes, Miss Angie, I am so proud of the five of them, including their father. They found an apartment with a dining room and three bedrooms. Can you imagine such a place? I can't wait to see it."

"The boys made wood frames for their beds, and we bought mattresses. Now, I'm looking for a dining room table. We're eating on an old door that we found in the trash, but that won't do for my Katie when she comes home," Mike, the father, said proudly.

"Where will we put the baby?" Patrick asked.

"That would be where you slept, my boy, and your brothers after you. We will make a comfortable bed using a bureau drawer for the first months."

"Not in a cradle?" asked Dave.

"No, I've never gotten around to making one," said Mike, the father.

"Well, maybe this time, we can buy a cradle for little Katie," Mickey said.

"Yes!" Sean agreed.

"What makes you lads so sure it will be a girl?" Katie Ryan asked.

"Well, you'll be well-deserving of a little pink bundle after us boys, don't you think?" Patrick declared, laughing.

"I wouldn't mind another boy child. You boys have made me so proud. I couldn't ask for more than to have yet another one like you around. We are blessed. Oh, I can't wait to go home." Katie Ryan said, with a tear welling up in her eyes.

"Merry Christmas to the Ryan family, I wish you all the best in the New Year with the new baby, and with your new life in America. It's been an honor to know you these past weeks," Angie said, making her way back to her desk.

From her desk in the middle of the room, Angie noticed that every patient was surrounded by a group of visitors except Fabiana Morales. She was sitting quietly on a chair next to her bed, looking sad and lonely. Angie was certain that she had seen her with a visitor earlier in the afternoon. Angie was always glad that Fabiana understood Sicilian so that she could talk easily with her. "Merry Christmas, Fabiana. Did you have a visitor earlier?"

"No, I would not call that boy a visitor. That was the fool who refused to marry me, Miss Angie."

"Why did he come here today?"

"He came to tell me that he has decided to do the honorable thing…to marry me. He did not tell me the whole truth. I know that my mother sent his parents a letter expressing her disappointment. She asked for her money to be returned. His parents were embarrassed by his actions. The honorable thing, indeed, he is a simple, scared, little boy. I will never marry the likes of him. He said that it was lucky for him that my goiter was smaller. Lucky for him? I told him that I had no intention of marrying a coward. I am no longer afraid to go back to

South America even if it means going home a failure. My great-uncle has not come. Time is passing quickly. Soon, I will have to face my deportation hearing. I will be strong and suffer the consequences of my decision today," Fabiana said, proudly.

"Fabiana, you are brave to make such a decision. I am very impressed. There are many women who would have married after coming this far, rather than face deportation."

"I am not afraid, Miss Angie. I have to do what I hear from my heart."

"You are very courageous. It is always right to do what your heart tells you."

"Thank you, Miss Angie. I will remember your kindness when I return to Paraguay to live with my mother." Fabiana stood to give Angie a tight hug. Angie looked up as she hugged Fabiana.

Walking across the ward toward her, were her two older brothers, Giacomo and Santino. Angie could not believe her eyes. "What are you doing here?" Angie cried. "What a surprise!" She ran to give her brothers a hug and a kiss.

"We came to see you, Sister," Santino said.

"Why aren't you home with the family on Christmas Day?" Angie asked.

"We brought the family with us. They are all downstairs in the lobby. We ate our holiday dinner earlier than usual this year. We have a surprise for you!" Giacomo announced. "Would you be able to leave the ward and come down to see everyone for a few minutes?"

"Yes, I was going to take the patients down to the auditorium in a half-hour, but I can start taking them now. I will ask Fannie to watch the ward while I am downstairs," Angie said. "There's a show scheduled at five o'clock this evening. Can you stay, Giacomo? I hope so. The children will love it."

"What kind of a show?" Santino asked.

"A young singer is coming! He is very popular downtown. He sings with his jazz band. I can't say exactly who. Well, if you don't tell..." Angie stood up on tiptoe to reach Santino, and whispered in his ear.

"Magnifico!" said Santino.

"Wait for me while I gather a few patients."

"We'll go downstairs, and wait with the family in the lobby. Don't be too long. We have a Christmas surprise for you. The children can hardly wait!" Giacomo said.

"Brothers, I can't imagine what you have planned downstairs, but it sounds wonderful. Both of you, being here, is the only surprise I need today."

"No, there is an even better one. You will see."

Angie found Fannie. Then, she gathered four ambulatory patients, and escorted them to the hospital auditorium. As she walked into the lobby, her three little nieces came running toward her. They were holding hands with a taller young lady.

Perhaps, they brought a mother's helper with them on their holiday outing.

"Aunt Angie! Aunt Angie! Merry Christmas!" They screamed as they crashed into her.

"Leea, Leea," the woman called out to Angie. In an instant, Angie recognized the woman who was hugging and kissing her.

It's Celestina. She still smells the same.

"My baby sister, I can't believe it's you." Angie started to cry. Celestina hugged her sister with all her might. "Celestina, you are here! How can that be? No one told me."

"We wanted to surprise you. Celestina arrived three days ago. She will be staying in New York, and going to college downtown," said Rosa, Santino's wife.

"You came through Ellis, and didn't stop to see me. I can't believe that." Angie said, with a frown.

"It was so close to Christmas. We wanted to surprise you." Santino explained.

"Let me take a look at you." Angie said, pulling away from her baby sister to study her closely. "How tall are you?"

"I am exactly one hundred and fifty-two centimeters," Celestina answered.

"Oh my, five-feet tall and how beautiful you are!" Celestina's dark brown hair was thick and long with a deep luxurious shine. Her dark eyes and olive complexion resembled Santino and Giacomo's coloring more than Angie's, who was fairer than her three siblings.

"We sent Celestina a Second-Class ticket. She is the first Bosco who did not travel in steerage. She was not required to stop at Ellis Island." Giacomo announced, proudly.

"Oh my, you should be very proud of yourselves. I am very proud of you. What a wonderful surprise. It's a dream come true." Angie could not contain her excitement. "I waited and prayed for this day to come. Oh, Celestina, I have missed you so."

"It seems like forever since I have been in your arms, Leea, my sister," said Celestina in English.

"Celestina, I just realized that you are speaking English."

"The brothers…they insist that I study in Sicily. They send the money for school and a special English tutor. Zia Dona has to search for a tutor to prepare me for America, and she finds one," Celestina said.

"You have thought of everything. What a wonderful family we have. Come, let's celebrate. Let's find seats for the show. The band has arrived. We are all in for a wonderful treat this evening." Angie led her family into the auditorium, and found seats for everyone. After she saved a seat for herself, she returned to the ward to bring more patients down to see the show.

The young performer, *Ragtime Jimmy*, turned out to be a spirited singer and an energetic comedian. Accompanied by his band, he sang a number of popular songs: *Balling-The-Jack*, *Dinah*, *Ain't We Got Fun* and *Yes, We Have No Bananas*. He told jokes between his songs and the audience howled with laughter. The hour-long show ended all too soon and with great applause.

Before long, everyone was preparing to leave and saying their good-nights. Angie walked her family down to the quay to bid them goodbye with kisses and hugs. She promised to see them in one week on New Year's Day. Celestina cried until Giacomo and Santino agreed to bring Celestina down to the ferry landing in two days to meet Angie for a dinner outing.

As the ferryboat filled with passengers returning to the city, Angie waved and blew kisses. Suddenly, Adeline was standing next to Angie with a strikingly handsome gentleman at her side.

Adeline took a deep breath. "Angie, I want to introduce you to Harry. Harry, this is my dear friend, Angelina Bosco."

"Enchante! I heard so much about you," Angie said as she shook his hand.

"You are French also, like Adeline?" Harry asked.

"No, I thought perhaps you were French," Angie said.

"No, Angelina, my family is originally from Germany."

"Call me *Angie*. I am so pleased that you came tonight. It was grand of you to give up Christmas with your family to be here with Adeline."

"My parents do not celebrate Christmas. We are the Steingolds, a Jewish family," Harry explained.

"….but you are the gentleman who sells gramophones, correct?"

"No, I am a jeweler," said Harry with a smile, "but I did buy a Victrola for the hospital."

"Are you related to the famous Steingold Jewelers?" Angie asked.

"Yes! That is our family business."

"That's most interesting, Mr. Steingold. It's a pleasure to meet you."

"It's been my pleasure, but you must call me *Harry*. Look, the ferry is about to leave. I hope to see you again, Angie. I'm sorry to go, but this is one of the last ferries returning to the city this evening." Harry kissed Adeline on the cheek. "Good Night, My Love," he said as he boarded the boat.

Angie and Adeline stood at the pier and waved goodbye. Angie's nieces and nephews shouted from the ferry boat railing, "Merry Christmas, Aunt Angelina!"

Angie turned to Adeline, and whispered. "Harry Steingold, Adeline." In a louder voice, she shouted, "MERRY CHRISTMAS, EVERYONE!"

"We love you, Angelina, see you next week!"

Angie said to Adeline, "Harry Steingold of the *Steingold Jewelers* is not exactly an ordinary salesman."

"MERRY CHRISTMAS TO ALL!" shouted Adeline, waving to the people on the ferry boat as it slowly left the dock.

"Correct me if I am wrong, but wasn't it Miss Adeline Fermè who gave me advice about only dating men who are the same religion?"

Angie turned to grab Adeline, but Adeline was one step ahead of Angie, and already running up the hill toward the hospital. As she ran away, Adeline called back to Angie, "I have lots of work to finish up tonight."

"You have lots of explaining to do tonight, Miss Adeline. You're not getting away from me that easily." Angie chased Adeline up the hill toward the entrance of the hospital.

"... and to all a good night, except you, Adeline Fermè. Just wait until I catch up and get my hands on you!"

Chapter Nineteen

❦

Christmas Evening

December 25, 1923
8:30 PM (20:30)

Sometimes, we hear their warnings whispered in our ear.
At times, we hear their callings come in loud and clear.

Each year, Sister Gwendolyn, Miss Elizabeth, and Miss Elsie did their best to make Christmas evening dinner at the Cottage a memorable one. Many of the nurses lived far away from home, and could not celebrate the holiday with their families. The supervisors planned the dining room decorations months in advance. They crocheted red scalloped borders on the round, white tablecloths, and made table centerpieces from gilded pinecones and gold-painted candles.

Outside, the harbor glistened. Inside, Christmas Buffet was beautifully displayed on two rectangular tables which were positioned directly in front of the largest window facing Lady Liberty and her holiday lights. The combination of the golden tabletop candlelight and the sparkling lights from Bedloe Island gave the dining room a cozy holiday glow. Platters of oven-baked ham, mashed potatoes, sautéed spinach, and candied sweet potatoes were arranged around fresh cranberries and holly leaves.

This year, as a special treat, Sister Gwendolyn hired a harpist who was available to play at the Cottage on Christmas evening until 11 pm.

Sister paid her from her personal savings account. The harpist had already begun to play soothing Christmas hymns in the Living Room. As the nurses came down the stairs for holiday dinner, they were greeted by Reverend Sanders, Sister Gwendolyn, and Miss Elizabeth. The supervisors stood at the double doors of the Dining Room. They greeted every nurse, wishing each one, "A Very Merry Christmas!"

The nurses had finished eating and were feeling relaxed, happily listening to the harp melodies coming from the next room. They were telling stories of past holidays when Miss Dorothy appeared. She looked pale and tired. Questions came from every table.

"Are you okay, Dorothy?"

"You look like you've seen a ghost."

"Why are you so late coming back from CD?"

"Is anything wrong?"

Dorothy sat down next to Adeline. She tried her best to smile, but couldn't. She looked away. She didn't want to spoil the evening for everyone by showing how upset she was feeling.

"What happened, Dorothy?" The group asked as Sister Gwendolyn approached their table. "Dorothy lost a patient this evening," Sister Gwendolyn explained, "only a few hours ago."

"My little patient died of scarlet fever. She was only four years old. She came in last week with a rash and a fever. She seemed to be getting better, but this afternoon her pulse raced. She appeared to be in pain. I gave her aspirin to comfort her. I prayed. I was certain that she would make it through, but her pulse began to slow down. She died three hours ago." Dorothy continued. "We notified her family this afternoon. Her parents came immediately. They were heartbroken. They told me that they had lost their son two months before they sailed for

America. The little girl's brother was trampled by a horse. After wrapping her body in the sheets that I soaked in disinfectant, I brought her tiny shroud to the morgue. I was all alone there. I cried and cried. I kept wondering why the poor parents should have to experience this kind of double tragedy. They were only trying to pursue their hopes and dreams by moving to America."

"I've seen that happen. A tragedy occurs, and another follows," Adeline said.

"By coming to America, the family was simply following their hearts' calling. Instead, they walked straight into heartbreak. Why does that happen, and on Christmas Day, of all days?" Dorothy asked.

"It is not for us to question God's plan," Miss Elizabeth said, sadly. "Perhaps, it is their work or destiny. We don't know. I don't have any answers for you tonight, but I know how deeply you are hurting."

Dorothy was crying. "My only Christmas wish was to make her better."

"I wish there was a cure for scarlet fever," Angie whispered.

Miss Elsie said, "I am certain there will be someday. They developed the diphtheria vaccine this year, and will start to vaccinate people against diphtheria early next year."

"I wish there were more vaccines available for everyone," Ethel sighed.

"That would be my Christmas wish, too." Gertie announced.

"Mine, too. I heard that they are working on a vaccine for pertussis, also." Maude added.

"Maybe our wishes will come true in years to come. Imagine, there could be a vaccine that could wipe out every known contagious disease, and everyone would be required to receive it." Adeline said.

"We would have to vaccinate everyone in the entire world. I don't know if that would be possible. There would always be pockets of the population without the vaccine, and they would continue to spread the disease." Sister Gwendolyn explained.

"Then, we need a medicinal agent that would kill germ cells before they multiplied in the body," Mabel said.

Imogene interrupted, "That's a foolish notion. Such a drug would kill all the cells in our bodies, the germ cells and the healthy cells."

"Oh my, that's a discouraging thought, Imogene."

"I think I've got it," Angie said, "a medicine that would strengthen our immune system. When a person begins to get sick, she takes this elixir. It strengthens and fortifies her white blood cells so that they gobble up all the germs in a matter of days, helping her to recover quickly."

"I think you may be on to something, Angie."

"Even if it is not possible or probable, I am wishing for it," Angie insisted.

"I will pray for it," Mabel said.

"Yes, let's say a prayer tonight for Dorothy's little patient. Let's pray for an end to these dreadful diseases," Sister Gwendolyn announced, before leading the nurses in a Christmas Evening Prayer.

After the prayer, all was quiet except for the soft music coming from the Living Room. The nurses left the Dining Room. They huddled together around the fireplace, listening to the soothing sounds of the harp. The harpist played until after eleven.

The nurses continued to quietly sit together long after the music ended. They lingered in front of the fire for another hour before they began to leave. Ruth and Rose left first, holding hands. The others followed. That's when Angie had her first opportunity to talk privately to Adeline. When they reached the third floor, she followed Adeline into her bedroom.

"Okay, Ad, tell me!" cried Angie. "Tell me everything."

"There is nothing to tell, Angie. You know the story: girl meets boy, girl falls for boy, they come from different backgrounds, boy doesn't marry girl, and they break up, the end."

"I need more facts, Ad, tell me more about Harry."

"We met at a fundraiser for Woodrow Wilson."

"When?"

"1912"

"Eleven years ago, you were just a baby. How old were you?"

"I was twenty-six when I met Harry," Adeline told Angie. "We fell in love. His family discouraged the relationship. You see, we practiced different religions. I was not about to change my religion because of a man. You know how headstrong I can be. I felt that I should be allowed to be who I am. We loved each other, and we foolishly dated on and off for more than four years. Finally, the romance ended. After that, the war started. I went overseas. We met again this past summer. I told you I was seeing him."

"I know, you told me about him last month. Where did you meet again?" Angie asked.

"We met at a party. He seems different somehow. I think he's more mature and confident. His family has become extremely wealthy due to many of his business decisions."

"I'm glad he came to see you today, Adeline."

"I invited him, but I didn't think he would come. I couldn't meet him on our usual date night this week because of the holiday schedule. I suppose that is why he came today," Adeline said.

"I didn't know you were seeing him every week. How do you manage to get a ferry pass from Sister Gwendolyn?"

"I do, but Sister's strict. She will only give me a four-hour pass from seven to eleven once a week. She insists that I return on the ten-thirty ferry. Harry has definitely grown. He's talking about starting his own branch of the business, specializing in diamonds. The business is doing very well," Adeline added.

"Well, at least, he will always be able to shower you with diamonds!"

"I haven't accepted any gifts of jewelry from him."

"Ad, aren't you attracted to his wealth?"

"No, I don't think I am. In fact, I believe it complicates things. It would embarrass me if people around here knew how wealthy he is. I think that his business responsibilities confuse his obligations to his parents. Perhaps, the business is the reason why he prefers to remain free and unattached. I don't know."

"Oh, this is so sad!"

"I feel I have to follow my heart."

"That's the third time someone mentioned that today. I suppose I'm being surrounded by strong women who are here to teach me a lesson."

"Thank you, Angie. I take that as a compliment."

"I wish I were as strong as you!"

"You are, Angie, believe me."

"No, Adeline, I'm not, but thank you for saying that. Now, tell me, how rich is he?"

"Very rich, like Fifth Avenue rich…mansion rich…limousine rich, Angie, you would not believe it!"

"Do you ever ride in his limousine?"

"Yes, he takes me to the ferry building in the limousine after our dates. Usually, no one is around at that time of night to see us. He wants to pick me up at the ferry, but I don't want the others to know. Oh, look at the time, it's getting late. We have to get up early for work tomorrow."

"Ad, wait. I have a problem."

"What?"

"There was more codeine missing from the medicine cabinet this morning."

"That's three times..."

"Yes, I discovered pills missing November 1st, November 30th, and again today," explained Angie.

"Did you report it to Sister Gwendolyn?" Adeline asked.

"I did. She doesn't seem to be taking me seriously."

"Who do you think is taking it?"

"I don't know, but I have suspicions."

"What are you saying?"

"I think Sister Gwendolyn is covering for someone."

"Is it someone at the hospital? You don't think *she* is taking the meds?"

"No, but perhaps this has been going on for a long time because she appears to be looking the other way."

"Tell me again. What are you thinking? Who do you suspect?"

Angie explained. "Well, I've thought about this for a long time. First, I thought it might be someone who worked the night-shift. I examined all the work schedules. There was no one aide and no one nurse assigned to work all three nights in question."

"You were looking specifically for someone who worked the same three nights when the codeine was taken?" Adeline asked.

"Yes. First, I looked for someone who worked the night-shifts. Then, I had another idea. I searched the schedule for someone who was assigned to work the same three day-shifts. There was no one nurse assigned to those days either, except..."

"Except who, Angie? Tell me. Who was there all three days?"

"Miss Elsie, Ad, Miss Elsie comes in earlier than anyone who works on the day shift. It's her habit to go on six o'clock morning rounds. Sometimes, no one is around when she goes from room to room because we are in charge of so many wards during the night."

"Miss Elsie? What are you saying? Angie, are you out of your mind? You suspect poor Miss Elsie?

"I'm not saying she did it. I'm saying that she was on duty every day the codeine was taken. She was on the units this morning, too."

"Yes, I met with her when she gave me her morning report. She was checking to see if everything was in order before she left the island to go to her sister's house for Christmas. Why would she take codeine?" Adeline asked.

"I don't know. I don't even know if she took the pills, just that she had the opportunity to take them. She does have arthritis. Ad, I don't know what to do? Should I go to Sister Gwendolyn, and tell her what I know? What do you think?"

Adeline advised Angie. "No, whatever you do, do not do that. Do not tell Sister Gwendolyn who you suspect. You may be very, very wrong. We are going to have to do a little more detective work before we point a finger at anyone. Write up the incident report. Submit it to Sister Gwendolyn. That's all you are to do, nothing else."

"I wrote up the report this morning, and put it in her mailbox. Are you sure I shouldn't do anything else?" Angie asked.

"Don't do anything right now. The two of us will have to put our heads together. We'll come up with a plan to catch the culprit in the act next month. I am certain that, together, we will think of something," Adeline said with determination.

"Yes, I know we will, Adeline!"

"Okay. Now, let's get some sleep. It's been a long day. Merry Christmas, Angie Girl. Sweet dreams!"

"Sweet dreams to you, too, Ad, and thank you."

"Night! Don't let the bed bugs bite, Angelina."

Angie could not wait to get into her cozy bed after she washed up and put on her nightgown. It had been a long day. Before she fell off to sleep, memories of Baby Celestina in the ancient town of Castelvetrano floated through her mind.

Chapter Twenty

∾

May 22, 1903

What do they call the message that comes from up above?
There isn't a real name for it, but it begins with love.

"Leea, Leea, Come!"

Angelina ignored Baby Celestina's calls from the nursery. Celestina had awakened from her afternoon nap. She was calling for her older sister from her crib. The temptation to go into the baby's room was hard to resist, but Angelina battled it with all her might. Angelina had chores, and she was not allowed in Celestina's room. Zia Dona told her many times that she was not to disturb the three-year-old after she had put her down to sleep.

"Leea, Leea, Come!"

Angelina continued to polish the silver, following her aunt's orders. Her aunt assigned her a job every day. She wished she could work outdoors like her older brothers. Zia Dona had found a position for Santino as a shepherd boy. He left the house at 6 am every morning. He did not return until after dark. Giacomo was gone all day, also. It was Zia Dona's idea to have him sell tin pots at the village gate.

"Leea, Leea, Come!"

Angelina wished she could take her baby sister outside. She wanted to wheel her around the village in her carriage like Zia Dona often did in the afternoon. Angelina knew Zia Dona would punish her severely, but she could no longer ignore her sister's cries. She quietly put down her aunt's precious silver. She tiptoed into the nursery. "Shh, baby! Shh!" She said, putting her index finger to her lips.

Baby Celestina smiled. "Out, Leea! Out, Leea!"

Angelina lifted the toddler out of the crib, and set her down on the wool rug. She rolled a ball to the baby, and laughed. The sisters quietly rolled the ball back and forth to each other.

Suddenly, Zia Dona walked into the room!

She stood looking down on them with her hands on her hips. Zia Dona scolded Angelina. "There you are, you disobedient child. I went to check on the silver, and found that you abandoned your duties. I had a hunch you would be here against my orders. You deliberately disobeyed me. You are a bad child. Get out. Get out of my house this instant. Leave now. Do not return until bedtime. I do not want to see you anymore today."

Angelina was happy to leave Zia Dona's house. She walked down the dark and narrow streets of the town until she reached Piazza Garibaldi, the park-like square in front of the church. The old men of the town were sitting on the benches in the square. They appeared to be absorbed in a discussion, and did not notice the little girl who walked past them. Angelina continued to walk until she reached the stone entrance gate of the walled town. There, a number of peddlers were gathered, selling stalks of artichokes, fava beans, and lemons from their wooden carts. Angelina found Giacomo among them. He was peddling tin pots from his tiny wagon.

"Ciao, Giacomo!"

"Angelina, what are you doing out here? Go home. You must go home or you will get in trouble."

"I am already in trouble, Giacomo. I have been banished by Zia Dona."

"For what, Angelina? What did you do?"

"I went into the nursery, and played with Celestina when she woke up from her afternoon nap," Angelina said.

"Oh, no, our Zia Dona found you with Celestina. Did she get angry?"

"Oh, yes, Giacomo, so angry that she turned red."

"Did she beat you, Angelina?"

"No, she would never hit me, but she does hate me." Angelina started to cry.

"Don't cry, Angelina. She doesn't hate you. She is overwhelmed with us. She is a spinster lady who does not know anything about children. She suddenly found herself with the four of us to care for."

"…And she can't wait to get rid of us. The only one she loves is Celestina."

"We must be grateful that she loves Celestina. She takes good care of her. Do not worry, Angelina. I am going to America. That is why I sell my pots every day."

"You will have to sell hundreds of these tiny tin pots to buy a ticket to America, Giacomo."

Giacomo outlined his plan. "Zia Dona promised me that she will pay for half of the cost of my ticket to America. That is my hope. We must all go to America. I will go first. I will earn money for you and the others to follow me. There, I will open my own store."

"Okay, I will go with you, Giacomo. I will do anything you say, but Zia Dona will never allow Celestina to come with us. She believes Celestina is her baby now."

Giacomo agreed. He firmly said, "I know, Angelina. You are right. Zia Dona thinks she owns our Celestina, but she is our mother's child, named *little star* after her, up in Heaven. Our mother wants us all to be together. That is why I have thought of this plan, Angelina. I will find a way for the four of us to go to America. I promise, one day we will all be together as a family in America."

Chapter Twenty-One

∾

January 13, 1924
6:45 AM (06:45)

I felt the babe. She called to me.
Safe and secure in her cocoon,
She hungered for some extra room.

The clock on the wall of Ward 220B read 3:45 am.

Miss Claire forgot to windup the clock last night. It must have stopped. I think it's been that time for, at least, three hours.

As the first slivers of dawn filtered through her window to reveal yet another crack on the ceiling above her bed, Katie Ryan was deep in thought.

How is it that I've never noticed all those cracks on the ceiling before tonight?

The two wavy lines directly above her appeared to connect, and reminded her of the rolling hills behind the train station in Ireland where she often played with her sister, Bridget. Katie Ryan lingered over the memory of Bridget's green eyes and thick red braids until the contraction she was feeling gradually ended.

Although she wasn't expecting her baby to arrive for another two weeks, Katie Ryan knew her labor had begun. She wasn't entirely sure when a vague stomach cramp woke her up at one o'clock in the morning. She had been having this type of cramping sensation, on and off, throughout the week. Now, hours later, she was absolutely certain her labor had begun.

Perhaps, I should be telling Miss Claire or should I wait for Miss Angie to come on-duty. Katie Ryan closed her eyes. *I don't want to be bothering the good ladies-in-white as yet. I think I still may have some time to go.*

Minutes later, she felt her abdomen tighten. The cramping started slowly at first, getting progressively stronger and stronger until the ache turned into a stabbing sensation. Katie squirmed, and pressed her left foot against the metal foot-railing of her bed. As the contraction reached its peak, Katie bore down on the metal bar, and pushed against it.

Hold on a moment longer, Katie. Seconds later, Katie Ryan felt a slow releasing as the sharpest pain morphed into a sick achiness.

Relax, Katie, like Aunt Fiona taught you. Relax. Don't tense up.

When she was pregnant with her first child, her Aunt Fiona, who had birthed ten children, instructed her to relax with each contraction. Aunt Fiona told her to unclench her fists, soften her shoulders, and to not squirm. Most of the time, Katie Ryan was able to do exactly that, starting with her face, her neck, shoulders, hands, and feet. However, as labor progressed, she liked to push against something in rhythm with the contraction. It was her secret. One that Aunt Fiona would not have approved. The stronger the contraction, the harder Katie pushed her foot against the metal.

Aunt Nola insisted the trick of surviving labor was not to relax, but to concentrate on something. "Concentrate hard on something, something near or something far. Find anything. Examine it. Study every detail," she told Katie. Katie was no more than twenty at the time.

Aunt Fiona argued with Aunt Nola until Katie's mother told the two aunts to stop harping on the girl. Katie could still hear the three sisters bickering as they walked home from Sunday Mass. "Don't tell the girl that, Nola. How can she concentrate on something when pain is ripping through her thin, little body?"

"Well, that's not the way to do it, Fiona. How can anyone relax when the labor pains attack?"

"Sisters, perhaps, you are both right. However, you must stop fussing this instant!" Katie's mother told her sisters, "You are confusing my sweet Katie. Katie will figure her own way through. Now, Katie, listen to me. Laboring is a doorway you walk through to get inside the house. That's all it is, child, like walking across a threshold. It's only a speck of time in your whole life. Simple as that, Katie, now you don't be worrying that it's anything more."

"Listen to your Mum, Katie. See all those people out there. See them all. See all the people in church this morning. Well, even all the people you don't see, they were all born." Aunt Nola added, "They were all born, slipping right though their mother's loins. If all the people in Ireland and all the people in the world were born, birthing is as natural as that."

Today, we'll be crossing a threshold, dear baby.

Katie Ryan was about to deliver her fifth child. She was sometimes relaxing, Aunt Fiona style; sometimes concentrating, Aunt Nola's style; and sometimes wiggling and pressing against the footboard, Katie Ryan style.

What didn't work for Katie Ryan was screaming. She did not want to wake or frighten the other patients who were sleeping in the room. She felt that she would lose the rhythm of the contraction if she screamed. She wouldn't be able to feel its ebb and flow. She needed to track each contraction to its peak, and wanted to feel the glory of relief when the pain began its descent. When Katie Ryan's current contraction dissolved, she dozed off.

Miss Angie was at her bedside when Katie Ryan woke up with a contraction. "When did your contractions begin, Mrs. Ryan?"

"At one o'clock this morning, I looked at the clock. Later, it seemed to have stopped. I lost track of time," Katie Ryan reported. "At first, I thought I was having false labor, but the contractions have been coming regularly."

"Did you feel your water break?" Angie asked.

"No, usually it doesn't, until later," Katie answered.

"I'm going to examine you to see how dilated you are, Mrs. Ryan."

"Yes, Miss Angie. I know."

Another contraction began. Angie reached for the pair of rubber gloves and the tube of lubricant that she kept stored on the bedside table. She waited until the contraction eased before she positioned Katie Ryan for a quick cervical check. With her gloved hand, Angie felt the opening in the thinning cervix and estimated that it was a little less than the size of four of her fingers.

"Seven centimeters, already, Mrs. Ryan, let's get you to the Delivery Room. When your water breaks, your cervix will dilate quickly."

Angie called Fannie to help her transfer Katie Ryan from the bed to the gurney. They wheeled Katie Ryan to the elevator, and rode up to the third floor.

"Morning, Gertie, Mrs. Ryan is fully effaced and seven centimeters dilated," Angie announced when they arrived.

Taking Katie Ryan's hand in hers, Miss Gertrude said, "That's good news, Mrs. Ryan. You will be going home with your baby sooner than you expected. Angie, let's use the Recovery Room until Dr. Collins arrives. It's empty at the moment."

"Do you have enough staff today? Do you need me to stay?" Angie asked. "I can arrange for coverage downstairs, if need be."

"No, Angie, we are fully staffed with only one surgery scheduled for early morning. We'll send word to you when it's time to receive the baby."

Angie returned to her ward. She resumed her routine nursing duties, knowing Mrs. Ryan was in the best of hands.

Two hours later, she was called to the Recovery Room to receive the new baby after an uneventful delivery. Angie found Mrs. Ryan holding her newborn. She looked up at Angie with sparkling blue eyes. Her smile was radiant. "It's a girl, Miss Angie."

"Congratulations, Mrs. Ryan. I am so very happy for you!"

Angie washed her hands for thirty seconds. She slipped a clean surgical gown over her uniform. "Ready, Gertie," she said, holding out her arms. Miss Gertrude placed the newborn baby girl in Angie's arms, and gave Angie a copy of the delivery information sheet. Angie turned to Katie Ryan, "I'll take her downstairs to wash and admit her. I'll bring her back to you in two shakes of a lamb's tail. Did you decide on her name?"

"I named her the moment I met her. She'll be called *Erin*, Miss Angie. It means Ireland. So we'll always have a bit of Ireland with us as we start our new life in America."

"That's a fitting name, and a lovely little one she is, Mrs. Ryan."

Angie took the elevator down to the nursery. She admitted the newborn, following the standard admission protocol. First, she unwrapped little Erin Ryan and weighed her. A clean square of white flannel was already positioned on the scale. Angie reset the weights to allow for the weight of the cloth, and placed Baby Erin on the scale. Positioning her left hand an inch above the baby to protect her from falling, Angie used her right hand to balance the weights of the scale…*2,750 grams…six pounds, one ounce.*

Angie set a tape measure on the scale, and positioned Erin's head at the zero mark of the measure. She gently straightened Erin's legs, and made note of where the heel of her foot ended...*fifty centimeters...nineteen and a quarter inches.*

Angie lifted Baby Erin, and carried her in her left arm while she charted the baby's weight and length in both metric and imperial measures. With her right hand, she reached for her stethoscope and a glass thermometer. Angie placed the newborn in a wicker crib, and draped a flannel blanket on the baby to prevent her from getting chilled while she took a rectal temperature. Then, Angie counted the newborn's heart rate and respirations for one full minute. She charted her findings.

Temperature: 97.8

Heart Rate: 142

Murmur: None noted

Respirations: 36

Muscle Tone: Mildly Flaccid

Umbilicus: Normal, 3 vessels

Angie measured the circumference of Baby Erin's chest and head. She palpated the fontanels checking for firmness, bulging, and depressions in the soft spaces between the separated skull bones. There were none. She noticed that the shape of Baby Erin's head was not perfectly round, but slightly flattened in the back. She stopped, and studied it.

Does her head appear abnormally flat?

Next, she prepared a tincture of silver nitrate solution, and dropped one drop of solution in each eye. Silver nitrate was used as a standard preventative treatment to kill bacteria, such as chlamydia and syphilis. Both infections could cause infant blindness if a baby descended through the birth canal of an infected mother. While doing this, Angie noticed a slight roundness in the corner of the infant's eyes instead of the more usual almond shape.

Is this an irregularity or a familial trait? Are the eyes of the Ryan brothers rounded in this manner?

She lifted Baby Erin, blanket and all, and walked to the sink. She wiped the baby's face with cotton using water that had been sterilized earlier by boiling and cooling. Next, Angie washed Erin's hair with ivory soap removing much of the thick white *vernix caseosa*, the waxy coating that protected the baby's skin from the amniotic fluid while she floated in her mother's uterus. Before continuing with the bath, Angie dried Baby Erin's head to prevent heat loss. Angie noted that Erin's ears looked a bit small and lower than the level of her eyes.

Dear Lord, tell me that I am imagining this!

Quickly, Angie rinsed Baby Erin under the running water in the sink, and dried the newborn thoroughly.

One distinctive sign left to check.

Before dressing Erin in a diaper and infant shirt, Angie opened the infant's hands, and looked for one large crease across the palm of her hand instead of two separate ones. She noted this as a *Simian Crease*.

One crease across the palm is another of the many signs which Professor John Down from England identified in his research study when he listed the characteristics of infants born with this type of syndrome.

Angie had worked with a number of babies with this condition. The many physical characteristics together alerted the trained eye of a medical practitioner to identify *Down's syndrome* in infancy. She knew that one in eight hundred infants was born with *Down's syndrome*. Many bore some physical characteristic of the Mongols of Asia. For this reason, the children were inappropriately labeled *Mongoloids*, meaning *resembling Mongols.* These infants were often born to older mothers. As children, they frequently showed lower than average scores upon intelligence testing. As a result, they were classified in an *idiot* category.

This classification meant only one outcome for Baby Erin Ryan. She would not be allowed into the United States of America. The newborn baby would now be subject to Ellis Island screening criteria. Mother and baby would be deported to Ireland. It was believed that a Down's infant would grow to be a dependent public charge. Due to the unique Ellis Island interpretation of the immigration law, a baby born at Ellis Island Hospital was not automatically granted citizenship. The Board of Special Inquiry would determine that Erin, although born on American soil, was not a citizen because her mother had not passed the immigration clearance requirements. She had not received her Landing Card prior to the birth of her baby. Upon disembarking her ship, Katie Ryan had gone directly to Ellis Island Hospital because of swelling and edema. If she had been discharged from the hospital prior to the birth of her child, even the day before, this would not be an issue.

If Angie clearly noticed the physical characteristics of this condition, others would too.

She looked up.

Through the nursery window, she saw Dr. Goodwin enter the ward. Angie thought… *especially Doctor Goodwin!*

Angie gently placed Baby Erin in her wicker crib, and went out to meet the doctor.

"Got word of the Ryan delivery, and only have a minute to do an admission exam on the newborn," Dr. Goodwin said.

"Oh, Doctor, I brought the baby upstairs to be with her mother. They're both in Recovery now."

"Listen, Miss Angie, I have a flood of exams to do this morning. I'm running late. How's the baby? Boy or girl?

Angie reported, "A little girl…six pounds one ounce…good color, good cry, vital signs within normal limits, no murmur…"

"What if I come back this afternoon, Miss Angie, would that be all right with you?"

"Fine with me, Dr. Goodwin," Angie said. The doctor turned, and rushed out of the room.

What was that all about, Angelina Bosco? What in the world are you thinking, lying to Dr. Goodwin? As if you could hide the baby from him. I suppose you wanted a moment to pretend everything was still perfect for the Ryan family, but, Angelina, to lie to him like that!

At noon, Miss Gertrude and her surgical aide wheeled Katie Ryan down to Angie's unit on the second floor. Angie brought the baby out to the mother. She positioned the baby's crib next to the mother's bed. Erin's physical characteristics were hardly noticeable to the lay person, but Angie was certain that an experienced mother, like Katie Ryan, would notice and question her.

However, when Angie helped Katie Ryan breastfeed her baby, Katie Ryan simply commented that Erin was the loveliest baby girl on the face of the earth. Katie Ryan told Angie that she couldn't wait to see how excited her sons were going to be when they saw their new baby sister.

"When do you think I can leave to go home?" Katie Ryan asked Angie.

"The usual time is two weeks, Mrs. Ryan."

"Two weeks, I don't believe I can sit still for another two weeks. I have been here more than two months already. I must go home. Please, Miss Angie, would you talk to the doctors to see if they would allow me to leave this week?"

"You need to rest and restore yourself here at the hospital."

"I feel as though I could get up right now, Miss Angie. If they would allow me, I would like to go home tomorrow."

"No, Mrs. Ryan, you must rest. However, I will talk to the doctor about discharging you a little earlier than usual."

Angie was on edge all afternoon and into the early evening. When Dr. Goodwin returned at 18:00, Katie Ryan was breastfeeding Erin. Dr. Goodwin appeared impatient, but knew not to interrupt the feeding. He told Angie that he had been called to the Contagious Disease Hospital and could not wait, but would return to examine the baby later in the evening.

When her shift ended at 19:00 hours, Dr. Goodwin had not appeared. Angie was upset and felt she could not leave the ward. She stalled, and postponed leaving the unit for two hours. She proofed her charting and nursing notes. She checked expiration dates on the sterile packs stored on the unit. She helped Miss Darla straighten up the ward after the dinner trays were served and collected. When she left, Dr. Goodwin still had not returned.

That night, Angie couldn't sleep. She tossed and turned in her bed, worrying about the future of the Ryan family. She prayed through the night. By morning, she had recited three rosaries. She begged the Blessed Mother for a mother's protection for Baby Erin. She asked for protection, happiness, and a fruitful future for the Ryan Family. The more she prayed, the more she knew she was desperately praying for a miracle...an impossible miracle.

Chapter Twenty-Two

∾

January 14, 1924
7 AM (07:00)

Often he will wonder. How can this really be?
She could look at him and into his heart she'll see.

When Angie walked into the Women and Children's Ward the following morning, she expected to see Dr. Goodwin gowned and in the process of examining Baby Ryan, but much to her disbelief, the room was unusually quiet. She walked to the chart rack to review the *Physician's Notes* and the *Doctor's Order Sheet* for Baby Girl Ryan. She found no notations on the newborn admission exam sheet. Angie quickly skimmed through the patient charts on the chart-rack to find that none of the patient progress notes had been updated, as well. It appeared that Dr. Goodwin had not returned to the ward the evening before. Angie sat at her desk, deep in thought, wondering what could have prevented him from his evening rounds. She didn't notice the small yellow envelope that had been placed squarely in the middle of her green desk blotter until Fannie called it to her attention.

"Look, Miss Angie! It's a telegram for Fabiana!" Fannie cried.

Angie picked up the envelope. It was addressed to Miss Fabiana Morales.

Both Miss Angie and Fannie rushed to Fabiana's bed. She was just waking. Fannie could not contain her excitement. "Wake up, Fabiana. Wake up. Look what has just arrived!"

"I found it on my desk this morning. It's for you, Fabiana."

Fabiana looked at them in bewilderment. "What is it?" she asked, opening up her eyes.

"Why, it's a telegram. It's addressed to you, Fabiana. Open it," Fannie ordered.

Fabiana carefully opened the yellow envelope. She looked down at it, and stared at the type-written words. Finally, she said, "I cannot read this. It is written in English." Fabiana handed the paper to Angie. Angie slowly read the telegram out loud, first in English, then in Sicilian.

```
MPA 191 R295CC IF FT
SCRANTON PA 842P JAN 12 1924


COMMISSIONER OF IMMIGRATION STOP
ELLIS ISLAND STOP
PORT OF NEW YORK STOP
NEW YORK NEW YORK STOP


CONFIRMING ATTENDANCE AT IMMIGRATION HEARING STOP
SCHEDULED JANUARY 14 1924 AT 09:00 STOP
TO SPONSOR NIECE FABIANA MORALES STOP
SIGNED MR ROBERTO MORALES
COPY SENT TO FABIANA MORALES ELLIS ISLAND HOSPITAL
STOP
```

"Why, that's this morning! Fabiana, your uncle is coming today, January 14th. That is today!" Fannie screamed, jumping up and down.

"Is it true, Miss Angie, or am I dreaming?" Fabiana asked.

"Well, Fabiana, you are not dreaming. The telegram says he is arriving today for your hearing. I'll go and check today's schedule. Do you know what this means, Fabiana? If your case is on the docket, your wait is over."

Fannie added, "You will soon be issued a Landing Card, and you will be on your way to Pennsylvania. I am so happy for you."

"What do I do?" Fabiana asked. "I must get dressed to meet him."

At that moment, Dr. Goodwin entered the ward. He walked toward them. "Good Morning, Ladies. Tell me. What's all the excitement about?"

"Dr. Goodwin, you will not believe it. It is just what we were hoping for. Fabiana's uncle is coming to Ellis Island today to sponsor her," Fannie cried.

"The hearing may actually be scheduled for this morning," Angie said.

"It's nothing short of a miracle, Ladies, and in the nick of time." Turning to Fabiana, Dr. Goodwin said, "Your thyroid levels have been normal for over a week. I don't believe we could have stalled a deportation hearing another month. How much time do we have, Miss Angie?"

"There is some confusion. I will inquire if her uncle is coming at nine, or if his Board Meeting is scheduled for nine. I was on my way to check the hearing schedule now." Angie handed Dr. Goodwin the telegram.

"If indeed, the hearing is this morning at nine, we have no time to waste. Miss Angie, please bring me the chart. I must begin a discharge exam, and collect the final blood test results at the laboratory for documentation. The discharge exam and the lab results will have to be processed for a formal hospital release. Then, the papers must all be reviewed by the Board. Let's get started!"

"Immediately, Doctor…"

Doctor Goodwin began Fabiana's discharge exam while Angie contacted Miss Gowan, the Secretary of the Board of Special Inquiry. She confirmed that the Morales Hearing was scheduled for that very morning. Angie told Miss Gowan that Dr. Goodwin would hand-carry the necessary discharge documentation to her office within the hour. "Will there be enough time to process the paperwork?" Angie asked Miss Gowan.

Miss Gowan assured her. "If Doctor Goodwin can bring everything to me by eight, I will have the file ready in time for the committee's review."

Dr. Goodwin finished his progress notes, and was headed to the laboratory by 07:30. "Now you can start to pack your things, Fabiana. I believe I have everything I need for your discharge. I'm going to submit your papers for processing, and will personally present them to the Board."

"The hearing is scheduled in Hearing Room C at nine o'clock," Angie announced.

"I'll meet you there, Fabiana!" Dr. Goodwin called out, as he rushed to the door of the Women's and Children's Ward with Fabiana's chart in hand. He disappeared from sight. Then, he reappeared, popping his head through the open door. "Oh, Miss Angie," he shouted from the doorway. "Wasn't there something important I had to do on the ward this morning?"

"Yes, Dr. Goodwin, but nothing that can't wait. See you later."

There, you've done it again, Angelina!

Angie was filled with guilt about yet another lie which, once again, postponed the inevitable examination of Baby Ryan. She forced herself to turn her attention to Fabiana. "Fabiana, off you go to wash-up and shower. After breakfast, I'll help you pack."

"Will you be at the hearing, Miss Angie?"

Angie was about to say 'yes' when she remembered Baby Girl Ryan. Ordinarily, nothing would have stopped her from supporting Fabiana, meeting her uncle, and giving her a warm send-off. Miss Elsie was always available to be called upon to cover the unit in her absence. However, today, Angie dared not risk leaving Baby Ryan with Miss Elsie, for she was a seasoned nurse who possessed keen assessment and observation skills. "I will walk you to the Registry Room, Fabiana, to meet your uncle, but I can't stay for the hearing. I know you will be in Doctor Goodwin's good hands."

Fabiana looked heartbroken. "But, Miss Angie, will we meet again? Can I visit you here at the hospital?"

"Yes, my dear, of course, you must write to me here, also. I will put your uncle's address in my notebook right now. Do you have any concerns about leaving so suddenly?"

"Oh, no, Miss Angie, my aunt and uncle visited South America when I was a little girl. They brought clothes and presents for me from America. I have many happy memories of their visit to the ranchero. I am sad to leave you."

"I will miss you, too, Fabiana!" Angie said, giving her a big hug.

"Fabiana, hurry, it's time to shower. It looks like today may be your special day." Fannie said.

Fabiana was packed and ready when Mickey knocked on the window of the ward door. He walked up to the nurse's desk in the middle of the ward. "Morning, Miss Angie. I am here to escort Miss Fabiana Morales to Hearing Room C," Mickey announced.

Angie accompanied Mickey and Fabiana to the Registry Building where she met both Fabiana's aunt and uncle. She hugged and kissed Fabiana good-bye, and showered her with good wishes. When Dr. Goodwin arrived, papers in hand and looking confident, she left Fabiana to return to the Women and Children's Ward. "Promise to tell me every detail of the hearing, Doctor." Angie said.

"Will do," he answered with a big smile and a thumbs-up. "See you at lunchtime."

Angie was jumpy and nervous throughout the morning for fear that Dr. Goodwin would appear, but she was saddled with work and the time passed quickly. Miss Gertrude brought down a post-op appendectomy who required close watch and vital signs every hour. After that, a woman was admitted with an unidentified rash. Angie recognized the rash to be impetigo, and felt an error had been made. She immediately arranged for the woman to be transferred to the Contagious Disease Hospital. An elderly lady was admitted for treatment of an infection on her index finger. Her nursing care kept Angie busy, boiling water for finger soaks.

Dr. Goodwin did not return at lunchtime as planned. After lunch, Angie was fraught with worry because the doctor still had not appeared.

Where is Doctor Goodwin? Why isn't he here? Did something go wrong? Perhaps, Fabiana's hearing did not go well. How will I ever explain my lies when he examines the Ryan baby?

Angie busied herself by taking afternoon vital signs on her patients. Angie took Baby Ryan's axillary temperature by holding a glass thermometer under her tiny armpit. She was charting the results when Dr. Goodwin startled her. She jumped.

Dr. Goodwin appeared energized and excited as he washed his hands at the sink, "Miss Angie, what a day this has been! Starting with Fabiana's case which, by the way, went like clockwork. Her hearing took less than ten minutes. Fabiana was off the island and on the ferry with her aunt and uncle by ten. Then, I was called to assist with exams. Suddenly, I remembered that I never completed the admission exam on the Ryan Baby. I rushed right over."

Angie slowly undressed Baby Ryan in preparation for the doctor's examination. She covered the infant with a small flannel blanket to keep her warm. Lifting the blanket, the doctor took a long look at the Ryan Baby as she squirmed in her crib.

"Muscle tone is slightly flaccid. Did you notice, Miss Angie?"

"Yes, Doctor.....slightly."

The doctor cradled the baby's head in his hands. "The shape of her eyes...ever so mild..." He turned the baby's head to examine her small ears. "Let me see. One would have to rule out..." He opened one of her little fists, and then the other, searching for the characteristic Simian Crease. "Ah, Miss Angie, this may mean."

"Yes, Doctor," Angie said, her eyes pleading.

Dr. Goodwin stared back at Angie. They stood frozen for what seemed like a very long time. Both were unable to utter a word for they knew the symptoms that the baby presented, and realized the consequences. Dr. Goodwin broke the silence. "Miss Angie, what am I to do? The baby has many of the signs that Professor Down outlined in his work."

"Doctor," Angie pleaded. "They will label her an *idiot*. They won't admit her. They won't allow her into the United States."

"I know, Miss Angie, I know."

"Are you absolutely sure? Is there a test you can order to be positive?" Angie asked.

"We are never positive. There are no tests to determine a diagnosis like this, perhaps someday, but not now."

"What if we were wrong?"

"That is always a possibility, but as a physician, I have an obligation to report what I see. These physical findings must be noted and documented to allow other practitioners to be on the alert to follow her appropriately."

"Doctor, the findings are subjective…in the eyes of the examiner."

"What are you asking, Miss Angie, to *not* document my findings?"

"No, Doctor Goodwin."

"I did hear of a case of a false diagnosis in which physical characteristics, such as these, were actually due to a familial resemblance."

"Doctor, there was a little boy in my village. He was blessed with a pure and joyful heart. His family treasured him. He brought happiness to everyone. He was the most innocent and sweetest of children."

"…but he was dependent on others to care for him. We aren't the only ones caring for the Ryan baby. Others will be assessing her and noting their observations. Unless…"

"Unless…?" Angie said.

"Unless…" said Dr. Goodwin, "…you distracted them! Is this what you have been doing, Miss Angie?"

"This case is breaking my heart. The family will be separated, and they are so deserving of the opportunities that America offers."

"It is not our call. The rules state…" Dr. Goodwin stopped. He walked to the window, and took a deep breath. He stood, deep in thought, for several minutes. Suddenly, he said. "We could discharge the baby to her mother's care tomorrow...even tonight!"

"That's impossible, Doctor. You can't send a postpartum patient home two days after delivery. It's not proper!"

"It's not proper but possible, Miss Angie. Mrs. Ryan requested to be discharged. She has always delivered at home with little or no postpartum care. Is she aware of the baby's condition?"

"No, but she is an experienced mother with a mother's instinct."

"I must talk to her in private. Miss Angie, please escort her in. I will complete the infant examination in her presence."

"Yes, Doctor, I will bring her to you."

Angie ushered Mrs. Ryan into the small nursery, and left the doctor and mother to talk in private. She couldn't bear to stay. She half-heartedly went about completing afternoon vital signs, frequently looking up toward the nursery window. Dr. Goodwin and Mrs. Ryan were deep in conversation for over twenty minutes. Finally, Dr. Goodwin waved to Angie to enter.

"Miss Angie, Mrs. Ryan is expecting a visit from her husband tonight. Mr. Ryan sent word that he is taking the five pm ferry to see his new baby. Mrs. Ryan has requested to leave the hospital this evening with him. This is not a prison. I see no medical reason why this mother and baby could not be discharged. I am writing the orders. I'll be taking the paperwork to medical records this afternoon to be processed."

"Yes, Doctor. I will start preparations. Thank you, Doctor."

"Thank you, Doctor," echoed Mrs. Ryan. "Thank you with all my heart."

"Miss Angie, I must talk to Mr. Ryan when he arrives. Will you notify me?"

"Yes, Doctor."

When Mike Ryan arrived at 5:30 pm, Angie called for Dr. Goodwin. The doctor immediately returned to the nursery to talk privately to both parents while Angie prepared Baby Ryan for her trip home. The baby cried loudly as Angie dressed her. Katie Ryan came out into the ward to assist Angie.

"Perhaps, you could breastfeed before you leave tonight, Mrs. Ryan," Angie suggested.

"That's a good idea, Miss Angie, because I don't know how long it will take us to get home."

Angie left the ward briefly to go downstairs to the hospital discharge room while Katie Ryan fed her baby. There, Angie received two copies of the baby's birth certificate; one for the parents and one for the chart. When she returned, she helped Katie Ryan bundle up the sleeping baby for the ride home on the chilly winter night.

At the Registry, the hospital discharge orders were processed and exchanged for two Landing Cards, allowing the mother and her infant admission into the United States.

Captain Taylor stood at the doorway, calling out directions to the last remaining immigrants in the Registry Room. "Next ferry's leaving in five minutes. Down the steps and to the right, this path will lead you to the quay."

As the Ryan family was about to leave, Captain Taylor shouted, "STOP!"

Angie froze.

"Do I get to sneak a peek at the beautiful baby?" Captain Taylor asked.

Angie showed him the sleeping baby bundle. "Ah," he said, "such a beautiful little one, the best of luck to the lot of you."

Dr. Goodwin and Miss Angie walked down to the quay with the Ryans. They watched and waited as the family boarded the boat. A moment before the ferry ramp was lifted up, Angie called out, "Wait! I forgot to give you Erin's birth certificate. Here it is." She ran onto the ferryboat, and handed Katie Ryan one of the two birth certificates she had in her hand.

"Good Luck, Ryan Family!" Angie shouted, waving good-bye from the dock as the ferry pulled away.

Dr. Goodwin turned to Angie, and said, "Well, Miss Angie, I suppose first thing tomorrow morning, I will be scheduling an eye exam with Doc Gibbons, for I am sure there will be talk that Doctor Goodwin is in need of spectacles."

"Yes, I believe so, Doctor."

"Seriously, Miss Angie, if this ever gets out, I think I will be labeled a most incompetent doctor."

"...Or a very wise one. What do you think will happen when they take the baby to the free public clinic for her examinations?"

"I instructed the Ryans to take the little one for her well-baby checks to a pediatric colleague of mine. He has a private practice on Tenth Avenue where they live. I will contact him in the morning to arrange payment."

"Someday, Doctor, you may be sorry I influenced you."

"Being influenced by an *angel-of-mercy* is nothing to be sorry about. No, I believe Baby Ryan is entitled to life, liberty and the pursuit of happiness, as is any citizen born in the United States."

"...but Baby Girl Ryan is not automatically a citizen. Her mother wasn't officially admitted to the United States prior to her delivery."

"Well, that's the Ellis Island interpretation of the law, but I believe the Supreme Court would rule in favor of the actual documentation on the child's birth certificate. Look, Miss Angie, you have a copy right there. Read it. Read Erin's place of birth."

In her hand, Angie still held the copy of the birth certificate that would later be attached to the baby's discharge chart. She looked down at the lower right-hand corner and read:

Place of Birth: *Ellis Island General Hospital*
Address: *Port of New York*
City: *New York*
State: *New York*
Country: *United States*
Recorded By: *New York City Department of Birth Records*

Chapter Twenty-Three

◦

February 21, 1924
6:20 AM (06:20)

Hopes and dreams evaporate and slowly disappear.
Gently, they disintegrate and vanish into air.

Although Angie was late for breakfast, she could not resist taking a moment to peek out of her dormer window. A thick layer of snow had fallen during the night. Both Ellis Island and Bedloe Island were blanketed in white. The snow was already piled high atop Miss Liberty's crown, and covered the ground beneath her.

"Good Morning, My Lady, I hope it's not too cold out there for you today."

Rushing from her room, Angie remembered she had forgotten her toothbrush in the bathroom. She made a quick detour to retrieve it. When she entered the bathroom, Angie found Adeline at the sink, coughing deeply.

"What's the matter, Adeline? Are you okay? You're coughing so hard." Angie looked into the sink. She noticed Adeline's mucus was tinged with blood. "Adeline, how long have you been coughing like this?"

"Only a few days, I was hoping I would get better, but I'm getting worse. I don't know what to do, Angie. I have to go to work."

"No work for you today, Miss Adeline, you are staying in bed."

"No, more patients were admitted yesterday. We are short of staff. I can't be a burden," Adeline moaned.

"A burden? That you can never be, my dear Adeline, off you go now." Angie put her arms around her friend. She assisted her back to her room and into bed. "You are burning up with fever. You cannot go to the hospital today. Here, let me tuck you in. Then, I'll bring you some breakfast."

"I feel so sick. I don't think I can eat a morsel of food, Angie."

"Well, then, you must drink lots of fluids, including hot tea. I will bring you some. Ad, do you have a sore throat?"

"No."

"Are you having any trouble breathing?"

"Only when I lie down, I've been sleeping sitting up," Adeline said.

"Stay right here in bed and don't move. I'll go over to the hospital, and report you *ill* to Sister Gwendolyn. I'll be right back with hot tea and lemon," Angie promised, and rushed out of the Cottage.

Angie went straight to Sister Gwendolyn's office. She was relieved to find the Nursing Superintendent sitting at her desk. Sister Gwendolyn greeted Angie warmly.

"Good Morning, Miss Angie. How are you today? Did you see the snow? It's beautiful, isn't it?"

"Yes, Sister, I did."

"What brings you to me bright and early this morning?" Sister Gwendolyn asked.

"Sister, Miss Adeline is very ill. She says she has not been feeling well for days, and is getting worse, not better. I found her coughing in the nurses' lavatory, and put her right back to bed. She has a fever." Angie reported.

"Did you take her temperature?" Sister Gwendolyn asked.

"No, there wasn't time. She felt hot to the touch, and her pulse was racing. She was having some difficulty breathing. I tucked her in and ran right over. Sister, I am worried. What should we do?"

"Don't you worry," Sister said, standing up. "I am going to check on her this very minute. You may go. Report to your unit. It's getting late. I must call for the house officer and have him order a Chest X-ray for Miss Adeline. I will take care of everything, my dear."

"I told her I would bring her tea," Angie added.

"I am going to the Cottage now to see what she needs. I will report back to you, Miss Angie, or send word to you this morning after I arrange for a doctor to examine her."

"Promise, Sister?"

"I promise, of course, my dear. I'm leaving now. Miss Angie, pick up something to eat before you report to work this morning."

"How did you know that I didn't eat?" Angie asked Sister Gwendolyn.

"Because so many of you young *ladies-in-white* are skipping meals; don't think I don't know. Grab an egg sandwich, at the very least." Sister Gwendolyn rushed into the hall with Angie still sitting in her office chair.

Angie left the office, and stopped at the General Hospital's Dining Room to eat a hard-boiled egg before heading off to the unit for morning report. As she was leaving, she noticed the clock in the dining room read 07:04.

"I'm late!" Angie said, and started to run.

Angie arrived at the Women and Children's Ward at 07:07, seven minutes late.

Fannie looked frantic. "Miss Angie, what happened?" She asked, excitedly. "You've never been late before?"

"I know, Miss Adeline was sick and I stopped..." Angie was interrupted before she could finish her sentence.

"No time to talk, Miss Angie. Miss Gertrude needs you upstairs immediately. She delivered a baby who isn't doing well." Fannie added, "The doctors haven't come in yet."

Before Fannie could say another word, Angie turned and ran. She called back to Fannie, "Fannie, find Miss Elsie. Tell her I am upstairs in Delivery. Ask her to cover for me. Please tell her Miss Adeline is ill this morning. Sister Gwendolyn left the hospital, and went to the Cottage to check on her."

"Yes, Miss Angie, I'll go right now."

Angie didn't wait for the elevator, but ran up the stairs to the third-floor delivery room. She found Imogene and Gertrude with the mother and newborn.

"The mother said she wasn't due for six weeks, but when I delivered the baby I was relieved to see that she was a nice big baby. She weighed almost eight pounds. I noticed some respiratory distress with sub-sternum and inter-costal retractions. I suctioned her, but it didn't seem to help. Her respirations were increasing. She seemed to be struggling more." Gertrude reported. "That's when we called for you."

"I've seen this before, although she's the size of a full-term baby, she's acting like a baby born a month early," Angie explained. "She may actually be six weeks premature like the mother reported."

"Why would that happen?" Miss Gertrude asked.

"They don't know exactly why the baby grows so quickly in-utero, but somehow it does. It may have something to do with the baby's metabolism or the mother's. I only know that we have to treat the baby as if she is premature. She needs oxygen and nourishment immediately."

"Mom's fallen off to sleep, but her vitals are stable. Do you want me to wake her to breastfeed, Angie?"

"No, I'll take the baby down to the nursery, and give her sugar-water. They used to think that feeding these babies early on was just an old wives' tale, but there may be some scientific merit to it. I've seen it work a number of times. It seems that these babies get accustomed to absorbing extra nutrients from their mother in-utero. They need to maintain that same level of nourishment. Sometimes, if they aren't fed, they begin to get sluggish, and may even forget to breathe," Angie explained.

"Oh my, Angie, that's amazing. What should I tell the Mother when she wakes up?" Gertrude asked.

"Tell her that her baby girl is a bit premature, and that we are observing her in the nursery." Angie instructed. "If the baby improves with oxygen and feeding, I'll bring her up. If not, in a few hours, I'll meet you on the unit when you bring the mother downstairs."

"Aye, aye, sir, right away," Imogene mocked. She stood in front of Angie to block her way.

"I apologize if I offended you, Miss Imogene. I didn't mean to sound as if I was giving orders."

"Well, it sounded like that to me."

Unmoving, the two nurses glared at each other without saying a word.

Gertrude broke the silence. "Imogene, don't forget the baby's ID bracelet."

The baby's identification bracelet, matching her mother's, had not yet been prepared and attached to the infant. As if nothing had happened, Miss Imogene opened a small case of tiny beads. Using tweezers, she quickly selected a number of white beads with the letters of the mother's last name. She strung them on a thin wire-like thread. After she finished off the bracelet with pink beads, she secured it to the baby's ankle. Angie scooped up the newborn and the chart. She left without saying a word, and returned to the second-floor nursery.

When Angie left, Gertrude said, "Imogene, don't pretend as though nothing happened! Why are you always giving the young nurses a hard time?"

"Because they are *know-it-alls,* and think that we are too ancient to still remember anything, especially that confident one, *Miss Perfect.*" Imogene answered.

"The nurses who are right out of school know what's current." Gertrude said.

Imogene interrupted. "…And we don't?"

"Is that what's bothering you, Imogene? There's still so much we can teach them. We have the experience that they yearn for and didn't get in nursing school."

"I suppose you're right," Imogene said.

"I am right. Try to be good, Imogene."

"I'll try, but it's not easy, Gertie!"

Down on the second floor, Angie placed the newborn in a crib while she turned on the oxygen, and removed the glass enclosure from her warming table. She transferred the baby to the table. She suctioned the newborn's mouth and nose, and placed the oxygen mask three inches away from her face. Then she carefully replaced the glass enclosure of her make-shift incubator, pulling the oxygen tubing through the openings in the glass. Angie grabbed the bricks and warm blankets that were neatly stacked on top of the radiator. She rolled them together tightly, and placed them along the inside edge of the glass enclosure, taking care that the blankets were far enough from the baby so that they would not touch her. Later, she would tuck in a hot water bottle to maintain the warm temperature of the incubator.

Angie took the baby's vital signs, including her temperature, and carefully observed her breathing pattern. She charted that the baby appeared to be in mild respiratory distress because when the baby inhaled, the skin between her ribs, as well as the small space beneath her sternum, retracted slightly. Angie needed boiled water to make sugar-water and to fill a hot water bottle. She took a Bunsen burner and an eight-ounce glass beaker, and put them on a metal tray. She called for Fannie.

Fannie came quickly, "What can I do for you, Miss Angie?"

"Fannie, I need boiled water to make sugar-water fast. I can't light the burner in this room because I have oxygen flowing on the baby. Take these to the utility room next door. I am certain no one is using oxygen on that ward. Fill the beaker with water. Light the burner exactly as I taught you. Carefully let the water boil before you bring it back to me. Watch the water as it starts to boil. Lower the flame slowly. Remember, the water heats up very quickly. Use a towel. Don't get burned. "

Fannie took the Bunsen paraphernalia from Angie, and said, "Yes, Miss Angie, that's no problem. I will be back in a flash with the water, nice and hot for you."

"Oh, Fannie, if you will, submit an *FRF* to request a big teapot of hot water so that we will have that in an hour's time."

"Will do, Miss Angie, anything else? Shall I call someone to help you?"

"Is Miss Elsie on the ward?"

"Oh, yes, Miss Angie, she is caring for your patients."

"Ask her to stop by when she has a free moment. Please send word to Dr. Goodwin that the baby has mild respiratory distress."

"Yes, Miss Angie."

When Fannie left the nursery, Angie measured one tablespoon of sugar into each of the two baby bottles that she had set out on the counter. While she waited for Fannie to return with the hot water, she sat close to the warming table, and charted her nurse's notes. She noticed that the baby's nose flared when the baby took a breath. She continued to watch and monitor the baby closely. Then, she observed that the baby lay still for many seconds with no chest movement. Angie put her hand through one of the little incubator openings and lifted the baby's leg. She shook it softly to wake her as a reminder to take a breath. "Wake up, Baby Girl," Angie said. The baby responded immediately to the slight stimulation of her nurse's touch. She resumed her irregular breathing pattern.

Fannie walked in, carrying the beaker of boiled water covered with a towel, just as she had been instructed. "Here you go, Miss Angie."

"That was fast, Fannie. Good job."

Angie took the beaker from Fannie, and measured two ounces of sterile water into each bottle. She put the caps on the bottles, and shook them to dissolve the sugar. Then, she took the caps off to cool down the water in the bottles. While she waited for the sugar-water to cool, Angie took another set of vital signs, and continued her charting.

She wrote: *08:00: Inter-costal and sub-sternum retractions with flared nares noted. Acrocyanosis noted yet centrally pink and somewhat active with good muscle tone.*

Fannie waited. She watched everything that Angie was doing. "She doesn't look premature to me. She looks like a nice size baby."

"Yes, that may be the problem. She grew quickly. She was in her mother's womb for only seven and a half months. She is over eight pounds. That is large for her gestational age of thirty-four weeks or six weeks early. It is a sign that alerts us to question why she grew so fast. It signals us that something was not completely right inside the mother's womb."

"That is so interesting, Miss Angie. I don't know how you know so much stuff like that. I wish I were more like you."

"It's just schooling, Fannie."

"Well, then, I am going to go to nursing school someday, too."

"I hope so, Fannie. I will help you. Did you reach Dr. Goodwin?"

"I sent a messenger to find him," Fannie answered.

When Angie was satisfied that the sugar-water had cooled down, she offered the bottle to the baby who grasped the nipple eagerly and sucked strongly. Angie pointed this out to Fannie.

"Look, Fannie, she is sucking and swallowing very well. That is a very reassuring sign." Angie knew that premature infants often had weak suck-swallow reflexes, but this baby eagerly took one ounce of the sugar-water. Angie stopped to burp the baby. While the baby remained in the incubator, she sat her up, and supported her head between her right thumb and forefinger. She gently tapped on her back with her left hand. When she heard two little burps, Angie offered her the remaining ounce of water. She was relieved to see that the baby continued to suck with gusto. Angie talked to the newborn as she worked. "Time to rest now, Baby Girl, and see if that agrees with you. If it does, you can have a little more in an hour."

She continued to watch the baby very closely, and took vital signs every fifteen minutes. The baby's temperature had fallen to 97.2 degrees which meant the incubator was cooling down. Angie was in the process of exchanging the cool blankets for warmer ones when Fannie came with the teapot of hot water.

Fannie reported that Miss Elsie was covering the wards, and would come as soon as she had a moment to spare. "She cannot leave. She is very busy. She sent in a request for more aides to help us. She asked if anything was urgent, Miss Angie."

"No, but you brought the hot water just in time, thank you, Fannie. I need to raise the temperature around the baby."

Angie filled the hot water bottle, wrapped it in a thin flannel blanket, and placed it at the foot of the handmade incubator. Then, she made four more bottles of sugar-water. She was giving the infant her second feeding when Dr. Goodwin came by. He went directly to the sink to wash his hands before he touched the infant. Angie stepped aside for him to examine the baby. He talked out loud as he concurred with Angie's assessment.

"Definitely premature...but large for gestational age...you have everything set up nicely. She seems to be breathing easier. Let's see how she does when we begin to wean her off oxygen."

"The sugar-water seems to make a difference, Doctor. I wish I knew why."

"There has been some research on this subject recently. It may have to do with how the mother metabolizes glucose. It is a very delicate process but the general idea is that there is extra glucose circulating in the mother's blood, and the baby receives it, making her grow bigger. When she is born, the higher glucose level should be maintained for her continued stability."

"How long will she need the sugar-water, Doctor? Her mother will want to breastfeed when she comes down from the Recovery Room. Should I encourage it?"

"It's been my experience that she will only need the sugar supplements today. If all goes well, she will be out of harm's way by this evening, especially in your care. By all means, let the mother breastfeed if the baby can latch on, but continue the glucose feedings into the evening. She seems to have a strong suck reflex, doesn't she?" Dr. Goodwin said.

"Yes, she took four ounces easily."

"Excellent. That's a good sign. It looks as though the baby may soon stabilize. Will you be all right alone with her this morning, Miss Angie, or would you like me to stay on the unit?"

"I can handle it, Doctor. If her condition changes in any way, I will send for you immediately."

The baby girl progressively improved throughout the morning. At noon, she showed no signs of cyanosis and no flaring of her nostrils. When her mother came down from recovery, Angie took the baby out of the incubator and placed her on her mother's chest, skin-to-skin. Angie told the mother that the baby needed to stay warm, and holding her close to her body would help increase her temperature. Angie helped the mother to breastfeed. The baby latched on to her mother's breast and began to suck. Angie explained that she would continue to give the baby girl sugar-water supplements between feedings. The mother nodded in agreement.

Later, when Angie was changing the baby's diaper, Sister Gwendolyn came into the nursery. She quietly waited until Miss Angie dressed the baby, and repositioned her in the incubator. "Your incubator system and frequent feedings has made a big difference in the quick recovery of this baby, Miss Angie."

"Yes, thank you, Sister."

"I want to ask you to remember to write down your nursing care. Your treatment discoveries should be included in Miss Elsie's procedure manual. It's very important for us to document what we learn for other nurses to use in the future."

"Thank you, Sister, I am honored to."

"Miss Angie…"

"Yes, Sister?"

"I do not have good news for you."

"Yes, Sister?"

"It is about Miss Adeline. She had a Chest X-ray this morning.

"Is she going to be all right, Sister?"

"No, Miss Angie, we found a suspicious spot on her X-ray. We believe she has tuberculosis. She was admitted to the *TB* unit an hour ago."

Chapter Twenty-Four

∾

February 21, 1924
10:30 PM (22:30)

Great deeds achieved but much is lost.
Achievements gained but at what cost?

Journal of Gwendolyn Hanover
Date: February 21, 1924
Entry Time: 22:30
Journal Notation:

Today, my worst fear has been realized. Miss Adeline Fermè (Miss Adeline) has fallen in the line of duty. I feel that I have failed her in every way. The health and safety of the women, living and working on this island, is my complete responsibility. Miss Adeline has been working at the Contagious Disease Hospital since 1919, and has extensive knowledge of our infection control procedures. I assigned her to work on the children's tuberculosis wards six months ago because we had experienced an increase in the number of children diagnosed with *TB*. Five percent of the children at the CD facility now have tuberculosis. I was confident that Miss Adeline had adequate years of training to safeguard herself and the children, but anyone can succumb to these airborne bacteria as the droplets stay alive and float in the air for hours. The children are highly susceptible because they are so active and playful. Miss Adeline has a tendency to want to soothe them, playing and holding the children in her arms. She believes in healing with laughter, song and games. I have often passed the wards and heard the children singing and laughing. I wonder if Miss Adeline was properly masked while she sang along with them.

I assigned Miss Adeline to a private isolation room with a veranda at the CD hospital this afternoon. She will need plenty of fresh air, rest and sunshine. I question if it is best for her to remain here at Ellis where we can monitor her nutrition, or shall I investigate the possibility of transferring her to an out-of-state sanitarium? It will take several months or even years at a sanatorium to effectively be cured. I have already contacted the Sea View Tuberculosis Hospital in Staten Island. Unfortunately, they are filled to capacity with a patient census of over a thousand patients. *TB* has now become the city's leading killer. We know why the disease was called *consumption* because it consumes its emaciated victims. I will write to the Hebron Sanitarium in Maine this week. I heard talk of a *TB* hospital opening in Middleton, Massachusetts, but when I investigated the rumor, I learned that the project is currently only in the planning stage. I pray that a vaccine for tuberculosis is discovered soon. They are vigorously working to find such a vaccine at the New York City Health Department Research Laboratory.

One of the most difficult tasks of the day was to inform Miss Angie of Miss Adeline's illness. She was completely devastated when I told her the news this afternoon. I felt a bit guilty because I have largely ignored Miss Angie's concerns over staffing, not to mention the campaign she has waged over a few missing codeine pills.

Miss Angie frequently questions me about the hiring freeze that was implemented in January. The 1921 Quota Law was renewed in 1922 and 1923, but it can no longer be extended. In light of this, the nurses are pressuring me to begin hiring additional nurses immediately. However, Miss Elsie and I feel that a new law may be passed with even stricter guidelines. Of course, the boys in this *old boys' club* will not so much as hint any news to the women folk running this hospital. I suppose Miss Elsie and I will have to wait until May before we learn of any changes.

Miss Angie has become a regular Harrison agent, and has developed a rather elaborate method of counting the number of narcotics on her assigned wards. She is able to execute her system efficiently. She asked me to support her efforts by implementing daily medication checks throughout the hospital. My feeling was that it was a waste of valuable nursing time until I reported this to Captain Higgins. He informed me that the hospital is now required to comply with the Harrison Act by tracking narcotics. Of course, someone could be stealing and selling drugs, which is against the law, but these days the authorities are really more concerned with stolen moonshine.

Ah, Gwendolyn, perhaps you solved Miss Angie's mystery. Is one of your nurses taking codeine as a substitute for her long-lost alcohol? Now, think, Gwendolyn. Which one of your ladies-in-white has a tendency toward the bottle, and has been missing her hooch during these dark days of prohibition?

❧

Chapter Twenty-Five

March 19, 1924
9PM (21:00)

Somewhere along the journey, the two of you will part,
But when you love each other, love lives within your heart.

"Angelina Bosco, I am going to keep repeating this until you listen to me. You do not need to be here every evening. You're wearing yourself out. You come here directly after working a twelve-hour shift, miss dinner every night, and watch over me until bedtime. Now, enough is enough, my dear friend," Adeline insisted. "You need to take time for yourself. I'm concerned about your health. You're working sixteen hours a day."

"I'm not the one who's sick, Adeline. You need me here."

"Why, Angie?"

"Because you do, that's why!" Angie said, resolutely.

"You know, I'm highly contagious. You could catch this germ at any moment, especially if you're fatigued. Then, where would we both be? You must be very careful."

"I know how to be careful. I'm gowned and masked, aren't I?" Angie said.

"I can understand coming for a short visit after supper every night, but you're devoting all of your free time to my recovery. When was the last time you requested a ferry pass to leave this island?" Adeline asked.

"I went into the city to meet my brothers." Angie answered.

"When was that exactly, Angie?"

"Umm, let's see...I went to meet them a few weeks ago. Well, perhaps you're right. It was the week before you got sick, but Ad, listen to me, you're getting stronger. Whatever we're doing is working. The bacteria are localized in one small spot in your lungs. Your last X-ray showed no further signs of disease progression. We're winning this battle. I can't lose you. I've had too many losses in my life."

"Now, Angie, don't be putting me in the grave. You must stop worrying. Sister is writing to everyone she knows, and is looking for a vacancy at sanitariums in Arizona, New Mexico, and even California. Wouldn't that be exciting?"

"Don't even think about leaving, Adeline. You're getting the best care right here, and you know it. You have plenty of fresh air, good food, and respiratory therapy, and, I might add, you will never find another nurse who gives you as much attention as I do."

"I know, for certain, that is true. Thank you, Angie. I know what you're doing for me, and I appreciate it. However, I want you to know that if I leave the island, I'm not leaving you. I will always be here for you. Angie, I promise."

"If only I can believe that. Adeline, I'm scared."

"Scared of what, Angie?"

"I'm terrified that you might die. Ever since I can remember, people who I love, leave me. My circle of loved ones grows smaller and smaller."

"Yes, I know that about you," Adeline said. "Perhaps, it's why you shy away from new relationships. It may also be the reason why you stay hidden away on this island."

"You're right, but how do I change?" Angie asked.

"You have to think positively and crash through your fear. Whenever you find that fear is preventing you from reaching something you want, you have to step through it."

"You're right. I know in my heart that you'll recover, but then the fear takes over."

"Be strong. Ignore it. Step through it."

"Like when we went on the roller coaster at Luna Park?"

"Exactly, Angie, if you let your fear take over, you will never get on the ride. You'll miss the good stuff, the fun and the laughter. Be positive. Before you go to sleep at night, imagine your circle of friends growing bigger and bigger, instead of smaller. You'll dream on that thought through the night."

"I like that image. Celestina came to America, and I have her in my life again. Perhaps, she will marry and have children someday. Then, there will be even more people to love and care for."

"Or, perhaps, *you* will marry and have children!"

"Oh, Adeline, do I dare imagine that, too?"

"Yes, Angie, you are allowed to include anything in your dreams. Hold it in your heart as a future intention. You deserve to be surrounded by family and friends who you love and who love you."

"Thank you for saying that. So even if you go out west, we'll always be together?"

"Right, Angie!"

"Okay, I'm going to work on being positive. You work on getting stronger. You're already showing great progress, and it's only been four weeks since your diagnosis. Your appetite has returned. You've stopped losing weight. We should be getting back the results of your test cultures early next week. If you show the same rate of improvement, I promise to relax. I won't hover over you as you say I do." Angie picked up a hairbrush, and began to brush Adeline's long brown hair.

"Promise, Angie?"

"I promise!"

"Okay, fill me in on what's going on at the hospital. Does Imogene still have it in for you?" Adeline asked.

"Oh, yes, but most of the time, I ignore her. She wants to make trouble. I figured out that if I react, it's just what she wants me to do, and I become the troublemaker. However, if she doesn't get a reaction from me, she gets to stew in her own juices."

"That's clever. How did you figure that out?"

"Remember, I was married once. I quickly learned to not reward bad behavior. When my husband was unreasonable, I ignored the behavior. Most of the time, it worked." Angie said, gently rubbing her arm.

"Angie Girl, sometimes you are so wise."

"…and sometimes so naïve," Angie added.

"Sometimes, so confident!" Adeline said, smiling.

"…and sometimes a scaredy-cat," Angie said, making a silly face at her.

"What else is happening around the island?"

"It's been very quiet this month. All the babies went home with their mommies. I've been covering on both the North and South Wings, you know, floating anywhere I'm needed. We've been very busy," Angie said.

"Have you discovered more missing codeine?" Adeline asked.

"No, it's strange. Nothing has been missing since Christmas. I've been keeping a watchful eye. I count the narcotics on my units daily."

"Angie, do you still suspect Miss Elsie?"

"I don't know. Could it be possible that Sister Gwendolyn tipped her off?"

"I don't believe that. Miss Elsie could easily ask any one of these doctors to write a medication order for her aches and pains. Let's think about this again. Angie, you studied the schedules and didn't find one nurse or one aide working the same three days. Have you ruled out a patient as a possible suspect?"

"No, I never considered a patient." Angie said.

"Now that I'm a patient, I can see how easy it would be for me to take anything I wanted late at night when the nurses are assigned so many patients. Were there patients in November and December who were discharged after Christmas?"

"Yes, of course, a number of them, but…."

"Well, that could solve your mystery. It may have been one of the patients on the ward."

"No, I can't believe that it was one of my patients. It would be completely out of character for someone like Mrs. Ryan or Miss Morales to steal narcotics."

"There were other patients besides Ryan and Morales."

"Yes, that's true, but…"

"Like you said, you can be very naïve, Angie Girl."

"I know, but I'm the one who suggested to Sister that we lock up all the narcotic drugs."

"What did she say?"

"Sister simply looked at me and said, 'Now, Miss Angie, Dear, you know I am waiting for the funds to purchase locked cabinets for the units'."

"It's the law, Angie."

"Sister doesn't feel it is urgent. You know how it is, Adeline. There's always the budget to consider. We are so short of staff and supplies these days. Sister says it's a temporary measure, but I feel something is brewing. I can feel it in the air."

"Like what?"

"I don't know, Adeline. Why does Sister continue to refuse to consider spending the full budget allotment? Why is there a freeze on hiring new nurses? Like I said, there's something going on that they're not telling us. Here, let me put a ribbon in your hair. What color do you want tonight?"

"Let me see. How about the purple one?"

"Perfect, you look great in this color."

"How is your baby sister doing?"

"She's not quite a baby anymore. She's twenty-four years old, and a beautiful young woman."

"Celestina is a beauty. I agree. We must stop calling her your baby sister."

"She's smart, too. She excels in school, but guess what?"

"What?"

"All she talks about is transferring to nursing school," Angie said.

"Oh dear, did you talk her out of that?"

"I've tried. I even signed her up to volunteer at the hospital two evenings a week. I was hoping that after she got a taste of hospital work, she would change her mind, but she hasn't. She started three weeks ago. I assigned her to lice detail. She loves it. She is determined to ask Giacomo for permission to transfer to nursing school in the fall."

"What do you think he will say to her?" Adeline asked.

"I can hear him now, 'Two spinster nurses in the family, isn't one enough, women?' "

"That's not true, Angie. Giacomo is very proud of you."

"I know, but he likes to tease me. Here, let me put some Vicks VapoRub on your chest."

"You aren't going to rub my feet with it again tonight, are you?"

"Yes, it's been proven to stop your night coughs. You know it works. The menthol in Vicks circulates throughout your body while these socks keep your feet warm."

"I think that's an old wives' tale but I must admit that it feels good. I love your foot rubs. Here, go to town, my feet are all yours if it makes you happy."

"It does!" Angie said.

"VapoRub on my feet, steam treatments, hot milk with lemon and honey...what else is on the treatment list for me tonight?"

Angie was finishing up her nighttime treatments, covering Adeline with two heavy wool blankets when the nurses heard a knock at the door.

"Come in." Angie called.

Dr. Goodwin's head peeked around the door before he entered the room. "Are you up for a short visit?" He asked.

"We sure are, Doc! Come in," Adeline said, smiling.

"I finished evening rounds, and I wanted to stop in to see how you are doing tonight. Good Evening, Miss Angie. I had a feeling I would find you here." Dr. Goodwin entered Adeline's isolation room, already gowned and masked.

Adeline laughed as she sat up in bed. "She's here every night!"

Out of habit, Angie instantly reached for the loose strings on the back of the doctor's surgical gown. "Here, let me help you, Doctor." She felt a wave of energy sweep through her as she approached him. Her heart began to pound. She had to concentrate to steady her shaking hands as she tied three neat bows on the back of his gown.

Why do I always feel so nervous and jittery around him?

"My, I can see you are looking stronger, Miss Adeline. I must say, that violet ribbon becomes you. Your private-duty nurse is taking good care of you tonight."

Angie blushed. Her body seemed to have a mind of its own, controlled by something other than her own brainpower. For Angie, these strange feelings were getting more and more uncomfortable, and her only thought was to run. Angie leaned over and kissed Adeline on the top of her head. Her voice cracked as she said, "Oh, look at the time. It is almost eleven. I must be saying, *Good-Night,* to both of you now. See you tomorrow, Adeline."

Dr. Goodwin spoke quickly. "Miss Angie, do wait a moment. I'll escort you to the Cottage. You shouldn't be walking alone so late at night."

Angie was already at the door with her hand on the doorknob. "Oh, no need for that, I'll take the inside passageway. There are still many people around. Do stay and visit with Adeline for a while. She loves having visitors." Angie opened the door, and disappeared.

Adeline smiled. "Well, she left in a hurry, didn't she?"

"As usual," Dr. Goodwin said.

"What do you mean?"

Dr. Goodwin looked deflated. "Miss Angie is always running away from me."

"No, she isn't, Doctor. She's bone-weary. She's been here all evening. She has to get some sleep." Adeline attempted to explain Angie's strange behavior. Then, decided it would be wiser to divert the conversation. She asked, "How are the kids in CD doing?"

"We lost another measles boy this week. He died of measles encephalitis."

"I heard. Many of the immigrant children succumb."

"They are so debilitated from travelling at sea."

"Outcomes are best when the children are admitted to the hospital early on."

The doctor agreed, "Yes, that's true. Ten years ago, the mortality rate was higher, one in eight. The immigrant kids in the city aren't fairing too well either. If they were stronger and better nourished, they might be able to fight back. These diseases wouldn't spread so quickly through their frail little bodies."

"At least, there are the Settlement Nurses working downtown, teaching, and making home visits."

"Those ladies are doing a wonderful job, but many immigrants are moving over the bridge to Brooklyn now. There's practically nothing out there in the way of low-cost healthcare and health education."

"Doctor, try not to worry so. You look so terribly troubled tonight."

"I am, Miss Adeline. I must admit, it's not just my patients. It's Miss Angie. I was hoping to walk her back to the Cottage this evening, but she wants no part of me."

"You mean, you didn't come to visit little old me tonight?"

"I did, of course, but when I saw Miss Angie. Oh, what's the use? She hates me."

"No, she doesn't, Dr. Goodwin. In fact, I happen to know that she holds you in the highest regard."

"Why does she always run from me? We work together so well, but whenever I attempt to get to know her on a more personal level, she disappears."

"Her training has taught her not to cross the *line.*"

"The *line*…what *line* is that?" Dr. Goodwin asked, looking puzzled.

"You know, the *line* that we are taught to maintain. It separates professional relationships from personal ones."

"Yes, I understand. I suppose that is true."

"…And also, you must not forget that she is a good Catholic woman."

"…And I am a good Catholic man!"

"A Catholic man? Forgive me, I thought you were of Jewish faith… your last name?

"My father is Jewish from Austria, but my mother is Roman Catholic from Bolzano, a town in northern Italy. My father promised my Italian grandparents that he would raise his children as Catholic."

"Oh my…!" Adeline said, falling back onto her pillows

"What's wrong, Miss Adeline. Can I get you something?" Dr. Goodwin asked.

"No, nothing's wrong, I just assumed…ummm," Adeline stopped in mid-sentence. "I was wondering, how are things over at the General Hospital? I do miss everyone."

"Everyone misses you. They feel badly that one of our own is down."

"Tell them that I am getting better slowly. They should come to visit me."

"I will do that. Recovery of TB is a very slow process, and you must be patient. It's good to see that you are looking stronger. I'll say, *Good Night*, for now, Miss Adeline. I don't want to keep you up late. Do continue to get well. May I stop in again to check on you from time to time?"

"Yes, Doctor. I will get well. I must. I just discovered that I have a few things to do, or rather, in this case...to *undo*!"

∾

Chapter Twenty-Six

April 19, 1924
11:55 AM (11:55)

You each agree to love and to protect each other,
An oath of loyalty pledged by sister and brother.

It was Saturday, the day before Easter and Angie's day off. Adeline knew that Angie would be knocking on her door in a matter of minutes. Not only did Angie visit every evening after work, she always appeared promptly at noon on her scheduled day off. Adeline glanced at the clock, and quickly jumped onto her bed. There was no time to waste. She poised herself as the dying Marguerite played so dramatically by Sarah Bernhardt in the play, *The Lady of the Camellias*. She carefully draped her right leg and right arm over the edge of the bed while her left hand went up to her forehead. She groaned softly when she heard Angie's knock.

"Who...is...it?" Adeline asked in a soft voice.

"It's me, Angie."

"Come...in...dear," whispered Adeline.

"Oh, Adeline, what's wrong? Aren't you feeling well? What happened?"

"No...I...think...I...took...a...turn...for...the...worse," Adeline said, very slowly.

"It can't be! It just can't be! You've been doing so well. Are you in pain, Adeline?"

"No…I…mean…yes…but…only…when…I…breathe…Ann…gee."

"No, I'll find the house officer. I'll get help." Angie rushed out of the room, and ran down the hall.

"Angie, wait! Wait!"

"What?"

"Wait, Angie, come back. I'm only kidding. Please come back. I feel fine."

Angie returned to Adeline's room with her mouth wide open. "Adeline, how dare you do that to me? You scared me to death. Don't ever do that again! Do you hear me?"

"I couldn't resist, Angie. I believe the devil made me do it. I'm sorry. You're always worrying and fussing. I was so tempted."

"Well, that was cruel, Ad, but the good news is that if you're feeling well enough to tease me, you must be getting better."

"I keep telling you that I am, Angie. If only this coughing would stop, but I am getting stronger every day."

"Then, why is Sister Gwendolyn sending you off to a nunnery in Arizona?"

"It's not a nunnery. It's a sanitarium run by nuns," Adeline said.

"That's almost the same thing, Ad. Why can't you stay here to recuperate?"

"Because Sister feels that I would do better in Arizona."

"Even though the warm weather is right around the corner?"

"You know that New York summers can be quite humid. They are not an ideal environment for healing TB," Adeline explained.

"Arizona is so far away."

"Angie Bosco, do not start crying that I am dying again. Remember, be positive. I'm going to Arizona, and the dry sunny weather will cure me. I promise to return to you. It is as simple as that. Sister went to much trouble to get me this spot. They usually only accept sisters, nuns, but they're making an exception for this nurse, fallen in the line of duty."

"What did Harry say?"

"Harry? What does Harry have to do with anything?"

"I am sure he will miss you terribly. What did he say when you told him that you were going out-of-town?"

"Angie, Harry doesn't know. I didn't tell him."

"Just as I thought, you are afraid to tell him you're leaving town."

"No, I didn't tell him that I am ill."

"What? He doesn't know that you've been sick all these weeks. Do you mean to tell me, Adeline, that you never sent word to him? He must be worried to death about you."

"I never told him, Angie, but he will be fine. He will simply think that I reassessed our relationship, and decided, for the fourth or fifth time, that I need something more, like the many other times we parted."

"Maybe you're wrong," Angie said. "Perhaps, he is still waiting, waiting, and waiting each and every week at your meeting spot. I can see the poor man now."

"Oh, yes, I can picture him at Keens, arriving before eight, and patiently waiting for me to appear. He comes religiously every Saturday night, our date night, and silently waits the entire evening until Mr. Keens closes up shop for the night. Reluctantly, he leaves for home with a heavy heart. No, I'm sure he gave up on me weeks ago, Angie Girl. That's the way it is. He doesn't need or want a burden. If he couldn't commit when I was well, he isn't about to now when I'm an invalid."

"You are not an invalid. You are getting better. You can be so stubborn sometimes, Miss Adeline."

"Yes, I can. Now, tell me Angie, what's happening on the wards? Got any news for me?"

"You're changing the subject, Adeline. I think you're being mean to not tell Harry about your illness."

"Perhaps, but..."

Angie interrupted Adeline. "But, what? Look who's scared now?"

"What are you saying?" Adeline asked.

"I was thinking that maybe you're the one who's afraid of commitment. Consider this for a moment. You go with a man who won't commit. You break up and part, but reconnect with him again and again. Perhaps, it's you who wasn't ready for a long term relationship all these years."

"Wow, you are getting good at this, Angie Girl. I suppose you're right. A few years back, I wasn't ready to be married. There were so many things I wanted to do. Staying home and having babies was not on my list. It didn't appeal to me at the time, but I feel that I'm a different woman now."

"You have to tell Harry. Give him the opportunity to know the truth."

"But...what if?"

Angie asked. "What if? What, Ad? What if he knows the truth? What if he runs? What if you're rejected? Is that what you are afraid of?"

"Yes, I suppose."

"But you will survive, Adeline."

"I'm just afraid. I don't even know why." Adeline said.

"Oh, no, someone taught me that when that happens, there's only one thing to do..."

"…Crash through the fear!" Adeline completed the sentence.

Angie laughed. "You took the words right out of my mouth, Ad."

"Angie, I see your point. There's still some work I have to do here."

"Yes, Ad, you deserve it. Harry deserves it. It's the right thing to do."

"I know, Angie, I'll give it some thought. It'll be my Easter duty."

"What's to think about? You write him. You call him, or you send me over to tell him."

"You would do that for me?"

"Of course, I would. I would do anything for you."

"Thanks, Angie. I'll think about it. Are you working tomorrow?"

"Yes."

"Too bad, I know how you enjoy family get-togethers on the holiday," Adeline said.

"I don't mind. We're going to have the family Easter dinner next Sunday. Listen, I forgot to tell you, I'm meeting my brothers and Celestina at the Ferry Building tonight. I would give anything if you were well enough to come with us."

"Angie, are you actually going out?"

"Yes, I didn't forget my promise to you last month."

"Where are you going?"

"The four of us are meeting for a quick dinner. Santino is picking up Celestina at school, and Giacomo is meeting us at the Ferry Building as soon as he closes his store."

"I'm glad you're finally getting off this island. Is the General Hospital decorated for Easter, like it is here?"

"Yes. Dr. Collins and Gertie are all dressed up. They will be going on an *Easter Parade* in the Registry Room to distribute Easter eggs this afternoon. Captain Joseph is coming in this evening. It's his day off, but he wants to deliver Easter baskets to all the patients in the hospital."

"He always volunteers for that duty."

"He told me at Christmas that he doesn't like to be alone on a holiday."

"Then, I suppose, he is a Catholic man."

"Yes, I assumed he was, or perhaps, he's Protestant."

"Well, we are nurses. We must not assume such things. Always remember Nursing 101 at Bellevue. Do not assume anything. Check. Verify. Ask."

"What are you talking about, Adeline?"

"Nothing, I was just thinking that we shouldn't assume that some people are a certain religion when they could be a different religion. We should ask. Inquire. Be certain."

"Okay, that's good advice. I'll ask him tomorrow when I see him. Are you feeling okay? What are you getting at?"

"I made assumptions. I'm not *always* right, you know. For instance, not *all* the doctors who train in the northeast are Jewish."

"Okay. What has that to do with anything, Ad?"

"Nothing, I just wanted to tell you…like Dr. Goodwin isn't."

"Isn't what?"

"His mother raised him as a Roman Catholic."

"Well, that's interesting. Why are you telling me this?"

"I thought that you might want to know, that's all."

"Okay, now I know. Look at the time. Come, let me help you up and out of bed."

Angie spent the rest of the afternoon with Adeline. She pampered Adeline with both a back rub and a foot rub. She cut and filed Adeline's toenails. She combed Adeline's long brown hair and picked out a white ribbon to tie in her hair for Easter Sunday. When she was satisfied that Adeline looked comfortable and tidy, she kissed her good-bye and hurried off to the Ferry Building to catch the 17:00 ferry to the city.

Angie waited for her brothers and sister at the entrance of the wooden Ferry Building at Battery Park. Giacomo was the first to arrive. "Happy Easter, Giacomo, you're right on time."

"Evening, Angelina, you're looking lovely and happy tonight."

"I am happy. I left Adeline a little while ago. She is looking better and getting stronger. How was business today?"

"Great. The store is doing very well. I am blessed. I closed promptly at five in order to be on time tonight."

"I'm glad. I have something to ask you, Giacomo. It's been on my mind for a very long time. At first, I couldn't figure out how you managed to get Zia Dona to loosen her grip on Celestina. It somehow seemed out of character for her to arrange for Celestina's English lessons, and then, actually allow her to come to America. I pondered on it. Over and over, I asked myself: 'How, in heaven's name, did Giacomo convince Zia Dona to release Celestina?' Then, it hit me."

"Is that right, Angelina? What conclusion did you come to?" Giacomo asked.

"I believe that you offered Zia Dona a great deal of money!"

"Well, Sister, now you know that every Dona has a price."

"I am certain that Zia Dona's price was a small fortune. In fact, I believe that you are continuing to send her money."

"You presume correct, Angelina. I threatened to stop the income if she didn't send Celestina," Giacomo explained.

"Stop what income? Have you been sending Zia Dona money all these years, Giacomo?"

"Yes, Angie, and it was worth every penny. Why do you think she allowed you and Santino to sail to America?"

"I assumed she was glad to rid herself of us." Angie jumped up to give her brother a big kiss. "Oh, thank you Giacomo, for keeping your promise for all of us to stay together."

Giacomo laughed. "Thank you, Angelina, for being my sister and loving Celestina so much. Look, here they are now. Ah, Santino! Celestina! Little one, you look beautiful tonight."

"Thank you, Giacomo."

"Where shall we eat this fine evening?"

"I would like to go to the Automat again," Celestina said. "I love to put the nickels in the slots, and take the food out through the little glass doors."

"Yes, that is fun, Celestina, but I was thinking of something a little more special to celebrate the holiday. There is a new restaurant uptown that I would like to try," Giacomo said.

"Where is it? Is it far?" Santino asked.

"It's uptown on Fifth Avenue and Forty-Fourth Street. We'll have to take a taxi."

"Is it where Delmonico's used to be?"

"Indeed, Delmonico's closed last May, but the Happiness Restaurant opened its doors in the same spot," Giacomo explained.

"Let's go!"

The brothers hailed a Checkered Cab for the ride up Fifth Avenue to the new restaurant. They enjoyed the dinner, the music, the service, and the camaraderie. Both Giacomo and Santino ordered Tournedos of Beef while Celestina had Chicken Vol-Au-Vent. Angie had Loin of Lamb with mint sauce. They all drank Turkish coffee, and had a big slice of apple pie, served with brandied pears, for dessert.

When it came time to say goodnight, Santino offered to escort his sisters to their destinations, but Angie insisted that he take the Third Avenue El uptown with Giacomo. "Go on, Santino, I will see to it that Celestina returns safely to the college dorm. Then, I will return to Ellis Island by ferry."

"Celestina, I thought you would come home with us tonight, and sleep over for Easter."

"No, I was able to obtain a pass only for this evening. I must return to the dormitory tonight, but I will take the train to your house in the early morning, Brother, I promise."

"I hope you will come in time to go to Mass with the family," Santino said.

"Yes, I will leave at eight am sharp, Brother."

Angie gave Santino a little push. "Go on, Santino, from here you will only have to walk four blocks to Third Avenue to catch the El. Go home to your family, Santino."

After much discussion and kisses, the brothers agreed to take the train together, but not before giving Angie the money for the cab ride home. When her brothers were out of sight, Angie turned, and walked downtown.

Celestina followed. "Where are you going, Angelina? You promised Giacomo you would hire a cab?"

"We will, Celestina, but first, there is something I must do tonight. It is eight-thirty. I suddenly realized that my errand is but a mere eight blocks away. I believe that it is serendipitous that we are so close to this destination. I must go. Come."

On the way, Angie told Celestina about her conversation with Adeline earlier in the afternoon. She told her the story of the long love affair between Adeline and Harry, and how they would meet weekly at Keens every Saturday night at eight o'clock.

"I see," said Celestina, "It is only thirty minutes past eight now, and it is Saturday. Is the Keens restaurant nearby?"

"Indeed, it is, Celestina. Who knew the brothers would take us uptown tonight? Keens Restaurant is on Thirty-Sixth Street between Fifth and Sixth Avenues. I must see if Harry is there. After that, we will go straight home like we promised the brothers."

"Let us go, Angelina, to see if true love waits." Celestina sighed.

Angie and Celestina entered Keens and found that the lighting was dim, the walls were dark, and the room was crowded. Angie could not find Harry in the crowd.

"May I be of assistance, Ladies?" asked a distinguished, bearded man in a tuxedo.

Angie continued to survey the crowd. "Yes, I am looking for Mr. Harry Steingold. Do you know him, Sir?"

"Yes, my dear, he is sitting at the small table for two near the wall. See him there. Please allow me to escort you," the man said. The two women followed him through the maze of white tablecloths.

"Mr. Steingold, how do you do? I am Angie Bosco, Adeline's friend."

"I remember you, Angie. You are from the hospital. We met on Christmas Day. How are you? Where is Adeline? Did she come with you? She has not been here for weeks. Is she well?" Harry asked.

"No, Mr. Steingold, Adeline is ill. That is the reason I am here. This is my sister, Celestina. We were having dinner with our brothers on Fifth Avenue tonight, only a few blocks away. I thought to come and see you."

"Angie, what has happened to Adeline? Please tell me. She hasn't answered my letters."

"I am sorry that I do not have good news to report to you this evening, Mr. Steingold. Adeline was diagnosed with TB one month ago."

"Tuberculosis," Harry whispered. He appeared to freeze as he stared into his cup of coffee.

"Mr. Steingold, are you all right? I didn't mean to alarm you. She is recuperating nicely."

Harry did not answer. All color drained from his face. For a moment, Angie thought that he would fall off his chair and faint. Instead, he stood up and waved to the head waiter. "I am sorry, Ladies, but I must go," Harry said, backing away from the table. "Rudwick, I have many things to do tonight. I must leave immediately. Please see to it that these ladies have a good meal, and escort them safely into a cab. Use my tab, Rudwick," Harry mumbled. Then, he turned, and ran out of the restaurant.

"Oh, Angie, where is he going?"

"I have no idea, Celestina."

"Harry was looking at us as if we had tuberculosis, and he was going to catch it if he stayed around a minute longer."

"No, Celestina, he ran out of here as if we had leprosy, and we were here to give it to him. Perhaps, Adeline is right. He looked so very scared. She says he wants no involvement or commitment. She knows him best, I suppose."

"How dreadful, Sister. This love story is a sad one." Celestina moaned.

"Now, Ladies, do sit down. Let me offer you a menu." Mr. Rudwick said.

"No, Mr. Rudwick, we have already eaten our dinner. We won't be staying."

Mr. Rudwick looked concerned. "Then, do let me serve you tea. Ladies, please stay and have tea while I call a taxi for you."

The sisters sat together, stunned. They drank their tea quietly while they waited for the taxi. When it arrived, they rode silently in the Checkered Cab as it made its way downtown. Celestina broke the silence, "My heart feels so heavy. I cannot believe the way that man acted tonight."

"Me, too, Celestina."

"What will you ever tell Adeline?"

"I don't know."

"Are you going to tell her that we went to Keens?"

"Not tonight, Celestina."

Moments later, Angie asked Celestina when she planned to ask Giacomo for permission to apply to Nursing School.

"Perhaps, tomorrow, time is running out. I am required to apply by the end of May. I am certain I want to transfer from the teaching program."

"Have you considered everything about changing your career to nursing, Celestina?"

"Everything. Why are you not more supportive, Sister?"

"The work is terribly hard."

"That does not scare me."

"What attracts you so?"

"Helping people, caring, doing good, making things right." Celestina answered.

"Hard work, long hours, and always being so fearful that you carry an ache in your heart each and every day you go to work," Angie added.

"What are you afraid of Angelina?"

"I fear for the welfare of my patients. I worry that I will make an error, so I check and double check everything I do. I am frightened that we will be so short of staff that the work will not get done, and patients will be neglected. Carelessness and neglect can lead to a death. I am always fearful, and always praying that I do the correct thing when my patients are entrusted to my care," Angie said.

"But, Sister, you never show that you are afraid. You always look calm and in charge."

"That's how it looks on the outside because of my training, but on the inside my stomach is in knots. Please think seriously about this, Celestina."

"I will. I promise. Look, we are here already. Good Night, Leea. I am sorry that Mr. Harry was so rude and ran away from us. He loves Adeline but he is scared. His love is not deep enough to face his fear. He is not able to come shining through for Adeline. What a pity. Kiss Good Night, Leea."

"Yes, Celestina, I am disappointed also. Good Night, Sweetheart. Try not to worry. Enjoy a Happy Easter tomorrow with the family. I will see you next Sunday." Angie kissed Celestina on each cheek. The sisters hugged, tightly.

Angie arrived at the Ferry Building ten minutes later. The 22:30 ferry was ready for boarding. Angie was able to hop right onto the boat. She arrived at the Ellis Island Ferry Station twenty minutes later. Angie began walking to the Cottage through the wooden enclosure connecting the Ferry Building to the General Hospital.

ELLIS ANGELS

As she hurried along the drafty hallway, Angie felt a chill. She remembered that she had forgotten her navy-blue cape on the back of the utility room door on Ward 240. When she arrived at the hospital lobby, Angie decided to hurry upstairs to retrieve her cape in case it was cold in the morning.

Angie walked up the stairs to the second floor, South Wing. All was quiet, except for the clicking of her boot heels on the tile floor as she walked through the corridor. Passing several hospital rooms, she looked through the door windows, searching for Miss Rose or Miss Ruth. They were nowhere to be found.

When she entered Ward 240, Angie surveyed the room. Everything was in order. All the patients appeared to be asleep. Angie noticed that there were Easter Baskets on every bedside table. The utility room door was ajar. She went into the tiny room, and immediately saw that the door to the medicine cabinet was wide open. There were three unopened medicine bottles on the counter.

That's strange. Why were these medicine bottles left out, and not put away?

Her instinct was to immediately close the door to the medicine cabinet, but she stopped. She felt something was wrong.

Someone is breathing. Someone is here.

Angie turned. Through the door window, she saw her cape hanging on a wood hanger. Angie held her breathe, and clutched the door knob.

Slowly, she opened the door to reveal an intruder behind her cape.

She screamed!

He screamed!

Angie steadied herself. "You scared me. What are you doing here so late at night? Why are you hiding?"

The two stared at each other.

Chapter Twenty-Seven

Easter Sunday

April 20, 1924
1 PM (13:00)

From the first moment, the attraction was so strong.
I was destined to sing it as my life's song.

Journal of Gwendolyn Hanover

Date: April 20, 1924

Entry Time: 13:00

Journal Notation:

I am writing this documentation on my lunch hour at 13:00 hours because much has occurred this morning, and I fear I will not remember all the facts accurately if I do not write them down immediately. I reported to work this morning at 06:15 to carry out Morning Rounds as I am covering House Supervision as substitute for Miss Elsie Archer (Miss Elsie), who was given the Easter Holiday off. After Morning Rounds, I returned to my office at 06:50 hours to find Miss Angie Bosco (Miss Angie) patiently waiting for me at my office door. Miss Angie reported that she returned to Ellis Island via the 22:30 ferry last night. On her way to the Cottage, she detoured to Ward 240 to retrieve her cape. At approximately 22:55 last night, she discovered Captain Joseph on the unit, hiding behind the utility room door.

"What happened next, Miss Angie?" I asked her.

"I screamed, Sister. He screamed, too. We both screamed. We woke up quite a few patients. You are going to receive a number of complaints this morning, I assure you."

"I already have, Miss Angie. I've just completed my morning rounds. I promised the patients on Ward 240 that I would look into the matter immediately."

"Oh, Sister, I'm afraid I scared him, but he frightened me so. Miss Rose came running to the utility room to find both the Captain and I in tears. Of course, when we realized what had happened, we closed the door and whispered. Oh, how he cried. Miss Rose ran to call the guards, but he stopped her. He begged us not to make a scene in front of the patients. Between sobs, he was able to give us an explanation. Captain Joseph admitted to taking the codeine tablets from the medicine cabinet. He confessed that he had stolen the drugs a number of times before. Captain Joseph promptly returned the pills, and promised to personally report his indiscretion to the Commissioner the first thing this morning. He confided to us that his wife and child had died five years ago. The holidays are an especially difficult time for him. He is still grieving his loss. He suffers so. Sister, what will happen to him?"

"Heaven only knows, my dear," I said to her.

Miss Angie submitted a hand-written report which accurately documented the incident as she related it to me.

After I read her report, everything became clear. Why didn't I see the pattern that was right before my eyes all these months? Perhaps, I would have, if I had paid closer attention to all the clues. How could I have missed the obvious? The drugs were taken on Halloween, Thanksgiving, and Christmas when Captain Joseph was on the wards delivering holiday gifts. I always received the incident reports in my mailbox the following day.

I decided it would be wise to wait until 09:00 to call the Commissioner at his home, as it is Easter Sunday. I did not wish to disturb him and his family too early on the holiday morning. As I was preparing my report for the Commissioner, a handsome gentleman appeared at my open office door. The man was very finely dressed in a suit of quality material. He introduced himself as Mr. Harry Steingold, proprietor of Steingold's Jewelry, a well-known retail establishment in New York City. I am familiar with the Steingold family, who were immigrants only forty years ago. Their story is a tribute to the opportunities available in America. They worked diligently, amassing a fortune in just one generation.

Mr. Steingold proceeded to tell me that he was the beau of Miss Adeline Fermè (Miss Adeline). He recently learned that Miss Adeline was ill with tuberculosis, and that she was a patient here at Ellis Island Hospital. Apparently, Miss Angie and her sister visited him last night at Keens Restaurant. Mr. Steingold said that he was desperate to speak to Miss Adeline this morning. He needed to see her immediately. I told him that wasn't possible. He would be required to wait until visiting hours at 14:00 hours this afternoon. At that moment, the gentleman pulled out a small black velvet box from his pocket, and opened it. It contained a ring with the largest diamond I have ever seen in all of my life.

He said that he had come to ask Miss Adeline to marry him, and begged me to arrange a meeting between him and Miss Adeline. He assured me that he would be a good provider, and would arrange for Miss Adeline to have the best medical care. He spent last night calling physicians around the country.

I did try to remain stoic to his request but the romantic in me could not resist, and I eventually succumbed to his pleading. I left my office at 08:55, and walked with him to the Contagious Disease Hospital where Miss Adeline is a patient.

When we reached Miss Adeline's private room on the Tuberculosis Unit, I instructed Mr. Steingold on how to properly gown and mask before entering the isolation room. Miss Adeline was in bed eating her breakfast. She had a pretty white ribbon in her hair. She smiled radiantly when he approached her bedside. Then, I was honored to witness Mr. Steingold kneel down on one knee, and propose marriage to the young nurse.

I am overjoyed to report that Miss Adeline accepted his proposal. All three of us could not contain the tears in our eyes. Miss Adeline and Mr. Steingold continued their conversation while Mr. Steingold remained kneeling on the floor. As happy as I was for the young couple, I interrupted them to insist that Mr. Steingold stand up and get up from the floor immediately, as the floor in an isolation room is one of the dirtiest places in the entire hospital. Mr. Steingold attempted to kiss Miss Adeline through his mask. She instructed him to keep his distance, and they both laughed. I could no longer stay in the room with them as I felt like a voyeur to their display of love. I left them to have some measure of privacy.

I returned to the Superintendent's office at 09:46. Soon after, I received a telephone call from the Commissioner of Immigration. He said that Captain Joseph arrived at his home this morning, and was presently with him. The Commissioner wished to alert me that Captain Joseph confessed his impropriety as he had promised Miss Angie and Miss Rose. I verified the story, and told him that Miss Angie submitted a written report at 06:55 this morning. He praised Miss Angie for a successful outcome to her intervention. Captain Joseph will be put on temporary probation until a hearing can be scheduled to determine his fate. He will, no doubt, be dismissed.

Next, I proceeded to seek out Miss Angie. I reported the morning's events to her, including the romantic proposal from Mr. Harry Steingold to Miss Adeline. Miss Angie was surprised and overjoyed, to say the least. She jumped up and down with excitement, and then, actually hugged me! Miss Angie is quite remarkable. How she managed to coordinate these developments with a mere six-hour pass is indeed noteworthy.

It is now 13:22 as I sit at my desk documenting these events. I pray that the next five and a half hours remaining on this shift will not be filled with any more Easter Sunday surprises.

Part Three

Changes

In a dramatic response to the demands of community organizations and labor unions, the Immigration Law of 1924 was signed on May 26, 1924 when the Temporary Quota Law officially expired. It would go into effect on July 1, 1924.

The new law permanently reduced immigration quotas to 2% of the 1890 census. In addition, it ruled that every immigrant was to be screened at inspection stations at the American Consulate offices in their country before traveling. This ruling had a powerful and lasting effect on immigration through Ellis Island, forever changing the number of people stopping there to be processed and registered.

Chapter Twenty-Eight

❧

May 26, 1924
7 AM (07:00)

Giving and receiving with ease and mutuality,
Two people, two hearts, one shared philosophy.

Angie woke up refreshed, and upon rising, opened the dormer window in her bedroom. A burst of morning air encircled her. She grounded herself at the window to wait for the exact moment when the rising sun ignited the water with a rich orange glow. Then, she dressed quickly, and ran down to the Cottage Dining Room to check if everything was in proper order. It was perfect. She grabbed a piece of toast from the serving table before stepping out onto the back porch.

Angie was eager to see Adeline. Although the enclosed walkway was the shortest route to Island Three, she decided not to take it. The tide was high, and a soft breeze was blowing that felt clean and refreshing. Angie couldn't resist walking outside along the water's edge. She took the longer path to the Contagious Disease Hospital. When she reached Adeline's room on the TB unit, Adeline was nowhere in sight.

"Adeline, where are you? I know you're in here somewhere!" Angie said with a chuckle.

Adeline was lost in a sea of white boxes. Coat boxes, dress boxes, hat boxes, and shoe boxes were scattered throughout the room, and piled high around two steamer trunks. The packages were addressed to *Miss Adeline Fermè*. During the past three weeks, five and six boxes had arrived daily during afternoon mail-call.

"I'm down here," said Adeline, rising to stand in front of the mirrored dresser.

Adeline was dressed in a wool suit in a soft, creamy, off-white color. Her skirt was mid-calf in length with delicate pleats running down the left side from the waist to the hem. A half-caped jacket wrapped gracefully across her chest, and buttoned at her left shoulder with a large pearl button. Five, tiny, white mink tails were attached to it, and draped down softly along the front of the jacket.

"Oh, Adeline, you look absolutely gorgeous! How are you feeling today?"

"A bit tired, but I'm happy. I'm glad you talked me into packing the steamer trunks last night. Do you think this is the outfit I should wear today?"

"You have so many to choose from, but this one is perfect. Adeline, you look absolutely stunning!"

"What about the shoes? I was trying them on."

Angie worked her way over to Adeline, skirting between the boxes that were scattered on the floor. She looked down at Adeline's elegant shoes. The creamy calfskin leather had been pleated and twisted into an intricate design that seemed to gently mold to Adeline's feet. "Oh, they are lovely. They look so comfortable, like they were made just for you."

"They were, Angie. They fit so well."

Angie read the name on the shoebox. "Oh my, they're Bartoli shoes made by the best shoemaker in all of New York. Your Harry certainly has thought of everything."

"Mr. Bartoli makes every shoe individually to fit each and every foot," Adeline said.

"I heard. Did he actually come to the Island to fit you?"

"No, Eugenio Bartoli says, 'If they want-a-my shoes, they have to come-a-to my store.'"

"How was he able to make them?"

"Mr. Bartoli still had my shoe lasts stored in his basement. Last year, Harry announced he was honoring my wishes by not giving me jewelry for my birthday. He joked that he had thought of an extremely practical gift for me. Because I was working long hours on the hospital wards, he wanted me to wear a good pair of shoes. His mother recommended the Bartoli Shoe Store on the Upper East Side."

"Those are the shoes you wear every day. I always admired them," Angie said.

"I wear them often, and they still feel like new. Harry wanted to buy you a present for coming down to Keens to find him. He still feels awful about upsetting you that night."

"It's not necessary, Ad."

"Well, I asked him if he would buy you a pair of Bartoli shoes, and he did. This is for you, Angie. It's just a little thank-you for all you did for us, and for being my maid-of-honor today."

Angie opened the envelope. She could not contain her excitement. "A gift certificate for *two* pairs of Bartoli shoes!"

"Yes, it's signed by Eugenio Bartoli himself. You simply take it up to his store. It's uptown, on Third Avenue between Sixty-Third and Sixty-Fourth Streets."

"Thank you, Adeline, it is so thoughtful. You didn't have to do this for me."

"You deserve the best shoes in the city, Angie Girl!"

"I am certain my feet will be forever grateful to you and Harry. He really surprised me when he showed up at Sister Gwendolyn's door last month. I can still remember your face when you showed me the sparkler he gave you on Easter Sunday. You were absolutely glowing. Let me see it again."

Adeline proudly displayed the ring on her left hand. The three-carat diamond ring sparkled under the hospital lights. "I love how it sparkles!" Adeline said.

"Me, too! Celestina and I were devastated when Harry ran out of Keens Restaurant last month. You should have seen our long faces that night. We didn't know that Harry was in a hurry to go out to find the biggest engagement ring in all of New York for you."

"That afternoon, after you left to go to dinner with your brothers, I thought about what you said. I hardly slept. I kept waking up and thinking of Harry, all night long. I remember eating my breakfast, and trying to compose a letter in my mind. Then, wondering if perhaps I should call him. I was thinking that what I really wanted was to see him again, and talk to him face-to-face. Suddenly, I heard a knock at the door. I looked up, and there he was. Thanks to you, my friend. I thought I was dreaming. I was stunned when he took out the ring, and popped the question. He did it just like that, with no hesitation. I surprised myself, saying *'yes'* even before I had a chance to think."

"You crashed through your fear, like *you* taught *me*."

"It's funny, Angie, but at that moment, I had no fear. I haven't had a moment of doubt or fear since."

"Oh, Ad, and he's hired a whole Pullman car to take the two of you to California after your wedding this afternoon. I'm going to miss you, but I know you will be in good hands in the house that he rented and staffed in Palm Desert."

"I will miss you, too, but my lungs are showing signs of clearing. We're hoping that we will be able to live there one year. If all goes well, we'll be back by next spring in time for Harry to open a new store on Madison Avenue."

"Another addition to the family chain of stores?" Angie asked.

"No, this store will be uniquely his own. He's making his own decisions, and his parents are slowly getting used to the idea."

"I know his mother came, and visited you last week. What did she say when he told her he was going to marry you?"

"What do you think? She *'oy-vey-ed'* for three whole weeks. Then, out of the blue, she asked Harry if she could come down to meet me. She came last week. She is absolutely adorable and an amazing woman. 'After all, I'm a modern woman,' she told me, 'and this is America, you know.' Harry said that she's slowly coming around. Both his parents will be coming to the ceremony today. His mother is already planning an anniversary party for next year to make up for not having a big wedding reception today."

"That will make her happy, Adeline."

"Angie, before I forget, you must keep your promise to me. I'm going to miss Election Day. It will be up to you to encourage the nurses to vote in the presidential election in November."

"I have everything in place. Sister Gwendolyn has already made the arrangements for the polling station to be right here on Ellis Island so that all the employees can vote."

"You are in charge of arranging for the *ladies-in-white* to take time off from their assignments to vote."

"Yes, Adeline, I promised you, didn't I? Don't worry. I will follow your instructions to the letter. Your only job is to recover and return to us. When you return to New York, you'll be an old married lady."

"Angie, I will be a married lady in less than a few hours. I still can't believe it. Love really does conquer all. I suppose the heart wants what the heart wants, and it doesn't matter what the rules are, like Dr. Collins and Gertie."

"What? Dr. Collins is married! There's nothing between Dr. Collins and Gertie." Angie looked shocked.

"Yes, there is, Angie. Just because they can't marry, doesn't stop the heart from loving, like Ruth and Rose, also."

"What are you saying, Adeline? Ruth and Rose don't love each other like that."

"Oh, really, open your eyes, Angie. Love is all around us…even our dear Dr. Goodwin."

"Dr. Goodwin? Who is he is love with, Adeline?"

"Why you, Angie Girl!"

"No, Ad, you're wrong."

"You should see the way he looks at you, Angie."

"No more talking nonsense. Enough of this silly talk, this is your special day, and you must enjoy every bit of it. No more about me."

"Angie, but…"

"No, I'm not listening to this anymore."

"Okay, Angie, don't listen to me, but when I'm away, promise me one thing."

"Anything, Adeline."

"Promise me that you will be brave, and that you will not be afraid to listen to your heart."

"Yes, I will try. At the very least, I promise to really try. Right now, we have lots to do. We have to finish packing so that you can be off to California."

"Angie, my trunks are filled to the brim already. Harry picked out so many beautiful clothes. I don't think we can fit another garment in."

"I'll do it, Adeline. That's why I'm here. Of course, whatever doesn't fit in the trunks, you can always leave with me for safe keeping!" Both Angie and Adeline laughed at the thought of Angie fitting into Adeline's clothes. Their laughter was interrupted by a knock on the door.

"Who is it?" Angie asked.

"Miss Pearl, Miss Angie." Miss Pearl opened the door, but did not go inside the isolation room. "Miss Elsie is requesting to see you before lunch. She seemed to be in a bit of a tizzy. She asked for your assistance at the Cottage."

"Of course, Pearl. I'll be right there."

"What do you think Miss Elsie wants?" Adeline asked.

"I have no idea, Ad, maybe she's not feeling well, and wishes me to cover for her."

"Not today, I need you."

"I can't imagine what she might need. I'll go. I'll see what the problem is. I'll be back before lunch to help you close up the trunks. Do try to rest a bit while I'm gone."

"Okay, but hurry back, Angie."

Angie rushed to the Cottage, taking the enclosed passageway, which was the fastest way back. She had a hunch that Miss Elsie's crisis concerned the wedding surprise the nurses planned for Adeline. The wedding was originally scheduled to take place at 13:30 hours in the small chapel of the Contagious Disease Hospital. The newlyweds planned to leave shortly after to catch the evening train to Chicago. However, as a surprise for the bride and groom, Sister Gwendolyn arranged for the ceremony to take place in the Cottage Dining Room with its beautiful harbor view. After the ceremony, the nurses planned a two-hour reception in the scenic front rooms so that medical and nursing staff could stop by if they were on-duty during the wedding ceremony.

Every nurse living at the Cottage had stayed up into the early morning hours to decorate the Dining Room with white satin streamers and bows. They rearranged the tables and chairs, and made white paper cones filled with silk roses for the back of each chair. They planned for the walkway outside the Cottage to be lined with hundreds of pale pink and white impatiens. The Ellis Island gardeners on Island One permitted the nurses to *borrow* the flowers before they were planted on the hospital grounds for the summer. In return, the nurses agreed to leave the flowers undisturbed in their little four-inch flower pots.

I wonder if Miss Elsie's crisis is that the gardeners forgot the impatiens.

As Angie turned the corner, she could see that the petite, delicate flowers were already in place along the walkway.

No, that's not the problem.

Approaching the Cottage, Angie found the entrance blocked by a sea of floral arrangements. Each beautiful bouquet stood five-feet high on a pedestal, and contained blush-colored peonies, pale-pink roses, and creamy lilies. "Miss Elsie, where are you? Are you here?"

"Yes, I'm here. Heavens, Dear, what do we do with all this? There's hardly time."

"Where did all the flowers come from?"

"They were delivered an hour ago by six messengers sent by Mr. Harry. Sister called him yesterday to tell him of the surprise. She asked him if he wished to invite more family and friends to the wedding in addition to his parents. He was delighted, of course, and said they would all be arriving on the twelve-thirty ferry. I suppose he thought to enhance the ceremony with a few flowers."

"Oh my, Mr. Harry does tend to be extravagant. Doesn't he, Miss Elsie?"

"Whatever will we do? The deliverymen were instructed to place them at the end of each row of chairs. I disagreed. I told them to leave them right here. The nurses worked so hard on their decorations. They look meager in comparison."

Angie weaved her way across the foyer in an effort to reach Miss Elsie who was standing at the entrance of the Dining Room.

"How many are there?"

"An even dozen."

"Ah, suppose we use half the flowers up front to frame the picture windows where the Commissioner and the Bride and Groom will stand."

"Good idea, then we can scatter the other six arrangements throughout the room."

"Let's leave two here at the entrance to the Dining Room, and put two on each side of the front door of the Cottage."

"Yes, and perhaps we can take the remaining two off their pedestals. We can put them on the center table in the foyer."

"That will look wonderful. I'll ask the nurses for help right away."

Angie ran up the stairs. She called upon any available nurse for assistance in moving the flowers. In no time at all, the room turned into a wedding chapel fit for a king and queen. The harpist arrived, and began setting up in the corner of the room.

Angie looked at the clock. "It's getting late. I've got to get back to Adeline. If I don't tell her the surprise soon, she will be waiting all alone at the door of the CD chapel."

"Angie, take this to Adeline. We made something *new* for the bride."

"What is it?" Angie asked.

The nurses were excited to show Angie their gift. "We embroidered a silk mask for her to wear today."

"Perfect!" Angie laughed, and rushed out of the room.

"Hurry, Angie, and don't return until you come back with our bride!"

At 13:25, Adeline looked radiant as she walked down the flower-lined path to the Cottage. Angie had never seen her smiling so brightly. The bride cried when she saw how the Dining Room had been transformed. The ceremony was serene and perfect in every way. The Commissioner officiated. Captain Higgins offered to be Harry's Best Man. Angie was Adeline's Maid of Honor. Many of the on-duty staff took a short break, and stopped by to see the newlyweds during the reception that followed the ceremony.

At 15:45, the newlyweds left the Cottage to catch the 16:00 ferry. They were followed by a small procession of family and friends. Angie, Sister Gwendolyn, Miss Elsie, Miss Elizabeth, Gertie, Imogene, Ruth and even Dr. Collins trailed behind the newlyweds to give them a big send-off.

As the ferry crew carried Adeline's steamer trunks onboard, the ferryboat Captain hopped ashore with three dozen copies of the afternoon newspaper tied in a bundle. He called out, "Hot off the presses! Read all about it!"

"I almost forgot!" Adeline shouted, throwing her wedding bouquet into the crowd as the ferry slowly pulled away from the quay.

Miss Imogene caught Adeline's bouquet!

"You're next, Imogene." Everyone cheered. Then, they saw something they had not seen in a very, long time.

Imogene smiled!

When the ferryboat sailed away and shrank to a dark dot on the water, Dr. Collins reached for a newspaper from the bundle. He read the headlines of the day.

NEW IMMIGRATION LAW SIGNED TODAY!

President Calvin Coolidge signed The Immigration Law of 1924 today. The new law will go into effect on July 1, 1924. The law will impact immigration to the United States of America. Immigration quotas will be calculated at 2% of the 1890 census. It is the strictest immigration policy of the century.

Chapter Twenty-Nine

June 30, 1924
7:30 PM (19:30)

Your life will change forever when new beginnings start.
You'll share your life together connected in your heart.

The All-Hands Meetings were scheduled in the auditorium of the General Hospital at 18:30 for night-shift employees and 19:30 for day-shift employees. It was mandated that all staff scheduled to work that day were required to attend one of the two meetings. Throughout the day, rumors flowed around the compound that the Commissioner would be revealing his plan to close Ellis Island and discharge staff.

However, in a very brief ten-minute speech, the Commissioner simply outlined the major rulings of the recent law. He presented potential ways it could impact future immigration. The new law was scheduled to go into effect the following day. It would permanently lower annual immigration numbers when quota numbers would be changed to 2% of the 1890 census.

The Commissioner reassured everyone that Ellis Island would not be closing anytime soon, and that no staff member was in danger of losing his job. In the upcoming months, the Commissioner and his staff would be working closely with Washington to outline a transition plan for medical screening abroad. A major aspect of the ruling was that an immigration candidate would be required to apply for a visa, and would be screened at an American Consulate Office in his country of origin prior to traveling. The Commissioner projected that it could take up to five years to fully implement screening overseas. Medical examiners would be taken from the present pool of public health officers.

It was obvious to the staff that not all the facts were to be revealed at the general meeting that evening. Dr. Goodwin was disappointed and deep in thought as he followed the staff leaving the auditorium. When he looked up, he found himself behind Miss Angie. They walked together toward the Lobby.

"He didn't tell us much, did he?" Dr. Goodwin said.

"No, Doctor, I have a feeling they really don't know what is going to happen or how things will change. I am certain that we will all know in due time."

Dr. Goodwin held the door open for Miss Angie as they exited the General Hospital. They walked down the steps to the sidewalk. "I suppose you'll be going to dinner at the Cottage now."

"Dinner is scheduled for eight-thirty tonight. They expected the meeting to be longer," Angie said.

"Well, Miss Angie, I suppose you'll want to wash-up and change before dinner."

Angie froze, and could only mumble, "Yes." As she turned to walk back to the Cottage, she felt her heart pounding. Her legs were like putty beneath her.

Why am I so frightened? Angie asked herself.

Suddenly, Adeline's voice popped into her head.

Don't listen to me, Angie Girl, listen to your heart. Go on. Be brave. Crash through your fear.

Angie took a deep breath, and turned around. Dr. Goodwin was walking away. Her heart was beating wildly. She opened her mouth to call his name. Nothing came out. She tried once again, but only heard an echo of her soft whisper as the doctor continued to walk away.

"Doctor Goodwin," Angie called out in a louder voice. "Dinner won't be served for forty-five minutes. It's a lovely evening. Would you like to take a walk?"

"Why, yes, of course, it feels good to be outdoors on this beautiful evening."

The twilight sky above the Registry Building was ablaze with brilliant bands of pink and red, casting a rosy glow on the water below.

"Rosso di sera, bel tempo si spera, rossa di mattina mal tempo si avvicina," Dr. Goodwin quoted.

"Red sky at night, sailor's delight. Red sky in the morning, sailors take warning." Angie looked at him strangely, and asked, "How do you know that expression in Italian?"

"My mother recited it, when she was lucky enough to catch a glimpse of a rose-colored sky on a summer evening. She was from Bolzano, Italy."

"I didn't know that about you, Doctor."

"There are a great many things we don't know about each other."

"Some things are not proper to ask, Doctor."

"Yes, I know, like our personal lives, and yet, we've been working together for more than four years."

"I know your heart, Doctor, and how you care."

"…and I know yours, Miss Angie," the doctor said.

They followed the path that circled Island Two until they came to a park bench near the Ferry Building, and sat down. Looking back toward the hospital, Angie said, "I wonder what will become of the hospital in years to come."

"I'm certain that the military will put it to good use. It will never be abandoned."

"Yes, I agree. Perhaps, they will convert it to a Tuberculosis Hospital."

"…Or a Veteran's Hospital," Dr. Goodwin suggested, and took a deep breath. "I suppose I will be transferred overseas if I were to remain in the service."

"Would you like to live in Europe, Doctor?"

"Perhaps, but at this time in my life, I'd like to continue my work with the immigrants. Two years ago, my pastor approached me with an idea of opening a settlement house clinic in Brooklyn. It would provide the same service to the community as the Henry House downtown. I haven't been able to get that idea out of my head since he told me the plan."

"There is such a need."

"Yes, Father is continuing his attempts to raise the funds. I doubt if it will ever become a reality, but it's something I dream about. Miss Angie, may I ask you something?"

"What is it, Doctor Goodwin?"

"Miss Angie, do you think you could ever call me *Abe*?"

"I don't know, Doctor, I…"

Abe Goodwin interrupted Angie. "Can you try?"

"Yes, Doctor, I think…I mean….*Abe*," said Angie.

"Miss Angie, I would like to get to know you better."

"Then, I must ask you to call me *Angie*, Doctor."

"Yes, Miss Angie, as I was saying, I would like to get to know you better."

"I would be honored, Doctor." Angie quickly corrected herself. "Of course, I mean *Abe*."

"Well, I was thinking of perhaps going out…Miss…um…*Angie*."

"This is a bit sudden…"

"Sudden, *Angie*? I believe I had feelings for you the moment I met you four years ago, but you always seemed to hate me."

"I never hated you. Well, maybe…on the first day." Angie couldn't resist teasing.

"Don't remind me of that day. I behaved badly. I apologize. *Angie*, I would be delighted if you would go out with me sometime." Dr. Goodwin gulped, "Would you consider going to Coney Island with me this summer? Perhaps, you could show me the Infant Incubator Exhibit at Luna Park."

"I would love to go there with you, Doctor Goodwin."

"*Abe*," the doctor said. "Call me *Abe*!"

Chapter Thirty

July 15, 1924
Noon

As long as cherries are in season,
There's no reason to be blue!

Despite the heat, Mulberry Street was in full swing by midday. The intense summer sun did not slow down the bustle of activity on the crowded street. Butchers and fishmongers periodically peeked out of their doors to catch the light breeze that occasionally blew in from the south. An iceman, wet from dripping ice, made a water trail in the street as he delivered ice blocks to the store owners.

Women sat on their tenement stoops with babies in their arms, and huddled in the small amount of shade that remained near the entrance doors. Black iron fire-escapes, used as summer balconies, cooled people on the second and third floors of the tenements. A group of women waited in line to have their scissors sharpened at the knife-sharpening cart for the cost of a nickel. Children scattered between them. The weather did not stop the kids from running, skating, and playing ball on the sidewalk, which was now so crowded that Abe Goodwin had a difficult time finding room to pass through. Instead, he walked in the middle of the street among the carriages and push-carts laden with ripening fruits and fresh vegetables. Cherries were in season, and he could no longer think of an excuse not to buy them. He took his place in line, and patiently waited his turn to buy a pound of the firm, dark-red cherries.

Enjoying his day off, Abe continued his walk toward Battery Park. He stopped to watch the city kids cooling off at a *johnnie-pump* that was gushing water from the municipal water supply. A *Johnnie* waited and watched the children as they ran in circles and screamed with delight. The firemen, called *Johnnies* by New Yorkers, often opened the water hydrants for the children to cool off on extremely hot days. Reaching Battery Park, he passed the Castle. He waited for the next ferry in the cool shade of the ferry building. The one o'clock ferry arrived. Abe Goodwin boarded. He had his pick of seats at the bow of the boat. Although it was a short ride to Ellis Island, he was relieved to sit in this breezy spot after his long walk.

When he arrived on the island, Dr. Goodwin walked to the General Hospital. He knew exactly where he was going, and who he needed to talk to.

As usual, Angie was in the nursery. Lost in thought, she was slowly dressing the infant she had placed near the window ten minutes earlier to expose him to light in an effort to reduce his ruddy coloring. "Hi, Miss Angie, you're looking a bit sad." Dr. Goodwin said, as he entered the nursery.

"I am. It's going to be hard to leave this special nursery of mine. We're starting to consolidate units. This ward will be closing at the end of the week. I miss it already," Angie said.

"Was the baby looking a little jaundiced?" The doctor asked.

"Yes, I'm dressing him to take him to his mother. Wait. How do you know about the nurses' treatment for jaundice, Doctor Goodwin?"

"I've watched you put the babies by a window for many years now. Do you think I don't know what you're doing? You know, of course, that there's no scientific basis for your treatment. It's an old wives' tale."

"Yes, but in this case, it's an old nurses' tale. Although sometimes I do believe it works."

"It works because you want it to work," Dr. Goodwin replied.

"I suppose you're right. I thought today was your day off, Doctor."

"It is, Miss Angie."

"What are you doing here? Doctor Winthrop is house officer today. He checked your patients this morning."

"I came to talk to you, Miss Angie."

"Is there a problem, Doctor? Is something wrong?"

"No, no problem at all."

"I can't leave the unit right now. I sent Fannie to lunch a few minutes ago."

"We can talk here, Miss Angie."

"Fannie was so excited. She received her acceptance letter from the Bellevue School of Nursing last night. She could hardly wait until her lunch break to tell everyone. She was offered a scholarship. Sister Gwendolyn and Miss Elsie wrote recommendations for her."

"I'm glad you encouraged her to apply, Miss Angie."

"My sister, Celestina, also applied. She'll be starting with Fannie in September."

"Well, Miss Angie, I know you had a hand in her decision, as well. It's no wonder. The whole world wants to follow in your career footsteps once they meet you."

Blushing, Angie turned, and reached for the wicker crib. She started to wheel the infant out to his mother. "I'll just take the baby out to Mrs. Sackaphee to start his feeding. I'll only be a moment. Would you mind if I brought in my sandwich? I'm running a little late today. I haven't had a chance to go to lunch, as yet."

"Good idea. Oh, I almost forgot. These are for you..." Dr. Goodwin offered Angie a crumbled brown paper bag, "...and of course, for the others. You can share them. I couldn't resist. I thought it would cheer up everyone."

"What is it?" Angie asked.

"Just a pound of cherries..."

"Just a pound of cherries is exactly what we need around here." Angie peeked in the bag. Then, she handed it back to the Doctor. "How thoughtful, this is a day to celebrate Fannie's success with cherries. I think I saw the perfect bowl in the kitchen. I'll be right back." Angie turned, and left the room.

Minutes later, she returned. "I couldn't find the bowl I wanted. It would have been perfect. All I could find was this," she said, holding up a white emesis basin. "It's the best I can do, but I think it will work." Angie put a cloth at the bottom of the enamel basin. She washed the dark, ruby-red cherries while Dr. Goodwin watched. "Can I offer you half of my ham sandwich?" Angie asked.

"I don't want to take your lunch, but I am hungry," answered the Doctor.

"Well, take half of my sandwich. We'll have your cherries for dessert," Angie suggested.

"Deal, Miss Angie."

Angie and the Doctor sat down on the only two chairs in the corner of the nursery.

Angie looked toward the window, and sighed. "It looks like a nice day. On days like this, I wish I worked outdoors. I'd love to be out in the fresh air today."

"It was quite hot in the city this morning." Dr. Goodwin reported.

"You were there this morning, and back already?"

"Yes, that's the reason I came to talk to you today, Miss Angie."

"What is it, Doctor? You look very serious. Did something happen?"

"Yes…no…nothing bad at all. Actually, it's good news. Do you remember that I told you my pastor was attempting to raise funds to open a settlement house clinic in Brooklyn?"

"Yes, Doctor."

"A week ago, he received an extremely generous donation from a benefactor. Father now has the money to realize his vision."

"I wonder who donated the money."

"He was obligated not to tell, but he did reveal that the benefactors were wealthy. They were immigrants in desperate need of healthcare at one time. When he showed me the bank transfers, I noticed that they came from California."

"Do you suppose that the newlyweds had something to do with this?"

"I couldn't help but think the exact same thing. I have no proof, but I'm certain we will find out one day. Enough money was donated to hire a full-time doctor and nurse for three years. Father chose me for the project, Miss Angie."

"How wonderful, Doctor. You're a perfect choice."

"We met this morning. I signed a three-year contract. We're considering a storefront rental in Williamsburg as a possible location."

"Oh, that is good news. A clinic is desperately needed. So many immigrants have moved there."

"Angie, would you consider working with me, starting the clinic?"

"Oh yes, Doctor, you are one of the finest doctors I have ever worked with. Would you really recommend me for the position?"

"Father gave me the go-ahead to hire a nurse today. I am offering the position to you. He's expecting more money to hire aides to assist us by the fall of next year."

"Thank you for considering me. I accept," Angie said, decisively.

"We haven't talked salary or working conditions or hours or..."

"Whatever they are, I accept."

"Do you have any questions, Miss Angie?"

"No. I know your heart, and I'm honored to work with you."

"Now, it is my turn to thank you, Miss Angie."

"You're most welcome, Doctor."

Angie and Dr. Goodwin sat in silence for a moment. Then Dr. Goodwin said, "Miss Angie, this is a very special day for me."

"For me, too, it's a day to celebrate with cherries. Let's have one." Angie reached for the stem of a red cherry from the cherry bowl. As she turned, Abe Goodwin took hold of her hand.

"Didn't we agree to call each other by our first names? *Angie*, do you think you will ever be able to call me *Abe*?"

"Yes...*Abe*, of course."

"*Angie*, what do you think will happen if we are working together and begin to cross the *line*?"

"What *line* would that be?" Angie said with a big dimpled smile.

"It's an imaginary *line* that Miss Adeline told me about. It's the *line* that prevents professional relationships from blending into personal ones."

"Did she explain *what* exactly could happen, *Abe*?"

"No, *Angie*, she did not."

Angie bit into a cherry. She found herself glued to the doctor's chocolate brown eyes. She could not turn away. "Well, then, perhaps we will just have to take it day by day, and discover what develops for ourselves."

"Anything can develop, you know," the doctor said, as he leaned in to be closer to her.

"Yes, Doctor Goodwin, anything can develop." Angie whispered just before their lips met.

THE End

Author's Notes

Tell your story with truth and tact, or Fact
Becomes Fiction and Fiction becomes Fact!

Ellis Angels is a work of fiction presented in a true, historical setting. Some people, places and events in this novel occurred in the past, and are not a product of my imagination. By weaving fiction into fact, historical fiction can be a fascinating teaching tool. However, it carries the potential to compromise real-life events, sometime enhancing history and sometimes distorting it. Because much of the historical data and medical records from Ellis Island Hospital were lost or destroyed, I relied on the documentation of oral histories and thousands of photographs to fit this history puzzle together. The following historical facts were incorporated into the fiction of Ellis Angels.

The Ellis Island Hospitals:

The Ellis Island Hospitals closed their doors over sixty years ago, but the buildings still stand on Ellis Island. The General Hospital opened in 1902, and the Contagious Disease Hospital in 1911. In the 1920s, it was one of the largest hospitals in New York, second only to Bellevue Hospital. When the hospitals closed in 1954, all the hospital records were archived and lost. When you come to New York or New Jersey, don't miss a visit to the Statue of Liberty and Ellis Island Monument operated by the National Park Service. For the cost of the boat ride, you can visit both Ellis Island and Liberty Island (formally Bedloe Island). Before landing at the Ellis Island Immigrant Museum, the ferry will pass Island Two and Three. Notice that the two islands are now connected! You'll see the buildings that were once the 450-bed Contagious Disease Hospital and the magnificent 275-bed General Hospital where my fictional character, *Miss Angie,* worked. You won't see the *Cottage* at the tip of the island. The residence cottage, where the nurses lived in 1924, deteriorated many years ago. It was demolished in 1934.

The non-profit *Save Ellis Island Foundation* was established to increase public awareness and funding to preserve the hospital complex as a future educational conference center. Visit their website for maps, pictures and more information on plans for the site. (www. saveellisisland.org)

Ellis Island Immigrant Processing Center:

Ellis Island served as one of the immigrant registration centers in the United States (U.S.) from 1892 to 1954. Screening guidelines were determined by a multitude of U.S. immigration laws that were passed between the years 1875 to 1946. (2,4,11) The Statue of Liberty and the Ellis Island Museum were closed for a year due to flood damage from Superstorm Sandy.

When you come to visit, arrive early and plan to spend the entire day. There are three floors of exhibits and displays. Sign up for the presentations given by the knowledgeable National Park Rangers, watch the movies, listen to the oral histories, and learn more about the screening procedures that *Miss Angie* studied during her week-long orientation. Christmas at Ellis Island is well-documented in photographs throughout the museum. The nurturing kindness of the *ladies-in-white* is frequently mentioned in the recordings of the Ellis Island Oral History Project. (12)

(www.nps.gov)

(www.ellisisland.com)

(www.ancestry.com)

(www.ellisislandimmigrants.org)

Events of the 1920s:

Women were first given the right to vote on August 18, 1920 when the Nineteenth Amendment to the U.S. Constitution was ratified. The presidential candidates for the 1920 election were Warren G. Harding and James M. Cox, both from Ohio. Theodore Roosevelt's sister, Corrine Roosevelt Robinson (1861-1933) was a poet and a suffragette who frequently spoke to women's groups concerning their voting rights and responsibilities. A nurse, Margaret Sanger (1879-1966), was an activist who founded the Birth Control League in 1921, which was to later become Planned Parenthood.

The Edison Company began experimentation with battery-operated lights.

The Morton Salt Company added iodine to salt production.

The Bartoli Shoe Store was established in 1890 by Eugenio Bartoli, my husband Al's grandfather. He sold high-quality, hand-crafted shoes on Manhattan's Upper East Side.

Delmonico's Restaurant closed in 1923 and the Happiness Restaurant opened in its place a year later. Horn and Hardart's self-serve Automat opened in 1912 in Times Square, New York. Keens Restaurant was established in 1885, and remains open for business on 36th Street in New York City (NYC).

Luna Park opened as an amusement park on May 16, 1903. With the biggest rides and best attractions of the 1920s, it was labeled *The*

ELLIS ANGELS

Heart of Coney Island. Coney Island was nicknamed *The Nickel Paradise* because the NYC subway system charged only five cents to ride the trains from Manhattan to Coney Island in Brooklyn.

(www.history.com)

(www.smithsonianmag.com)

Bellevue Hospital School of Nursing:

Bellevue Hospital Center can trace its origins to a six-bed infirmary in New York beginning in 1736. Bellevue Hospital was the largest city hospital in the 1920s. Currently, it is an 828-bed member of the NYC hospital system affiliated with New York University (NYU) School of Medicine.

The Bellevue Hospital School of Nursing was established in 1875 as a three-year diploma school. In 1969, the school merged with Hunter College to offer its graduates a four-year Bachelor's of Science in Nursing. The Bellevue Hospital Nursing School pin is a Tiffany design. The Bellevue Nursing Cap has been described as a hat that resembles an upside-down pleated cupcake liner.

(www.nyc.gov)

Celebrities:

The Ellis Angels fictional character, *Fiorello,* is modeled after Fiorello LaGuardia (1882-1947), the popular mayor of New York City from 1934 to 1945. LaGuardia spoke five languages and worked as an interpreter at the Ellis Island Immigration Center until he graduated from NYU law school in 1910. Before he became the NYC Mayor, he held positions as a NYC Alderman and an U.S. House Representative. LaGuardia was influential in building LaGuardia Airport in Queens, New York.

(www.nytimes.com/obituaries)

(www.nyc.gov)

Entertainer Jimmy Durante (1893-1980) was nicknamed *Ragtime Jimmy* in the 1920s when he performed with his jazz band at speakeasies throughout New York City and Coney Island. There is some documentation that he sang at Ellis Island with Bob Hope for wounded soldiers during World War II but not on Christmas Day in 1923!

(www.redhotjazz.com/durante)

Another entertainer and famous film-actor, Cary Grant (1904-1986) worked part-time as a barker at Coney Island's Luna Park during the day and on Broadway in the evenings. Before he changed his name to Cary Grant, he was born Archibald Alexander Leach in England.

(www.imdb.com)

(www.americanheritage.com)

1911 Fire at the Triangle Shirtwaist Factory:

On Saturday, March 26, 1911, a fire erupted on the eighth floor of the Triangle Shirtwaist Factory. It quickly spread to the roof. Within minutes, 146 people were killed. The majority were young immigrant women. Locked exit doors, an unstable fire escape, short ladders and machine oil on the floor contributed to the loss of lives. This disaster served as the catalyst for workplace safety legislation, fire-department inspections, and the creation of the Garment Workers Union.

(www.ilr.cornell.edu)

Infant Incubator Exhibit:

The fictional characters, *Dr. Martin and Madame Louise*, honor Dr. Martin Couney and his head-nurse, Madame Louise Recht. In 1903, Couney opened the *Infant Incubator Exhibit* at Coney Island's Luna Park following the strict guidelines he learned in France from his mentor, Dr. Pierre Budin. Labeled by some *The Father of Neonatology*, his life-saving techniques were highly efficacious. The money he earned from the exhibits financed the care of the infants. After forty years of service, he closed the exhibit. He felt that he had completed his mission when New York Hospital (New York-Presbyterian/ Weill Cornell Medical Center) opened the first hospital center for babies born prematurely in the NYC tri-state area.

(www.neonatology.org)

(www.pediatrics.aappublications.org)

(www.prematurity.com).

Medical Discoveries:

There were no antibiotics to treat pneumonia, tuberculosis or trachoma in 1920. The mass production and use of antibiotics began after World War II in 1945. The treatment of favus scalp infections described in Chapter Nine was the state of the art treatment until anti-fungal medications proved to be highly effective in controlling the fungus in the 1950s.

Although English nurses experimented with fresh air and sunshine to decrease newborn jaundice, the use of phototherapy for the treatment of neonatal jaundice was first documented in 1958. Research on gestational diabetes and its link to diet and a baby born LGA (large-for- gestational-age) was published in 1946.

Vaccines for cholera (1879), rabies (1885), tetanus (1890), bubonic plague (1896) and typhoid (1897) were discovered in the 19th Century. Research began on vaccines for diphtheria (1921), tuberculosis (1921), scarlet fever (1924) and whooping cough (1926) in the 1920s with widespread use of the vaccines occurring five to ten years after preliminary testing. Vaccines for polio (1952), measles (1963), mumps (1967) and chicken pox (1974) followed.

With the discovery of karyotyping in 1958, genetic researchers obtained the ability to study human chromosomes. Trisomy 21, once called Down's syndrome, is now accurately named because of the discovery of the presence of a third copy of Chromosome 21 (instead of a pair). A clinical diagnosis of Trisomy 21 is now confirmed by genetic testing.

(nejm200.nejm.org/timeline)

(www.historylearningsite.co.uk)

Statue of Liberty:

The Statue of Liberty has been standing in New York harbor on Liberty Island (formally Bedloe Island) since it was dedicated in October, 1886. The structure was designed by French sculptor, Frederic Bartholdi (1834-1904), and engineered by Gustave Eiffel (1832-1923). Called *Liberty Enlightening the World*, it was offered as a gift from France to the United States, and remains a symbol of democracy.

(www.statueofliberty.org)

(www.nps.gov)

Story of the Quota Baby:

Chapter Seventeen tells the story of a family caught in the technicalities of the 1921 Quota Act. This is loosely based on the real *Quota Baby* story documented in Ellis Island history. Emmy Werner recounts this tale in her book, *Passages to America* (9). The father was a Pennsylvania coal miner who had emigrated from Poland with his wife. Years later, his wife traveled to Poland when her parents became ill. She returned to America on the SS Lapland sailing from Antwerp, and delivered a baby girl on the ship. When Ellis Island inspectors admitted the mother and rejected her newborn, a debate ensued. Included in the arguments was the country of origin of the steamship. The Ellis Island Commissioner of Immigration was called upon to make the final judgment. His decision was to admit both mother and baby because the mother's intention was to return to the U.S. to deliver her baby.

Superstorm Sandy:

When Hurricane Sandy hit land on October 29, 2012, it was no longer a hurricane, but was downgraded to a tropical storm. Because of the unusually high tides, storm surges and winds, it is labeled *Superstorm Sandy*. The damage to New York, New Jersey, Staten Island, Ellis Island and Liberty Island are real, but *a long-buried file cabinet* found on the hospital grounds is fiction fabricated by the author.

Acknowledgments

I wasn't aware of the Ellis Island Hospitals the first time I visited Ellis Island. My attention was directed toward the magnificent Registry Building, both its exterior and interior. I was awed by this historic place. The great arched and vaulted tiled ceiling and the distinctive glass windows *flooded the Great Hall in a pearly light* just as I had seen in photographs and movies. I was excited to find my grandmother's name on the Immigrants' Wall of Honor. (Years before, my sister, Patty, ordered the inscription as a birthday present for my Mother.) I wandered through three floors of exhibits and learned about an immigrant hospital, but never realized that the actual hospital buildings were standing right across the ferry dock.

Days later, I opened Lorie Conway's book, *Forgotten Ellis Island*, (13) and was captivated by the photographs before I reached Chapter One. On the second page, there is a photo of one white shoe, well-worn by a forgotten nurse, dropped and misplaced in an empty hallway. Next, is a group picture of thirty-one nurses in their white uniforms, the actual *ladies-in-white*, as they were lovingly called by their immigrant patients. From aerial shots and photos, I was able to identify each building in the complex. The pieces of the hospital puzzle were falling into place, and I was hooked. Although we've never met, I am forever grateful to Lori Conway and her work for giving me a blueprint for my novel, and being my very own *Miss Elsie*, leading me through the hospital grounds.

ELLIS ANGELS

I couldn't have written this novel without other valuable resources. I frequently referred to Vincent Cannato's *American Passage: The History of Ellis Island* (3) and used it as my very own Ellis Island reference bible, especially for Chapters 2, 3, 6, 7 and 8. Peter Coan's *Ellis Island Interviews* (1) gave me a wealth of information about the small towns and villages many immigrants traveled from. Nevada Barr's descriptions of the decaying hospital buildings in *Liberty Falling* (14) proved helpful. Barry Moreno, Librarian and Historian with the National Park Service, authored a collection of photography books. (15,16,17) The pictures on these pages helped me visualize my story. One afternoon, I called him, out of the blue, and am grateful that he took the time to talk to me. He gave me valuable information about the nurses' residence cottage, the training of Red Cross nurses during World War I, and the ferry-passes that the nurses were required to obtain in order to leave Ellis Island.

Because I worked and studied at a number of New York City hospitals that were built in the early twentieth century, I could actually see the nurses working on the wards, walkig through the hallways, and caring for their patients. Stories kept coming to me, but what was I to do with them?

I am most grateful to my two Alberts, Al and Albert, my husband and my son, who never stopped encouraging me. "Just write it down," they told me. "You'll go back and fix it later." Both fluent wordsmiths, they pulled me out of literary quicksand numerous times. One evening, at my husband's insistence, I took a break and watched the HBO's mini-series, *Boardwalk Empire*. A quick sweep of the *Boardwalk Empire* movie set provided me with a glimpse of the façade of the Baby Incubator Exhibit on the Atlantic City Boardwalk. Later that night, I began my research of Dr. Couney's work.

I thought I knew about character development but my clever daughters, Caroline Limata and Michelle Lathrop, had more to teach me. Their questions kept coming: "Why is she so unemotional? What is she feeling? Are all nurses like that? Why is she afraid of romance? What do the characters learn from each other?" They got so tired of reading chapters, over and over, that they finally asked me to read the chapters out loud to them until they approved the story. What beautiful daughters I have! Thank-you for your patience, your time, and the support you gave me. Caroline, you were my inspiration for Adeline. Brendan and Brooke, my son-in-law and granddaughter, thank you for sharing your Michelle with me.

Thank you to my sister, Dr. Patricia Ann Marcellino, who read and re-read the story from start to finish a great number of times. When everyone was getting tired, you kept going and going. You are always my salesperson, always finding ways to be more precise, and always encouraging and cheering me on. Another thank-you goes out to my sister, Madeline Dittus, for your proofing, support, and encouragement. Thanks, Mom (also named Madeline), for the family stories you told me, and for giving me permission to use my grandmother's married name, *Angelina Bosco*, as my story's main fictional character.

The cover photo is the art work of Frank C. Marcellino, architect and artist and the brother of my brother-in-law, Carl. He paints beautiful nature scenes of classic Florida. Two of his paintings are hanging in my living room. When he learned of my book, he offered to read it, and then shared his inspiration on what the cover could be. Frank, I can't thank you enough for the hours, days, and weeks you spent getting the right art work for the cover of Ellis Angels. After his wife, Marilyn Marcellino, read the story, she called to tell me about the mini-series and book, *Call the Midwife: A Memoir of Birth, Joy and Hard Times* by Jennifer Worth (18). I bought the book, and devoured it. I had neglected to include the practice of holding the newborn baby upside down after birth, and revised Chapter Eleven accordingly. It prompted me to re-read Helen Dore Boylston's *Sue Barton: Student Nurse* (19), a book I treasured as a child. Thank-you, Frank and Marilyn!

I am grateful to my friends who offered to be early readers. Thank you, Evelyn Lane, Patricia Paretta, and Martha Hodges for your helpful comments and your encouragement. I knew you ladies would tell me if I wasn't going in the right direction.

A thank-you goes out to Wesley Clapp, MD, retired Kaiser Permanente Pediatrician of 40+ years who recommended that I change the section on phototherapy as a preventative measure for newborn kernicterus. Although nurses experimented with natural sunlight for the treatment of jaundice for many years, phototherapy wasn't approached scientifically until the 1950s.

I am most thankful for my friends and colleagues who were part of the early RN Review Committee: Terry Campisi, Mary Callahan, Elaine Eastman, Susan Mansi, Jennifer O'Keefe, and Judith Sanderson. All are experienced nurses with Labor and Delivery, Postpartum, or Nursery clinical training who I worked with through the years. Some read the story quickly, and offered their suggestions. Elaine encouraged me to continue. Terry gave me permission to use her famous night-shift story of the wandering patient in the hospital hallway. Jennifer offered a full page critique, including her ideas on character development. Mary felt the nurses in my first draft were too sweet. She suggested including a grouch. Thus, *Miss Imogene* was created. Thanks for your ideas, your support and your encouragement.

Lastly, a very special thank-you to the nurses I worked with during my forty years in nursing. From your kind hearts and generous spirits, I learned so much, including how to communicate with my patients.

Heart To Heart

The infant in the isolette
Struggled all night long,
While oxygen and monitors
Hummed a hopeful song.
In the morn's wee hours,
His mom came around his bed.
So gently did she look at him,
Both arms reached above
   his head.
The muscles of his face went
   limp.
Frail little legs did the
   same.
His lower lip relaxed to
   pout,
"Mom, I'm glad you came!"

There is a kind of language
That only two can share.
If you listen closely,
It comes in crystal clear.
What do they call this
   language
It's power from above?
There isn't a real name for
   it
But it begins with love.
It's love that makes this
   language
An uncomplicated art.
Simply close your mouth
   and ears
And listen with your heart.

By Carole Lee Limata

319

Resources

(1) Coan, Peter M., *Ellis Island Interviews: Immigrants Tell Their Stories In Their Own Words*, New York: Barnes and Noble Books, 1997.

(2) Immigration Law of 1891: Session II Chapter 551, 26 STAT. 1084, 51st Congress March 3, 1891.

(3) Cannato, Vincent, J., *American Passage: The History of Ellis Island*, New York: Harper, 2009.

(4) 1921 Emergency Quota law: An act to limit the immigration of aliens into the United States H.R. 4075; Pub. L. 67-5, 42 Stat. 5, 67th Congress May 19, 1921.

(5) Brick, Michael, *And Next to the Bearded Ladies and Premature Babies*, The New York Times, New York Region, June 12, 2005.

(6) Liebling, A. J., *Profiles: A Patron of the Premies*, The New Yorker, June 3, 1929, pp. 20-24.

(7) Silverman, William A, M.D., *Incubator-Baby Side Shows*, Pediatrics 64 (2): 127-141, August, 1979.

(8) *The Coney Island Baby Laboratory: Incubators for Newborn Infants Were Developed Not in a Medical Research Facility but Amid Barkers, Sideshows, and Gawking Crowds*, Innovation and Technology Magazine, Fall 1992, Vol 10, Issue 2.

(9) Werner, Emmy E., *Passages to America: Oral Histories of Child Immigrants from Ellis Island and Angel Island*, Washington D.C.: Potomac Books Inc., 2009.

(10) Leighton, Maxinne R. and Nolan, Dennis, *An Ellis Island Christmas*, United States: Penguin Group, 2005.

(11) 1924 Immigration Act: An act to limit the immigration of aliens into the Unites States. H.R. 7995; Pub. L. 68-139, 43 Stat. 153, 68th Congress May 26, 1924.

(12) Oral History Project: 1892 to 1973. A collection of two thousand oral histories by the Ellis Island Oral History Program of the Ellis Island Immigration Museum.

(13) Conway, Lorie, *Forgotten Ellis Island: The Extraordinary Story of America's Immigrant Hospital*, New York: HarperCollins Publishers, 2007.

(14) Barr, Nevada, *Liberty Falling: An Anna Pigeon Novel*, New York: Penguin Books, 1999.

(15) Moreno, Barry, *Ellis Island, Images of America*, California: Arcadia Publishing, 2003.

(16) Moreno, Barry, *Children of Ellis Island, Images of America*, California: Arcadia Publishing, 2005.

(17) Moreno, Barry, *Ellis Island Famous Immigrants, Images of America*, California: Arcadia Publishing, 2008.

(18) Worth, Jennifer, *Call the Midwife: A Memoir of Birth, Joy and Hard Times*, England: Penguin Books, 2002.

(19) Boylston, Helen D., *Sue Barton, Student Nurse: The Story of a Likeable and Courageous Girl and a True Picture of Life in a Great Hospital*, Boston: Little Brown and Company, 1938.

About The Author

Carole Lee Limata graduated with an Associate Degree (AAS) in Nursing from Queens College, New York in 1968. After taking her Nursing Boards that summer, she worked as a Registered Nurse at New York City's Metropolitan Hospital, and then, at the City's Premature Nursery Center located at Elmhurst Hospital before moving to Northern California. She received a Bachelor's Degree (BSN) from Sacramento State University, and earned a Master's Degree (MSN) from the University of California at San Francisco (UCSF) in 1980. She is a member of the Nurses Honor Society, Sigma Theta Tau International.

Throughout her forty-year nursing career, Carole worked as a staff nurse, supervisor, maternity instructor, and prenatal educator before becoming a Director of a Maternity Department. In 2008, she retired from her final position as Supervisor of the Screening Programs at the Kaiser Permanente Genetics Department in Oakland, California. Ellis Angels is her first novel since retiring from clinical nursing.

Carole has three wonderful grown children, a terrific son-in-law and two beautiful grandchildren, Brooke Marie and Hunter Neil. With her husband, Al, she divides her time equally between both coasts.

Carole Limata can be contacted at EllisAngelsNovel@aol.com

Discussion Guide One

1. Miss Angie is nervous on her first day reporting to work on Ellis Island. Do you remember having similar feelings on your first day of a new job? (Chapter 1)

2. Miss Angie recalls her memories of coming to America and seeing the Statue of Liberty for the first time. Does your family have a *Coming-to-America* story that was passed down from one generation to another? (Chapter 2)

3. First- and Second-Class steamship passengers were not required to go through Ellis Island for screening and processing. Do you think this policy fulfilled the screening criteria outlined in the law of the day? Do you feel it was fair that only steerage passengers were required to go through the Ellis Island registration process? (Chapter 2)

4. Have you ever had the experience of traveling and meeting someone who did not speak your language, nevertheless, both of you discovered a way to communicate? How did you do this? (Chapters 2 and 4)

5. When the Ellis Island uniforms are delivered to Miss Angie, she is excited to try one on. Her uniform consists of the traditional starched white dress, white cap, navy blue wool cape and white shoes. It is much different from the *scrubs* that nurses wear today. Why did registered nurses stop wearing their traditional uniform? As a patient, would you prefer that nurses had continued to wear the classic white-capped uniform? (Chapter 3)

6. How did you react to the mental health research questions at Ellis Island that Miss Elsie described: "Do Englishmen have higher IQ levels than men of other nationalities? Are certain facial features reflective of intelligence?" (Chapter 3)

7. Women were allowed to vote for a U.S. president for the first time in 1920. Imagine not being allowed to vote in the last presidential election because you are a woman. (Chapter 4)

8. In the 1920s, a marriage of two people from different religions was frowned upon. Have modern-day norms changed around this topic? (Chapter 4)

9. Abortion and contraception were controversial subjects in the 1920s. Has public opinion changed since then? (Chapter 4)

10. The design of Ellis Island Hospital was modeled after the European concept that fresh air and sunshine promotes healing. Do you think these factors contribute to a healing environment? Do modern hospitals take these concepts into consideration? (Chapter 6)

11. What do you think of the immigration policy that did not allow a single woman into the United States unless she was claimed or sponsored by a spouse or relative? (Chapter 12)

12. Do you feel that the premature infants at the Luna Park Exhibition were exploited because they were exposed to the public in order to fund their growth and development? (Chapter 15)

13. How do you feel about Sister Gwendolyn's policy revision to allow for a private space and time for parents to grieve for their baby who had died? (Chapter 18)

14. The holiday gifts for the immigrants came from donations from the people of New York City, the very ones who were strongly opposed to immigration. How would you explain this? (Chapter 18)

15. There were a number of important medical discoveries since 1924. How could antibiotics, anti-fungal medications, and modern-day vaccines have helped the patients at Ellis Island Hospital? (Chapter 19)

16. Do you think that Dr. Goodwin and Miss Angie did the right thing is allowing the Ryan baby to leave the hospital without documenting their findings? In your opinion, were they breaking the law? (Chapter 22)

17. How do you feel about Angie telling Harry about Adeline's illness without the go-ahead from Adeline? Do you feel she acted impulsively? What would you do if you were Angie? (Chapter 26)

18. There is a recurring message to *follow your heart* throughout the book. Have you ever *followed your heart* but experienced an outcome different from the one you hoped for? Adeline advises Angie to listen to her heart. How do you do this? What things often get in the way of hearing your inner voice? (Chapter 28)

19. Angie and Abe share their ideas on how the hospital could be used in the future. It is inconceivable to them that the buildings would ever be abandoned. What uses would you suggest for a state-of-the-art hospital built on an island? (Chapter 29)

20. Have present day attitudes toward immigration changed in this century? How are they different? How are they similar?

Discussion Guide Two

For Nurses and Nursing Students

1. Although the Superintendent of Nurses, Sister Gwendolyn Hanover, was desperately short of nurses, she arranged for a week-long orientation for her new nurse, Angie Bosco. Why did she do this? How important is a proper orientation when starting a new position in an organization? Do you feel Miss Angie received a thorough orientation? In your opinion, was anything missing from her Ellis Island orientation? (Part I)

2. In a hospital setting, patients often cannot communicate to their caregivers with words. Give an example of how you used non-verbal communication when caring for a patient. (Chapter 2)

3. Miss Angie explains the meaning of the symbols that are on her nursing school pin. Examine your nursing school pin. Do you understand the meaning of the symbols on the pin? Do the symbols represent the overall philosophy of your nursing school or perhaps, the location of the school? Does your nursing school still have a student pinning ceremony? Do you currently wear your nursing school pin either on your scrubs or on your name badge? Why or why not? (Chapter 3)

4. When the Ellis Island uniforms are delivered to Miss Angie, she is excited to try one on. Her uniform consists of the traditional starched white dress, white cap, navy blue wool cape and white shoes and stockings. It is much different from the *scrubs*

that nurses wear today. Why did registered nurses stop wearing their traditional uniform? What were the advantages and disadvantages of the classic white-capped uniform? (Chapter 3)

5. Explain centralization and decentralization as it relates to a department or a system at your hospital. What considerations are taken into account when a system or unit moves from decentralization to centralization or the reverse? Identify and describe one centralized department at your hospital. (Chapter 3)

6. The design of Ellis Island Hospital was modeled after the European concept that fresh air and sunshine promotes healing. What other factors contribute to a healing environment? Have modern hospitals taken these concepts into consideration? (Chapter 6)

7. The discovery of antifungal medications has wiped out favus scalp infections except in the most remote parts of the world. Why does a high incidence of fungal infections, like athlete's feet, still exist? (Chapter 9)

8. Outline the nursing organizational structure at Ellis Island Hospital. Compare and contrast it to the organizational structure at the hospital you are currently working or studying at. (Chapter 10)

9. Compare the delivery of Baby Girl McGuire to a modern-day delivery. Why did the nurses wait patiently for the placenta to deliver? Why did Miss Gertie examine the placenta immediately after it delivered? Why did Miss Angie hold Baby Girl McGuire upside down when she was born? (Chapter 11)

10. Do you think it was appropriate for Miss Gertie to give Fannie an explanation of the delivery while Mrs. McGuire's was present in the room? (Chapter 11)

11. Upon arrival at Ellis Island, Katie Ryan's prenatal symptoms of edema and high blood pressure caused her to be admitted to the Ellis Island Hospital. Why was bed rest ordered? (Chapter 12)

12. Have you ever had the experience of working the night shift? What was it like for you? What are the advantages and disadvantages of the three eight-hour shifts: days, evenings and nights? Compare a twelve-hour shift to an eight-hour shift. (Chapter 12)

13. The first neonatology units in a hospital setting were actually *centers* for a group of hospitals? Why did this occur? (Chapter 13)

14. Locate the protocol for a neonatal death at your facility and compare it to the addendum to the protocol that Sister Gwendolyn authored in 1923. What considerations are now made for grieving parents? (Chapter 16)

15. Do you think Miss Angie's system of checking narcotics was efficient? How are narcotics currently tracked at your facility? (Chapter 17)

16. Down's syndrome is now called Trisomy 21. Why? What prenatal screening tests and procedures to detect Trisomy 21 are currently available to prenatal mothers? (Chapter 21)

17. Were Dr. Goodwin and Nurse Angie on the right track in their care of the LGA baby? What is the rationale for an LGA baby (large-for-gestational age) and an SGA baby (small-for-gestational age). (Chapter 23)

18. Did you ever feel like Angie when she said: "I fear for the welfare of my patients? I worry that I will make an error, so I check and double check everything I do. I am frightened that we will be so short of staff that the work will not get done and the patients will be neglected." (Chapter 26)

19. How do you feel about *crossing the line* between a professional and a personal relationship? What is your opinion about romance in the workplace? (Chapter 27)

20. Were the nurses correct in believing that exposure to sunlight was an appropriate treatment for jaundice? (Chapters 10 and 30)

ELLIS ANGELS ON THE MOVE

Making A Difference in Brooklyn

A Novel by Carole Lee Limata, RN, MSN

Thank you for reading *Ellis Angels!*

Ellis Angels On The Move: Making A Difference in Brooklyn is the continuing story of the nurses of Ellis Island Hospital. Nurse Angie Bosco and the ladies-in-white continue their work, caring for newly-arrived immigrants. However, 1925 finds Miss Angie moving from Ellis Island to a section of Brooklyn called *Williamsburg*. There, she begins working closely with Dr. Abraham Goodwin to establish the Nativity Settlement House and Health Clinic.

Before Angie begins her journey, she meets with Lillian Wald, the founder of the New York Visiting Nurses at the Henry Street Settlement House. Lillian teaches her the importance of establishing trust with the residents in the neighborhood. As Angie "settles" in Williamsburg, she lives at a nearby church convent, and quickly immerses herself into the culture and the customs of the diverse community. She connects with Visiting Nurse Maureen O'Shaughnessy and her long-time friend, Nurse Adeline Fermé.

Nurse Angie and Doctor Abe begin to have many unanswered questions about the mysterious activities of their neighbors. They slowly uncover answers, and learn the vital contribution a settlement house can make in helping the immigrants achieve their American dreams. In the process, they achieve their own dreams, as well.